Praise for *The Shores of Tripoli*

"Mr. Haley's research has been so completely absorbed as to be unobtrusive. He has mastered the politics of the period and the business of sailing a ship. . . . There is much charm and humor, as well. . . . Meanwhile this is a book that, like so much of the best fiction, makes you both think and feel." —*Wall Street Journal*

"It's a rare novelist who has a commanding grasp of history, and it's a rare historian who has an intuitive understanding of how to bring fictional characters to life. Fortunately for us readers of *The Shores of Tripoli*—and (please!) of the next book about Lieutenant Bliven Putnam—James L. Haley fuses historian and novelist into a spellbinding storytelling whole. There could be no better captain to sail this ship."
—Stephen Harrigan, author of
The Gates of the Alamo and *A Friend of Mr. Lincoln*

"Historical fiction has to work simultaneously as history and fiction. Rarely do the stars align, but in this case they have. *The Shores of Tripoli* is a terrific novel, elegantly written, and grounded in first-rate research."
—Ian Toll, author of *Six Frigates*

"It's no surprise that Haley's command of historical detail here is superlative, and his adrenaline-inducing descriptions of cannon-fueled sea battles are also first-rate." —*Booklist*

"This is one more naval historical fiction series worth reading."
—*Good Old Boat*

"Rich with historical detail and cracking with high-wire action, *The Shores of Tripoli* brings this amazing period in American history to life with brilliant clarity." —BookReporter.com

"Thanks to Haley, America now has its own Captain Horatio Hornblower in midshipman Lieutenant Bliven Putnam, who would sail the seas fighting the Barbary Pirates. . . . Readers will savor the pacing and the wild ride across the seas with a young man making his mark on history." —*Romantic Times*

"An award-winning historian who also writes fiction can be expected to deliver excellence, and Haley doesn't disappoint. With poignant echoes of today's horrors with terrorism, the book sadly reminds us this conflict is not new. The novel concludes with a dramatic, event-filled ending which brilliantly sets the stage for the following books in this new series. This wonderful book is, in historian Barbara Tuchman's words, 'a distant mirror.' An absolute must read."

—*Historical Novels Review*

"A highly readable blend of fact and fiction . . . Rich with historical detail and filled with action, *The Shores of Tripoli* brings this amazing period in American history to life. . . . The first entry in James Haley's new series seems a fitting successor to the seafaring sagas penned by Forester and O'Brian." —*Herald-Dispatch*

THE SHORES OF TRIPOLI

LIEUTENANT PUTNAM

and the

BARBARY PIRATES

JAMES L. HALEY

G. P. PUTNAM'S SONS
NEW YORK

G. P. PUTNAM'S SONS
Publishers Since 1838
An imprint of Penguin Random House LLC
375 Hudson Street
New York, New York 10014

The Library of Congress has catalogued the G. P. Putnam's Sons hardcover edition as follows:

Names: Haley, James L., author.
Title: The shores of Tripoli / James L. Haley.
Description: New York: G. P. Putnam's Sons, 2016 | Series: Lieutenant Putnam and the Barbary Pirates ; 1.
Identifiers: LCCN 2016010831 | ISBN 9780399171109 (hardcover)
Subjects: LCSH: United States—History, Naval—19th century—Fiction. | United States.
Navy—Officers—Fiction. | Battleships—Fiction. |
BISAC: FICTION / Historical. | FICTION / Sea Stories. | Fiction. / Sagas. | GSAFD: Adventure fiction. |
Historical fiction. | War stories. | Sea stories.
Classification: LCC PS3608.A54638 S55 2016 | DDC 813/.6—dc23
LC record available at https://lccn.loc.gov/2016010831
p.   cm.

First G. P. Putnam's Sons hardcover edition / November 2016
First G. P. Putnam's Sons trade paperback edition / October 2017
G. P. Putnam's Sons trade paperback ISBN: 9780425278178

Printed in the United States of America
1   3   5   7   9   10   8   6   4   2

Book design by Meighan Cavanaugh

To the Blivens, with love,

Brent and Gina

and Lucas and Annika

———◆———

All nations that have not acknowledged the Prophet are sinners, whom it is the right and duty of the faithful to plunder and enslave, and every Moslem who is slain in this warfare is sure to go to Paradise.

SIDI HAJI ABDUL RAHMAN ADJA,
TRIPOLITAN AMBASSADOR

Perhaps no service, either in the way of ships or officers, ever had so large a proportion of that which was excellent in it . . . as the navy of the United States, the day peace was signed with Tripoli.

JAMES FENIMORE COOPER,
The History of the Navy of the United States of America

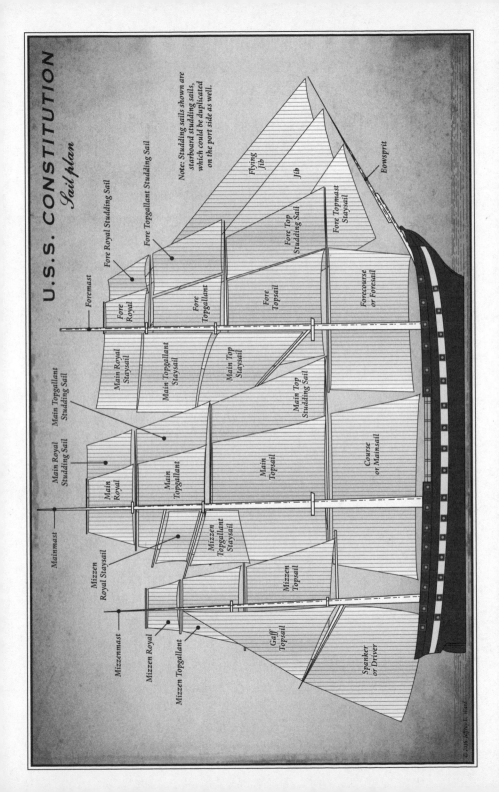

U.S.S. CONSTITUTION
Sail plan

Note: Studding sails shown are starboard studding sails, which could be duplicated on the port side as well.

Flying Jib

Jib

Fore Royal Studding Sail

Fore Topgallant Studding Sail

Foremast

Fore Royal

Fore Topgallant

Fore Top Studding Sail

Fore Topmast Staysail

Fore Topsail

Forecourse or Foresail

Bowsprit

Mainmast

Main Topgallant Studding Sail

Main Royal Studding Sail

Main Royal Staysail

Main Topgallant Staysail

Main Top Staysail

Main Royal

Main Topgallant

Main Topsail

Main Top Studding Sail

Course or Mainsail

Mizzenmast

Mizzen Royal Staysail

Mizzen Topgallant Staysail

Mizzen Royal

Mizzen Topgallant

Mizzen Topsail

Gaff Topsail

Spanker or Driver

© 2015 Jeffrey L. Ward

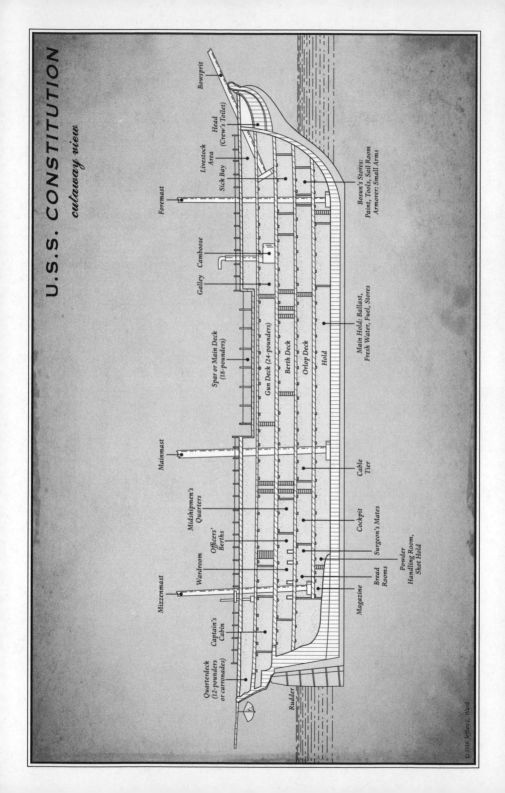

U.S.S. CONSTITUTION
cutaway view

Bowsprit

Head (Crew's Toilet)

Livestock Area

Foremast

Sick Bay

Galley

Camboose

Spar or Main Deck (18-pounders)

Gun Deck (24-pounders)

Berth Deck

Orlop Deck

Hold

Main Hold: Ballast, Fresh Water, Fuel, Stores

Bosun's Stores: Paint, Tools, Sail Room
Armorer: Small Arms

Mainmast

Cable Tier

Midshipmen's Quarters

Officers' Berths

Wardroom

Cockpit
Surgeon's Mates

Mizzenmast

Bread Rooms

Powder Handling Room, Shot Hold

Magazine

Captain's Cabin

Quarterdeck (12-pounders or carronades)

Rudder

© 2016 Jeffrey L. Ward

CONTENTS

THE SHORES
of TRIPOLI

Atlantic Ocean

FRANCE

EUROPE

45°

Leghorn

Toulon

Corsica

PORTUGAL

SPAIN

Sardinia

40°

Mediterranean Sea

Cape St. Vincent

Cádiz

Cabo de Gata

Algiers

Tunis

Algeciras

Gibraltar

Tangier

Jeb el Musa

ALGIERS

35°

Salé

MOROCCO

TUNIS

OTTOMAN

Mogador

30°

AFRICA

0 Miles   500

0 Kilometers   500

Scale at 40° North Latitude

© 2016 Jeffrey L. Ward

1.

THE MORNING WATCH

———◆———

June 6, 1801

Before he went to sea, Bliven Putnam had wondered why men personify ships, name them, ascribe temperaments to them, refer to them in the feminine. It took only one day at sea in a stiff blow to understand it. When the sails of the *Enterprise* bellied out and the masts bent before the wind, when the ship buried herself in a trough and then vaulted to surmount a swell, she took on the life of the most spirited filly. A ship at sea—you ask things of her, sometimes difficult things, tricky things, and she responds, although not always in the affirmative. She becomes your home and your safety—your only safety—in the middle of an ocean. And she not only crosses that ocean, but does so with a grace and touch that is nothing if not feminine. To seamen this relationship with their vessel becomes embedded in their nature. Those who do not go to sea cannot understand it; they accept it readily enough, and they mimic the sailors' reference to a ship as "she," but they do not comprehend it, really. That is the seamen's bond alone.

And who can understand an ocean who has not crossed one? A body of water so vast that months peel from a calendar as one dares to traverse it, so mysterious that antediluvian creatures yet to be discovered swim in it, a sea so primal and so powerful that when it rises up in its fury, the tallest and proudest ship is at its mercy—no wonder, he thought, that ancient peoples worshipped sea gods.

Probationary Midshipman Bliven Putnam was fourteen by the calendar, but he appeared and acted years older. The wind was following, lifting the curly, sandy-brown hair on the back of his head, his three-inch standing collar keeping the morning chill off his neck. He was already as tall as many men and as broad in the chest, with a square set to his jaw, his blue-gray eyes conveying determination and quick intelligence.

He stood his trick at the wheel, his fourth, as he would note with pride in the diary he was required to keep and lay open for Lieutenant Porter, who oversaw his and the other midshipman's schooling. This was the first watch that Bliven had stood alone, the morning watch, the coldest and darkest, with the sparest number of men to watch over the vessel while most of the crew slept. It frightened him badly at first, the responsibility, not having an officer observing him, but in the peace of the wee hours he came to appreciate how little attention a vessel in a good wind requires. He stood with his feet just wider apart than his shoulders, as Lieutenant Porter had shown him, and was aware that he was learning to trust his ship. She was easy to guide, but if he had to force her into a turn it would take all his strength. Five bells brought first light; at six bells the bosun's mate clattered below to light a fire in the galley. The partially stove-in old jack-tar who served them as cook had been on the ship since she was commissioned. He had been an able seaman until a wrench of his back in taking a French privateer had left him with a permanent list to his gait. Thus he had been given the lighter duty as cook and in three years had acquired a skill at it. Seamen valued a cook who could prepare edible food from stores that became progressively more foul the longer they were at sea, and those in the morning watch were content to allow him an extra half-hour's sleep by firing up the camboose for him.

From his stance at the wheel, Bliven watched the ship come to life. The day bid fair, and crewmen and marines who had been piped awake filed onto the deck, blankets wrapped in their hammocks to be stowed in the netting. The bosun, Josiah Merrick, quietly inspected the sheets and shrouds for any adjustments and directed a detail to set up the elm-tree pump with which they *clack-clock, clack-clocked* the night's accumulation of water up from the bilges and out the scuppers. Merrick was a small man, but wiry, with auburn hair that tended to fly wild and whiskers that he often had to be reminded, after twelve years of merchant service, were not permitted in the navy. He, too, had been on the *Enterprise* since her commissioning. He was efficient and even-tempered, a good buffer between the sailors, who were often inexperienced, bewildered, and hostile, and their often irascible officers. His too was the office of schooling the midshipmen in practical seamanship and boat handling.

With the sun up and obliquely in his eyes, Bliven understood anew that the *Enterprise* was a small ship, and they would feel every slap and lurch of the ocean more keenly than they would in a larger vessel. Thus naturally they would cling tighter to her for their safety, but the larger the ship and the greater her reputation, the more intense was her sailors' devotion. That was central to understanding seamen, and with Bliven's ambition it took little for him to imagine his future at the helm of a mighty man-of-war.

A majestic ship of the battle line, ninety-eight guns that spread over three decks, masts that tower course on course of sail up to topgallants and royals and then even skysails—and, especially when she is girded for fighting, her pennants snapping, guns rolled out, marines in her fighting tops priming their muskets even as they lean against the swell, she inspired a near reverence among her sailors. It is a love that could ignite tavern duels if a ship's worth or virtue were in the least part questioned.

But now embarked on his first cruise, Midshipman Putnam was assigned to the *Enterprise*. Smaller even than the twenty-gun sloops, she was a mere schooner of 165 tons, the smallest class of warship in the American navy. She had only one-tenth the displacement of their flagship, the forty-four-gun frigate *President*. *Enterprise*'s single-stick masts had just been rerigged as a jackass brig, and she mounted only a dozen guns, little six-pounders. She was eighty-five feet long and seemed barely capable of sheltering a crew of ninety officers and men. There had never been so many, but they had taken on an entire company of marines. The orders that sent them to the Mediterranean were to show the flag and escort American commercial vessels, but no man on board doubted that they were sailing into a war.

For a decade, the United States had been paying an annual "tribute," as it was disgracefully called, to the four Berber states of North Africa: Morocco, Algiers, Tunis, and Tripoli. They were collectively known as the Barbary states. Piracy on the open sea had been the mainstay of their national economies for some three centuries. In that time they had taken hundreds of thousands, perhaps more than a million, European Christians captive, held them for ransom, and if they were not ransomed sold them into slavery. They apportioned the women among the warlords' harems to spend their youth in sexual bondage, and after that consigned them to drudgery. This the Berbers justified by their religion: Mohammedanism, known also as Islam. Its adherents were called Musselmen in America, from confusion over the correct name of Moslem. Boldly they proclaimed that their Prophet had given them, the faithful, the right to capture infidels as they pleased, and use them—enslave them, kill them—as they pleased. In the West, piracy was the criminal act of desperate bands of outlaws; on the Mediterranean, it was the state policy of the Mohammedan countries that claimed the right, exceptional from all other nations, to mastery over the lives and liberty of other nations.

Mr. President Adams, whom Bliven's father had voted for, supported this policy of tribute and appeasement, with a mind to protect American trade for less cost than building and maintaining a seagoing navy. Thomas Jefferson had been the first to advocate resistance, some fifteen years ago, but his threats were idle, for there was no fleet. The Revolution had been fought at sea almost entirely relying on the French, aided by our own privateers and small warships belonging to the several states. With the federal government created by the 1787 Constitution came the possibility of a national navy, but it was only in response to the Berber pirates, who began attacking American ships at about that time, that the Congress passed the Naval Act in 1794. It provided for the construction of six heavy frigates, with the acquisition also of support vessels. With governmental wavering over the cost, it took years, but now that Mr. Jefferson was president, the pirate states were demanding higher tributes and ransoms, and the United States had drawn a line.

The *Enterprise* had left Baltimore on Tuesday, the second of June, 1801, after a delay in fitting the new masts. They were bound for Gibraltar with the most impressive squadron that their young nation had ever put to sea—and that alone said a great deal for the United States, that they could deploy three frigates together so soon after having none. They showed well together, and this was a brilliant morning, the sea reflecting all the interior blues of a sapphire, laced with rolling whitecaps.

ONCE THE JUNE SUN GOT HIGHER he knew he would be happier not to wear the coat, but now that they had a navy, the officers were keen to display all the polish and discipline of the European fleets. Respect they had already won, when their new ships and green crews mauled the French in the recent battles that they called the "Undeclared War," the "Quasi-War." This present sortie would be America's first into a theater of action in another part of the world, and the Barbary pirate states were the first enemies they would face that were not of a familiar culture. Stories of American fighting prowess must necessarily precede them, and running a tight ship—being seen to run a tight ship—would be indispensable in compelling the deference of the renegade Moorish states.

The *Enterprise*'s lieutenant commandant, Andrew Sterett, had given him the course, southeast by east, and only occasionally did Bliven glance at the compass to ascertain that he had not veered more than a point or two before boxing back to the proper heading. Like all midshipmen, he had a tendency to overcorrect, but the one time this was pointed out to him he learned to steer more conservatively, nudging back to course with the merest suggestive tugs at the wheel. Lieutenant Sterett had marked what a quick study he was, and without being aware of it accorded him a place advanced from his other midshipman. *Enterprise's* action this morning was lively, invigorating, but not dangerous—an ideal time for a probationary midshipman to turn his trick at the wheel. Sterett was careful to keep out of sight and not make him feel too closely hovered over.

Only fourteen he may have been, but this was far from exceptional. Many boys went to sea when only twelve, and if they persevered they could expect to be commissioned lieutenants at fifteen. Bliven heard steps mounting the single ladder, and saw Sterett's fiery red hair appear, for he did not secure his bicorne hat snugly to his head until he was clear of the hatch. "How are you faring, Mr. Putnam?"

Sterett had a penetrating voice, and Bliven started at the sound of it. "Very well, sir. I think." Standing his first watch alone at the wheel, it would have been pointless to try to sound confident. Since coming aboard he had paid the strictest attention to the operation of the ship, committing to memory as fast as he could the nautical vocabulary that was the sailors' daily language, but which to those on land might as well have been Greek. The best he could appear to be was game to learn, and that at least was accurate.

Lieutenant Commander Sterett was a spare man, and slim-waisted. He had a reddish mop of hair, wavy and unkempt no matter how much vanity he expended on it, and bushy combs of red—brilliant, almost to orange—whiskers, worn straight down the sides of his face in front of his ears, down to his jawline. He had an arcing, beaked nose, a noticeable overbite, and a receding chin—an avian countenance not helped by his tendency to move in starts and jerks. There was nothing lacking in his courage, however. Among the crew it was quietly spoken that Sterett, when his blood was up, drew near to madness in his ferocity. During the late Quasi-War with France, when Sterett was serving on board the famed frigate *Constellation*, he had killed one of his own gun crew, run him through with his sword, when the man flinched from his gun while receiving fire.

It was no thing to boast of, and Sterett was not the only American officer to have ever done so. The crew of the *Enterprise*, more than half of them new to the sea, spoke of it somberly, in the manner of an admonition. Their gameness for battle had better match his, or their lives would be equally forfeit. For this summary deed Sterett was savaged in the newspapers, and he was compared to French and even British officers who governed their crews by terror. The journalists found his conduct inconsistent with the principles that led to the revolt against those British. The American navy itself shared this revulsion of the Royal Navy, to the degree that in their own service they determined to recognize no rank higher than that of captain. To have to address anyone as admiral conjured up too many memories of British outrages committed by Admiral Lord This One or That One.

Lieutenant Commandant Sterett sailed above this storm concerning his conduct. Indeed, he assured one newspaper with perfect equanimity that on his ship, "We put men to death for even looking pale." The crew of the *Enterprise* feared that he meant it, and Bliven knew that the navy would sustain him if he did it again. The day he received his provisional appointment, he also received a pamphlet of the navy regulations, and before reading even beyond the first page he learned that cowardice was a capital offense—for officers as well as for the lowly jack-tars.

Still, Bliven felt it odd for one so young to be in command of a ship. Sterett was twenty-three, which meant that he had just turned twenty-one when he summarily executed one of his own men. But then it seemed that every navy man Bliven had encountered was unlikely in his sheer youth. Since its inception the navy had been undermanned; perfectly good ships were laid up in ordinary for want of sufficient crew.

Sterett surveyed the deck, hands clasped behind him, and started to go below, but stopped and turned and regarded how much canvas was set. "Shorten sail, Mr. Putnam, we are outrunning the squadron again."

"Aye, sir." He appreciated the fact that Sterett went below and did not superintend him further—a step doubtless calculated to build a midshipman's confidence. "Mr. Merrick!" Bliven called forward to the bosun. He was still learning the proper address of their stations; seamen ordinary and able were called by their surnames only; warrant officers were entitled to the dignity of "mister." His voice no longer squeaked, but it was not done changing, bridging that awkward gap between the boy and the man. "Take in your tops'ls, if you please."

"Aye, sir."

Bliven watched with some interest as Merrick sent the men aloft; the experienced ones skittered up the swaying ratlines as easily as lizards up a wall, followed by those less sure of their footing and then a few whose hearts were clearly in their throats. Their foresail and main were rigged fore-and-aft, and the men ascended higher to the topsail yards, spacing themselves out and in unison hauling in and making fast the canvas. He glanced over his shoulder, where, alternately visible and not visible beyond the taffrail, according to its rise and fall in the following swell, four hundred yards astern was a sight to make any American's heart leap in sheer pride—three of the proudest frigates on earth, the *President*, forty-four guns, in company with the *Philadelphia*, thirty-six guns, and the *Essex*, thirty-two guns.

No sooner had he turned his gaze back forward—the cause he knew not, perhaps there was dew on the line, or the man's shoe was too large, but Bliven saw the outermost starboard man on the main topsail yardarm lose his footing; his feet shot sideways out from under him and heels over head he plummeted down, issuing a plangent screech the whole distance.

With a helpless gasp Bliven steeled himself to hear the crunch as he struck the deck, but being the farthest outboard he and his shriek sailed past the railing until silenced by a terrific splash of water.

At the top of his lungs, the tar next to him shouted, "Man overboard!" and the cry was taken up, and every man in the rigging was crying, "Man overboard!" until they must sound like monkeys in a tree spreading an alarm.

"Mr. Putnam!" shouted Merrick.

"Mr. Merrick, lower your booms, I will come about!"

"No!" A heartbeat later Merrick sprinted aft toward him, waving his arms. "No! For God's sake, do not turn until the booms are down! Do you hear?"

"Yes! Hurry, then!" Bliven waited, his heart pounding. From no more than Merrick's warning, he understood that if the supremely maneuverable *Enterprise* heeled over in a turn, and the following wind had caught the main fore-and-aft sails broadside, she might have lain right over. "Lower your booms, then finish taking in your tops'ls!"

He squeezed the blood from his hands in gripping the wheel, until he saw the fore and main sails collapsing down their masts, before pulling the wheel hard to starboard. *Enterprise* heeled sharply over; her momentum carried her through the turn and to a stop a moment after heading into the wind. In seconds, as others of the crew furled the topsails to prevent her backing ship, Merrick had a crew in the cutter being lowered into the water and was pulling toward the sailor flailing in the frigid water.

Bliven heard Lieutenant Sterett before he saw him, bounding up the ladder two steps at a time, in breeches and waistcoat, without his coat. Even as he stalked toward Bliven he turned and looked up to see the masts now bare and the cutter stroking away.

Sterett came toward him, his hands clasped behind his back, striding in a manner that told Bliven they must have been clenched into a single fist. He did not speak until he came very near, and then with low, throaty force that Bliven found unnerving; he would rather have been shouted at. "Well, Mr. Putnam. You have taken a great deal upon yourself without my being on deck."

Bliven was near to hyperventilating. "Yes, sir. The man fell from the tops'l yardarm. I judged it a matter of life and death to stop the ship. I could not leave the wheel to come get you."

Sterett grunted. "Why did you come about and not just take in your sails?"

"To stop our forward speed, sir. Our momentum might have carried us past rescuing him."

"Why did you turn to starboard and not to port?"

"Sir, our cutter is mounted on the starboard side. The men can get right to him without rowing around the ship."

Sterett appeared astonished. "You thought of that?"

Bliven's instinct to defend himself snagged on the knowledge of his inexperience. "Well, no, sir, but as you see, it was a fortunate turn."

Sterett's voice rose to a bellow the deeper into the question he got. "Did you think about three big frigates close astern who might run us over when you wheel about right in their way?" They looked up and saw that *Essex* had cleaved several points to starboard to give them room, and it was obvious that their distress had been observed.

Bliven was caught and dropped his head. "No, sir, I confess I thought only of the man in the water."

As the men in the cutter rowed their hardest, in a moment Sterett and Bliven saw Merrick twirl a float several times over his head before flinging it out to the thrashing sailor. He seized it, Merrick began pulling him in, and all knew that the incident would have no mortal cost.

"Do you require assistance?" It was the voice of James Barron, captain of the *President*, his voice tinnily amplified by a speaking trumpet as she billowed past them to port.

Sterett had left his trumpet below, and so cupped his hands. "Thank you, no," he shouted. "We will catch up to you."

Barron waved to indicate that he understood, and the *President* left them slowly behind.

Alone with Sterett on the quarterdeck, Bliven began to feel sick to his stomach. "I am sorry, sir. I judged it a situation that called for the most instant action."

Sterett pursed his lips, looked Bliven down and up, and sighed deeply. "Well, Mr. Putnam, in an emergency at sea instinct can serve you as well as forethought, you may find. Better to have called me, even as you took action, but you have done well. You saved that man's life. I am going below for my coat. Please, no more theatrics until I return." It was as close to humor as Sterett ever came.

"No, sir," said Bliven quietly. "Thank you, sir."

Once on the quarterdeck, Bliven's knees began to shake. How fast it can all change, he thought, mortality that can strike at any moment, from any quarter. Vigilance must never cease. He must learn faster.

He saw Merrick standing at the cutter's tiller, confident, his experienced sea legs absorbing the swell. The stricken sailor was stripped of his wet shirt and wrapped in a blanket that he clutched tightly about himself, no doubt sending aloft his prayers of thanks that he had not been left to drown, terrified and alone and freezing.

Before three-quarters of an hour had passed, Sterett in complete uniform had them under way again, had overtaken the squadron and resumed their position in the van, before leaving Putnam alone again to see out his watch.

The emergency passed, and he allowed himself a smile; he was conscious that after only three days at sea, he already felt the magic that a ship works on her sailors. Their *Enterprise* could not match the frigates in firepower, but she was swifter and more nimble. She had been fresh from the builder's yard when she sallied into the Undeclared War with the French, and by the end of that conflict she had bested eight French privateers and liberated eleven American merchant vessels. It was a peerless record and there was no sense of inferiority to sail in her. Little schooner turned jackass brig she may have been, but she was every inch a fighter and everyone knew it.

ON THE QUARTERDECK OF THE *PRESIDENT*, Commodore Richard Dale wedged his knee against the starboard rail and observed the *Enterprise* through his glass. He was glad to have her with him, and wished he had more like her, but smaller vessels to support the frigates were becoming a rarity. President Adams had sold out the *Pinckney* before he left office; *Enterprise*'s own sister ship, the *Experiment*, was now laid up in ordinary, and even with the sudden conflagration in the Mediterranean she would likely also be sold out before the year was over. Mr. Jefferson had begun his term as the enemy of high expenses and a powerful military. In fact he had turned his famous avocation as an architect to designing a grand covered dry dock for the Potomac, where their expensive ships could be laid up, safely out of the water, and then refloated using the power of the tide when they were wanted. *Ass,* thought Dale. He could preserve his ships, but where would he find officers and sailors who knew what they were doing after he dispersed them into civilian life? Save money, indeed. If we are going to fight, Dale had written his superiors, let us fight, for God's sake. Half-measures would cost much, avail little, and ultimately must only postpone an inevitable conclusive action.

Such ancillary vessels as schooners and brigs did not command the notice and respect from foreign powers that the frigates did, but the *Enterprise* could fight where he could not. Dale well knew that the *Enterprise* drew nine feet of water; his smallest frigate, the *Essex,* over twelve feet. That could be a critical difference if it came to blockading or perhaps even fighting in Tangier, or Algiers, or Tunis, or Tripoli— harbors of which they had only the most dubious charts, and which surely were strewn with rocks and reefs and three thousand years of wrecks of which they knew nothing. If he ran one of America's great frigates aground there, the disaster must be incalculable.

"MR. PUTNAM?" Bliven recognized the voice of Samuel Bandy, the other midshipman of the *Enterprise.* "Your watch is relieved."

Bliven held the wheel as Bandy stepped up to take it. "Course sou'east by east," said Bliven. "She rides well. I have shortened sail; keep an eye on the squadron and let Mr. Sterett know if they come up too close."

"Thank you," said Bandy. He grasped the wheel with hands as much fat as strong. Bliven felt the strain drain out of him, happy to surrender the forenoon watch; he had been at the wheel since four o'clock that morning. Yet he found the etiquette amusing, standing there at fourteen in their standing collars and bicorne hats—hats that were excessively snugged down, for in this wind they were at risk any moment of blowing off, but as mere midshipmen they were unsure whether they might be allowed to remove them. Perhaps it was necessary for the smooth operation of the ship, but he found it extraordinary, the degree to which they were expected to comport themselves as any other officers. They were not even done growing. At home they should be racing or wrestling or hunting when they found leisure time. Or rather they would, if they were neighbors, but Samuel Bandy was from the other end of the Atlantic seaboard, from South Carolina.

He was a stout lad with straight hair of reddish blond, fair skin that tended to burn rather than tan, and blue eyes slightly popped and very clear that seemed to always express expectation. South Carolina seemed as distant and strange to Bliven Putnam as the African shores where they were bound. The Putnam family came close to sufficing for themselves on their farm at Litchfield, growing and laying by sufficient crops for themselves and their stock, selling apples and cider and dairy products for the cash they needed. Bliven's father also operated a livery stable and drayage, putting to good use their two giant shire horses in hauling goods and merchandise for people. Though they both came from families that worked the land, Bliven was instantly aware that Samuel held himself a class higher, for the Putnams worked with their own hands, where the Bandy family commanded slaves in doing the hard labor. Bliven could not help but wonder whether this was a cause of Sam's lack of physical toughness. He could not be called weak, particularly, but Bliven's personal acquaintance with ax and plow had honed his strength to a higher degree. It was a greater effort for Sam to get aloft or haul lines, but he was game for it and always applied the necessary effort at a task until he succeeded. They had boarded *Enterprise* and begun their careers on the same day; no doubt sea duty would slim Sam down and toughen him.

Bliven went below to their one impossibly crowded berth deck. After four hours on watch he headed straight through the wardroom, easing himself out onto the narrow stern walk and then into the absurdly small officers' privy. He peed for several seconds down into the open water, when the door flew open and a voice barked, "Haul that in, sir! I need this space." He knew and had already learned to dislike the voice of the second lieutenant, Phineas Curtis.

"Yes, sir, I'm just fin—"

"Now, damn your eyes! You want to stand about exploring yourself, go for'd to the heads and amuse the rest of the degenerate swash on this vessel."

"Yes, sir, I'm very sorry." Bliven had covered himself enough to retreat back into the wardroom. He had heard it said of lieutenants that one of their primary tasks was to make life hell for midshipmen, and he was grateful that Porter had principal charge of him and Sam Bandy. Curtis enjoyed his superiority entirely too much.

Enterprise's bottom curved up steadily from the midships aft, making her slick as grease over the water while giving her a deep, sharp keel for stability, but this was at the cost of interior space. The midshipmen's berth in the steerage, which necessarily conformed to the curve of the hull, was little larger than a burial crypt, and he shared even this tiny compartment with Sam. It was lit by a single battle lantern, its small glass panes solidly clamped by iron strapping. There was a bucket of sand in which to place a heated shot for warmth when needed, hooks for their clothing, ropes' ends to practice tying their knots, books to study mathematics and navigation. There was no point in feeling they had been cheated in their accommodations; the cabin opposite the wardroom, of identical proportions, was that of the surgeon's mate and the chaplain.

It was the latter, a smallish, gray-haired minister of the old Episcopal faith named Pelham, who discreetly balanced out the cruelty of the lieutenants. He could not be seen to contradict them, much less quarrel with them, for navy regulations did not spell out the specific relations between line officers and those with ancillary functions— the clerk; the purser; the surgeon or surgeon's mate, depending on the size of the ship; and the chaplain. Within bounds tolerated by the captain, a lieutenant could make life equally unpleasant for them. But with the dearth of Pelham's listed duties—conducting divine services, and helping the surgeon's mate tend to the sick, and after a battle the wounded—he found circumstances behind the lieutenants' backs to take the midshipmen under his wing for some kindness and encouragement. It was after Bliven's first humiliation at Curtis's hands—he sent him aloft for two hours their first night out, for daring to read a book that was not about navigation or seamanship—that Pelham told him it was likely because Curtis was merely a second lieutenant, and had been for a number of years without promotion, that venting his frustration on the only officers aboard who were beneath him took on such a great importance to him.

Already Bliven had learned to hate their lessons in swordsmanship, for Curtis's special gift was to cloak his mania for cruelty in the guise of training. When he and Sam Bandy first came aboard ship, each found on his blanket a U.S. navy regulation cutlass, with scabbard, belt, and buckle. Bliven withdrew the slightly curved thirty-inch blade and found it stunningly sharp. No sooner had they found them than Curtis had them buckled on and was leading them up the ladder.

"Come on, now," he said. "What young boys do not love to play at sword fighting?" He squared them off on the quarterdeck, had them strike their blades together a couple times to hear the *ting* of steel on steel. "Now, boys," he took pleasure in saying, "a cutlass is ever so much more lethal than a foil. A foil can only pierce, but a cutlass can hack and slice as well, as facilitated by the curved blade. The design is copied from the Moorish scimitar, but lighter and more maneuverable." Curtis faced Bliven and Sam against each other. "Feet apart," he said, "weight on the back foot unless you are advancing. If your opponent lunges at you, merely step back out of his way. If you can't do that, deflect the blow with a sideways strike of your own. Remember, economy of movement is a great advantage. All right, let's see you go at each other."

Sam and Bliven looked at each other, bewildered.

"Oh!" exclaimed Curtis suddenly. "No, wait, wait. Here." From the netting he extracted two wooden practice swords of the same dimensions. "Wouldn't do to have you bleeding all over the nice clean deck, would it?"

Worse than practicing with Sam, Bliven came to loathe training with Curtis himself, for although Curtis also used the wooden cutlass, his experience was such that he easily won, and when he struck he struck hard and called it good training to learn to defend themselves.

Safe in his berth from Curtis for the moment, Bliven gave a quick glance at a one-page inclusion in the pamphlet of regulations. This was his first Saturday at sea, and there was much still to accustom himself to. He traced his finger in the dim light down the schedule of prescribed rations—today there would be peas and cheese to augment the pound of salt pork and pound of bread. He nodded in satisfaction; they would get cheese only twice a week while it lasted, and as the bread turned foul they would turn to the infamous rocklike biscuits. Their ration also included a daily half-pint of rum. At fourteen he was not allowed the rum, but the purser credited his account four cents for every forgone ration of alcohol; Bliven had already calculated that if they were away for a year, there would be near fifteen dollars extra pay when he returned. That was an even exchange, for he felt no attraction to drink—but another morning like this, he thought and sighed, and that case may alter itself.

Bliven lay down in his tiny berth and closed his eyes, but he did not sleep. Instead he pondered how close he might have come to wrecking his naval career, less than a week old. In his mind's eye he saw the man fall from the yardarm again and again. Bliven did not know his name, but surmised he was one of the new recruits who went to sea, as many did, one jump ahead of the law. Bliven had seen him clinging uncertainly to the rigging; ought he to have drawn Merrick's attention to him? Surely it was not for a midshipman to tell a bosun of fifteen years' experience who to send aloft. Again he saw Merrick running toward him, waving his arms and shouting at him not to come about until the sails were down. Might he have capsized the vessel? Likely not, really, for she was well ballasted, and it was part of the bosun's job to help train midshipmen. His first three watches at the wheel, either the second or third lieutenant was nearby. He could not have been expected to respond as a seasoned officer would have.

Bliven rubbed his eyes and shook his head, hoping to place it behind him. He thought again of the majesty of a ship of the line, and wished that he had seen one, but he had not, he had seen only pictures. At a time when England and France deployed scores of them, the United

States possessed not one. He knew they had built one, once, but straightaway awarded her to France as thanks for their help in the Revolution, and to replace a French vessel lost in that conflict. This seemed like a grandly generous gesture, to public perception, but over time the real reason became clear, that our infant country had no money to maintain such a powerful ship in peacetime, and in this gift to France they divested themselves of that ruinous expense. The largest ship Bliven had seen was a frigate; he had boarded the *President* once, briefly, to receive his commission, and was breathtaken at even her size and complexity. He had heard it widely stated as fact, and it was universally accepted, that America's frigates were incomparably better than any of their class in the European navies; even the great Admiral Lord Nelson had remarked his consternation at ever having to fight one.

ONLY THREE DAYS AT SEA, but home seemed a world away. Bliven's brawn and self-reliance had slowly accrued with dawn-to-dusk labor on his family's farm near Litchfield, Connecticut, and his late start as an officer in training resulted from the bargain he had made with his father. Unlike many of their neighbors who could apportion chores among four or six or many more children—a circumstance common even elsewhere in his extended Putnam family—Bliven, despite his parents' prayers and assiduous effort, was an only child. He had agreed with his hardworking father, laconically in their spare-spoken New England way but not altogether tacitly, that Bliven would work long and without complaint to bring their farm to self-sufficiency, and when the time came he would be free to seek a larger destiny, to travel, to learn things of the world that did not come from cultivating corn and root vegetables, or pressing cider from the apples in their orchard.

The world held wonder for him, and he read books ahead of his years on history and geography. He had proven only a moderately successful student at mathematics and the sciences, but he applied himself to learning of the rest of the world, the places, the people and how they lived.

In that two years since Bliven voiced his interest in the navy they had increased their orchard to an acreage ample for commercial production, enlarged the garden, and brought two new fields into production. In this condition they needed only to hire a single helper, paid for with the sale of cider, and his father proved as good as his word.

Bliven's choice of the sea was new within his family. New England had always had sailors, but far fewer as so many turned to farming and commerce. The perils of the North Atlantic were all too well known, as townspeople observed lonely matrons strolling the widow's walks atop their harborside houses, forever gazing out to sea for the rise of approaching masts. Most of their men eventually returned, but all too often they did not. Yet the Revolution and the Quasi-War clarified to all the need for a fleet, whose paucity of seamen was well publicized, and for Bliven it was his best chance to enlarge his own horizons. There was little to prepare him for the sea in Litchfield, but this placed him at no disadvantage from other midshipmen, for many entered the service having read less than he had. Bliven had seen several of the memoirs written by officers who had accompanied Captain Cook in his explorations. Only recently had he acquired a recent edition, though not the latest, of *The Practical Navigator*, but he did not consult it as often. He was no great hand at mathematics, and he could only trust that the trigonometry required for the subject would come to him with age.

A midshipman's appointment was impossible without a recommendation from a senator of the candidate's home state, and the senior Mr. Putnam had approached Uriah Tracy, who had long maintained a law office in Litchfield. It was in Bliven's favor that the celebrated Revolutionary War general Israel Putnam had been his grandfather's brother, and moreover that the navy wanted men, desperately. Mr. Putnam recounted his family's hardship during the Revolution—and it surely also helped that Tracy was an enthusiastic consumer of Putnam cider. When Bliven's appointment to the navy issued, he left the farm without guilt and with his father's spoken blessing, but in Bliven's quiet moments he worried about them.

Bliven knew that with the afternoon watch they would beat to quarters for gun drill. Lieutenant Sterett was mad for discipline and efficiency from the gun crews, but then, as one of the few on board who had seen action, he had reason. With twelve guns and three messes that the crew had formulated their first day out, the labor was evenly divided: first mess to service the first four guns port; second mess the first four guns starboard; third mess the last two guns each side. Each gun had a crew of four, which, as each six-pounder weighed three quarters of a ton, was barely sufficient to run them out and in, and a boy for each three guns to shuttle powder and shot up from the magazine. The lieutenants had command of the guns in action; Bliven was assigned to help Porter with port guns one through four.

Sterett drove the crews hard, but after three days, from the initial tattoo of beating to quarters the crew were at their stations, tompions pulled, guns rolled out, powder horns at the touch holes ready for priming powder, second cartridge and ball waiting to reload, wet sponges and ramrod ready—all in three minutes. Mistakes the first day were met with a tongue-lashing; mistakes the second day were lashed with a cat; the third day there were no mistakes, and when Sterett praised them, it meant something. Almost never did a ship fight both sides at once; thus, when the starboard guns were engaged, the crews of the port guns were available to manage the rigging and replace casualties. Every man knew his action station and his duty, and Sterett pressed on them that confusion in battle was fatal.

On their fourth day out they suddenly encountered a north wind, stiff and chill, that blew stronger during the course of the day. The frigates held their course but lost speed, hauling repeatedly closer to the wind until it seemed they must lie on their beam ends, while the *Enterprise* skimmed ahead on her fore-and-aft main rigging.

Sterett was visibly vexed at the prospect of having to shorten sail even more to keep from outrunning them, when a cry came from the lookout that the *President* was running up signal flags. He put the glass briefly to his eye and hissed, "Damn." He sent a boy to run and fetch his speaking trumpet.

He could see the bosun was aware something was afoot, and was awaiting instruction. "Mr. Merrick!" called Sterett.

"Sir?"

"The flagship desires to speak us. You'll need to change your set. We will run on tops'ls and jibs until they catch up."

"Aye, sir."

Lieutenant Porter was in the small wardroom when he heard the new orders, and clattered up the ladder to the quarterdeck.

"The commodore desires to speak us," Sterett told him.

It took the *President* an hour to maneuver up, fifty yards off *Enterprise*'s starboard beam—alee, which would be harder to speak into but a safety precaution; should an errant gust push the great frigate off her heading, she would not run the schooner over.

"Steady as you go, Mr. Bandy," said Sterett quietly.

"Aye, sir." Sam Bandy wished he could run below and tell Bliven to come have a close look at a forty-four in all her majesty, but he knew he must stay rooted at the wheel.

Sterett and Porter beheld a clot of officers on the *President*'s quarterdeck, carrying their hats, which would have blown off had they tried to wear them. In their center was one noticeably older, close to fifty, with iron-gray hair and soft, intelligent eyes above a finely turned mouth. That one strode to the rail and put a speaking trumpet to his mouth, and called into the wind with distinct syllables, "Good morning, Mr. Sterett."

Sterett put the trumpet to his lips, a brass cone nearly two feet long that did not just direct his voice but amplified it with its brassy vibration. "Good morning, Commodore." In fact, Dale's rank was captain, no higher than the other frigate captains, but by universal consent a captain in overall command of a squadron was addressed by the honorary rank of commodore.

They noticed that the *President* did not alter her canvas after catching up; the visit would be brief. Dale put the trumpet to his lips again. "My compliments, I instruct you to go ahead of us to Gibraltar. Make contact with our supply ship, if possible, and the American consul. Inform them of our imminent arrival, gather what information you can, and wait for us there."

Sterett's heart leapt. "Aye-aye, sir."

"Very well," said Dale. "Godspeed."

"Thank you, sir," he concluded as he lowered the trumpet. "Mr. Merrick!"

"Sir?"

"Make all sail! Mr. Bandy!"

"Sir?"

"Think you can handle her with all the canvas set?"

Sam Bandy grinned broadly. "Yes, sir."

"Mr. Porter, if you will come below with me." As they reached the head of the ladder, Sterett said where only Porter could hear, "Keep a good eye on Bandy this watch. I would feel better if he showed just a little doubt in himself."

2.

GIBRALTAR

————◆————

July 1801

The first hint that they were entering troubled waters came on June 28, as the coasts of Spain and Morocco began to narrow in the approach to the Straits of Gibraltar. Cádiz lay behind a British blockade, unseen over the northern horizon. Ahead of them they spied a French squadron of three sail, inbound, and ninety minutes later they heard the rolling booms of a furious battle as the French ships attempted to break through to their garrison. Spain, her own imperial glory a fading memory, lay prostrate between them.

The United States was neutral in this newest manifestation of Anglo-French bloodletting. Their hatred for each other had simmered for centuries, often boiling over into war. America had found little to choose between them in the Quasi-War; indeed, there had been as much sentiment to fight the British as the French. That they chose the French produced a happy result now, for English friendship vouchsafed them resupply in the British colonies at Gibraltar and Malta, which could prove indispensable if it did come to war with the Barbary states.

The officers on the *Enterprise* studied the northern horizon the rest of the day for any sign of who had won the unseen battle, but sea met sky undisturbed until night fell and they contented themselves with the mystery.

Enterprise began to thread the Straits of Gibraltar early on June 29. Bliven waited until Lieutenant Curtis had the watch, and he furtively pulled his Rollins *Geography* from beneath his blankets. The ancients called the mountains on either side the Pillars of Hercules, and he wondered whether indeed the flanking peaks should look as if they were holding up the sky. In the morning he saw Africa sliding by, three and a half miles to starboard, and Spain three and a half miles to port.

When he spied the Jeb el Musa of Morocco he nodded. The ancients had let their imaginations carry them away; it was a high, rearing massif of a hill, but did not live up to such an expectation. They had passed Cádiz on their north, and then five miles ahead off their port bow he saw, shimmering in the salt air, the white south face of Gibraltar, a sharp peak like a lion's tooth. There, he thought with satisfaction as though the earth had resumed its order, that one is holding up the sky—ah, no, the ancient writers had caused him to mix his metaphors, and he decided to prefer the lion's mouth. But sailing between Gibraltar and Jeb el Musa, he was aware they might be sailing into a lion's mouth in an entirely different way.

In books Bliven had seen engravings of the famed Rock of Gibraltar rearing thirteen hundred feet out of the water, but he had read nothing to tell him, and he was surprised to discover, that the harbor and the town lay on the west side of the rock, which sloped gently, not dramatically, up to the heights, so his first close view of that celebrated profile would have to wait until they left the harbor and penetrated farther east into the Mediterranean.

They tacked north into the Bay of Gibraltar, shortening sail as they took on a pilot who guided them through a gap in the mole into Gibraltar's basin that was ample but by no means huge. Sterett inquired into the confused etiquette of a salute, but the pilot assured him, upon learning that *Enterprise* was merely in advance of a squadron, a salute would be rendered by his flagship and not him. All officers were on deck, surprised at how empty the harbor was. There was not a single British man-of-war to be seen, and only a couple of merchantmen, one of which they learned was the American *Grand Turk*. She was laden with a cargo of the infamous tribute for the dey of Algiers, and was sheltering in Gibraltar, awaiting an American warship to escort her safely across lest the riches intended to purchase the peace of one pirate be spirited away by another more brazen. Also anchored in the harbor were two of the oddest curiosities that Bliven had ever seen. The pilot took them a few hundred yards off the beam of the larger vessel before signaling to stop; the block was knocked from the chain and the anchor plunged into the water with an enormous crashing rattle.

The bizarre ship that so arrested their attention was low-waisted like a schooner, although much larger than the *Enterprise*, and with a raised quarterdeck, rigged as a brig, and despite the nine open gunports along her main deck she presented the most unwarlike appearance imaginable. She was painted yellow with a broad white stripe, her stern a brilliant green, and the muzzles of her guns painted red. She flew the red and yellow stripes of Tripoli.

"There, boys!" Bliven heard one of the tars call out, as a hairy sunburnt arm pointed her out. "Look'ye over there, I know that ship!"

Bliven strode to the rail. "What ship is it, Murfin?"

"Ha! Do ye not know a Boston brig when ye see one?"

Bliven would have died before admitting that he did not. "Yes, but what ship, Murfin?"

"Why bless me, sir, it is the *Betsy*, taken by pirates five, seven year ago."

Bliven heard Sterett come up behind him. "Sir, Murfin says it—"

"I heard him, Mr. Putnam, thank you." Lieutenants Porter and Curtis followed him, prompting Bliven to retire from the conversation but remain within hearing.

"Shall you hail him, sir?" asked Porter.

"No, we should wait for the squadron. Commodore Dale will decide what to do. I suppose we had best go ashore and look up the American consul. Then we'll see if we can find some fresh food and water for the men."

IT TOOK FIVE DAYS MORE for the squadron to arrive, in late afternoon inching past the mole under topgallants; as they nosed into the harbor the British batteries saluted them with seventeen guns, which placed Dale at ease, for he desired to be correct in his formalities but there was no international convention on how many guns to salute to whom. A naval squadron entering a friendly port, however, was surely a requisite occasion. To the British, twenty-one guns was a royal salute, seventeen guns less so, but Dale knew that it was an average and acceptable salute for a monarchy to render the flag of a republic. The *President* returned the salute, gun for gun, which was always a safe policy. The pilot eased the flagship—Sterett thought it must have been at Dale's request—between them and the gaudy Tripolitan brig, within hailing distance, before dropping anchor, with the *Philadelphia* and the *Essex* close behind.

Sterett took his cutter over at once to report, and found Captain Samuel Barron of the *Philadelphia* and William Bainbridge of the *Essex* already there, as well as James Barron, who commanded the *President* while Dale concerned himself with matters of the squadron and the question of how to position his four ships to protect American commerce in the entirety of the Mediterranean. He had need of at least twice that many.

They could see that their arrival had engendered a lively commotion on the Tripolitan, whose port side swarmed with staring, open-bloused Moors, and a quarterdeck whose officers clustered about a large, black-bearded man in a red fez and black tunic whose front was emblazoned with gold filigree.

Dale put his speaking trumpet to his lips. "I am Captain Richard Dale, United States frigate *President*." The other officers found that typical of Dale's modesty; he could have stated his rank as commodore but did not.

"I am Murad Reis, grand admiral of the Tripolitan navy," answered the impressive bearded man. "Warship *Meshuda*."

The American officers looked at one another, dumbfounded, until Bainbridge said, "He's no more an Arab than I am."

"Why, he's Scottish. What in hell?" wondered Samuel Barron.

Again Dale spoke him. "We are five weeks at sea. Are Tripoli and the United States at peace, or at war?" There was no risk in the answer, for they were in a neutral port.

"Why, at peace, Captain."

"And our consul in Tripoli, Mr. Eaton, he is well and on his station?"

"At last report, he is well and had gone to Tunis at his own desire."

"Excuse me, sir," ventured Sterett. "That is a lie. Tripoli declared war on the United States while we were at sea, according to the consul."

"Indeed?" Dale seemed only mildly surprised; they had suspected this was where events were headed, and needed only the confirmation. "Well, let's see if we can draw him out a little." Again he raised the trumpet. "Will you accept our hospitality and dine with us this evening?"

There was a pause, a little too long. "Thank you. Regrettably, I cannot." There was another pause. "Welcome to Gibraltar." They saw the admiral hand his trumpet to a boy and retire.

Every American on the *President's* quarterdeck perceived the danger in the first instant, and their stroke of good fortune in the next. Of the four Barbary states, Morocco on the Atlantic had made peace some time back, if it still held, and in former years, theirs were the majority of pirates in the open ocean. Algiers, Tunis, and Tripoli usually sought prey only in the Mediterranean. Tripolitan ships even being in Gibraltar might well signal their design to spread their aggression into the Atlantic. There this Scot of a grand admiral could fly English colors, hail American merchant ships in his jovial Highland accent, and pounce on crews before they knew what hit them. But there was another side to it.

"We've got him, by God," said James Barron with satisfaction fairly dripping from his voice. "We've got him."

Dale nodded. "It is obvious that we were not expected, and now two of their principal ships are trapped here. I will need to leave one of you here to bottle him up, and sink him if he tries to break out."

"Oh, he won't try." The unfamiliar voice caused all five officers to turn. "Permit me, I am John Gavino, United States consul in Gibraltar. You are Commodore Dale, I presume?"

They bowed and shook hands. "Captain Samuel Barron of the *Phil-*

adelphia," Dale introduced him, "the other Captain James Barron of the *President*. Captain Bainbridge of the *Essex* I believe you should already know, and Lieutenant Commandant Sterett of the *Enterprise*."

"I do indeed know Captain Bainbridge, and Lieutenant Sterett and I are also acquainted now."

"You think he will not attempt an escape?" asked Samuel Barron.

"All our information suggests he has no stomach for a fight—he is grand admiral largely because he is the son-in-law of the bashaw. But we can discuss all if you will come to my house for dinner. If you are free, we can go in my boat now."

"Well, apparently"—Dale rolled his eyes at the Tripolitan—"we have no other engagements." The other captains laughed.

As the oarsmen pulled away, Dale directed them first around the *Meshuda*'s bow and down her starboard side before pulling to the quay. He estimated twenty-six to thirty guns, the main battery of nine-pounders by the look of them, plus carronades and bow and stern chasers. The vessel was large enough to carry them—barely—but having been built as a merchantman, she could never take punishment. She was no doubt a deadly commerce raider, but someone was thinking grandly to regard her as the flagship of a navy.

Dale conveyed these sentiments to Consul Gavino, even as they saw a couple of Berber officers staring down at them from the *Meshuda*'s quarterdeck, and the others followed Dale's example in lifting their bicornes in acknowledgment.

"So in essence," said Dale as he settled himself for the pull to the wharf, "she is a large pirate ship. She is not a warship."

"Yes." Gavino held tightly to the gunwale; he was a thoroughgoing landlubber and did not like being on the water, even in the harbor. "You might well say the same of their crews. Like all navies, the

Berbers take their rank and file from the worst of society—beggars, drifters, criminals—and to be at the bottom of society in North Africa is a different and worse condition than in Europe or America. Most of their men were cutthroats by nature before being put aboard ships to become pirates in fact."

Dale glanced over his shoulder to judge the distance to the wharf. "Mr. Gavino, I was given to expect that we would meet our supply ship here, but save our squadron and the *Grand Turk*, I see no other American ships in the harbor. We want water and provisions. Have they not arrived?"

"Water, we can give you some," Gavino answered, "probably not as much as you need. Spain is near desert in summer. We will do what we can. Your supply vessel has been detained by the Spanish at Algeciras."

"For heaven's sake, why? Our business with the Berbers does not involve them."

"Well, they are caught between the British and the French; I imagine they just need to feel they can still bully somebody, even if it is just an American merchantman."

"Yes," Dale said, nodding. "We saw a French squadron of three sail just off Cádiz, headed in to try to break through the blockade. We heard battle but don't know the outcome—"

"Look here, Mr. Gavino," Samuel Barron interrupted. "You seem to know these Berbers, all these different Berbers, better than we do. What are they like? Can they fight?"

Gavino shrugged. "If you corner them I suppose they could, but they are not known for it. Simple thievery is much more their business." The oars dipped in time to the small chop in the harbor, setting the boat into easy rocking. "I do know from several sources, when they attack a merchantman, they will fire one broadside, usually high, to get their attention. Then they will all line the rail, brandishing dirks and cutlasses, and shout and threaten in the loudest and vilest way they can. That usually suffices for an unarmed merchant ship to surrender, and accept that they will be captives and slaves until they are ransomed. I have a letter with more detail of their fighting tactics, I will read it to you when we arrive at my house."

"It's outrageous," growled Bainbridge. At twenty-six he was the youngest of the captains, ten years younger than Samuel Barron and seven years younger than the latter's brother James. Bainbridge had curly brown hair around a lumpy sort of face, and an underbite that made him look always like he was about to spit. "The whole system is outrageous."

"Well," said Commodore Dale with an exaggerated idleness, "you certainly have more cause to feel that than the rest of us, God knows."

The other captains laughed quietly as Bainbridge scowled. All knew that the previous year, when Bainbridge was in command of the *George Washington*, twenty-four guns, he had been entrusted with delivering the United States' annual tribute to the dey of Algiers. That man, a perfumed old silk-swathed potentate, Mustapha VI, compelled Bainbridge after he had once lain to outside the mole of Algiers, to anchor his light frigate within the harbor under the guns of his fort. He not only commandeered the American ship to transport his ambassador to the Sultan's court in Constantinople—along with his wives, concubines, servants, male companions, and a menagerie that included a dozen lions—he forced Bainbridge to do so while flying the Algerine flag above the American.

Bainbridge would have happily died that day, could he have done so vindicating his country's honor. He protested with the greatest vehemence that he had no authority to lower his country's flag to any nation, but Mustapha Dey assured him that the choice was either that or war, and Bainbridge and his crew should be the first prisoners. With the consul advising cooperation and no other American firepower within five hundred miles, he did as he was bidden, though striking his colors meant court-martial. But he was hardly finished.

He held his gorge through the whole voyage—nearly six hundred miles from Algiers to the Sicilian straits, then eight hundred miles on to Crete and the turn into the Aegean, and three hundred miles of meticulous navigation through the Greek islands to the Dardanelles—a long time to seethe while being faultlessly correct to the ambassador and his retinue. As he approached the castle on the European side of the narrows a lighter came alongside and demanded that he anchor and submit to inspection. God only knew, thought Bainbridge, what kind of game might be afoot there to make things even worse. He knew that the fortress was armed with gigantic antique cannons that fired eight-hundred-pound round stones, but they could barely be aimed and had a fixed elevation. He eased the *George Washington* within range of the castle, moving only under topgallants as though he were making to anchor. He fired a full salute of twenty-one guns to the fort, which they were compelled to answer. Unlike the Western navies, the Turks still fired shotted salutes, a holdover from the days when salutes were meant to demonstrate that one's guns were empty. Bainbridge and his officers watched the white geysers erupt from the bay where the gargantuan stone balls landed, and while his ship was shrouded in smoke, Bainbridge suddenly made all sail and scooted into the Sea of Marmara before the Turks could do anything about it.

He safely delivered his passengers and cargo to Constantinople, where he was granted an audience with the sultan himself—to whom Bainbridge gave such an earful about his treatment that this ruler of the Mohammedan world expressed his respect of the captain's manliness and sense of duty. He voiced as well his annoyance with the dey of Algiers, who Bainbridge learned had a history of flouting the imperial authority. The sultan sent the *George Washington* back to Algiers, where Bainbridge incurred the wrath of the dey when he declined to undertake another errand. Mustapha Dey threatened to place Bainbridge's head on a pole at the harbor entrance—until he handed over the sultan's letter, after which the old dandy could not do enough for him. And to top all, the dey had declared war on France, and Bainbridge was able to bargain the freedom of all the French citizens in Algiers and took them with him to safety—despite the undeclared war between their two countries.

Unsure of what reception he would receive at home, Bainbridge found himself lionized, praised for his cool head, initiative, and ultimate vindication of American honor. Though young, he was a pride of the navy, and he took Dale's dry witticism in good part.

They discovered that the American consul in Gibraltar lived and worked in a very ordinary house, only a short walk from the wharf, but in this small enclave, everywhere was a short walk. After five weeks at sea they almost swooned over the table he set—roast beef, potatoes, English peas, a generous pouring of a very fine Madeira, and quantities of the fresh fruit for which the south of Spain is so famous.

"You have a gruesome fine cook," said Dale.

"English." Gavino nodded. He confirmed for them that Tripoli had declared war on the United States. "Now," he said, "I am informed that the dey of Algiers will not join the war, but I don't trust the old rapscallion. Your real trouble is with the bashaw of Tripoli, he's a real brute, named Yusuf Karamanlis. Mark me, he is an evil one, he is. He was born a third son, which did not suit his ambition, so he murdered the eldest brother, shot him twice, and when he wasn't dead stabbed him until he stopped twitching. As you can imagine, that deed attracted some unfavorable notice, so when the old bashaw died, Yusuf had to stand aside and see his second older brother, Hamet, become bashaw. That lasted only a couple years. Then Yusuf seized the throne last year, exiled Hamet, and now he's in Egypt somewhere; some of our people are trying to find him. Yusuf began demanding the same level of tribute as we pay Algiers, even though he is supposed to be vassal to the dey. Our consul there, Mr. Eaton, stalled for as much time as he could, but eventually Yusuf sent a gang of thugs to the American consulate and chopped down the flagpole. Now you will understand that Mohammedan countries do not issue written declarations of war, like civilized people. In Tripoli they chop down your flagpole!"

Dale and the captains laughed. "Well, surely that conveys the message; that is all good to know," said Dale. "At least now we can drop all this damned silly pretense and start shooting." He swept his glass of Madeira above his plate as he gestured.

"Well, yes and no," said Gavino, his tone suddenly turning serious. "They have declared war on us, but unless we declare war on them, and you are officially notified of it, you are limited to your existing orders. You will protect American shipping, you will defend yourselves if attacked, but you will undertake no offensive operations; you will take no prizes. You must understand me rightly here: no offensive operations. Are we clear on this point?"

Dale stared at him, disbelieving. "Damn me," he spat. "Damn me if you're going to put me on a sea with enemies and tell me I can't attack them. Can Jefferson even be trusted to declare war back home? He wants us all to become farmers and get sunburns and read that damned Rousseau fellow."

Gavino reached around the table, filling the glasses with Madeira. "Well, now, do let's be fair. After all, it was Jefferson who was the first to advocate resisting the Barbary states, fifteen years ago. It was Adams talked him down until we got us a navy. Now we have a navy, and Jefferson takes your part before the Congress, maybe more than you know."

Samuel Barron waved off more Madeira. "No more for me, I thank you. If that be true, why are we here with just four ships? How in bloody hell are we supposed to blockade"—he made a fist before him, extending his fingers one at a time—"Tangier, Algiers, Tunis, Tripoli, convoy American shipping—"

"And tie down these two buggers here in Gibraltar," added his brother.

"With four damned ships? Who is that going to impress?"

Gavino began to feel defensive. "Gentlemen, please. In the first part, a second squadron, a larger one, will be forming up soon to come relieve you next year, let us hope with a declaration of war in hand. The government is aware that our sailors enlist for only a year at a time, so you will not be left in the breach for very long. In the second part, as far as we know, Morocco is satisfied with what we pay them, and they will observe our treaty with them. The bashaw of Tunis is not that interested in war, either. Your main worry is Tripoli, and again, perhaps Algiers, although that is not certain."

Dale scowled at the table, thinking. "Tripoli," he said at last. "How many ships have they got, anyway?"

"Well, that is the good part," said Gavino. "You surprised their two best ones here. *Meshuda* is a large brig, twenty-eight guns, reasonably fast, but not strong. The smaller brig that accompanies her does not have a name; they do not name their small ships. Apart from that, they have another small brig, and about five small polaccas and xebecs. In Tripoli harbor itself they have some gunboats and bomb scows."

"No frigates?"

Gavino shook his head. "No, but the Algerines do have one small frigate; that was the special tribute that they required of us a few years ago."

Samuel Barron folded his arms in disgust. "God. I forgot about that."

"But by tying down the *Meshuda* and the small brig here," continued Gavino, "you've cut the heart out of their navy." Quickly they calculated that of a total strength that they estimated at 106 guns, they had captured perhaps 40 there in Gibraltar, including *Meshuda*'s nine-pounders, which must have been the largest they had. The remaining small vessels aggregated 66 guns, not larger than six-pounders. The three American frigates alone mounted 118 guns, mostly twenty-fours, plus the dozen six-pounders of the *Enterprise*. On paper, at least, it should be a fly-swatting contest to destroy the Tripolitan navy.

"Now, whether we can consider Tripoli defeated without taking the city is another question," ventured Samuel Barron. "The fort guarding Tripoli harbor has over a hundred big guns, bigger than ours, and they cannot be engaged from open sea, only from the confines of the harbor. That is an entirely different matter."

"Well, for better or worse, your orders do not go so far," said Gavino. "You are to try to maintain the peace and fight only if necessary."

"Now, what about that admiral?" asked Dale.

Gavino laughed suddenly out loud, the first time he had done so. "Ah, Peter Leslie." He laughed again. "He was a just deckhand on the *Betsy* when she was captured. He converted to the Mohammedan religion to escape slavery, and he entered the old bashaw's service, courted and married his daughter, and next you know, he is the grand admiral. Quick advancement, eh?"

"It's disgusting," said Dale.

Gavino opened his hands in conciliation. "Well, now, let us be fair. Leslie's shipmates on the *Betsy* were imprisoned in the bagnios for five years before they were ransomed; many of them were barely alive after that time. The Berber religion forbids Mohammedans from enslaving each other, so he escaped the fate of his shipmates. I can't blame him for thinking out a better living. But he's a lover, not a fighter. If he tries to escape, whichever of you is left here to watch him, just put one broadside into him and he'll be done."

"That will be you, Samuel, and the *Philadelphia*," Dale said. "Mr. Gavino, have you a map?"

"Yes, yes." As he fetched one from the study the officers cleared dishes to the sideboard, and then they weighted the corners of the map with saucers as Gavino unrolled it.

"What is your thinking, Commodore?" asked Bainbridge.

Dale took a deep breath. "*Philadelphia*, I think, will stay here and pin down our Scottish lover boy. Mr. Bainbridge, you will take the *Essex* and escort the *Grand Turk* to Algiers with the tribute." He traced his finger the five hundred miles east to the Algerine capital, then smiled wryly. "You being such a warm friend of the dey already, he should be glad to see you again."

"I hope the old bugger has died of his own meanness," said Bainbridge.

"No," said Gavino, "he is still quite alive, and just as sneaky."

Dale moved his finger an equal five hundred miles farther to Tunis and Cap Bon, then a farther three hundred miles southeast. "James and I will take the *President* to Tripoli, along with Mr. Sterett and the

Enterprise. Now, Mr. Gavino says they are at war with us, but we are not at war with them, yet." He shook his head at the idiocy of it. "I am carrying a letter to the bashaw from President Jefferson. It says that we are not there to open hostilities, but merely to escort our merchant ships and to offer him ten thousand dollars to forbear going to war—but if that does not gain a favorable result, we will brook no nonsense from his ships. Now, you can tell me"—Dale looked at Gavino—"whether under the circumstances this is proper, we will offer him the ten thousand dollars to call off his war. We will tell him that we have been given to understand that he has declared war on us, but we have not reciprocated as of our knowledge. Thus, we will take no offensive action, but if he does, we will defend ourselves to the uttermost."

"Yes," agreed Gavino. "That would be quite appropriate in both content and tone."

"Forgive my interrupting"—Sterett had sat quietly through the conversation, as became a lieutenant among captains—"but lest we forget, I believe you said you were going to give us further information about their fighting tactics."

"Ah, yes," said Gavino. "Thank you." He continued speaking as he rose and walked into his parlor, remaining well visible from the dining table. "I received a copy of a letter some time since from our consul, Mr. William Eaton. He had occasion to learn some facts firsthand, and I thought it might be useful one day, one moment—ah, here it is."

Gavino resumed his seat at the table. "Mr. Eaton says that the Berber ships are almost never comfortable engaging in cannon duels, broadside to broadside. That is understandable, given their lack of expert training in gunnery." He searched rapidly through the letter. "Here it is: 'Their mode of attack is uniformly boarding. Their long lateen yards drop upon the enemy and afford a safe and easy conveyance for the men who man them for this purpose. They throw boarders in from all points of rigging and from all quarters of the decks, having their sabers grasped in their teeth and their loaded pistols in their belts, so they have the full use of their hands in scaling the gunwales or netting of their enemy.'"

"So," said Dale, "they are brigands, and they fight like brigands."

All murmured in agreement. "Oh," said Gavino, "one other matter. I took the liberty of contacting Mr. Leslie—oh, forgive me, Grand Admiral Murad Reis." The captains laughed appreciatively. "I anticipated that you would desire an interview with him. However, he positively declines to meet you on your ship, here in the consulate, or on his ship. He will meet you only in a public tavern of his choosing."

"Ha!" exclaimed Dale. "So he is cheeky as well as no Christian."

"True, but I have heard that his taste in taverns is quite discerning."

"Well, to hell with him. We'll just cork him up here for the duration. The only thing that maddens me is he won't mind at all being left out of the war. We call that cowardice."

"Indeed," agreed Gavino.

"Well." Dale slapped his hands on the table. "With thanks to you for your hospitality, and our compliments to your cook, whose name is—"

"Mariah," said Gavino.

"Ah." Dale extracted a small gold pin from his lapel. "Will you thank her for us, with this?"

"She will be delighted." Gavino saw them down to the quay and into his boat. "Communicate with me as much as you will; I will do all I can for you."

"Water is our great need," Dale repeated.

"I will do what I can."

. . .

THE NEXT DAY, Dale took the *President* across the bay to Algeciras, where the presence of a forty-four-gun frigate did much to facilitate access to his detained supply ship, a private vessel, the *Algonquin*, contracted to the navy. Afternoon found Commodore Dale deep in her hold, inspecting her bill of lading in the dimness of a single lantern, in company with her captain, whom he would happily have killed.

"Look at this!" sputtered Dale. "The bread is alive with weevils. There is no cheese at all, there are no candles, there is no—and what is this? Rice! We do not want rice!"

"We are carrying the rice for a civilian client; it is bound for Toulon."

"Damn your civilian client, I have to fight a war—with this? And where is water? We want water most of all."

"I am sorry, Captain, the navy gave us no order to bring water. I imagine they believed you could water your ships when you arrived in Europe. Europe is not known as a desert."

"Spain is, in summer, I am told."

"Captain, as you can see, I brought every commodity that the navy contracted of me. I am sorry that the bread is somewhat spoiled."

"Somewhat!"

The *Algonquin*'s captain swelled up for a moment. "I daresay it is in no more foul a condition than your own, after your crossing."

Dale hung his head for a moment, defeated. "Well, have everything that is consigned to us transferred to my ship at once. No more than it is, it should not take very long, should it?"

That same afternoon, Bainbridge led a victualing party through Gibraltar's markets. Backed by the pursers' silver, they bought whatever the vendors would sell them of fresh fruit and vegetables, a live pig, and some hens for each ship. When Dale returned the next day his dismay over their supplies was shared among all the captains as they divided what there was of salt meat and wormy biscuit.

Over three days they were able to water the ships, one lighter at a time, until the frigates had taken on ninety tons each, almost replacing what they had expended in crossing, and the *Enterprise* twenty tons. Dale dared not sail with less; they could not be certain of watering anywhere on the coast of Africa, and the closest friendly port was Malta.

3.

A TASTE OF BATTLE

July–August 1801

On his cutter back to the *Enterprise*, Sterett decided to hold close that part of his orders directing defensive battle only. She was a little vessel, but every man of her crew knew her reputation, of her having bested eight French privateers and taken them as prizes. For the men to learn now that they were forbidden to take prizes could be a mortal blow to their fighting spirit.

The squadron weighed anchor on July 5, exchanging salutes with the British garrison as they left. Samuel Barron took his *Philadelphia* out into the bay, remaining within sight of Gibraltar. He had his lieutenants run drills with the gun crews, letting the Tripolitans safely behind the mole listen to the deep roar of his twenty-fours, daring them to run for it. The wait was diverting for a day, but then settled into glum boredom, realizing that the pragmatic if not cowardly Scot who had "gone Turk" would never challenge them. Trapping the two largest Tripolitan ships in Gibraltar was of critical service, but there would be no glory in it.

Bainbridge shortened sail in the *Essex* so as to remain in company with the heavily laden *Grand Turk*. They departed Gibraltar in company with the *President* and *Enterprise*, but soon fell astern of them and eventually dropped from their sight. As they turned east, Bliven finally saw, a distance to the north, the famous Rock, its beetling white cliffs plunging from the heights perpendicularly to the sea. It is justly famous, he thought, it does not disappoint, it was one of the sights of the world that he desired to see, and now he had done. The winds were light and Dale was in a hurry, at a disadvantage in keeping up with the *Enterprise*; therefore, James Barron set studding sails for extra canvas, giving Bliven the thrill of seeing a frigate at her most majestic, plowing along under an absolute cloud of canvas. They noisily dropped anchor in the harbor of Algiers on July 9.

Commodore Dale obtained an audience with old Mustapha Dey, who received him and James Barron on his dais in the courtyard of his palace. Situated at the crest of the hill overlooking the harbor, it was surrounded by the crowded warren of the casbah. "My intention is to honor my agreement with your country," he told Dale through an interpreter, who was a black American. "Thus you will understand our great anxiety, that your country should fulfill its part of the treaty, which, as of this moment, it has not done."

Dale thought he had never seen such brilliant light as reflected off the limestone walls of the palace courtyard, intensifying the July heat, the more keenly felt for being in their most formal dress uniforms. *He must be doing it deliberately;* Dale thought, *he must enjoy watching us wilt like lettuce.* "I have the honor to inform Your Highness that the treasure ship *Grand Turk* left Gibraltar with us, accompanied by another frigate. The *Grand Turk* is carrying all the tribute that was agreed for this year, and she should arrive on tomorrow."

Mustapha stroked his voluminous white beard as he listened both to Dale and to his black interpreter. He nodded and said, "That is good to hear, and good to know that our American friends value our continued good will. Will you please to take some refreshment before you go?" He made a small gesture, at which a servant approached them with a tray. Dale and Barron each took a large porcelain cup, cold to the touch, and the servant took up a silver ewer and filled them with cold, clear water.

Dale stared at his cup, disbelieving, and then drained it. It was cold and delicious. In what other way could hospitality and mockery be so exquisitely combined? He knew that the old dey was waiting, just waiting, for him to ask to water his ships, but by God he would die of thirst before asking anything of this horrid, simpering old tyrant. Barron followed his lead in replacing their cups on the tray. "Your Highness is very kind. The ship that will arrive tomorrow is escorted by the frigate *Essex*, under command of Captain Bainbridge, whom Your Highness will remember from last year. He will oversee conducting your tribute ashore."

"That will be most satisfactory." The slight inclination of the dey's head was their cue to withdraw; they stood to attention and saluted, and were escorted by janissaries back to the wharf.

"Did you forget to ask to water the ships?" asked Barron.

Dale's sudden glare at him revealed in an instant that he was joking. "God rot him."

The jetty where their cutter had tied up was lined with the bagnios, the infamous dungeons that had confined countless thousands over the centuries. They were empty now because the European slaves were dispersed to hard labor around the city. There were not supposed to be any Americans among them, since the crew of the *Betsy* had been ransomed, but Dale wondered if that was true. They were met on the jetty by the American consul in Algiers, Richard O'Brien, who accompanied them out to the *President*.

He wore his disdain for the Berbers on his sleeve. Mustapha would growl, he said, but he thought would not bite. He made no secret of the fact that he would prefer to see all the Barbary lords swinging on gallows. "Oh, my," he said repeatedly as they approached the *President*. "You have no idea, after two years in this godforsaken place, how it cheers me to see such a testament of American power. Won't you have someone show me around your ship?"

"With pleasure," Dale answered. "I will conduct you as we talk." In the first half-hour of their interview they descended from spar deck down to gun deck to berth deck to orlop deck, and then back up to the commodore's cabin.

"Tunis should present the least of your difficulties," said O'Brien. "In fact, I am told you may water and provision there." He echoed, however, Gavino's warning about Yusuf Karamanlis and Tripoli. "Understand me rightly, that man is a killer, and no mistake. Do not present yourself in the city as you did here, or you will have to be ransomed."

At the first sight of the *Essex* and *Grand Turk* the next day, Dale and Sterett weighed anchor, east for Tunis, where indeed they were welcomed, quickly watered and provisioned, at handsome profit to the bashaw there, but that was to be expected. They conferred quickly with the consul, William Eaton, who confirmed with further particulars his account of the mode of Tripolitan warfare that Gavino had read to them.

Throughout these days, Bliven Putnam and Sam Bandy gained in their apprenticeship as midshipmen. They stood their watches, studying the function of every sail and every line, as willing to learn from the lowly tars as they were from the lieutenants. David Porter had main charge of them. He was twenty-one, with a taut face, thin lips, black hair over fair skin; he was severe but usually decent. He gave their lessons in navigation and seamanship, and even tested them with mock questions of the very kind he knew would be asked of them on their lieutenant's examinations. He imparted his facility with sextant and chronometer, at which Sam Bandy excelled, and with the guns, at which Bliven showed the greater aptitude, perhaps because good shooting required an art and an instinct that went beyond the rote calculations of navigation. There was an indefinable feel that told when a ship was nearing the end of its uproll or downroll, how long the match would take to catch the primer, how far to the target and how to gauge its roll with his own, how far a ship would travel between firing and the ball striking—and all that was the difference between shivering or breaking a mast, and wasting a shot into thin air. Bliven seemed to have been born with this, but Sam was his master at trigonometry.

Second Lieutenant Curtis, whom they had both learned to fear, continued to instruct them in what he knew best: fighting, with saber and dagger. After their most elemental lessons, each session seemed to degenerate into a genuine fight for their very lives. After two weeks Curtis took away the wooden swords and had them fight with their real cutlasses, to accustom them to the desperation of it, the gravity of it. They could not be certain whether, given a weak moment in their guard, Curtis would actually kill them, but neither would take that risk. Like being dropped in a foreign land with none to speak their own language, it astonished them how quickly they became proficient with swords. And beyond one's own proficiency, Curtis hammered it into them how one day their lives would depend on being able to read the eyes of an opponent, to take swift advantage of just the slightest second's hesitation. A poor lesson inevitably resulted in an extra watch, or a stint aloft, or standing at the bow with a ball in each hand. He refrained from whipping them, but they always knew it was a possibility, and it disturbed them to see his eyes shine when the ship's company had to turn out to witness punishment of some luckless tar.

By the time they raised Tripoli off their starboard bow on July 25, Baltimore and innocence seemed a lifetime behind them. The *President* and the *Enterprise* anchored outside the harbor, and Dale, heeding all he had been told, sent a letter ashore for the bashaw. He offered the friendship of the United States and of its president, and a cash gift of ten thousand dollars, if the bashaw would terminate the war. If not, he wrote, "The Squadron under my command will do Every Thing in its power to distroy the Corsairs and other Vessels belonging to Your Excellency." Dale could fight, but he could not always spell. His reports were always straight from his pen, never corrected by a clerk, but the secretary of the navy could always depend that Dale could get across his meanings with exceptional clarity.

For three long days there was silence from the city, before a boat returned with a truculent and insulting letter from Yusuf. Trying a second tack, Dale wrote again, reminding the bashaw that under the terms of their treaty, disputes were to be submitted to the dey of Algiers for his arbitration. Unknown to Dale, that was the worst thing he could have done, for the whole point of Yusuf's demanding greater tribute from America was his assertion that he was now the equal of the dey and entitled to equal tribute.

It was now two-thirds through the summer, and the heat coming off the African desert was sweltering. They had topped off their casks in Tunis, but by the end of the month water was again running dangerously low. Dale called Sterett over for a talk. The nearest fresh water was at Malta, although they could not be sure how much they could obtain. It might be delicate. British friendliness to the Americans could vary from port to port, according to the inclination of the local commander; they had been fortunate in Gibraltar. Dale ordered Sterett to Malta, and he filled *Enterprise*'s hold with empty casks. Cautioning him to be faultless in his salutes and formalities with the English, he dispatched him on July 30.

For hours after he left Tripoli harbor, Sterett stood on his small quarterdeck, immovable as a golem, marveling angrily at being put to such an errand as fetching water. He respected Dale and would not cross him, but the *President*'s capacious hold could lay in forty-five thousand gallons of water. He could go to Malta and take on water until his deck was awash and not come back with half so much. The *President*'s four hundred fifty hands received the approved ration of one gallon per day, per man. The navy cared little what they did with it; they could drink it or clean themselves with it or wash their clothes in it, but in this brutal heat they drank it, and they could not do with less. Four hundred fifty gallons per day, plus changing the water in the steep tub four or five times each day—for if the men were fed meat that was not rinsed of its salt their thirst would become ravenous. Calling it five hundred gallons per day and starting from a full hold, Dale must replenish after ninety days, with some of that expended in reaching a port for water. Eventually, unless he had a supply ship in continual attendance, Dale must withdraw to Tunis or back to Gibraltar.

Shortly after setting the forenoon watch on August 1, a cry came down from the lookout: "Sail ho! Sail! Ho!"

Sterett had not even finished climbing the ladder when he asked sharply, "What do you see?"

"A funny little bastard of a ship, sir. Square-rigged on the foremast, lateen-rigged on the main and mizzen. Not very big. Queer-looking thing."

"Do you see her colors?" Sterett shouted up.

"Tripolitan, sir."

Sterett took out his glass and looked for himself. "Indeed she is," he said almost hungrily, seeing the three red and two yellow stripes of that Berber state's pennant. In the circle of the glass Sterett made out the rigging of a polacca, which for more than a century had been one of the favorite raiding vessels of the Barbary pirates. It was plain that she was steering obliquely for them. Sterett's breath quickened as he pitched himself up for a fight. "Beat to quarters," he ordered tightly. "English colors, Bosun, run them up."

At the drumbeat Bliven and Sam Bandy were studying in the ward-room. Even as they leapt to their feet, they could see forward beyond the galley the surgeon's mate laying a plank on a line of sea chests and spreading a cloth over it. On it he opened his valise of instruments—probes and tourniquets, and the dreaded saw. Pelham the chaplain was out of his berth, already in his vestments, ready to hold down the wounded as they were treated, to comfort them as they died. Sam and Bliven were on the deck within seconds, armed. On large vessels midshipmen might be afforded some measure of protection, but today if there was a fight it promised to be even and every hand would be needed.

They watched the polacca gain on them, coming slowly up their port quarter. Sterett put the speaking trumpet to his lips. "Ho, the ship! Ahoy! What ship is that?" he said, affecting his best imitation of an effete, upper-class British accent.

"His Highness the bashaw's warship *Tripoli*," the voice floated back with an Arab accent. "What ship is that?"

"His Majesty's warship *Enterprise*," Sterett called back. "What is your mission?"

After several seconds the reply came back loud and jovial. "We are hunting Americans. Have you seen any?" The laughing of the Berber crew was audible.

Sterett looked down the deck and saw his marines lying flat, each with musket and pistol in hand. "Yes!" His eye caught the bosun's mate, the Stars and Stripes fastened on and ready to haul aloft at the order.

"Excellent!" cried back the Berber. "Most excellent! Are they close by?"

Sterett paused, gathering his fury. It was nine o'clock on a clear morning, the cliffs of Malta just visible some miles to the east. "Yes!"

"Where shall we find them?"

"Colors!" Sterett bellowed. The British naval ensign fainted down the line as the American flag raced up just as fast. "Right here, you thieving bastards! Marines!" The company leapt to their feet and aimed. "Fire!"

The rattle of musketry took the Berber ship completely by surprise. There were cries from the wounded, and there came the cacophony of what Sterett took to be a mixture of orders, curses, and exhortations. Her gunports opened, but only three guns fired; in their haste to respond the Moors fired at the extremity of their uproll, and even at this short distance their shot flew through the *Enterprise*'s rigging.

And now she must reload. "Mr. Porter!"

"Sir!"

"Open fire on her gun deck."

The ships were so close abeam that after the musket volley the marines discharged pistols at the Tripolitan gun crews. *Enterprise*'s ports snapped open and the six-pounders rolled out. Porter sighted each one on an opposite gunport before firing, the concussive boom followed a split second later by the sickening crunch of hull and railing that they knew must be showering lethal splinters among her gun crews. And then there were screams. Porter fired each six-pounder and moved on, leaving Bliven in charge of the crew reloading each.

Broadside to broadside, the *Enterprise* was outgunned seven to six, but the initial pandemonium on the corsair that Sterett had caused with his surprise negated any advantage.

"Sir!" called Porter. "Look!"

The corsair had suddenly luffed her sails, causing *Enterprise* to leap ahead, and then set the sails again, stealing the wind from her and bringing the pirates rapidly upon their port quarter. Brigands, dark-skinned and exotically attired, inched out onto the lateen yard, ready to leap aboard as soon as *Enterprise* was overtaken.

Sterett begrudged his admiration at this bit of seamanship; clearly this was a captain who had taken vessels before. But neither did Sterett think himself incapable. "Mr. Porter!"

"Sir!"

"Your aft starboard gun has no target; set it aft as a stern chaser, right now! From where they are now, our mains'l will cover you from sight. Load with grape. We'll rake those bastards from the yard when I turn. Tell me when you're ready; you will have leave to fire when you come to bear. Mr. Bandy! When I order the starboard turn, lean on the wheel and be distracted by nothing! All depends on shearing clean away!"

"Aye, sir!" Sam Bandy set his eye and his jaw. If the pirates managed to drop boarders, he must be one of the first targets. He glanced down at the decorative hilt of his saber. In its scabbard it would be useless, but instinctively he knew not to withdraw it now. Sterett had commanded all his attention to the wheel; that could mean only that he was meant to die at the wheel if needs be, and it would convey weakness if the lieutenant saw him prepare to defend his life before they were upon him. Mentally he calculated the posture he would need, to hold the wheel over with his left hand, while using his sword with the right.

With wind stolen from the *Enterprise*'s sails the polacca was on them before Porter was ready. She sheared hard to port, swinging her lateen yard over the *Enterprise* just fore of the quarterdeck; only the polacca's lack of bowsprit kept her from snagging in the spanker rigging. As she swung she dropped six pirates onto the deck. Others tried to swing over on ropes, but the polacca's turn had been too severe, and they swung out over blue water in wasted motion before dropping back onto their own deck.

"Repel boarders," roared Sterett. "Hard astarboard!" Sam Bandy spun the wheel to the right and *Enterprise* answered with a sharp heel away from the polacca, clearing them of the overhanging yard. Once it came to bear, Porter fired his new chaser, raking the pirates' deck with grape. But those six eager Moors had landed on their own deck, and the marines had discharged both muskets and pistols, and were engaged in reloading.

One of the Berbers landed five feet from where Bliven Putnam was reloading one of the guns—a labor that was quickly forgotten because the closest marines were engaged with two other pirates. In a heartbeat Bliven had his saber out of its scabbard and was fending off the first of the Moor's strikes. He was very dark, with yellow teeth showing against red gums; Bliven saw that he had a pistol wedged in his belt, but he did not draw it; therefore he must have already fired it.

Bliven drove the Moor back with a couple offensive strikes of his own, then drew his own pistol. The Moor froze at the sight, suddenly overmatched. If both men hesitate in a fight it remains even, Curtis had drilled into him, but if only one hesitates, it must mean his death. The instant Bliven saw the dark, heavily browed eyes fix on the pistol in his left hand, he lunged forward with his right, his saber sticking him mid-chest below the rib cage, lower part of the heart, surely, to a depth of perhaps eight inches—as far as he could reach. The Moor grimaced and grunted; even a dying man can strike a final blow, and before he might raise his scimitar Bliven raised a foot and pushed him off the blade, spinning him down to the deck, where he curled into a ball, as though that might stanch the course of blood that followed the blade as it withdrew. At Bliven's last sight of him he was breathing in short gasps, pinkish spittle edging out onto his cheek.

The polacca checked her port turn to try and stay within boarding distance, but the schooner's maneuverability was too great for her, and Sam's hard starboard turn opened enough distance between them that the six who dropped off the yard were now stranded, and their fate sealed, but they could wreak much damage before being dispatched.

Bliven saw one of his gunners, new to the navy, his eyes wide, fending off scimitar blows as each one came down on him, but unable to mount any offensive. At last when he was backed over the cascabel of his gun, Bliven thought it time to expend the one shot in his pistol. As the Moor raised his scimitar Bliven pointed the gun at his side, midway between waist and armpit; indeed, he had begun to pull the trigger, but the boom that he heard was not from his own gun but that of a marine who fired the instant he had reloaded. The ball struck the Moor square between the shoulder blades and exploded out of his chest, showering the astonished gunner with gore as the pirate's arms flung out to the sides. He crumpled like a marionette and never moved, and the gunner stared at him as the foreign blood trickled down his face.

"Shot your gun, man!" shouted Bliven. "Shot your gun!" The gunner regained himself, rolling and ramming a six-pound ball and wadding home down the barrel. The center of the action was in the waist of the ship; even Sterett had leapt down to be in the thick of it. Beyond the melee Bliven saw Sam leaning hard on the wheel with his left hand, his sword raised in his right hand as he stood off a furious assault from a loose-bloused pirate who was intent on taking the wheel and stemming their turn.

One shot—the thought raced through Bliven's mind and terrified him—*one shot and I must not miss.* Each of his gun captains had cried ready and were awaiting the order to roll out guns, but Bliven realized that with the turn they bore on no target at this instant. "Down!" he screamed. The crews either fell flat or crouched low; Bliven was able to race four steps toward the quarterdeck. Both the wheel and the Moor were between him and Sam; the pirate was assaulting him with the wheel between them. *Stupid man,* thought Bliven. *It's harder to reach him that way;* but he could not shoot him lest the ball pass through him and kill Sam as well. Bliven leapt to his left, almost tripping over the lanyard of the Number Four gun, but steadying himself over the breech of the gun he found an angle in which Sam was not in danger. Somewhere in the farthest reach of his mind he knew he was about to do something he had never done, pass through a portal from which there was no returning. He leveled his aim and fired.

The ball caught the pirate high in the side, beneath the armpit. He staggered to the side as though hit by a heavy weight, and just in the instant that he stood bewildered Sam ran him through. As he fell backward he took Sam's sword with him, and he could not retrieve it without releasing his grip on the wheel, which he dared not, so he let it go.

Sam's eyes met Bliven's before the smoke had blown clear of his pistol, and each realized that Bliven had saved his life, a turning point of their friendship that must bear pondering over, but later, for the fight still ran hot.

Discovering the ninety men of the *Enterprise* too well able to repel boarders, and the six who had jumped prematurely all sacrificed, the *Tripoli* stood off two ship lengths away, seeming content to settle the matter with the weight of their broadsides. Sterett regained the quarterdeck after making certain that his own ship was secure. "Twenty degrees back to port, Mr. Bandy. Bring our broadside to bear."

"Aye, sir!" hollered Bandy.

Fighting with broadsides was not what Gavino said they would do. "Let her have it, boys!" roared Sterett. A full six-gun broadside seemed to crush the polacca, as railing and gear and chunks of cabin wheeled into the air, after which there was an eerie silence. For the first time they noticed the black holes in her thin hull—the inevitable consequence of using a light vessel as a warship.

The red and yellow flag lowered, replaced with a white one. The tars manning the *Enterprise*'s guns may not have been from the upper classes, but they knew a victory when they had one, and they cheered lustily.

"Let her come up alongside, Mr. Bandy." The polacca approached within thirty yards, and Sterett put the trumpet to his lips. "Do you surrender, sir?"

Porter pointed suddenly with his saber. "She is hoisting colors again!" The Tripolitan standard raced aloft once, as a line of pirates leapt to their feet and emptied their assemblage of muskets and blunderbusses toward the *Enterprise*.

"What!" screamed Sterett. "Damn you! Damn you to hell!" He waved his saber over the gun deck. "Marines, fire! Fire at will! Back to your guns, boys! Hole her!"

The *Tripoli* managed to answer with a desultory pepper of four-pounders, but seemed almost to shatter under the weight of two more broadsides that sent great chunks of hull and railing spinning through the air. She steered off a hundred yards and rocked quietly, and after a few moments raised the white flag again.

"Not likely," muttered Sterett.

Five and then ten minutes passed, the polacca rolling in the swell, her white flag curling slowly in the breeze. Porter joined Sterett on the quarterdeck. "Sir, we must do something, we can't just leave her there."

"I know, but I don't trust him."

"Nor do I."

"Mr. Bandy, two points to port, come up slowly," said Sterett quietly. "Mr. Porter, have your full broadside ready."

"Aye." Porter hopped down to the gun deck. "Mr. Putnam, what is your status?"

"Guns primed and ready, sir." Porter saw the gunners blowing their matches.

With *Enterprise* carrying more canvas, she inevitably passed by the polacca's starboard side, and the instant she did so, the Berber hoisted all sails again and came for them, once again on their port quarter, intending to repeat their earlier maneuver, more pirates scooting out on the lateen yard to board.

"I don't believe it," Sterett whispered. "Waterline, boys!" he roared.

"Aim for the waterline! Sink the villain!" Porter left Bliven to keep up the fire from the six-pounders as rapidly as the crews could reload, and joined Sterett again by the wheel.

Bliven seized the long iron crow and levered the heavy breech up from where it rested on the carriage. "Hand spikes!" he shouted, and looking down guns Two through Four, he called again, "Hand spikes!" The swabber jammed a heavy wooden wedge between the barrel and the carriage, depressing the barrel six or eight degrees. It was a crude system of aiming, and the rest depended on Bliven's judgment of the ships' respective rolls, but it lowered the whole amplitude of possible strikes closer to the water, and the polacca sat lower than the schooner.

"Roll out!" The gun's crew, plus Bliven himself and a man from this gun's starboard mate, heaved mightily on the lanyards, and aided by a port roll the fifteen-hundred-pound gun slid home against the blocks of the gunport. "Clear!" The crew scrambled to the gun's sides, away from the coming six-foot recoil that would crush them like a hammer if they were struck.

He estimated three seconds for the priming to reach the pierced cartridge; he waited until the *Enterprise* just started her downward roll, his aim halfway between the polacca's railing and her waterline. "Fire!" he screamed.

Together Sterett and Porter knew the polacca was taking a horrific splintering belowdecks from the four-gun salvo, for from without they clearly observed the holes in her hull, one of them two feet above the waterline. She must now take on water with every starboard roll. Port guns Five and Six under command of Lieutenant Curtis followed seconds later. Number Six gun hung fire just long enough to elicit a curse from Curtis, before flame and wadding exploded from its muzzle on the uproll. It was a lucky shot, though, for the corsair's mizzenmast shivered and then slowly heeled over, draping its lateen yard and sail into the water. At length they saw a white flag hoisted a third time.

Bliven saw it, too, and looked up to Sterett for an order. "Keep firing," he roared. "Sink the son of a bitch!"

"Sponge your guns!" screamed Bliven to his four crews. By the time swabbers stood at attention, signaling their completion, the powder monkey had emerged from below with three cartridges in the crook of each arm. "Load your cartridges!" It was done, and the powder rammed home followed by wadding, and the chief of each crew called that he felt the powder beneath his touchhole. "Shot your guns!" A six-pound iron ball was rammed down each barrel, followed by a second wadding to keep it in place.

Another deafening full round sent the powder monkey scurrying below for new charges, as a man whom they took for the corsair's captain appeared at the shattered rail in a bloody tunic. With his hands in the air he called out, "Cease your firing! For the love of God, stop!"

Seconds ticked by in silence. The corsair had taken on a visible starboard list; one more broadside at her waterline and she must capsize. Sterett anticipated the wash of pleasure at seeing her sink, her crew floundering in the sea.

"Mr. Putnam!"

"Sir!"

"Cease your fire." Rage must give place to reality, he thought. If he sank her, he would make himself responsible for her wounded, and prisoners. That he could not do on his overcrowded vessel.

Sterett turned his fury on the corsair captain. "Well, sir! What trick have you this time? Why should I not send you down, damn you!"

The captain extended his hands in the air. "My men are killed and wounded. We cannot steer. We surrender, for the love of God!"

Sterett chewed on it for a few seconds. "Very well, send your boat over. We will take your surrender."

"We cannot! You have shot our boat to pieces. Send your boat over here!"

"My God," Sterett said to Porter, "does he really think we're that stupid?"

They saw the captain fall to his knees. "We surrender, in the name of God!"

"Prove it to me!" bellowed Sterett.

They saw the captain give an order, and a limping sailor brought him their ensign. "See! I cast our flag into the sea! We cannot raise it again! When was the last shot you heard from us? The battle is over! I swear before God you will not be harmed!"

Porter said quietly aside, "Let me take the boat over with some marines. We'll find out if they're really finished."

Sterett nodded. "Mr. Merrick," he called out.

"Sir!"

"Get your boat into the water."

Porter and half a dozen marines boarded the corsair and strode through the carnage of naval warfare, splinters from the wooden shower that killed and maimed. They took stock of the dead and wounded, rounded up the unhurt, and searched below to make certain there were no more tricks in store.

"It's all right, Mr. Sterett, you may come across." He sent the cutter back for him.

Sterett swung over the rail and descended the netting. "Mr. Putnam, come with me; you may be wanted."

"Aye, sir."

As he climbed up the polacca's netting and over the rail, Bliven's first thought was of the blood; he had no idea there could be so much. Each starboard roll brought a thickening of the course of blood that spilled over from half a dozen places; he had always read of blood running from the scuppers, and now he had seen it. The corsair's deck was thick and slick with it. On the farm he had helped his father with slaughtering pigs when cold weather came, so he had seen pools of gore before. But this, men were wounded not with a bullet but with a shower of grape, or a cloud of splinters as a ball crushed in a section of the hull. Men were not wounded, they were rent in pieces.

That was his first thought. His second was of Lieutenant Sterett. He knew he must show no horror, no thought that tended toward pity. Swinging over the rail, his feet met the deck squarely as the ship topped a swell. It would not do to slip and fall in the blood; Sterett would mark him most favorably if he strode through it, confidently, taking no notice that twenty men had bled out their lives in it.

Bliven's duty was at Sterett's side, and the lieutenant commandant and two marines as soon as their feet touched the deck rushed toward the stern, swords drawn, to where a man in a black tunic heavily corded with gold reclined against the stump of the mizzenmast. He had black hair and a trimmed white beard.

"Who are you?" demanded Sterett.

"I am Reis Mahomet Rous," he answered, "admiral in the service of His Highness, the bashaw of Tripoli."

Sterett was silent for a tense second before he fairly spluttered, "You are another damned Scotchman!"

"The captain was badly wounded," continued the admiral, "and has been taken below. It is I who surrender the ship to you, Lieutenant—" He paused for a name.

"Sterett! You are another damned bloody Scot. Explain that to me!"

"I can't bloody well help where I was born!" the admiral roared in pain. "Can you?"

"Well, you are a man of no honor, sir! You surrendered and resumed the fight!"

"And you drew us out under false colors, Mr. Sterett. Do you think you have the right to make accusations about honor?"

"We raised our own flag before we commenced firing!"

"So did we, both times."

"You surrendered!"

"No, we drew you in."

"Don't bandy words with me, I could hang you this minute and be within my rights."

The admiral gave a single, sighing laugh. "Proceed, then, if you will. It will be more merciful than to return home vanquished."

Sterett had spent the worst of his fury and looked about the carnage on deck. "What are your casualties?"

Admiral Rous collected a breath. "Twenty dead, including the surgeon. Thirty wounded, including the captain. I do not include myself, I am not that dangerously hurt. Twenty are unharmed. Can you send your surgeon aboard to care for my wounded?"

"Mr. Porter?" Sterett looked to his side.

"Sir?"

"Can you report on our casualties?"

"None, sir." Sterett looked at him, confounded. "Not one," he repeated. "Not a scratch."

Sterett shook his head in wonder. "Very well. Admiral, we have a chaplain aboard. Do you desire spiritual comfort?"

"No. All my men are Moslems, they would not take it kindly."

"I was thinking of you, you damned turncoat."

Even seated against the remains of the mizzenmast, Rous drew himself up. "All that I have done, I did to stay alive. I will not become a hypocrite now."

Sterett pursed his lips. "As you wish. Mr. Putnam?"

Bliven snapped to, alert at being wanted. "Yes, sir?"

"Take the boat back to the *Enterprise*. Return with the doctor and tell him to bring his kit. There are thirty wounded for him to sort and care for best as he can. And bring the carpenter, and as many men as he can get in the boat."

"Very good, sir." He turned to obey almost before he was done saluting, and was over the side.

Sterett observed his boarding crew disarm the remaining twenty pirates who were not wounded, binding them and sitting them back to back about the mainmast, where they could be easily watched. A second detail gathered the thirty wounded in the main berthing area below, tying those still capable of moving about, and making up a platform for the surgeon's mate to work on them when he came over. They searched thoroughly for weapons, which they deposited near Sterett on the quarterdeck, a growing pile of dirks and cutlasses and scimitars, old muskets and blunderbusses, and four large daggers of a curious manufacture, with polished handles, elaborately worked scabbards, and wicked, curving blades nearly a foot long and half as wide.

"The ship is ours, sir," reported the marine lieutenant at last. "The wounded are gathered and awaiting the surgeon."

"Very well," responded Sterett. "Rest your men, give them a ration of grog while we wait." He looked impatiently back to the *Enterprise* and saw Putnam, the surgeon's mate, and the carpenter, with four others, more than halfway returned; in a moment they were up the netting and on deck.

"Begging your pardon, sir," said the marine. "There is no grog below. No rum, or whiskey, or wine or anything."

"We do not consume alcohol," growled the admiral. "Our religion forbids it."

"Well," huffed Sterett, "it is a queer religion that allows piracy and murder and pillage, but no drinking." He sheathed his sword. "What ship is this, again?"

"The *Tripoli*," said the admiral. "Fourteen guns, one hundred eighty tons." Then he added disdainfully, "A nice prize for a young lieutenant."

To Porter's ears, the pirate admiral had said a yearned-for word. "Yes. Mr. Sterett, sir. Will you be naming a prize crew?" he asked. As first lieutenant, he knew it would have been pointless to conceal the hope that he would assume command of her.

"No," said Sterett curtly.

"Sir?" Porter was incredulous.

Sterett could not mask his own disgust with what he had to say. "Our orders are to protect our commerce and wage defensive battle only. They do not provide for the taking of prizes."

"What!"

Sterett held up his hands. "Don't complain to me about it, take it up with Congress. We cannot act offensively until there is a declaration of war, and they don't know yet that war exists. Admiral"—he turned his attention again to Rous—"my further orders are specific. I am to leave you the means to reach a port, and there you see Malta. I recommend you make for there. Mr. Putnam?"

"Sir?"

"Take these four you brought, roll their guns and carriages overboard. Then go below, carry up their shot and powder, and throw it into the sea as well."

"Aye, sir. Come on, boys, let's start with this one."

"Mr. Lanford?"

"Aye, sir," answered the carpenter.

"Saw off his mainmast at a height of six feet. Rig him one sail, enough to make for that island."

"Aye, sir."

It took more than an hour for the surgeon's mate to bind the wounded and lay out the dead and the parts of the dead, then the cutter returned him and the carpenter and his men to the *Enterprise*. When it returned, he, Porter, and Bliven gathered in the polacca's waist to follow. In an unseen moment as the marines were casting the entire assemblage of pirate weaponry overboard, Bliven leaned down and plucked up one of the enormous curving daggers with the carved handles that he had marked earlier. He did not remove it from its worked leather scabbard, but slipped it under his shirt. One of the marines found and lowered a boarding ladder, which he meant to make their descent easier, but it missed its purpose, for the blood on their shoes made them more likely to slip on its steps than they would have in simply climbing down the netting.

Once back on his own deck, Bliven was aware for the first time that his knees had begun to shake.

"Mr. Putnam." It was Sterett's voice.

"Yes, sir."

Sterett looked him down and up. "Well done, by God."

Bliven laughed just once, a single, almost hysterical "Ha!"

"And Mr. Putnam."

"Sir?"

"Regulations be damned, you have earned your first rum. Now get you below."

"Aye, sir."

"And what now, sir?" asked Porter.

"On to Malta," said Sterett, "and pick up water for the squadron. They will be getting thirsty."

OUTSIDE THE HARBOR OF TRIPOLI, Dale, James Barron, and the *President* encountered the *Tripoli*, limping home to port, before the *Enterprise* reached them. When Barron hailed the battered polacca, Rous told him he had been beaten by a twenty-four-gun Frenchman. Not allowed to take prizes, Barron allowed him into Tripoli harbor. It was not until he encountered Sterett and the *Enterprise* the following day, riding low from the thirty tons of water in her hold, that he learned of the battle.

"By God," Dale kept saying as he read Sterett's report, "by God," and he handed the pages as he finished them to Barron. "This is signal. This is—you expect gallantry from Sterett, but these boys, this, Bandy, sticking fast at the wheel as a pirate tries to cut him to pieces, and Putnam, kills one himself and then shoots the one hacking at Bandy. I tell you this is the stuff of which navy traditions are made. I want to meet those midshipmen."

Sterett sent them on board the *President*, where they were taken down the ladder to the gun deck, where they were dumbstruck by the neat, curving line of deadly long twenty-fours, their lanyards coiled, their swabs and rams hung overhead. They saw the next ladder down to the berth deck, but were led aft to the commodore's cabin. In their wildest imagination they could not have conjured such a spacious ship.

Dale and Barron spoke to them alone for more than half an hour before sending them out to the wardroom and ordering the best dinner the ship could provide. "Young men such as you are the pride of the navy, the future of the navy," said Dale. "You have begun great careers on this voyage. We shall follow you with the keenest interest." Dale said this outside the door of his cabin, and within the hearing of several lieutenants, both naval and marine.

Thus it was a great shock when, forty minutes later, Barron answered a frantic knock at his door and discovered the cook in a terrible state of agitation. "Beg pardon, sir, but you better come quick. There is a big fight down on the berth deck."

Barron grabbed his sword and clattered down the ladder. On gaining the berth deck he saw a gathering of young officers forward, and he heard the unmistakable pinging of saber blades.

"Tell other men that I am a coward?" It was a boy's voice that reached Barron as he approached; it was shrill, almost hysterical. "I'll show you for a coward!"

"Sam, stop this! I never—ha!"

Barron heard a staccato of metallic blade strikes, and the first voice repeated, "Damn you! Damn you!"

"All right, then, damn you!" the second voice shouted, and Barron could tell from the flurry that he had assumed a furious offense. He discerned from the accusations and protests that it was not a duel, really, for in duels there was little or no talking; that had already come and gone. This must be a very amateurish brawl indeed.

"Belay that!" Captain Barron's voice rolled, booming, down the gun deck even as they heard the hard soles of his shoes closer and louder. "Hold there, by God!" They heard the slink of his sword from its scabbard.

Their blood up, neither Bliven nor Samuel trusted to lower his saber, even at the captain's order. They stood frozen, their blades crossed, hearing his voice but neither taking his eyes from the other's. They heard the staccato of footsteps draw nearer along the planks but did not look away, seeing only Barron's blade slash between them, knocking their sabers down to the deck.

"What!" demanded Barron. "By God, how dare you? What do you mean by this?" From the corner of his eye the captain detected the ill-suppressed smirks among the lieutenants and assessed the true case, that the boys had been goaded to the confrontation. God only knew what malevolent whisper had set the violence in motion. "So! So!" He was a ball of fury seeking a place to strike, and a couple of the junior officers stepped almost imperceptibly toward the rear of the clot.

Sam Bandy spoke up as manly as he could. "It was a matter of my honor, sir."

"Your honor, sir?" roared Barron. "You are fourteen years old!" He started to add that questions of honor should come only after being old enough to shave, but he stifled it, because even in this moment he knew that might not really be the case. In this navy that sent boys to sea with the prospect of fighting and dying like men, that might not be altogether true at all. "You two," he growled. "Go to my cabin, this instant." Sam and Bliven turned to go, but then Barron nodded down at their swords. "Give me those, both of you."

They retreated meekly toward the ladder and then up, as Barron's gaze flashed among the junior officers. "Well amused, are you?" They knew better than to speak. "Well. Let us hope that your entertainment was worth the cost of what will come." They knew he was noting down who was there and who was not.

Barron regained his cabin, joined by Commodore Dale, who had heard the disturbance from the head of the ladder but had not descended. Sam and Bliven were still flushed, but calming down enough to be afraid of what they had done.

"I am shocked," sputtered Barron; Dale stood to one side, silent. "What in God's name was this about?"

Both boys looked at the floor.

"Speak!"

"Sir," said Sam haltingly, "I heard one of the lieutenants say that Mr. Putnam, well, asserted that I played little part in taking the *Tripoli*, and that my part was not as gallant as his, that the pirate he killed was about to kill me and take the wheel."

"I never did," Bliven protested.

"Be quiet," ordered Barron. "From whom did you overhear this?"

Sam started to say that he did not know their names, he was not acquainted with them, but then realized that speaking against a lieutenant, even an anonymous one, could land him in such grief as he had never known.

"Speak up, boy. Who said it?"

"The responsibility is mine, sir, no one else's."

"And did some other of the lieutenants impart to you that you must challenge and fight him or lose the respect of all the officers?"

Bliven and Sam looked at each other.

"Well?"

"Whatever I say, I'm doomed," muttered Sam.

"How do you mean?" Dale stepped in.

"Sir, we've been at sea long enough to know how it works. We've seen it. One lieutenant will order a sailor to do this, then a second will come along and order him to do something else, and then he will be whipped for whichever order he neglects. Then they laugh about it."

Barron folded his arms.

"Sir, the sailors do not deserve that," said Bliven. "And forgive me, sir, neither do the midshipmen. Forgive me, sir, but is it not well known in the service that the lieutenants abuse all their inferiors most terribly?"

Barron's voice softened. "I know the conditions at sea. Young men, full of fight, and the fight might be months away. And then not everyone gets to fight. You two fought the enemy and you both behaved superlatively. But now can you imagine the jealousy of the junior officers stuck here on blockade? I don't defend them, but I understand them. I know that midshipmen are caught under the thumb of the lieutenants." He gestured at Dale. "We all know they abuse you, but it is the naval tradition; it binds you to the service."

"Yes, sir," they muttered almost together, although neither one saw any connection between the abuse and loyalty to the service.

"So, will you agree to hold each other blameless?"

Sam and Bliven glared at each other intently until Sam finally swelled back up. "Sir, I don't know what he said."

"By God," said Barron, "I'll tell you what you are going to do. You are going to shake hands." Sam and Bliven eyed each other.

"Shake hands this instant!"

At least there was no issue of who would extend his hand first. They went out simultaneously and they clasped hands for about two seconds, Bliven looking over Sam's shoulder and Sam looking at the floor.

"No, by God," growled Barron, "you'll not get away with that. Take hands again and keep them there."

The midshipmen obeyed, embarrassed.

"Now repeat after me: I swear."

They knew better than to provoke him further. "I swear," they said.

"That I will never fight you again," said Barron.

"That I will never fight you again," they answered.

"For any pretext or provocation whatsoever."

"For any pretext or provocation whatsoever."

"I will defend you in battle."

"I will defend you in battle."

"And I will be as watchful for your honor."

"And I will be as watchful for your honor."

"As I am for my own."

"As I am for my own."

"So help me God."

Both boys swallowed. "So help me God."

"All right."

They released hands and took a step apart, shaken. Barron thought they must be religious enough to appreciate the gravity of an oath before God.

"I take it, then, that I no longer have to worry about you two flying at each other like a couple of hotheads?"

"Yes, sir," they answered together.

Barron pointed to his desk. "Take up your swords."

They obeyed, slipping them into their scabbards right away.

"Now"—Barron crossed his arms—"the commodore and I had a mind to transfer you here to the flagship, but that is impossible now. I am going to have to do something to punish you, so the other officers will feel that they have succeeded in landing you in trouble. I know they goaded you into fighting."

"What will happen to them?" asked Sam.

"That does not concern you." Barron chewed on his decision for several seconds. "Gentlemen, you will spend until four bells in the next watch, in the foretop, together. I advise you to discuss your differences, and if you cannot resolve them, I expect only one of you to come down."

"Yes, sir," they said again together.

"But if you both come down, I expect never to hear of such an altercation again. If I do, it will be very bad for you. Now, up the ratlines with you. When you come down, I will send you back over to the *Enterprise* in our cutter."

"Yes, sir."

"Now," said Dale, "nothing in what Captain Barron has told you will forbid you from stopping by the galley on your way forward. Take some food and water up with you."

"Thank you, sir."

4.

LIEUTENANT PUTNAM

October 1801

After their gory victory over the *Tripoli*, the squadron's activities in the Mediterranean descended into a litany of boredom. At Gibraltar, the *Philadelphia* kept her watch over the grand admiral and the *Meshuda* for months. The crew of the small brig eventually mutinied, owing to the British refusal to sell them stores, causing the crew to storm ashore and ransack a bakery. It was not known until well after the fact that the officers of the *Meshuda* gave up their ship, slipped off, and made their ways disguised as Moorish traders back to Tripoli. Still, the Tripolitan flagship could not be seized because she was in a neutral port.

On September 3, Dale relaxed his blockade of Tripoli. Out of provisions, he made for Gibraltar, sending the *Enterprise* to find the *Essex* and rendezvous with him there. Bliven was standing the second dog watch when the British pilot came aboard and guided them into the harbor; there both the *President* and the *Philadelphia* swung quietly at their anchors.

Immediately after breakfast the next morning, the *President*'s cutter came alongside the schooner and a warrant officer sought out Lieutenant Sterett, who led him to Sam and Bliven. "The commodore presents his compliments," the warrant officer said to them, "and requires you aboard the flagship at once."

Bliven tried to hide his surprise. "Very well. Give us one moment to polish up, and we'll be right along."

They closed the door to their tiny berth and avoided each other as best they could in sharing their small mirror, combing their hair, and straightening their uniforms. "What do you suppose he wants?" asked Sam. "Do you think he's still mad at us?"

Bliven shook his head. "I've no idea."

The cutter eased its way up to the *President*, and they climbed the boarding ladder. They saluted a lieutenant who approached them. "This way, if you please." They descended the waist ladders to the gun deck, where Sam and Bliven removed their hats so as not to knock them on the low beams, and then were led after to the commodore's sea cabin, at which the lieutenant knocked and entered.

He returned in a few seconds. "Gentlemen, if you please," and held the door open for them. There behind a table stood Dale in the middle, and the two Captains Barron, one on either side. Papers, pens, and inkwells lay before them.

Bliven and Sam saluted, which the captains returned and seated themselves. "Gentlemen," said Barron, "it is my duty to inform you that you have passed your period as probationary midshipmen, and you are here by these presents"—he scooted a large and official-looking document at each across the table—"commissioned as midshipmen in the United States Navy, with the rank to run from the date of your original enlistment. Congratulations."

Bliven wondered if his relief was visible. At first sight of the captains and the arrangement of the room he thought they would be court-martialed. "Thank you, sir," they said, almost together.

"Be seated, please." Dale indicated two chairs opposite the table from himself and the Barrons, who gathered their sheaves of paper closer to scrutiny and took pens in hand. "Now, Mr. Putnam, tell me, how would you determine the southing of the moon?"

"Sir?"

"The southing of the moon, when she crosses the meridian."

"Truly, sir? The first thing I would do is search to see if there is a table in the navigational manual."

The captains smiled wryly. "Mr. Putnam," Dale continued, "you are Captain Bligh. You have been cast adrift in your longboat with aught but pencil and paper. Now, how would you determine the southing of the moon?"

"At what time of day, sir?"

Dale pursed his lips with satisfaction. "It is in the afternoon, Mr. Putnam."

"Well, sir, first I would need to know age of the moon, how many days since she was new. One should always know this; today is seven. This number I would multiply by forty-eight, and then divide by sixty. The quotient and the remainder will tell me the hours and minutes when she is on the meridian past noon."

"Mr. Bandy, suppose now you are Captain Bligh, and it is the next morning. How would you calculate it?"

"Sir, I would multiply the age of the moon by four and divide by five for the hours, and multiply the remainder by twelve for the minutes in the morning."

"Very good, Mr. Bandy, and why is it important to determine the southing of the moon?"

"Because this is how we determine when will be high tide."

"Very well." He turned to Samuel Barron. "Captain?"

"Mr. Putnam," said Barron, "suppose a distance to zenith of ten degrees north, and a declination of twenty degrees. What latitude are you in?"

Bliven thought for a moment. "Ten degrees north, sir."

"Mr. Bandy, suppose the sun is in your zenith. Then what latitude?"

"The equator, sir."

"Very well."

Dale turned to James Barron. "Captain?"

Barron folded his hands before him. "Mr. Putnam, suppose you are hauling close to the wind, the weather is moderate, all your sails are set. How do you tack your vessel?"

Bliven's blood flushed cold. These were questions of the lieutenant's examination. He closed his eyes and swallowed, imagining that circumstance. "Sir, I would stretch along the lee bow lines, weather sheets, and lee tacks, then put the helm alee, let go the foresheet, lee foretop sail, brace and foretop bow line, jib, and staysail sheets. When the foretop sail touches, brace to and help her; when aback, brace up and help her. When the wind is out of the aftersails, I would raise tacks and sheets; shift the staysail tacks, and haul over the staysail sheets. When the wind is about half a point on the bow, I would haul the mainsail if I am sure of coming about. Now, if she has sternway, I would shift the helm and top the spritsail yard; haul on board the main tack and aft the main sheet. When the aftersails are full I would brace up the main yard; haul off all, and haul on board the fore tack; keep in the weather braces forward and let her come to, then brace up. Then haul aft the foresheet, jib, and staysail sheets, and haul the bow lines; then haul taut the weather braces, lee tacks, and weather sheets, and have the braces let go at once. Then when I give the word to haul mainsail, the yards should swing of themselves. Sir."

The faces of the three captains bore no expression whatever. "Mr. Bandy," said Dale, "how do you find the true azimuth?"

Thank God, Sam breathed; he had just reviewed this. "Sir, I add the complement of the latitude, the complement of the altitude, and the sun's or star's polar distance into one figure," he recited. "From half this sum I subtract the polar distance, keeping note of the half-sum and the remainder. Now, to the arithmetical complement of the cosine of the latitude, I add the arithmetical complement of the cosine of the altitude, the log sines of the half-sum, and the remainder. The sum of these four logarithms will give the cosine of half the true azimuth. The true azimuth is this figure doubled, expressed from the north when in north latitude. Sir."

After an hour and a half, Dale said, "Gentlemen, do you need a few moments to refresh?"

Sam and Bliven both shook their heads. "No, sir, thank you."

"Then let us proceed." Commodore Dale knew the lie of the national politics better than perhaps any other officer in the squadron. Their appearance in the Mediterranean had quieted the Barbary states to the point that there was a faction in the United States to call off the hostilities. Ships would be laid up in ordinary, officers would be furloughed on half-pay, but midshipmen would simply be turned out. Dale knew in his bones that as soon as their backs were turned, the dey and the bashaws would be right back up to their old tricks, and it would be all to do over again. There must be a whole new crop of midshipmen. He could think of only one sure way to bind Putnam and Bandy to the service, and that was to pass them through their lieutenants' examinations without delay. Their value to the service, as demonstrated by their actions on the *Enterprise*, would sustain him in any haste or irregularity.

After three hours Dale looked searchingly left and right at both Captains Barron, who nodded slowly, their lips compressed. "Gentlemen," began the commodore, "the situation of our navy is such that we think it well to not just recognize your past conduct, but ensure your future connection with the service. Your appointments will be provisional, of course, but until such time as they are formalized, you are to regard yourselves as holding the rank of lieutenant, although your duties on your own vessel will remain the same. Now, if you will be advised by me, apply to our purser here on board for needle and thread. Have a chair in the wardroom and sew these on at once." From the box Dale extracted two epaulettes with dangling gold cordage, which looked strangely large when disembodied from a coat. "He will also provide you one month's lieutenant's wages. It is just past noon; we give you the afternoon ashore to reflect on your new responsibilities and recreate yourselves. Your boat will pick you up on the wharf at eight tonight." The captains stood.

"Forgive me," stammered Bliven. "I am amazed."

"As am I," added Sam. "We were midshipmen for three hours."

"Not at all." Dale shook his head. "Your commissions date from the time of your enlistments. You have been midshipmen these four months. You distinguished yourselves in action, which gives you more experience than half the lieutenants in the service. Leave the details to me. I am confident that your commissions will be approved."

"Yes, sir." They saluted and departed carrying their epaulettes, their already outdated midshipmen's commissions in their pockets. It required an hour to transact with the purser, sew the epaulettes onto the left shoulders of their coats, and be deposited on the Gibraltar wharf for an afternoon's liberty.

Once they got home, Dale knew they would not see service again until they were well past their fifteenth birthdays, and sixteen was more likely. The navy had plenty of junior lieutenants of that age—a fact of which the captains regularly complained in begging the Navy Department to give them more seasoned junior officers. But here would be two lieutenants who were already tested in battle.

Hard by the wharf, Sam and Bliven found a tavern called the Dolphin, which was run by a barrel-chested Englishman named Duckworth. "I served ten years," he imparted after learning their situation and selling them a loaf of fresh bread, "then settled here as you see. Once we took this ruddy rock from the Dons, it will be British for centuries, so no need to worry about slack business as long as there is a navy, what? Yours or ours, all are welcome."

Duckworth proceeded to instruct them on the best vantage points to see the most famous profiles of the celebrated Rock. "Reserve the larger part of your bread," he advised. "You will want it once you reach the rock. Then, if you are able to buy a good supper, come back at six."

"Why should we save bread?" asked Bliven.

Duckworth smiled. "You will see" was all he would say.

They had ascended some three hundred feet to a small park, which left them gazing upward a thousand feet to its summit. Among the others taking in the sight was a thin, fit, black-haired British lieutenant named Showalter who engaged them in conversation.

"So," said Bliven with satisfaction, "this is one of the Pillars of Hercules."

"Indeed," said Showalter. "But hardly solid as a pillar. A honeycomb would provide a better analogy."

"Truly?" asked Bliven.

"Most certainly. I have no other business. Would you like to see the inside?"

"Most surely, yes, that is very kind."

Showalter led them down a street to a guardhouse in the side of the rock, at the entrance to what appeared to be a great cave. As they drew near, Sam and Bliven looked up and could see muzzles of guns, enormous guns, protruding from limestone ports as though from a gigantic white ship of the line.

Inside, Showalter conducted them through a maze of tunnels past their gun emplacements. Until that day Bliven had never thought of the famous Rock of Gibraltar as anything but solid stone, yet much of it, as he learned, is limestone and honeycombed with caverns. In the nearly one hundred years of their occupation, the British had fortified it in the most fearsome way, with guns far larger than any he had ever seen. In the tunnels they began to be trailed by a troop of apes—small, inquisitive apes, the males of which weighed perhaps thirty pounds and the females two-thirds that size. They were not tame, but their lively dark eyes evinced their anxiety to be offered morsels of bread.

"So that's why he said save the bread." Bliven smiled. Wherever they stopped, the apes stopped and crouched or sat down, unnervingly close, but they seemed discreet, almost polite. But once they offered a piece of bread, an ape would snatch it in a flash of greed and presumption. There was no end to the amusement. "Have you trained them to fetch powder when you exercise the guns?" he asked.

"True powder monkeys," Showalter laughed. "Now, that would be something."

Sam and Bliven regained the wharf, and the Dolphin, more than two hours before the boat would come from the *Enterprise*. Duckworth set before them bowls of a savory stew as the tavern began to fill with British sailors and townspeople.

"Now," said the tavern keeper, "you shall see something! To entertain the sailors I have hired this couple of *gitanos*, who play and dance their gypsy music most lively. You shall see!"

There was no stage, but a man and woman in what Bliven took to be native costume strode with some ceremony to a heavy trestle table in the center of the room. The man began to play a guitar in the most blazing manner, and singing to accompany himself—high, nasal, impassioned, and ornamented, unlike anything he had ever heard before. To Sam and Bliven's amazement the woman stepped onto a bench and then mounted the table, keeping first time and then double time with stamps of her feet on the table, before launching into a controlled staccato of the hard soles of her shoes on the table, even as she accompanied herself with castanets and occasionally joined in the song, throwing herself into the music in the most vehement way. By the time she finished she glistened with sweat, the press of her dark nipples prominent beneath the damp white linen of her blouse, her eyes fiery with the emotion of the performance, which left Bliven breathtaken. Never had he imagined a woman capable of such fire and passion, such a lack of inhibition that it seemed her very soul was crying out in song. Quietly Bliven rose from the table and motioned for Duckworth to lean over the bar. "What music is this?" he whispered. "Has it got a name?"

"Why, bless you sir," said Duckworth quietly. "I don't know as how it's got a name, it's just what the Spanish gypsies do. Sort of their national music. Do you fancy it?"

"It's on fire," gushed Bliven. "I've never heard the like at all."

Duckworth nodded. "That's just the way with the *gitanos*. Andalusia is full of them."

Andalusia, Bliven reflected. He had heard of it, read of it, and now he was here. To so experience the world was a marvelous thing. Sam and Bliven judged it a wonderful day, and luckily done, for the *Enterprise* was ordered home the next day, carrying dispatches from the squadron.

Their westward passage fought both current and prevailing wind, seven weeks of hard sailing and constant tacking. They did not dock in Boston until early in October, lucky to have come ahead of the winter storms. They would not sail again before spring, so the officers were placed on leave until they should be recalled. Sterett was neither extravagant nor sentimental in sending off his midshipmen, but the spare fact that he told them they had done well made it all the more meaningful. Bliven and Sam took trouble to thank Lieutenant Porter for his tutoring in the academics, but Bliven spent a few moments lingering over the irony that it was Curtis's harrowing bouts of swordsmanship that probably saved their lives, yet he had come to dislike him so intensely that he felt relieved that Curtis had already quit the ship and he was saved the experience of a farewell. The only other one that Bliven took the trouble to see was Pelham the chaplain. During his boyhood, God and religion were concepts that he had accepted, but the existence of different denominations and the competition among them over which was the correct path to salvation were not part of the family discussion. Pelham taught him that kindness and solicitude were virtues not confined to the Congregationalist church they attended when farmwork allowed. Indeed, he found in Pelham, who was of the old Episcopal stamp, a comfort often lacking in the judgmental certainty and frost of his own church.

Their victory over the pirate corsair *Tripoli* had made them famous; the Congress presented Lieutenant Commandant Sterett with a sword on behalf of a grateful nation, and President Jefferson himself wrote Sterett an extravagant letter. "Those Barbarians have been suffered to trample on the sacred faith of treaties, on the rights and laws of human nature!" it was widely published. "In proving to them that our past condescensions were from a love of peace, not a dread of it, you have deserved well of your country."

It was gratifying to know that they enjoyed the approval of their enigmatic president, but for the letter to have been published seemed odd. It must have served some purpose. The remainder of the crew were given shore leaves with an extra month's pay, and that was when the game became known. Their leaves were open-ended, and none of them knew when, or if, they might be recalled. The Congress, ever wary of hemorrhaging money to maintain the fleet, provided that if peace were reached with the Berber pirates, the navy must stand down. That news, and subsequent orders, would take months to transpire. Jefferson's letter must have been intended to let the sailors know he was not ungrateful, and to sustain them through a furlough of indefinite duration.

Bliven sought out the purser on the receiving ship to make certain they would know where to find him. "Where bound, Mr. Putnam?" asked the purser.

Bliven waited until the purser dipped his pen. "My father's farm, Benjamin Putnam, South Road, Litchfield."

"Ah," the purser said, and nodded in approval. It was a common reaction, for Litchfield, in western Connecticut, was one of the most desired residences in all of New England. "Have you a secondary residence in case we don't find you there?"

"I will be nowhere else."

"Very well." He counted out the money—nine months' active service, paid in Massachusetts notes, and the one-month bounty in silver that could not be depreciated wherever it was spent.

Bliven shouldered his sail-canvas sea bag, heavier than anyone else's because it contained his books, and set off to the stagecoach depot to learn how long he must wait. Had he known when he would land, his father could have sent a man with a horse, for stage travel was an extravagance. But now, sending word home and waiting would cost more nights in an inn than the stage would cost.

He discovered that there was a new-cut turnpike southwest to Hartford, which was the straightest route, from where it was only nine hours more to Litchfield. But that coach ran only weekly, and its proprietor was keen on earning back his investment with exorbitant fares. Bliven instead settled on the south stage to Providence, then west along the post road to New Haven, thence north via Waterbury. That one left on the morrow; he read the handbill carefully and smiled. "NO NIGHT TRAVEL!" it boasted, and then in the small print of the itinerary he saw that the coach departed at three o'clock in the morning; those who missed the stage received no refund. *Great God,* he thought, every year it was some new trick; how much deception and sharp dealing must we take from our common carriers?

The coach was full to its capacity of twelve passengers; it was a great rumbling conveyance, more like a large farm wagon fitted with seats than a proper coach. The proprietor charged extra for more than fourteen pounds of baggage, although there was plenty of room for more than any twelve people could carry. They moved at barely a walking pace, less where the road was bad. The third day of travel brought him to New Haven, where Bliven switched to Mr. Strait's coach north through Waterbury. As the turnpike approached Litchfield it widened into the South Road, and with only a moment's pause Bliven was deposited at his parents' door. His father, Benjamin, owned both a mercantile and a draying and transporting company in the town, and the house lay on enough ground to be considered a small farm, with an apple orchard. They lived adequately, although they had not come to it easily. They had lost everything during the British occupation of Boston and moved inland to start over.

BLIVEN PASSED the fall and winter with them, not needing to earn his keep particularly, but happy to lay his uniform aside and occupy himself with making improvements to their farm, for his father was no longer young and there were no other brothers or sisters to assume responsibilities. He was noticed about town as he helped at the draying stable, for as he turned fifteen he seemed older, nearly six feet tall and powerfully built, his sandy-brown hair now tied back in a short queue, his clear blue-gray eyes now more than ever making his natural expression one of interest and curiosity. He laughed easily and could make others do so.

On those occasions when he was seen in uniform, the students at Miss Pierce's School for Girls noticed him particularly, enough to merit him an invitation to the school's spring social, even though he was not one of Mr. Reeve's law pupils, and they were the usual clientele for events at the Pierce School. The same post that brought the invitation also brought, at last, orders from the navy to report to Boston by the end of April.

In front of the oval mirror, Bliven donned his one dress uniform. Until the previous year a uniform might be whatever an officer fancied;

only a few months since did the navy issue a formal regulation. Thus he donned his white knee breeches and stockings; black shoes; white shirt; white waistcoat; dark blue coat, with tails and a standing collar with gold cordage; and long lapels with nine brass buttons down each side, narrowing toward the waist to accentuate the breadth of the chest—which in Bliven's case was quite unnecessary. There was lace to accent the coat cuffs and pockets, although not so much as on a captain's coat, and to the left shoulder he affixed his single lieutenant's epaulette. From his large canvas sea bag he extracted a neatly collapsed bicorne and pulled it open. At the time he ordered it, the fashion was to wear it athwart, with the corners over the shoulders. The growing tyranny of Bonaparte and his association with that style had spoiled it for everyone else, however, and now the custom was to wear them fore-and-aft. There was no front or back to the hat, except as defined by the small badge of red, white, and blue ribbon, which he wore on the right side. He debated with himself and decided it would be needlessly showy to wear his sword, and he left his eagle-hilt saber hanging from the ladderback chair by his bed.

Bliven borrowed his father's saddle horse for the occasion; if this was to be his farewell to Litchfield society, he did not care to look like a country bumpkin and plod up to Miss Pierce's school on one of their enormous dray shires. Riding through Litchfield Green, he could see the two steeples, one of the Presbyterian church, and one of the Congregationalists', where the famous Reverend Beecher came to preach on occasion. Litchfield was an important community for Beecher to maintain support in. The census had descried 4,285 souls; only four towns in Connecticut were larger, but none had a greater reputation for learning and society.

Bliven turned up the North Road and soon passed Tapping Reeve's law school on his left. Old Mr. Reeve was now a justice on the Connecticut Supreme Court, but this owl-like little man of sixty still gave most of the lectures, from a high stool at the front of his one classroom. In years past, one became a lawyer by apprenticeship. Mr. Reeve was the first one with the wit to realize that by systematizing a course of study and lecturing an entire classroom on Blackstone, or Coke, he could turn out lawyers like ginger cookies and make an entire second living by doing it. Such was his reputation that four in five of his students sought him out from other states, but from Bliven's exposure to them, they seemed to dwell in a continuous atmosphere of such aggressive pettifoggery that he really desired no truck with them. And they who knew him only as the drayman's son did not feel rebuked.

Within distant sight of the law school and across the road, Reeve's dear friend Sarah Pierce and her sisters and nephew ran their school of even greater reputation, among females, than the law school. She was an arch, hard-looking spinster of forty who divided her time between teaching and raising funds and support in the community. At both tasks she was successful, for the school was new-built for $385 that she had raised from her patrons, and it was located next to the house that she shared with her other spinster sister, and where she had held classes until the separate school was constructed.

After tying up his horse, Bliven crossed the yard, aware of the gazes of admiration that his uniform drew to him. He entered and paid his respects to the Misses Pierce and poured himself a glass of punch. The school was a large single room, the middle partition of which was partially closed to create two connected chambers. He made his way through, assaying the young ladies, smiling and bowing to those who acknowledged him. Near the back door was a steep stair to the loft, around which was gathered a small clot of young men that could only have been from Mr. Reeve's school.

One had blond hair and three brown; the blond had blue eyes and the others brown—but what they all had in common and what Bliven noticed was their hands, white as lilies and, if he could have been induced to shake hands with one of them, doubtless as soft. They looked to Bliven as though they had never done an honest day's work, nor were likely to. His own large, strong hands, even at fifteen, the sun and salt spray had cured like hams into the hands of a man twice his age. As he crossed the room it was apparent that in some of the young lawyers, who looked down and up his uniform, he was sure he detected the slightest pang of envy. There was, he thought, no need for jealousy. The navy would greedily accept any of them into the service. The navy was short, chronically and painfully short, of sailors to man its six new frigates and growing support fleet of brigs and sloops and schooners. The frigates were famous as the best of their class in the world, but their operation was crippled for want of experienced crews. Any of these Latin-spouting dandies would do, thought Bliven, but it would cost them their lily hands.

"How refreshing!" exclaimed one of the group by the stairs. "Here is someone who does not look to be studying law." Bliven could not place the accent exactly, but he recognized the languid vowels and slurred consonants of the Deep South.

"Gentlemen," he greeted them.

"What ship, sir?"

"*Enterprise*, sir, twelve guns, Lieutenant Sterett."

Of the four Southerners grouped at the foot at the stairs, the one to whom they seemed to defer as a leader—whom Bliven took to be taller, but then realized he was really standing on the first riser—had a startling countenance. Features that tended in most men to be handsome were so exaggerated in him as to make him seem mistakenly assembled. He had thin lips across a wide mouth, but so wide that it extended end to end of a too-square jaw. He had a penetrating gaze, but of such scowling intensity as to betray the essential frost of his nature. He had ample hair, but so much that it erupted from his head wiry and unkempt and standing on end as though he were facing into a gale. There was something about him that was part John the Baptist, part lunatic. This odd young man rolled his eyes. "Oh, well, then."

Bliven was unused to such a reaction. "Is that not a welcome name, sir?"

"No fault to you, sir," said this specterlike man. "You were not in command. But it has been all over the papers of late that Lieutenant Sterett is dismissed."

"Really? I have not seen it."

"Is it not true that before you engaged the *Tripoli*, you were flying English colors, to draw her out?"

"It is."

"Does that seem quite honorable to you?"

Bliven took some pride to have served, even if only as midshipman, on the vessel that fired the first shots of the Barbary War. They engaged, bested, and captured the corsair *Tripoli* of equal strength, killing twenty and wounding thirty without suffering a single casualty of their own. There was no fault in it. "Perhaps no one has explained to you, sir, that pirates fight without honor. Trickery is their biggest weapon; one has no choice but to fight on their terms. Did you know she struck her colors twice, and when we came close abeam to take her surrender, she resumed fighting, trying to assassinate our officers? Tried to

board us, for God's sake. Then we shot her to pieces until the lieutenants were dead and the captain was wounded and helpless."

"A well-won prize," ventured the blond boy.

"No, sir, it was against our orders to take prizes, for we had not yet
the benefit of a declaration of war. After the fight we sent her into
Malta, which was nearby. She had eighteen holes in her and we rolled
her guns overboard; she will cause no more trouble for a while."

"Why did you not just sink her and be done?" demanded the wild-
looking one. "No question, then, of more trouble."

Bliven cast his eye about the room, seeking an escape, seeing no
point in explaining that such a course would have left them responsible
for the care of thirty wounded and thirty more prisoners that they
were ill-equipped to assume. His gaze met that of a girl seated alone by
the pianoforte, looking about the room without expression. She was
spare of figure, but her face was porcelain beautiful, her hair the
color of fine honey, done up fashionably, a cameo mounted on a lavender ribbon about her neck. "Excuse me, gentlemen, there is someone
I must speak to."

Bliven approached the pianoforte. "Good afternoon, miss."

She looked up, regarding his single epaulette. "Lieutenant, good
afternoon."

"Forgive my intruding—in my branch of service, there is a maxim
that a sailor may seek shelter in any port in a storm."

She smiled wryly. "Our South Carolina boys seem to have put you
to flight."

"They have the weather gauge on me, when they generate all the
wind."

"Especially the skinny one on the step, I'll warrant, the one with
the gleam in his eye."

"Is he quite mad?"

"He wants to be president one day, and often says so."

"Good Lord, how will he run the country? He can't govern his own hair."

A deep chesty laugh exploded out of her before she stifled it with the fan that concealed her from the nose down, even as heads turned away from their glasses of punch to look at her.

"I mean, look at him," he continued. "He looks like he was hit by lightning. What is his name, anyway?"

"Calhoun," she laughed. "John Calhoun."

"Ah, Miss Pierce." Bliven turned and greeted the headmistress as she approached; he acknowledged her with a bow.

"In default of anyone else to introduce you properly," said the matron, "allow me. Miss Marsh, may I present Lieutenant Putnam? Lieutenant Putnam, Miss Marsh." The schoolmarm backed away and turned her attention to others, seeming for the moment less severe than she had when he'd first greeted her.

"Miss Marsh," he said. "Related to the town founder, I imagine."

"My great-grandfather, yes."

"A large family, I hear," said Bliven.

"Yes, very."

He nodded thoughtfully. "It must make your gatherings quite damp."

Her face clouded. "How do you mean, sir?"

"Well, wading through the marshes, you see."

She smiled and rolled her eyes.

"Perhaps it would enable me to distinguish you from so many others, if I may know your Christian name."

Her gaze at him was even and pleasant. "Clarity," she said.

"Charity." He bowed. "How very lovely."

"Sir, no, Clarity." She enunciated it with greater emphasis.

He paused for a moment, embarrassed. "Ha!" he said at last. "A name that requires itself. Well done."

A smile flickered across her face. "And your Christian name, Lieutenant Putnam?"

"Bliven," he said.

"Bliven? Is it from the Bible?"

"No, ma'am, it is from Wales, a family name from my mother's side."

"Ah."

Bliven had already admonished himself not to let any silence extend into awkwardness. "I do say, this is a handsome pianoforte. Do you play?"

"A little, yes."

"Would you play for us?"

"No."

The abrupt refusal startled him into a slack face.

"There are other young ladies here who play much better than I. Do let us allow one of them to show off, if she likes."

"My apologies, ma'am. I did not mean to—well. Miss Marsh, forgive my frankness, but you did seem ill at ease before I came over. I hope I have not offended you."

"No. No, quite the contrary. But—"

Bliven inclined his head in earnestness to hear what criticism she would offer.

She recovered herself. "Do you know, I have it on good authority that Miss Pierce only pretends to host these spring socials for the purpose of stirring together the young and the eligible."

"Indeed?"

"Yes, her true object is to show off her garden. Would you care to see it?"

"Yes, very much." She led him out of the building, but tactfully through the front door so they would not pass the Carolina boys again. They rounded the school to the rear and found themselves at the head of a parterre of neatly trod earthen paths intersecting in a pattern of diamonds that covered half an acre. At the far end a small bench—vacant, she noticed—reposed beneath an arbor, and they walked leisurely.

"Four times a year Miss Pierce hosts a social for the students of Mr. Reeve's law school," she said. "We put on our best dresses and pinch our cheeks, and they come look us over. Sir, I think it is a cattle show, and yes, you judge me aright, I am ill at ease with it."

"Fair enough," he announced. "Ah"—he stopped abruptly where a rosebush was just producing its first flowers of the spring. He selected a large bud, deep wine red, and pinched it off, taking care to bend over and remove its two thorns before handing it to her.

Clarity touched it to her nose and they walked on.

"And who is that watching us from the rear door?" he asked.

Clarity glanced, though not obviously. "Miss Pierce's married sister, Mrs. Brace. She must approve of you, or she would not allow us to wander such a distance. She might yet come after you with a rake for pinching one of her roses."

"Well worth the risk." Bliven bowed slightly back to Mrs. Brace even as they walked. "Apart from your Carolinians, your lawyers really don't seem like such a terrible lot," he said. "Mr. Reeve's school is quite famous for producing the best lawyers in the country, is it not?"

"Mr. Vice President Burr is a graduate," she said, as though she disagreed. "Is he an example you would choose for honor and integrity?"

Bliven chuckled. "Well, no. But, correct me if I am wrong, did not the abolition of slavery in New England come about because of Mr. Reeve?"

They reached the vined bower with a stone bench beneath it. At his gesture she took the seat and he stood, one foot on the step and his hands clasped behind him—a pose that he had practiced in the mirror and knew that it showed his uniform to best advantage, and also showed his profile to the back door so that Mrs. Brace would know he was not attempting any liberties.

"It did, yes," she admitted. She was surprised he was so well informed. "Is the evil of slavery a concern of yours?"

"Well, ma'am, a sailor at sea has little time for philosophical matters, but when I do think about it, I dislike it and disapprove of it, yes."

She had almost forgotten he was a sailor. "Surely it is not a philosophical exercise. It is a matter of daily cruelty and injustice for thousands, for hundreds of thousands, of human beings in a country that claims to be a beacon of freedom."

"I would pay money to hear you say that to your friend, Mr. Calhoun."

"I would not waste my breath. Do you think me dreadful?" she asked.

"Hardly. Your candor does you credit, I think, and is surely good for your health. I mean, if there is ever in the land some disease caused by nervous timidity, you shall never suffer from it."

She laughed, suddenly and heartily. "And you? Do you know any other Carolinians who could have prepared you for their peculiarities?"

"Yes, I do know one. He was my friend and fellow midshipman when I first sailed on the *Enterprise*."

"And how did you find him?"

"Hot-headed. Always knows best. Has trouble taking in the opinions of others."

Clarity nodded.

"And in fairness I should add he says the very same things of me."

"Accurately?" she asked.

"Sometimes."

"Yet you called him your friend."

Bliven paused to assess the deeper meanings of the term. "Yes. There was no one more reliable in a fight." He omitted that they had tried to kill each other and had been compelled to swear their friendship to each other.

Bliven inclined his head toward the school. "What do they teach you in there?"

"English, literature, history—the history is fierce. Miss Pierce has compiled her own text of world history, in four volumes. Nothing easy about that, let me tell you. Miss Pierce is of the opinion that mothers are their children's first teachers, and they should be educated to the equal degree as their husbands."

Bliven knew that was a controversial doctrine, advocated by some strong-minded New England women. "She's right."

"You think so?"

"On board ship, I have to hide my books. Junior officers are supposed to be all fight, fight, fight. But fighting must be for a reason. History teaches the reasons, I think."

"My family," said Clarity, "pays a surcharge above the tuition for me to study art, and French, and needlework. And Reverend Beecher comes over from East Hampton to lecture on religion several times a year. The Beechers and the Pierces are great friends." She paused, unsure of her ground. "Are sailors religious?"

"Have you ever been in a storm at sea?"

"No."

"Let me assure you, nothing will lead you quicker to believe in God."

She turned suddenly serious. "Are we to become friends, Lieutenant Putnam?"

"As I stand here breathing, I do hope so." Even as he said it, he felt the barrier rising that separates sailors from sweethearts. He had not experienced it yet, but he had heard of it often from older men, and here it was. "But Miss Marsh"—he paused for breath—"I must tell you, the war against the pirates is not over. I have received my orders. I leave for Boston in three days' time. My ship sails in two weeks."

"Oh! Are you such a sailor, then? 'Enchanted to meet you, ma'am,'" she mimicked. "'How very charming you are, ma'am.' 'Perhaps I shall see you again in two years' time.' Ha! Ha!"

"Oh, it would be just one year, more like."

"Oh!" She was unmoved.

"No, really, the enlisted sailors only sign up for a year at a time. Well," he said more gently, "I can see you are not a young lady to pine away, waiting for her man to come home. But I should be very sorry to think that I have wasted your time today."

"You have not."

"May I write to you?"

She lifted her head. "Yes. We should go back inside." She rose and descended; he walked beside her, hands still clasped behind him. "Will you be in danger?" she asked.

"As wars go? Oh, I think not. Corsairs have only guns enough to take unarmed merchantmen. They could never stand up to our frigates, or even the sloops; I should be surprised if they dare try." It was better that she not know, at least not yet, that when the crew of the *Tripoli* tried twice to board the *Enterprise* after first striking their colors, Bliven had himself fought desperately with saber and pistol, and had himself accounted for two of the Berbers' twenty fatalities. He had not even told his parents of that, nor of the surprise in a man's eyes when he looks at you knowing you have killed him. Bliven reasoned that if he had no conscience, it would not haunt him, but it did haunt him, and would until he could share it with someone.

"Well," said Clarity, "will you write me about your adventures? Perhaps I can write a novel about you."

"What, you want to be a novelist?" He feigned shock. "Do your parents know this?"

"Are you going to betray me?"

"And miss being in it?" he teased. "Never." They had reached the front steps. "But if you publish a novel," he said, "being about my adventures, we must share the money."

She extended her hand. "Done."

He took it. "Well, in my time I have known a Charity or two, but never a Clarity."

"Indeed." She pressed his hand with unexpected earnestness. "What a poor, muddled life you must have lived to have never known Clarity."

"Yes, I do confess I begin to think so."

After they took hands he stepped back and bowed, and she dropped into a curtsy, but his eyes never left hers.

5.

DUNGEONS OF THE WHITE CITY

———◆———

November 1801

The sharp defeat of the *Tripoli*, and the regular presence in the Mediterranean of American ships ten times the size and firepower of the Berber polaccas, led to a sudden quiet in that sea. American merchantmen began venturing once more out of Spanish and Italian ports without waiting for escort by a warship. Though some captains were more wary than others, trade, by and large, resumed.

Joseph Barnes sat writing at the small table in the best cabin—although in a three-hundred-ton brig, having the best accommodation did not imply luxury. To say it was adequate met the case.

The morning began with a favorable wind off the port quarter, but during the day, as the *Mary Lovejoy* plowed through the blue Mediterranean a hundred miles north of Algiers, it increased and came more from the north, forcing the captain to haul in closer to keep his course. The crewmen looked northward, and smelled and studied. A chill wind on a warm autumn day, all trace of haze blown away, leaving the sky clear as crystal: It was from a mistral, no doubt about it. It must be roaring out to sea off the French coast to be felt this far out, pushing the sea into six-foot swells. Now the ship was near broadside to them, rolling obliquely. His daughter Rebecca, fifteen, lay seasick in the next cabin.

It was not easy to write through the ship's lurching and heaving, but Barnes dipped his pen again. Newly accredited, the United States consul to the Kingdom of the Two Sicilies was composing his response to the welcome he expected to receive from the king as they established formal ties. The kingdom had proven herself a steadfast friend in aiding America's conflict with the Berber pirate states of North Africa. Although they still called it the Kingdom of the Two Sicilies, once Napoleon had placed his brother Joseph on the throne in Naples the Italians were down to really only one proper Sicily, the island, with the capital of Palermo lying perhaps seven days east across the open Mediterranean.

Barnes thought the captain a timid man. Wilfred Hawley had wanted to take a much longer route, calling at Barcelona and Marseilles and Leghorn, but Barnes wielded his authority as the owner's business partner to insist that they run straight east from Cartagena. Their company had never lost a ship to the Barbary pirates, and with a favoring wind, Barnes calculated that their swift brig could not be caught.

Directly over Barnes's head on the quarterdeck, Hawley stalked back and forth, worrying. The captain of the *Mary Lovejoy* was a short man with a powerful chest and a round face, his smooth-shaved cheeks framed by beard on his chin and jowls. He squinted into the wind, studying. If it shifted even a point more to the east, he would risk being blown too far south to make the straight, safe north coast of Sicily. If he was forced south into the Sicilian Strait, he would have to work around the whole island, exposing himself to the pirates from Tunis and Tripoli. Hawley did not like it; the summer mistral never blew for more than a day, but this was not of the summer variety. This one might become stronger yet.

Barnes worked through the afternoon, entering his daughter's cabin at intervals to check on her. Rebecca was miserable but stoic. He hoped she would develop some poise and polish in Italy, and find diversion from her unhappiness back in Virginia. It was apparent that she would not be pretty, and occasionally she hurled thunderbolts of her mother's foul disposition. Perhaps Palermo, and Naples if it was recaptured, would give her a chance to cultivate a happier direction.

Writing at his table, Barnes jumped at the concussion of a cannon shot, not from their own deck and not close, followed by running and shouting and cursing from the deck above him. He rested his pen in the inkwell, tied up his cravat, put on his coat, and made a quick check in the mirror. He was forty-eight, tall, with curly, iron-gray hair. Not a sailor, he ascended the ladder carefully. By the time Barnes reached the quarterdeck, the captain had ordered sails trimmed back to only the topsails and they had slowed to where they just had steerage. "Here, Hawley!" he demanded. "What is all this?"

"Well, I hope you're happy now," growled the captain. Handing his glass to Barnes, he pointed off the starboard quarter. Barnes raised the glass to his eye and saw, a thousand yards out, an exotic-looking ship approaching, low-cut and lateen-rigged. "That, my greedy master, is an Algerine xebec. A pirate ship."

Barnes looked fitfully up at the sails. "Are you mad? You can outrun them!"

"Not a chance. In this wind the only way to open a distance would be to run straight south, and that would take us on a line to Algiers, which they would think rather funny, wouldn't they?"

"You're not going to surrender!" roared Barnes.

"I am."

"I forbid it!" Barnes gesticulated at four small, shrouded cannons on the *Mary Lovejoy*'s deck. "Is there not a reason this ship is called an *armed* merchantman?"

"Oh, yes," Hawley said grandly. "I have four guns; they have twelve or fourteen. I have twenty-two lazy merchant sailors who might give an account of themselves in a tavern brawl; they have eighty to a hundred trained fighters. Lateen sails—they can make double our speed hauling this close to the wind. We are done, Mr. Barnes! I am going to surrender and do whatever I have to do to keep my head attached to my shoulders. Now, you had best get below and break the news to your daughter that she is going to be spending a few months in Algiers before she gets to Italy."

"Good God!"

"When they board us," said Hawley, "I will tell them that you are an important American diplomat and that you will be well ransomed. You won't be harmed, but hear me now, and make no mistake: If you resist they *will* kill you."

Barnes thrust the glass back in the captain's hand and stormed back to the ladder; the captain just heard him mutter "Coward" as he disappeared. And Barnes just heard the words "Pompous ass" follow him below.

He forbids it, thought Hawley. *Silly man, who is he to forbid anything? There is no rank where we are going.* Hawley had been in Algiers before, and had seen the bagnios, the crumbling, fortified baths on the quays where captive sailors were held like goats in a pen when they were not chained together and used as slave labor by the dey or those he favored. Immediately out of the same hatch came a crewman, who approached the captain bearing a white bedsheet taken from Hawley's cabin. "Bring down our colors," ordered Hawley with resignation. "Run them back up with this above them. Jump to it, now."

"Aye, sir." Then the sailor hesitated and turned. "Sir, what's to happen to us?"

"I expect we will be locked up with the other American hostages in Algiers. But no fear, the owner is rich, we will be ransomed." The sailor turned to his task, and Hawley thought, *Damn the owner, and damn this ship.*

The *Mary Lovejoy* was Boston-built to the specifications of her owner, Franklin Lovejoy, the wealthy merchant. He had been particular in his preference for brigs to carry his cargoes. Brigs were square-rigged and fast running before the wind, never mind that she was slow and cumbersome in tacking or hauling. *Mary Lovejoy* was also fat and deep, her large hold too ambitious for her size. It was a fault committed at Lovejoy's insistence, for he meant her to carry every possible ton of cargo short of sinking her—lumber, sugar, rum—whatever needed transport from one wharf to another. Her too-great beam had caused the keel to hog by several inches over the years, as the weight of the bow and stern pulled down against the buoyant midships. Warned that one day she would mount a swell and her back would break, Lovejoy settled on a simple remedy: Keep the hold well ballasted with profitable cargo and the problem would correct itself. He had a knack for making money, Hawley allowed, but he cared little for the stresses on a ship's timbers. Or the dangers run by his crews, damn him.

BELOWDECKS, Barnes rapped twice softly before entering Rebecca's cabin. She was awake as he sat on the edge of her berth and laid his hand on her forehead. "How are you feeling?"

"Not as awful as before, thank you, Papa. What is all the commotion?"

He held her hand in both his own. "Becky, I want you to prepare yourself. You have to be very brave. We are going to be, well, diverted. We are not going to Palermo just yet. We are going to Algiers."

She took this in for a few seconds, that Algiers could mean only one thing. "Is it pirates?"

"Yes, I am afraid it is."

Her breath quickened. "Have we been boarded?"

"No. Not for twenty or thirty minutes yet."

She assimilated the news for nearly a minute and then nodded. "Go back to your cabin, Papa. I will get dressed and come to you." As soon as he was gone, she peeled back the covers and got to her feet, but then immediately sat back on the mattress as the ship's roll toppled her backward. She looked about the cabin, assessing what, if they were taken off the ship, she would need to take with her. She saw two novels lying on the table, and as she stared at them she realized that her father could not have been more wrong about her in his exhortation to be brave. She felt no fear at all. *To hell with silly novels,* she thought. She was about to live an adventure of her own. She felt apprehension, to be sure, but that only sharpened her determination to breathe in each moment of it.

Her only jewels were two rings and a small brooch, better not to wear and show them. There was no time to sew them into her clothing, as she had read a wise hostage would do, so she poked them down her stockings. And she had a small locket on a gold chain, which held a curl of her mother's hair. That she would wear. She thought if they took it, they might be satisfied and not search her further. She tied back her long brown hair and pulled on a green muslin dress, packed a small bandbox with her toiletries and as many clothes as would fit, and went to her father's cabin.

The remarkable thing about taking the *Mary Lovejoy* was the lack of violence; it was, if anything, businesslike. The corsair captain, whose name was Achmed Faisal, inquired into what cargo they were carrying, and upon learning that it was rice and sugar, burst out laughing and remarked how polite it was of them to bring their own rations into captivity.

From their cabin, Barnes and his daughter heard activity overhead, but nothing in any detail, and both leapt to their feet when the cabin door was kicked in. In rushed a large Berber, with no turban and almost Western in dress but for the looseness of his blouse, and wielding a scimitar. Seeing there were only two in the cabin, he advanced, the sword ready.

Rebecca's nerve deserted her and she buried her face in the breast of Barnes's coat. "My God, they're going to kill us! Papa!"

Barnes looked over his daughter's brown curls and saw the Berber raise his sword, but upon finding them unarmed, he stood up straight and swung the blade away from them. "No, no, dear. I think we shall be quite safe." She pulled away an inch and looked up at him searchingly. "They are corsairs," he said. "Pirates. They live on the ransom they take." He raised his gaze from her to look directly at their assailant. "The more of us they kill, the less profit all around."

"Girl," said the Berber, then repeated it, louder. "Girl!"

She turned partly around and saw his cotton-bloused figure over her shoulder as he lowered his sword. "The old man speaks truly. Do as you are bidden, no harm will come to you." She understood from Shakespeare that Moors were supposed to be dark, but she had not thought how dark until he took another step toward her and reached out, taking hold—he was surprisingly gentle—of the gold locket with her mother's hair between his thumb and forefinger. With a quick jerk he broke the chain and slipped it into a pocket. "Thank you," he said and nodded.

In a moment Hawley, with the guard assigned to him, was in the cabin with them. "The ship has been taken as a prize," he said. "I will be going as a hostage on their vessel, my crew has been confined, and their men will sail this ship and follow us to Algiers. There is no need for you to remove from your cabins until you are taken ashore. We will get there in about two days."

THEY RAISED THE AFRICAN COAST on the morning of the second day, and by noon the captives in the *Mary Lovejoy* were brought on deck and saw they were passing a masonry mole several hundred yards long, slipping into a capacious harbor. The city was on the harbor's western shore, facing east across the bay. Algiers was stunningly white, as virtually all its buildings were whitewashed, rising rank on rank, street on street, some four hundred feet in elevation up to the casbah. *Alger la blanche*, the romances called it, Algiers the white. *What a perfect target for bombardment*, Barnes thought when he saw it. There could be no hiding anywhere; every house, every shop, rose behind the one before it, every one exposed to the bay. He wished he could be there to witness the vengeance that the United States would wreak for his seizure.

As they landed, janissaries shouldering impossibly decorated muskets, inlaid with marquetry of ivory and jasper, led Rebecca away into the warren of whitewashed confusion that led up to the casbah. She called out once, "Papa!" as they pulled her away, and he called out once, "Don't resist! I will find you!" as he was led into the bagnio on the mole.

A guard opened Barnes's trunk, and on finding it packed tight with clothing uttered one guttural but very satisfied syllable as he motioned for the guards to take him within, and Barnes realized he would enter captivity with only the clothing he wore. In the large, echoing cells of the bagnio he counted more than a hundred other Americans, mostly common sailors and some commercial passengers; the one he found who had been longest in confinement had suffered there just under three years.

THE JOSEPH BARNES WHO EMERGED four days later was a gro-tesque of the one who went in. It was the same face, but unwashed, unshaven, caked with the salt of four days' sweat. His clothes were of the same elegant cut, but soiled and sweated through, shiny in places where he had wiped his hands after eating rice and greasy strips of mutton for four days. He could have been ill at the pasty density of his own smell. His hands were tied before him with a leather thong, and between two fantastically pantalooned janissaries he was led into the whitewashed maze.

The streets were only about ten feet wide, often made narrower by wares set out for sale, the sunlight partly blocked by overhanging upper stories, and passing every several houses they would turn and ascend more steps. After twenty minutes he began to catch glimpses of the fortress that overlooked the city, the casbah, and the jumble of connected houses around it. As they passed through the wall, he thought for purposes of imparting future intelligence he would count the cannons along its crenellations, but he could not in the few seconds he could see them. At least fifty enormous guns commanded the bay, and Barnes realized how idle was his earlier ambition to see the city reduced by bombardment. Algiers was beyond gun range from the open sea, and American ships in the bay would be blown out of the water before they could fire a second salvo.

As they crossed an ancient and irregular courtyard Barnes looked up at the dey's palace, integral to the fortress, rising three stories above a whitewashed stone ground floor, but there was no symmetrical façade. Very apparently it had been expanded incrementally over centuries, the stone varied in color as to when and where it was quarried. The temperature dropped several degrees as they entered a stone portal, which proved to be a chicane entrance, a baffle that protected the privacy of the palace interior.

The splatter of a fountain grew louder as they approached its far end, made a turn, and found themselves in a stair hall. Opposite them stood a medium-sized African wearing billowing red trousers and a loose white silk blouse, both secured by a black sash. "Mr. Barnes," he said.

"I am Joseph Barnes."

"My name is Jonah, chamberlain to His Highness the dey, Mustapha VI bin Ibrahim. You are shortly to be granted an audience."

Barnes was so shocked he thought he must only be imagining—the voice carried the soft drawl of his native Virginia. "Why, you're an American!"

"No, I was an American," Jonah said coldly.

"For what purpose is this audience?"

"You will be allowed to publicly claim your diplomatic status and plead for your release."

"Where have you taken my daughter?"

"She is safe. It is time. You will address the dey as 'Your Highness,' and you will bow as you answer any questions he may have."

Their footsteps echoed up the stone staircase and they passed into an inner court, surrounded by colonnades along all three floors, with latticed wooden balconies protruding from above the northeast corner. Opposite them rose a dais, richly carpeted, the style of chair that was mounted atop it he could not tell, for it was draped with bolts of the richest velvet, red, yellow, and green. On this chair sat an old man with a luxuriant white beard, his face as tan and weathered as Morocco leather, so swathed in white cotton that no part of him was distinct except his face and his hands, the right one dipping occasionally in a brass tray of figs. He was flanked on either side by a file of janissaries, each one with a scimitar through his sash, and each one holding a lavishly inlaid musket taller than himself.

As they approached the dey, Barnes took his cue from Jonah on when to stop and bow, and then Jonah mounted the first step of the dais and stood at the side of the dey, who leaned over to hear a soft aside from him.

The dey opened one hand in recognition. "Mr. Barnes."

"Your Highness." He bowed. "I am the accredited consul of the United States of America to His Majesty, the King of the Two Sicilies. My ship was seized at sea, and I and my daughter were brought here in arrest. Since the beginning of civilization, the law of nations has established that diplomats are exempt from such seizure. I am willing to recognize that this may have been done by mistake, but I respectfully ask our release, and passage to our original destination of Palermo."

It took Jonah a moment to render this into Arabic and hear the dey's response. "Regrettably, that is not possible at this time."

"My country has done you no injury," asserted Barnes. "By what right do you seize people of other nations on the open sea and hold them for ransom?"

Jonah had another inaudible exchange with the dey, who gave a longer response. "You are infidels, Mr. Barnes. Our Holy Koran places upon us, the faithful, the right and the duty to subdue and enslave unbelievers at our pleasure."

"But what if all religions claimed this right? No one could travel anywhere!"

"Perhaps. But this is the will of Allah, peace be upon him."

"Then may I know Your Highness's intention toward myself and your other American prisoners?"

The richly pantalooned African produced and read from a sheet of paper, whose words Barnes recognized instantly.

*My best friend Mr. Jefferson, three days before sailing from
Portsmouth I learn'd from perusing the newspapers that your
administration of the country is so warmly regarded in our former
mother country, that I resolv'd at first opportunity to apprise you
of your deserved popularity. And of course, to thank you once more
for the confidence you have reposed in me, as United States consul to
the Kingdoms of Naples and Sicily. From Portsmouth we called at
Gibraltar, from whence we sailed three days ago bound for Palermo,
where you may rest assured, my every effort will be bent to cementing
the continued friendship and alliance of His Majesty King Ferdinand
in quelling the disruption of our trade by the Algerine pirates of the
Barbary Coast.*

*The Dey of that state, and his brother brigands the bashaws of
Tunis and Tripoli, at this moment hold a dangerous face—but the*

trade of the Mediteranien is of such Magnitude, that these Robbers should be satisfied—one Ship with a Valuable cargo, & the Liberty of our fellow citizens are of more importance than the money they demand. Two or three frigates, with an intelligent and well informed Agent, might settle immediately a lasting Peace—or at Least as Lasting a Peace as these Pirates make with any Power.

Jonah lowered the letter that he had been reading from. "Do you deny being the author of this letter?"

Barnes glanced around the sun-bleached limestone courtyard, at the file of janissaries with their pearl-inlaid muskets, and concluded that his best hope was to make a brave show of it. If his only remaining act was to die, word must not get back to Virginia that he died less than a gentleman. His country would avenge him. "Of course not," he said. "Thank you for saving my papers for me."

The dey's dark eyes never left Barnes's sweating figure as he fished in the brass bowl for another fig, selecting one by feel. He spoke a few words of Arabic to Jonah. "His Highness says your insults condemn you."

The old dey shrugged slightly and spoke again at more length. "But the fact that you write so familiarly to the American president, and you appear to be his friend, commends you to our mercy. You may withdraw."

As they reached the edge of the courtyard, the air was suddenly rent by a terrible animal roar that made the paving vibrate beneath their feet. Then they heard a second, and then a violent combat between unseen beasts. "What on earth?" Barnes gasped.

Jonah led him on into the stair hall. "Lions. His Highness has a menagerie beyond the south wall. At feeding time, the lions fight over their food. The strong ones will prevail; the weak ones"—he shrugged—"will become rugs. As in life, the weak are walked upon."

Jonah accompanied Barnes and his guard back through the cool chicane to the street. "The dey has decided to let you live."

"Only because I am worth more alive than dead, I'll warrant."

Jonah stopped and folded his arms. "It is widely known that Mr. Washington and Mr. Adams agreed to pay the tributes every year to our Tripolitan states. And everyone knows equally well that Mr. Jefferson opposed the practice, vociferously. In your letter, you urge him to a more moderate policy. It is your reasonable attitude that has saved your life."

Barnes stared at him. It was astonishing to hear such speech from a black man.

"Now, if it was up to me," continued Jonah, "I might have you executed for not being able to spell 'Mediterranean.' When you return to the bagnio, you will be given pen and paper. Write a letter to your superiors, let them know your location and your circumstances. We will see that it is safely delivered to your consulate in Palermo."

They reached the entrance portal. "Please, where is my daughter?" asked Barnes.

Jonah pointed upward to the top floor of the palace. "She is in residence, in the dey's harem. It is pleasant and has a roof garden."

"The harem," he repeated sickly.

"Don't worry, the guards of the harem are all eunuchs."

Barnes started to go, but turned back a final time. "Jonah, where did you get your education?"

Jonah stood unnervingly close and looked right into this eyes. "Mr.

Barnes, black people in Africa have been reading and writing for centuries. Only in your Southern states are we condemned to plant rice and pick cotton. That is only your view of us."

Barnes and his guards descended through the city to the waterfront, and walking along the mole he saw in the distance the building that he had come from. They stopped him a hundred yards short of there, showing him into a different cell before locking the door behind him. He found himself alone in a large stone chamber, at the opposite end of which he found an enormous stone basin, recessed into the floor and surely as old as the bagnio itself, two-thirds full of water, with soap and a towel and his trunk of clothes. He lifted the lid just long enough to see that they had been undisturbed. There was a table with paper, pen, inkwell, and a platter of food—rice, mutton, chickpeas, figs, grapes, and an orange. He removed a cloth from atop a chilled pitcher and found it full of goat's milk, half of which he drank greedily before bathing, reaching out for food even as he washed himself. He found his shaving kit within his trunk.

At length he sat down to write, telling himself that if they thought he would be so awash in gratitude that he would soften his account of what conditions the other Americans were held in, they were grievously mistaken. But then he realized, of course, they would read everything before sending it on, if they did send it, and he must be measured, and moderate, to have a hope of bringing rescue.

6.

SWORD AND PLOW

March 1802

T hree days after parting from Clarity Marsh, Bliven donned his freshly laundered uniform. His mother's farewell at the door was affectionate but stoic; whatever volcano of fears and pain she suppressed, she knew the importance of making his going as genial, and seem as hearty and unconcerned, as his coming. She was well satisfied of his affections; making his heart heavier at parting would have evidenced the alleged weakness of her sex, and she was determined to prove worthy of better praise.

She reduced her storm of fears to one act, one remedy. "One thing only I will ask of you," she told Bliven in parting.

"Yes?"

"That you will read in your Bible daily. Not great chunks of it, just something, each day. Will you promise me this?"

He embraced her and kissed her cheek. "Yes."

His father rode with him to Captain Bull's tavern, which served Mr. Strait as his depot. They spoke quietly of the spring planting, which they had begun but not completed. "I have heard it said," Benjamin ventured, "that with Captain Bull no longer living, his family is thinking to close the tavern."

Bliven considered it; the tavern had been a steady buyer of their cider. "Well, we should have no difficulty selling the cider elsewhere."

"Yes, but perhaps we could take it upon ourselves to open a cider house, if that happens. The east road to Farmington and Hartford bears more traffic than where we live; it might prove profitable."

"It might, it might." They were interrupted by the clatter of the stage arriving southbound from Torrington. With naval enlistments still limited to one year, and with good luck, Bliven might be home in time to help with the pressing and fermenting. "Well, God willing, I shall be back in the fall, and we will take up the subject again."

"Write to your mother, she worries about you."

The three days and two nights of travel between Litchfield and Boston seemed interminable, but Bliven used the time to reconcile himself to again losing the comforts of home—no more his mother's care and cooking; their sharp white Vermont cheddar must transform into blue-green mold on cheese brought up from the hold. Her rich, dark, fragrant bread must become the ship's biscuits, those stone cobbles of flour and water paste twice baked, inedible except they be pounded to gravel and soaked in hot tea. In place of her savory apple pie he could only look forward on rare occasions to plum duff, a disgusting boiled pudding of flour, grease, and raisins. And after a few weeks any food on their plates might wriggle with worms. The foot warmer of coals in his bed must become a bucket of sand with a hot shot in it; the associations of his childhood must evaporate once more into the violence and stench of ninety men in a seventy-foot schooner. He steeled himself to the coming hardships, stern in the conviction that if he wished to have the greater reputation and social presence of a naval officer, this was what must be done. At least, he consoled himself, he now bore an epaulette on his shoulder; the bored and malicious misfits who occasionally passed for other lieutenants must take greater care with him.

Bliven had acquired several more books during his winter at home, bought from the printer on Litchfield's square who was attempting to inaugurate a subscription news sheet, but who supplemented his income by selling books acquired wherever he could do so cheaply. The new volumes weighed down his sea bag. It was round, of white sail canvas the breadth of a barrel but taller, with a drawstring pulling it closed at the top. The coach company required him to pay a stiff fine for its exceeding fourteen pounds, and then upon arriving he was compelled to rent a barrow from the stage company to trundle his sea bag to the navy yard, for now it was too heavy to shoulder for any great distance.

Bliven approached the gangplank of the receiving ship, sizing her up fore-and-aft, from the flagpole to the waterline. They must have their offices somewhere, he admitted, but what a tragedy for any ship to end this way: dismasted, with the stumps rising above the gabled roof of a barnlike building that belonged on land, the railing gone and windows cut into her hull, the bowsprit gone and only the curl of her prow to protest that she had seen graceful days, fighting days.

Leaving his barrow and sea bag at the foot of the gangplank, he found the receiving clerk, saluted, and handed the letter he had received across the desk. "Lieutenant Putnam, reporting as ordered."

The receiving clerk was a pasty white blond little lieutenant, who could not have been much older than Bliven was at the time of the Tripoli action, except he looked as though he had never been out of doors. He seemed a spectral clerk in these derelict remains of a once-proud ship; perhaps this was the entrance to the sailors' underworld. The clerk's barely visible eyebrows knitted. "There must be some mistake," he said, almost to himself.

"Is something amiss?" asked Bliven.

"We are fully manned at present. We have no place for you."

"That cannot be; are you quite sure?"

"A moment, let me inquire." The clerk pushed back from his desk and took up a crutch from the back of the chair that Bliven had not noticed before. He got to his feet and Bliven saw that he had no right leg below the knee.

"Oh, good God, I am sorry," Bliven said, before he could stop himself.

The blond clerk stopped and turned. "Sorry?"

"To . . . trouble you to inquire." He knew very well that what he was apologizing for was judging the man for a history he had only imagined from a first sight. Never must he do such a thing again.

"No trouble. Certainly it was our mistake and not yours. Wait one moment, please." He disappeared into an adjoining office, then returned to his desk. "You will forgive me if I sit back down."

"Of course," said Bliven. "How did you—"

"French cannonball in the West Indies, in the Undeclared War. Took it right off, never felt a thing. One minute I had two legs, the next minute I fell, fainted from loss of blood; no terrible amputation to remember, thank God. But"—he gestured around—"this is now my quarterdeck."

"I see." *That could be me,* thought Bliven, *one day*—instant injury, or instant death, or, as he saw, instantly maimed in a way that would never end.

The clerk arranged himself again. "There is a lieutenant in the *Adams*. Our information was that he would remain on sick leave, and you were sent for as a replacement. After we sent your orders, he reported for duty and will sail. I regret that we neglected to countermand this order."

But he busied himself writing now. "We want to retain you, however. You will continue on half-pay until we recall you." He handed up the hasty new order. "Send us a voucher for your travel expenses, here and home; you will be recompensed. You see my name, Lawrence Todd, Lieutenant—at the bottom. Send your expenses to my special attention. I shall tend to it at once."

"I thank you, although I was prepared for duty," protested Bliven. "I am at a loss what to think." He did not try to mask the lack of comprehension that he knew must show. "How is it this other man sails and I do not?"

"He has seniority. Mr. Putnam, as you well know, the size of the navy was slashed once we made peace with France. My God, we went from twenty-eight captains to nine! We had upwards of a hundred lieutenants; we now have billets for thirty-six. You and that other midshipman from the *Enterprise* were the latest to be commissioned, and therefore are the most junior. Your reputation was such that Commodore Dale especially recommended your recall, above several others of greater seniority."

"He did?"

The clerk nodded. "Directly before he retired."

"Retired? I was unaware."

"It was sudden. He had such a rocky time, as it were"—the clerk smiled vaguely—"in the Mediterranean, he was quite undone by the time he returned. He was to go back this spring, but he laid down certain conditions that the secretary of the navy could not accept, so he retired."

"He was not so disarranged when I left him. What has happened?" asked Bliven. "I have heard nothing." It did not sound like Dale to give the navy an ultimatum.

"Ah, no, you might not have heard. After he sent the *Enterprise* home, he went to Port Mahon to collect dispatches. There was an idiot of a Spanish pilot, ran the *President* aground in the harbor, sheared off the whole forward part of her keel. She stayed tight, but crossing the Atlantic was out of the question. He spent the winter in Toulon, seeing to the repairs. Managing foreign workmen in such an undertaking left him quite exasperated."

"And the ship? Was she permanently damaged?"

"No, thank the Lord."

Bliven nodded. The *President*'s massive internal strength would have kept her watertight. "What conditions did he lay down?"

"That the government support the squadron more effectively."

Bliven agreed. "Yes, he would."

"That, and I believe there was a quarrel over his duties. You know the navy is finally going to start building up to meet the Berber threat. Captain Barron—James—who had command of the *President* while Dale commanded the squadron, was needed for another command. Mr. Dale was informed that he would have to both command the new squadron and run his own ship without a captain on board. He would not brook it."

Bliven considered this sadly. "I am sorry to hear that they could not accommodate him. He was very kind to me on a number of occasions." His mind drifted back to the duel with Sam that they were goaded into by the lieutenants on the *President*. "But it is good hearing that they are going to increase the fleet. I was afraid we had made a peace with the pirates of which I was unaware."

The look on the clerk's face showed resignation, betraying his preference that they should have continued fighting until they brought home a conclusion. "It will take time. Your squadron under Commodore Dale rather did its job. You let the Barbary pirates know that we mean business, we have enough sail to escort our commercial vessels, so the government is hoping that a modest continuing presence will be enough. Commodore Morris sails with a new squadron to relieve the ships that have been longest on station."

"So I am to go home and wait."

"Enjoy your time with your family. I am certain that you will be wanted again. Perhaps you have not heard—the Algerines have taken one of our diplomats, and his daughter. He was to have been our consul to the Sicilies. Up until now we have had some trouble getting the State Department to go all in for a war, but they seem to be on board now. The wheels of government turn very slowly, but be patient. As they measure time it will not be long."

"I thank you for your attentions, Lieutenant"—Bliven looked at the paper—"Todd. You have been very kind." He turned to go, but paused. "By the way, I heard it said in Connecticut that Lieutenant Sterett has been dismissed. Can this be true?"

Todd registered surprise. "Hardly. It is true he has been relieved of command of the *Enterprise*, but he has been ordered to Hampton Roads to oversee fitting out a new twenty-gun brig, which he will command. In effect, he has been promoted."

Bliven nodded. "I am glad to hear it."

"Yes, you served under Sterett, did you not? Perhaps your source in Connecticut heard merely that he had been relieved of the *Enterprise*, and concluded for himself that he must have been dismissed."

"Perhaps so," said Bliven. That lay squarely within the likelihood of John Calhoun and the other Carolinians at Tapping Reeve's law school to set sail on a conclusion with only half a cargo of facts.

Bliven had planned to eschew an inn that evening to save money and carry his sea bag direct to the stage depot, intending to doze at their door to take the predawn coach for the return journey. But with the new order in hand authorizing his reimbursement, he dined and slept well. This also relieved him of the annoyance of paying for the weight of his books on the coach, and thus he called at a bookshop and acquired the six volumes of Gibbon's history of Rome for himself, for they had a used set for a reduced price, and a fashionable novel to present to Miss Marsh, when he could gain her company.

When Mr. Strait's coach paused again at the Putnam farm long enough for Bliven to disembark with his sea bag, his mother spied it from her keeping room, where she had been kneading dough. That chamber had been added to the side of the house and had a window onto the front road. She met him in the front yard, leaving wet strings of dough on her apron as she wiped her hands; she embraced him with a quizzical look on her face. "I had prayed of God to deliver you safely home to me again," she said. "But He does not usually answer so quickly." Benjamin was also out of the house before she was through speaking.

"Well," said Bliven, "in this case His instrument was a lieutenant on the *Adams* who first was too sick to sail, but was miraculously healed."

They went into the house, then into the kitchen, where they partook of a corn pudding just out of the oven. "How did you find Boston?" asked Benjamin.

"Boston thrives and is busy," said Bliven. "But the navy yard, Father, it is a disgrace. You should see the ships laid up, one after the other, even some of the frigates, beached like whales. We could crush these pirates in a stroke, but the government will not spend the money to send a whole fleet. Commodore Dale retired; he told them he would lead a squadron back only on condition that it was adequately supported."

"And they would not give him that assurance?"

"They would not."

Bliven's father packed tobacco into a long-stemmed Dutch clay pipe. He was not particularly fond of the Dutch, whose settlements dotted the Hudson Valley thirty miles to the west, but he appreciated that they knew how to smoke. Poughkeepsie was the closest of their towns, and he knew the leading families, the Van Kleecks and the Van Oosteroms, whose notorious thrift had left them very well off. They could buy what they wanted, and that included Putnam's hard cider, though he sometimes felt he had to shake the coins from their pockets.

"Well." Putnam rose, took a lighted brand from the kitchen fireplace, touched it to the bowl of the pipe, and puffed. "There is no need to be surprised. That is our government for you, what? They are willing to have a war, they love the rewards of a war, but they do not want to pay for a war. Probably at this moment someone has gone to Mr. Hamilton to ask his advice, how to arrange the figures in columns to make it look like it is paid for, but will not in truth cost them anything."

Benjamin Putnam sat heavily in a Windsor rocker with thin cushions on the seat and hung on the back. "It is the business men, you see? They want the trade with Spain and Italy and the south of France, even

Greece and the Levant. And they don't want to have to pay the pirates. So they send the navy, too few ships, mind you, and men whom they feed"—he censored himself, mindful of his wife's presence—"stale bread and cheese, to do their dirty work for them."

Bliven was astonished to hear this. "I had no idea you felt this way, Father."

Benjamin sucked pensively at the fragrant Virginia tobacco in his pipe. "This is why I opposed your entering the navy. Not that I want to keep you here forever, not that I feared that you would fail to acquit yourself honorably, but because your life is worth less to them than the moldy cheese they send you."

"But surely, Father"—Bliven set his bowl of corn pudding on the table though he had not finished it—"the piracy is indeed a fact. These Mohammedan states capture and kill and enslave white Christians by their thousands. The men are put to hard labor until they fall dead, the women"—he glanced at his mother—"far . . . worse. Surely it is honorable for any nation to put an end to that."

"And that, you see, is why I let you go." He let that register. "But look you, where are the British, the French, the Portuguese, the Spanish, the Sicilians? They all pay tributes and ransoms, do they not? Even while they fight each other! They ought to be paying us to fight the Berbers for them, as they shall reap the benefit of free seas."

Bliven nodded. "Yes, that I grant you. As cynics and insincere cads, the Europeans make Americans seem innocent as babies. But I had no idea that you had considered all this so deeply."

"Where the life of my only son is concerned? Yes, I have thought much on it. And when this war with the Moslems is over, it will not be long before the British or the French are back at our door, that's the kind of devils they are. We will need a navy then, rightly enough, so let us build all the ships we can, sail them or lay them up, it doesn't matter, so long as they are there in the future." There was quiet for a moment. "Dorothea, have you naught to say in the matter?"

She began to collect the dishes. "Trade, war, honor, that's all men's business. A woman's business is to want to keep her family alive." She would not speak her bitterness, but she hoped very much that it would carry in her tone of voice.

"How shall I explain myself now?" asked Bliven suddenly. "Everyone is expecting that I have gone to sea. It will be humiliating to be seen again as though I were not wanted."

Benjamin tapped the warm ashes of his pipe into a ceramic bowl. "I think not. I shall have a word with the news printer. He feels as stridently as you about the navy being left to languish, and now being sent forth in only part strength. He can announce your return and light off on their maladministration in one piece. He will be glad of it, and will excite sympathy for you." He patted the palms of his hands down on the chair arms. "Well, home you are, and home you are like to stay for some months, now. Is it not so?"

"Yes, it seems your fledgling is back in the nest a while longer."

"Spring is not half over. The widow Baker spoke to me about renting her back field that adjoins the end of our orchard. I declined, thinking that I would be full occupied this year. But if you are here to help work it, we can make good use of it. If you agree I shall go see her at once."

"Yes," said Bliven. "Yes, by all means."

They rose together, Benjamin kissing his wife on the cheek. "I hope she has not let the field to someone else. I shall hasten."

"That will be well, my dear." Dorothea Putnam did not need to be told that an additional field rented on any fair terms would be more corn, which meant more chickens, more winter hay, perhaps pumpkins.

"I remember that field; I shall go and have a look at it," said Bliven. "We must know how much preparation it will need." From the back of the house he walked through the garden, past the chicken yard and pigsty; he stopped in the barn and picked up a digging trowel. Beyond the barn, leaving the house and road farther behind, he looked in the small stone building that housed the cider press. It was instantly familiar, the crusher, the press, the rows of earthen crocks to ferment the hard cider, now clean and dry, awaiting the autumn.

Bliven took his time walking through the orchard. His father's father had been the first to bring Roxbury russets from Massachusetts down to his great-uncle Israel Putnam's farm near Brooklyn, in the very east of Connecticut. Now these golden leathercoats were their own staple, so sweet that they needed but little sugar when placed in the fermentation crocks.

Many of their Litchfield neighbors had added the peculiar codicil to their religious creeds that equated the consumption of alcohol in any measure, be it ever so mild and harmless, as sinful. This they carried to a point surely of pride—an irony that Benjamin Putnam was not shy to point out, for pride should also be taken for a sin. Nevertheless, for them in season he also prepared sweet cider, for which his golden Roxbury apples were so perfectly suited that even those most partial to the hard cider conceded that the juice, sluiced directly into cups beneath the press, was of astonishing sweetness. The mash they consumed as applesauce, and even the tough skins the hogs competed for.

But these were not the apples that Bliven most remembered from his childhood. Nearest the house his father had planted four rows of Baldwins, brilliant scarlet woodpeckers, tart and hard. One of Bliven's first associations was of the first frosts of October with fat slices of apple pie, hot and topped with melted cheese; such a breakfast fortified him well into the school day.

It was a young orchard, he was happy to note; with time and proper care its growing production would provide them a comfortable living. As he reached the far end of it he saw on his right the split-rail fence that separated their land from the widow Baker's. He swung easily over it and judged the parcel to be near ten acres or somewhat less in extent. It had not been planted since her husband's death seven years before. Much but not all had gone to brush, but that and the small trees that had started would not be difficult to clear; the stones had been plowed up years before. With spring half gone, planting quickly took precedence over orderliness; the field could not be seen from the road, in any case.

He knelt and thrust the trowel into and through the grass, pulling up a clod of earth that crumbled from the roots. It was dark and reasonably moist. He put his nose to it and inhaled the rich, dank fragrance. *Yes,* he thought, *I remember this.* He could think of only two primal smells, aromas that must extend unbroken back to the Creation. One was the fresh salt air of the sea, the other rich, moist earth; he dreaded having to choose between the two, and wondered how he might manage to keep both, as he had both now.

As he returned to the house, the wind brought the scent of bread baking and he thought, *Oh, very well, there may be three primal smells.* Benjamin returned with a year's lease on the field, renewable by mutual agreement. That night they ate roast venison, parsnips from the root cellar boiled and mashed with butter, and fresh greens new from the garden. This was Thursday, Bliven reflected with satiety, and the men at sea were eating salt pork with a half-pint of beans, and biscuit, and the worms in the biscuit. What stripe of fool must he be to even consider leaving this place again?

DURING THE LATE SPRING Mrs. Baker's field became Bliven's domain, and he was racing to clear it and plow before the season left them behind. He planted four acres in corn first, then cleared and planted four acres in hay, which was not so dependent on the calendar. There was room left for beans and squash, and pumpkins that his mother had such a taste for. It was hot work, even for a strapping fifteen and a half; occasionally he thought of bracing mornings at sea that appealed to him, but almost at once he would remember an important advantage of home.

Two days after the announcement of his return appeared in the local broadside, Bliven penned a letter to Clarity Marsh, explaining his return and asking her permission to call on her. In return he received an invitation to attend church with them on the first Sunday in May. They were Congregationalists, and it raised Bliven's hackles when he contemplated too close an association with them. They were an authoritarian church, long since stripped of the compulsion of law they had formerly enjoyed in the days of the Pilgrims. They also had no overarching governing structure; each local consociation controlled the churches in its area, which professed according to their leaders' persuasions. Thus dissenting sects now proliferated on questions of scripture and doctrine, free now of the threat of stocks or ducking stools.

To families such as the Putnams, who believed sincerely but practiced pragmatically, rancorous debates on the nature of the Trinity or who enjoyed the guaranty of salvation seemed wholly unconnected to the practicality of living honorable lives, helping their neighbors, and practicing hospitality and charity. Yet these were arguments that ended friendships and provoked condemnation to eternal flames. In the Putnam household, on Sundays when there was not time to attend church, Benjamin read passages from the Bible before supper, and almost always ended with Micah the prophet: What does the Lord require of thee? To act justly, to love mercy, and to walk humbly with God. For the nature of the Trinity he could spare neither time nor attention.

Such an attitude was as foreign to the Marshes and their class as the muezzins of Arabia, and Bliven was aware that he was entering dangerous waters; if Clarity was a siren, she was surrounded by the family shoal of needing to speak and act, and profess, correctly. The first Sunday in May was a signal day for Litchfield's Congregational church, for the learned Dr. Beecher had crossed the Sound from Long Island for one of his visits. It dawned brilliantly, and Bliven's uniform was spotless as he walked his father's saddle horse up to the Marshes' front door. It was a large house, two full stories, of white clapboard with shutters, in a style that was coming to be called Federal, although when it was built two generations before no one had yet thought to give it a name.

A maid, a young black girl, answered the door and led him to Clarity's father, who greeted him in the hall. He was a tall man with a full head of gray hair, a wealthy man of property, a man of authority, descended from leaders and himself a leader of the community. He showed Bliven into the parlor, where he bowed to Mrs. Marsh. In her, Bliven was sure he could see Clarity a generation hence, and was encouraged at the prospect, for she was a handsome woman. When Clarity descended the stairs they exchanged bow and curtsy; she did not take his hand until her parents were through the door. "I am glad you have come," she whispered.

The Marshes rode in their carriage, with Bliven walking his horse alongside. He thought their arriving in such process extravagant, for the church lay a bare two hundred yards from their house, but then he supposed that such a family must maintain its state.

After Bliven secured their horses, Clarity took his arm as escort, and they could see the visiting reverend greeting his flock as they entered the church. She waited until she saw Beecher was free and Clarity drew Bliven up to him. "Reverend?"

"Miss Marsh." He bowed and took her hand.

"May I present my friend, Lieutenant Bliven Putnam?"

They bowed. "Lieutenant Putnam, the hero of the *Enterprise?*" His smile showed teeth remarkably fine and even; he shot out his hand and Bliven took it. "Well, I am pleased to meet you, sir."

"Hardly a hero, sir, but I thank you." *So,* he thought, *this is what it's like. Being a hero paves a road ahead of you.*

Beecher's youth startled him; he must be only in his latter twenties, hardly time enough to have gained such a reputation as a doctrinal divine, as the conservative wing of the denomination was hailing him. His hair was dark, slightly wavy, and combed back; his dark-brown eyes slanted down away from his prominent nose, one more than the other, as though they were tired, and Bliven was certain that he caught in them the same glint, the same hint of possession, that elsewhere he had seen only in the Carolinian, Calhoun, he had encountered at Miss Pierce's social. Beecher had a prominent lower lip beneath a wide mouth, which when closed made it look like he had bitten into something bitter. "Are you a friend of the Marshes?" he asked.

"A new one," answered Mr. Marsh, coming up behind the group and shaking hands with Beecher. "Lieutenant Putnam's father is the proprietor of the drayage and livery stable, and has an admirable little farm on the South Road."

Despite himself, the "little farm" lingered in Bliven's ears.

"Yes, I have seen the livery stable," said Beecher. "Mrs. Marsh, good morning. Are your parents with you, Mr. Putnam?"

"No, sir, I came with the Marshes."

"Of what faith are your parents?" Beecher asked him this with stunning directness and with no hint of motive, whether it was out of friendly curiosity or guarded suspicion.

Bliven was taken aback. "Well, we are Congregationalist, albeit my mother tends to the Unitarian persuasion."

"Oh, I am sorry to hear it." Bliven had had no warning that Beecher was an avowed enemy, a passionate enemy, of Unitarianism. Harvard had gone over, and most of the churches in Boston, to this grievous doctrinal error. He looked upon his churches on Long Island and in Connecticut as bulwarks against this spreading heresy.

How quickly he raises a wall, thought Bliven, how quickly the welcome becomes more guarded, how certainly he expects you to be like him.

"And your father? Does he not attend services?"

Bliven blushed and looked around for help, but there was none. "Well, sir, he believes that he pleases God by not letting his family go hungry."

"He works on Sundays?"

"Often he does, yes, sir."

Beecher frowned, accentuating the bear-trap aspect of his mouth. "God's holy word tells us that the Sabbath is a day of rest, set aside unto Himself."

Bliven stiffened, but then smiled. "And yet I understand that you do some of your best work on the Sabbath, do you not, Reverend?"

Beecher's eyes registered an icy flicker before he boomed out in laughter. "Well, arguably that is different, but yes, so I do! Come, it is time to go inside."

Clarity separated from him as she and her mother went to the women's side of the church, but not before he saw the color drain from her face like wine from a glass, and he knew he had stepped amiss. Her father betrayed no feeling, but led him into a forward pew, to the far end, where Bliven found himself squeezed between him and the wall.

That morning Bliven Putnam came to understand why Lyman Beecher had become a standard-bearer for the Trinitarians. He preached a persuasive sermon, an angry and convicted sermon, on the sure damnation of those who fall into doctrinal error, but those who at the last hour, if they made the most abject confession, might yet achieve blessed salvation. Bliven felt every bone in his body taking offense. Had he been sitting next to Clarity, he did not know how he would contain himself.

"I am very pleased to have met you, Lieutenant," said Beecher as the congregation filed out. "Perhaps you might settle here, do you think?"

"And perhaps you might join the navy," he answered. "We have need of good chaplains on our ships." He would have loved to know that on some dark night Beecher had been hooded and buggered in the heads. That would take some of the starch out of him.

"A kind thought," said Beecher, "a very kind thought."

At the Marshes' house it was Clarity's father, descending from the carriage, who took hold of Bliven's horse's bridle. "Please, come in, take some tea with us before you go home."

Bliven had been nursing his insult and dreading what consequence he would face with Clarity. "Yes, thank you very much, I will."

Their black maid knew to have tea and cakes ready by the time they returned, which they took not in the parlor but in the library on the opposite side of the hall. Bliven could not stop himself from exploring the shelves before he sat. "Such a fine collection of books," he said quietly as Clarity handed him his cup—which he instantly set down. "Oh, look, you have Rollins's *Geography!*" He removed the first volume, then took up his tea and joined Clarity on the sofa. He remembered the page. "Look here, the Straits of Gibraltar, you know, when you sail through there you can see both shores. See where it says the Pillars of Hercules? Well, they aren't really. The Jeb el Musa—here—is just a little hill compared to the Rock of Gibraltar."

"Malta." Clarity pointed. "You were there."

"Yes."

"And where did you fight the pirates?"

Gently he moved her finger a quarter-inch to the left. "Just here, about ten miles west."

Clarity's parents had sat quietly through this exchange, until Bliven looked up again. "Such a fine collection of books."

Her father nodded. "I am pleased that you appreciate them. You must make a point to come visit us and gratify your curiosity further."

"May I?" Surely the man knew there were not just books in the balance.

"Certainly. Come, Martha, let us leave the young people to themselves for a moment before he returns home." Bliven thought that exceptionally well done, conceding them some privacy even as he signaled that it was time for him to conclude the visit.

Suddenly they were alone in the library. "I could have throttled you when you talked back to Reverend Beecher," hissed Clarity.

"When did I?"

"When you said he worked on Sunday."

"Oh, he took it in good part." Bliven shrugged. "Did you not see? Besides, it will serve him to learn that he cannot run over everyone as easily as he imagines."

She seemed unmoved. "It could only be seen as a lack of respect."

"Lack of his respect, not mine. Please understand, sixteen for a sailor"—well, near sixteen, but he was anxious to be older—"is not the same sixteen as for your law students. I cannot live as a man for a year, with a man's duties and expectations, and the sea is a hard life, and return to a state of pupilage when I come home. I no longer see the world as a child, and I will admit it, I can become resentful when I am treated as one."

Clarity grew thoughtful. "I'm sure you understand, his sermon was already prepared. He did not deliver it for the purpose of insulting your parents."

Bliven nodded. "I know. But all the same, I am glad they were not here."

"My parents like you. This is well begun."

It was a discreet time to withdraw. "As is the new shed on the side of my parents' barn, which I must go work on. May I call on you again?"

"Oh, yes."

7.

LITCHFIELD

———◆———

1802

Summer for Bliven passed congenially after this. He finished adding the shed onto the barn to store up the additional hay he would harvest from Mrs. Baker's field, and he enlarged the corn-crib, dug and roofed a second root cellar, and watched a bountiful crop of apples slowly grow plump. He took to attending church with the Marshes, which even his mother approved of, for she understood that he was thinking of his future.

Clarity came to accept that his embrace of faith was that of a strong young man; it was not as meek or humble as she would have thought proper, but it was on her father's counsel that she determined not to make an issue of it. She could find prospects at Mr. Reeve's law school who were wealthier and more gifted in sophistry, and if she selected a husband there, he would honor her choice. He also made it clear, however, that if she yielded her affections to her lieutenant, he would think that her choice of young Putnam's honesty and hard work was not an inferior one. This surprised her, for her father seldom crossed the lines of class.

It was hard for her to guess what turned him to favor him. At the first frost he invited Bliven to shoot geese with him on land he owned in some marsh country, but Bliven declined, on the grounds that he was not a very good shot, and he would likely maim more than he killed. Mr. Marsh declared he had heard it said that Bliven was quite a famous gunner. Bliven, nonplussed, replied that if Mr. Marsh wished him to bring his own guns from the *Enterprise*, they had best be uncommonly large geese, which caused her father to seize up with laughter whenever he tried to repeat the story.

More likely, she concluded that they shared a mild view of alcohol, of which Reverend Beecher disapproved without reserve. Marsh drank sweet cider when it was in season, but as apples ripened only once a year, he was willing to enjoy hard cider at other times of year and think no ill of it.

When he turned sixteen Bliven was judged old enough to visit Captain William Bull's tavern on the east road toward Farmington. Captain Bull himself was dead these past three years, but the family maintained the business and it was the most congenial stopping place in the town. There he could lift a tankard of ale and be sure that he would meet one or another of his family's friends and new acquaintances who wanted to hear of his exploits on the *Enterprise*. Bull's tavern was also the first place where the newspaper from Hartford could be found lying freely about. From the travelers and from the newspapers, Bliven was able to keep reasonably abreast of the conflict in the Mediterranean.

The year began well enough, for although Congress did not declare war on the Barbary states as President Jefferson had strongly suggested they should, they did—for whatever the subtle difference was worth to them—recognize the state of war. The point was, the navy was authorized to take prizes, and that would be a sure motivation to the crews. They also raised the pay, to ten dollars per month for an able seaman and proportionately less for ordinary seamen and boys. Much of the good done by these steps, however, was undone by doubling the term of enlistment to two years.

America had never fought a war so far abroad, and law providing for one-year enlistments had been enacted with the view of service close to home shores. Two years was a necessary change, but of men who were so down on their luck as to consider serving in the navy for a year near home, very few indeed even of the most unfortunate could be induced to sign on for two years. Nor did it help that it became better known generally that American officers, especially junior officers, had little to learn from the British in wantonness and cruelty in governing their crews. More than one captain, unable to make up his ship's company in Boston, was given leave to sail for New York and troll the docks and alleys there for derelicts—the class of sailor on whom the worst disciplines were inflicted, which thus deepened the cycle.

Bliven heard as much news from New York as he did from Boston, and while he felt certain that the navy never employed the press gangs for which the English were infamous, some of the stories he heard in Captain Bull's tavern trod so close to the line that one could be forgiven for losing the distinction. And all this was before the fighting even began.

Such fighting as there was, for the commodore who replaced Dale, Richard Morris, seemed to have little taste for it. News of fighting was mightily scarce, but the public was well informed of the fact that his wife, his young son, and a maid accompanied him on his flagship, and there were accounts of their sparkling presence in society, in Gibraltar, in Port Mahon, in Leghorn, and Naples, and Palermo, and Malta, where Mrs. Commodore Morris gave birth to their second child. News of fighting, however, was precious scarce.

After the harvest was in, Bliven heard one day in the livery stable that a letter was waiting for him with the postmaster. A short walk, and payment of a quarter dollar in postage, saw him holding a folded letter, with a postmark from Abbeville, South Carolina. Sam Bandy's hand he knew well enough.

"Bliven Putnam, Lieut., USN," it began.

My dear sir,

With matters well in hand on our plantation, I have in mind to come to Connecticut and visit you. Would this be well? The navy here is very dull, who can say when I will be recalled? Indeed, if you have gone back to sea, I expect your father will be kind enough to reply to this and advise me of it. But if you are in residence, I should be glad to gratify my curiosity for I have never seen New England, and it would be pleasant to talk over Barbary times with you. Be pleased to address a reply to me at Rosemount Plantation, Abbeville District, South Carolina.

> *Very Resp'y,*
> *Yr. Obt. Servt.,*
> *Samuel Bandy, Lieut.,*
> *USN*

Bliven wrote out his reply that night after ascertaining that his parents were as keen to meet Sam Bandy as he was to see him again. "My dear Sir," he wrote by candle in his upstairs bedroom:

> *I fear I have no similarly grand address from which to answer your kind correspondence, but my family will welcome your visit. Come when you can, and do not neglect to inform the navy in Charleston of your location. From what I can learn, it would not surprise me to hear that we had been called to duty. If I may advise you, you will find it faster to sail from Charleston to Boston and take the stage from there to Providence. There engage Mr. Strait's coach, and you need tell him only, 'Putnam Farm, South Road, Litchfield,' and you will arrive on our very doorstep. He knows us well. Any day is as good as another for your arrival, but you might tell us an approximate day, that we may be expecting you.*
>
> *Very resp'y., &c.,*
> *Bliven Putnam, Lieut.,*
> *USN*

Bandy arrived the second week in November, in a cold rain that had turned into snow. He descended from the coach with a large trunk as well as his sea bag, finely dressed but not in his uniform. "Sam!" cried Bliven as he opened the door. "Sam, come in, let me help you with those. I judge you have not seen snow in a while; we ordered it especially for you."

Benjamin greeted him, pipe in hand. "Well, young Mr. Bandy, you are welcome. Now, here is how it is. You see there the parlor, with the polite furniture, the bric-a-brac, and a fireplace that could not heat a dollhouse. Through there leads out to the kitchen, which has a blazing fire, and has food and tea, and the comfortable furniture. I leave it to you, sir, would you be company or family?"

"Family, by all means!" They settled in the kitchen, where Sam opened the trunk. He brought with him a selection of gifts for Bliven's mother from his own far-removed life—a sack of sweet nuts called pecans, which Bliven judged superior to walnuts, preserves made of strawberries, a ham cured in sugar instead of salt. She accepted these as rare delicacies, but he would not be thanked for them. "I am the one who is imposing on you," he protested. "The least I can do is help you feed me!"

It was apparent from Sam's clothing and accessories, and even more from the way he wore them, that he came from great wealth. It left Bliven embarrassed that the best hospitality they could offer him was to share his room in the attic eaves of their house, but Sam gave no evidence of feeling superior.

In the mornings, after chores, they hunted or fished. Bliven showed him the town, Tapping Reeve's law school, and was surprised to learn that Sam and John Calhoun knew each other, though not well; both were from Abbeville. "Why are you not as insane as he is?" asked Bliven. "Do you have better water at your plantation?"

"We just call him peculiar," said Sam.

Bliven introduced him to friends at Captain Bull's tavern, but not to the Marshes for they were away. Sam took to helping him with chores, to finish quicker and gain free time. "Do you and your parents really work this place all by yourselves?" Sam asked.

"Occasionally they hire one worker, but otherwise yes, we do."

"No wonder you are as strong as a bear."

Bliven leaned on the split-rail fence. "Do you remember what it was we fought about, back on the *President*?"

Sam considered it. "I think it was about what somebody told me, that somebody told him, that somebody told him, something that you said about me."

"We were fools. One of us might have killed the other."

"Well, I tried." They laughed.

They spent ten days together before Sam departed. The day before he was to leave, Bliven inquired and obtained an invitation to bring Sam to visit the Marshes, who had returned. Bliven had put it forward as a chance for Sam to see how the really well-to-do New Englanders lived, but in truth it was a chance to present him to Clarity.

They arrived for tea; it was now by habit that her father led them into the library. "Ordinarily," he said to Sam, "we take tea in the parlor, but when our young lieutenant comes calling, we know this is his favorite room, so we gather in here."

Sam was taken aback by the sheer number of books. "I can well believe it is his favorite room. You have to pull him out with a rope, I'll wager."

Clarity greeted him cordially, but with a reserve in her bearing that Bliven thought a little more than her custom. Their young black maid wheeled in the cart with the tea service and cakes, and Clarity rose and took control of it as she entered the room. "I will pour, Becky, thank you."

Marsh raised a hand and touched the maid's as she left and asked quietly, "Becky? How is your mother today?"

"Thank you very kindly, Mr. Marsh, I believe she's a sight better today, but the ague still has a pretty powerful hold on her."

"Does she need a doctor?"

"Oh, no, sir, thank you, she's strong, I'm sure we just keep her warm, she'll be fine."

"Well, you will let us know if she needs anything?"

"Yes, sir, thank you kindly." Marsh released her hand and nodded slightly to dismiss her. Sam took in this exchange without comment.

Clarity asked Sam pleasant questions about his family and his friendship with Bliven and their life at sea, but both boys noticed she inquired nothing of the plantation, or what they raised or how it was run. It was her father who learned from him that it was some four thousand acres in extent and grew the full range of crops suitable to the climate. "Well, between our wool and your cotton," Marsh said at last, "we ought to have a more lively commerce between our sections, don't you think?"

"Perhaps we shall," said Sam. "I hope so." He changed the subject suddenly. "But look, here we are, just a few weeks until Christmas. Have you special plans? How shall you celebrate it?"

The pall cast was as silent as if it had suddenly snowed in the library. Marsh's brows arched visibly, while his wife's eyes flew open like window sashes. Clarity looked helplessly around the room and then focused down on her tea cake.

"Hm, Sam," Bliven stammered. "Christmas . . . is not held to be such an event in New England as it is elsewhere in the country, or the Christian world."

"Do you not celebrate Christmas?" Sam asked incredulously.

"Mercy, no," hushed Clarity. "Why on earth would we do such a wicked thing?"

"What? Forgive me, I am amazed." Sam laughed nervously, aware that he had fallen off a social cliff, but astonished as to why. "Was not General Washington famous for his Christmases at Mount Vernon?"

"He was a Virginian," said Marsh, tempering his disapproval with his understanding that not everyone lived as they did. "And an Episcopalian. In our church, we regard the passion of Christ as the important matter, not his birthday."

"Oh. Well, please forgive me, I have never perceived any harm in it."

"It is popish," mumbled Clarity.

"If you read your Bible carefully," said Marsh, "you will observe that Jesus was born at the time of the Jewish Passover, and that is in spring. December was chosen because it was a pagan festival in ancient Rome. The entire concept was artifice."

Bliven was sure he detected one of Reverend Beecher's sermons in the cadence of it.

Sam heaved a helpless sigh. "Oh. I confess, I had no idea."

"And look at the time!" exclaimed Bliven. "Sam, come, we must go get you packed." They said their good-byes as quickly as propriety allowed and walked together south across the green. "You know, Sam, when you put your foot in your mouth, it is a good policy to leave the other leg free to hop away on."

Sam stopped abruptly, shot Bliven a cold look, crossed his left foot over his right knee, and hopped the next several steps, until he nearly fell and Bliven caught him roughly. "Never mind. I still like you as well as before."

That next morning Bliven's mother had packets prepared to take up the space in his baggage where Sam had loaded the Southern delicacies, and she presented him with walnuts, choice apples from their orchard, and a large jug of maple syrup, which Sam had opined was infinitely superior to Southern molasses. Bliven saw him out the door and put him aboard the coach, with exchanged promises that they would write more often.

ALONE IN HIS ROOM he quaffed a tankard of hard cider, and then rode to the Marsh house. He found Clarity seated with books before the fire in their library. "What are you reading?"

She smiled as her gaze rose to his. "It is a book of ladies' correct manners and deportment." She rose and they exchanged curtsy for bow, and they sat together. He spied a second book lying at her side, and as she did not call attention to it, he judged it must be a novel.

"After spending half your life with Miss Sarah Pierce, deportment is the last subject upon which I should think you need advice. Tell me, what did you think of Mr. Bandy?"

She grew thoughtful. "I will like him, for your sake. But in all honesty, the fact that he and his family own slaves must probably prevent my ever regarding him with great warmth."

Bliven shook his head. "They live in a different world, Clarity."

She was unmoved. "They speak the same language and worship the same God."

"But in the South, they preach that God approves of slavery."

She stared at him icily. "I do not understand how that is possible."

"Well, this is a mountain that I will not attempt today. Tell me, what are you learning about deportment?"

She smiled, but checked it. "It says here that ladies must never laugh aloud. They may smile with reserve, but only coarse women laugh."

"Well, that is sad news," he said, "for you are never prettier than when you laugh."

Their eyes met. "We are well matched, then," she said, "for you are never more handsome than when you scowl."

"I hope you will not cause me to scowl today."

"I hope that also, but why should I cause you to scowl?"

Bliven felt his heart pounding so hard it must make the vessels in his neck stand out. "Because you hold it in your hand today to make me either the happiest young blade in New England or the most wretched."

Clarity closed the book, suddenly very solemn. "So that is where we have arrived?"

Bliven shook his head and shrugged at the same time; it made him feel stupid, and the silence grew long. "I don't read novels," he blurted finally. "I have no idea how a fellow, well, declares his . . . love . . . for someone. I throw myself on your mercy—you have read about these things, I have not."

"Ah." She took his hand to calm him. "You must be the most unusual young man in Connecticut to fall in love with a girl and have to appeal to her greater . . . experience."

He understood that she was making a witticism but was in too great anxiety to play with it. "Yes, I am a clod, I know it." He glanced fitfully down at the second book lying beside her. "But tell me, what would your—Maria Rackrent have me do?"

She burst out helplessly, "Oh, now you have made me laugh; I am a coarse woman. Her name is Maria Edgeworth, her book is *Castle Rackrent*. I cannot say what she would advise. I can only say what I would advise." She fell silent.

"I am hanging from a yardarm here, tell me before I die!"

"I should want you to be completely honest with me," she said.

"How could I not? That's why I'm here!"

"Do you love me?"

The question startled him. "Yes, of course I do!"

"Then perhaps you should tell me."

"I love you. I adore you. I have loved you since the moment I saw you at Mrs. Pierce's spring social, sitting by the pianoforte, wearing your lavender ribbon. Which you are . . . wearing again today."

"Well, see now? That was actually quite a good start."

"Augh!" Bliven's neck went limp and his head fell forward, his chin bouncing on his chest.

Clarity let go of his hand, passed her arm inside his, and took it again. "My dear, kind, handsome Lieutenant Putnam. Are you trying to ask me to marry you?"

He heaved a sigh of gratitude for her rescue. "Yes."

She patted his hand. "Well, let us give you a moment to recover yourself before I must answer."

"Augh!" He breathed quietly for several seconds. "I suppose the real question, Clarity, is whether you love me. Whether you *could* love me."

She tightened her grip on his hand. "I think I do. But, at only seventeen, how can I be certain when my family, all those who advise me best, are united in the opinion that I am too young for such a step?"

She surprised him. "You have asked their advice, then?"

"No, but they have offered it all the same."

Ah, he thought, *that will include Reverend Beecher.* If she is enamored of a scowl, he must set her heart racing. If Beecher asked her, he thought, I'll bet she'd know quick enough. But jealousy was one emotion he must not show. "I am more interested in your own doubts."

She softened visibly. "How am I to do without you for years at a time, and then when you come home you are here only long enough for your ship to replace powder and balls and dead men? Of whom you may one day be one."

"I have been home for well over a year. Is that so little? And the navy is a likely field for ambition. A young man does have his ambitions."

"So you will end like Nelson, with one arm and one eye?" She flung one arm across her breast as though it were in a sling and closed one eye in the ugliest fashion of which she judged herself capable.

"My dear Clarity"—he heard himself say it, aware that it was the first time—"there is also such a thing as duty, which some of us must take upon ourselves."

"Hm!"

"You were born here in Litchfield and always lived here."

"I was, yes."

"We were born too late, you and I, to remember the Revolution, and my family has only lately settled here. But Litchfield was behind the battle lines. It was never fought over, nor occupied. Your families and property never knew that destruction. My father came here to start over because he lost everything in Boston. Everything, you understand. We cannot suppose that war will never come again. Our country is young, and must be kept strong. The navy, too, is young, and wants seamen badly. There are nowhere near enough ships even to safeguard the coast."

Clarity was quiet for a long moment. "I have said I want you to be completely honest with me."

"Believe me, I am trying."

"Can you admit to me simply that you love ships, and the sea, and sailing?"

"Yes, I do. And for myself, I want that."

"And battle?" she probed.

He thought on it. "No. There is the noise and the sting, and it is exciting, at least when you are certain of victory. But I have seen the dead and the wounded. And, Clarity, I should tell you, when we took the *Tripoli*, I killed two men."

"I know," she said quietly.

"You know?" He was incredulous. "How?"

"My father has read everything about the navy since you began passing time with our family. He told me. I believe he approved of you better after he learned it, but for myself—" She shook her head. "I don't know."

"I killed one Moor to save my own life, the other to save Sam. Had I not done it we would both be dead, but killing another man—it made me sick and ashamed. War will come again, without respecting whether or not I relish it. I am a good officer, and I am wanted to help guard the country. Is that not honorable?"

"It is"—she nodded—"but you will not be the only one called to serve. If you serve, I must serve, but not with you. I must serve without you, serve whole seasons without you, perhaps raise our children alone." She added flatly, "That is no small price."

"I know." Bliven felt an urgent need to lighten the air. "Or once I become a captain, I could take you with me, like Mrs. Commodore Morris. Would you fancy that?"

She hesitated. "I might, one day, but that is many years hence."

"But now, really, in truth," he protested, "if your father rejects me because you are yet too young, and you reject me because you believe you shall be an old maid before you see me again, then truly I am between the rock and the whirlpool. My cause can only founder."

She smiled, with reserve, just as instructed by the manual of deportment. "Make me a bargain," she said. "You go to sea again, and finish this war if you can. While you are gone, I will consider everything you have said. While we are apart we will consider ourselves engaged. But only as between ourselves; we will tell no one, but we will undertake no other friendships. When you return, if you still feel the same about me, and if I have made peace with myself that I can pay the price you ask"—she searched the depth of his blue-gray eyes—"I will marry you. Can you accept this as an answer?"

"The kindest and wisest I could wish for." He moistened his lips as discreetly as he could. "As we are now engaged, at least as between ourselves, may I leave with your kiss?"

He believed her smile the mildest he had ever seen, and their lips met, barely touching, then more firmly. When they parted, each could barely breathe.

"You will wait for me, then?" he asked.

"I will, but do not keep me in suspense. You must still write me of your adventures."

"I will, I promise."

"And it says here in the manual of deportment that a letter of fewer than five pages is to be considered a slight, so do not be excessively brief."

8.

THE *CONSTITUTION*

———◆———

June 1803

For junior officers such long furloughs were not unheard of, as the navy tried to hang on to good officers while their ships were hove down, or refitted, or even paid off and replaced. True, they were only paid half their wage, but knowing they would be home for large blocks of time left every opportunity to find gainful employ. If nothing else, the navy could point to it as a kind of seagoing militia, saving the country the crushing burden of a full-strength fleet while keeping an adequate number of good officers subject to recall.

Bliven received new orders to report to Boston on May 15, after a year and a half at home. The spring of 1803 came and went quickly, and the planting was finished by the time Bliven packed his sea bag and repeated the stage journey to Boston. He took less regard this time of the hulk that served as their receiving ship, and was pleased to learn that Lieutenant Todd was still on duty there.

When he entered his office, he dropped his sea bag in astonishment. "Bandy!"

Sam turned, as blond and boyish-looking as he was when he was a midshipman. "Well, look here!" he said. They shook hands tightly. "How in the world?"

Bliven shook his head. "My orders just said report here today. Good day to you, Mr. Todd."

He nodded.

"I just got orders to sail from Charleston to Boston on the *Vixen*," said Sam, "and then report here. I am amazed to see you."

"Mr. Todd," said Bliven, "are we bound for different ships?"

Todd looked down his lists. "Gentlemen, you are both assigned to the *Constitution*, Commodore Preble."

"Preble!" exclaimed Bliven. "I thought he was home, in Maine, sick."

"So he was," answered Todd, "but he improved miraculously after he was summoned to a dinner with President Jefferson and the navy secretary. They made him commodore of the new squadron; he's been here some few months, getting *Argus* ready to sail, getting *Philadelphia* and *Constitution* back into commission. *Constitution* has been a terrible headache, they hove her down, recoppering her bottom. Mr. Revere had to open a shop here in the navy yard to hammer the plates to shape. The commodore was in fits until she was finished."

"So," said Sam, "his temper lives up to its reputation?"

"Well," said Todd, "his ulcers have not gotten any better, they cause him much pain. His diligence in fitting her out has been amazing. He knows the difficulty you had with carrying enough water in the *President*, and he has increased water carrying to fifty-four thousand gallons."

"Really, how?"

Todd shrugged. "Well, he saw no point to carrying rations for six months and water for only three, so he converted two of the smaller bread rooms for water casks. Many other details. He had the remaining bread rooms lined with tin to try and seal the vermin out. How is that for an idea? Biscuits with no worms! Time will tell whether that succeeds."

Bliven nodded. "Still, he is not the senior captain. How did he get the command?"

"They tried to bring Dale back," said Todd, "but now he demanded that they create a rank of admiral for him. That was impossible, of course. Then there is Morris, but he is being relieved of command and won't be allowed near a ship ever again. Rodgers is senior, but they want somebody who will get in there and fight and settle this thing. Preble certainly made the most of his dinner with the president, won his confidence completely."

"Well," said Bliven doubtfully, "Commodore Rodgers may have something to say about that once we get to Barbary."

Todd smiled. "Well, Preble has been cautioned to be diplomatic in his assumption of command. One idea is to leave Rodgers in command of two ships, so he can still be considered a commodore, and detach him for his own operations." He shook his head. "Such delicate feelings to have to accommodate."

Bliven chuckled. "Accommodate the commodores. The words probably come from the same root."

"So is Preble truly half-mad?" asked Sam. The man's temper, and his ferocity, were a legend, and the apprehension registered on his face.

"Oh, he's not as bad as that. He is a hard man," Todd allowed, "but fair. One measure of his success is he has let his reputation for hot temper spread before him so that it is only seldom tested, at least by the men under his command. When it is, be on your guard. That fellow Ayscough on his last cruise disliked mutton and poisoned the ship's sheep. He was discovered when he was drunk and attempted to desert. Preble had him flogged through the squadron, a hundred and thirty-six lashes."

"My God," said Sam. "It is a wonder it did not kill him."

"No, it was spread out over a month, to let one round heal before the next. That is not typical. Only thrice have I ever read of Preble meting out lashes to a sailor."

"Thank God," said Bliven.

"But I advise you, if you find yourself crossways with him, if you have done something for which you are culpable, own up to it and accept the responsibility. That is the surest way to his favor. He hates nothing in the world more than sitting in a court-martial. He believes in rehabilitation. If you accept his personal and informal verdict, I assure you it will be more lenient. If you ever exercise your right to demand a court-martial, you shall have it, but he will bear the whole broadside of the law on you."

Bliven and Sam looked at each other. "We understand," said Sam.

"Now," said Todd, "it is hard to judge how long you will be here before you sortie. We know that things in the Mediterranean are reaching a crisis, and we are urged to haste in getting a new squadron ready." He paused. "Have you heard about the *New York*?"

Sam and Bliven looked at each other blankly. "We have not," said Bliven.

"Some spoiled powder was being transferred from the filling room to the bosun's storeroom. Some lunatic left a candle burning while he went to retrieve something and the powder flashed, which set off a store of cartridges. Fourteen men were killed, the ship was badly burnt, nearly all the stores destroyed. It will take weeks to fit her out again."

"How awful!" said Bliven.

"And Morris himself—" Todd stopped and shook his head. "It is not for me to say."

"What?" urged Bliven. "We won't pass it further."

"Very well, then, in confidence, he has made a most famous disaster of everything. At one point, he was patrolling off Tripoli in the *Constellation*, a mile offshore, when a Tripolitan pirate ship brought in the brig *Franklin* as a captive. Morris himself had assured the captain of the *Franklin* that he was in no danger, and then when his ship was taken, they passed into Tripoli harbor right under the guns of the *Constellation*, and Morris did nothing! And then when he pressed the other ships of his squadron for greater action, what did they do? *John Adams* overhauled and boarded the *Meshuda*, which was flying the Moroccan flag but was carrying weapons and contraband bound for Tripoli. So they took the *Meshuda*, and now the emperor of Morocco is demanding reparations or he will join the war."

"Wait, please." Bliven held up a hand. "Is that the *Meshuda* that was the Tripolitan brig, twenty-eight guns, that *Chesapeake* bottled up in Gibraltar when we were there?"

"The same. You do not know that story? Ha! Poor Barron sailed back and forth at Gibraltar for months, waiting on her to come out— never knowing that the admiral and his officers abandoned the ship and tiptoed their way back to Tripoli. Then there was a fast and mysterious exchange of papers. Tripoli sold her to Morocco, who is neutral, so we had no more right to blockade her. Dale and Barron were fit to be tied at having to let her go. Then Morris had to go to Tunis. The

Enterprise, in her zeal, took a prize ship, except she proved to be Tunisian, not Tripolitan. Morris had a quarrel with the bashaw there and turned his back on him as he left, in consequence of which he and his first lieutenant spent three days in jail before the consul bailed them out—with twenty-three thousand good dollars, thank you very much—and had to give the Tunisians their ship back. And then Morris did the same damn thing in Algiers. There are over a hundred Americans rotting in the bagnios in Algiers, but he never even landed. He went on to Tripoli and tried his hand at negotiating with the bashaw, who now wants two hundred thousand dollars in cash plus twenty thousand a year in tribute. Morris pretty well offered him pocket change and left—he went to Malta, to attend the birth of his son, do you believe it? So in a year, he has got us probably in war with all four Berber states instead of just Tripoli, all the consuls are screaming for his removal, and something dispositive must happen soon."

"Well," Bliven sighed, "I am glad you are not the one to say."

They laughed, and Todd continued, "They were able to talk Preble into command by giving him more small ships, of the kind that can follow the corsairs inshore. He will have the *Constitution* and the *Philadelphia* for their firepower, but the others—*Siren* and *Argus*, and *Nautilus* and *Vixen*—none of them have more than sixteen guns. They can get into shallow water and flush the villains out. *Enterprise* will be there already."

"Will Mr. Sterett be in command of one of them?" asked Bliven.

"No." Todd hesitated. "In fact, Mr. Sterett has ended his connection with the navy. There was a dispute about a promotion; he resigned rather abruptly and has gone into the merchant service."

"Really?" Bliven was surprised, but only mildly. "He is a fighter and his abilities will be wanted—but he always was a stickler for his prerogatives." He did some quick calculating. "That is two frigates, and five brigs and schooners."

"More frigates, too," said Todd, "if we can round them up. *Adams* and *John Adams* will likely stay on station, and *New York*. That will be a very respectable force."

"I should say so!" said Bliven, almost with a gasp. "If Dale had had such a squadron, we would have finished the job the first time 'round, and not be going back now."

"I take your point," said Todd. "But the government has seen the light now. The new squadron will sail as each ship is ready for sea. It is too early to know exactly when each will sail, all depends upon finding enough damned crewmen."

Bliven nodded. It was the same old obstacle. He and Sam lugged their sea bags down the quay. "That is all very remarkable," said Sam. "Do you think Dale really demanded to be made an admiral?"

"It's hard to say," answered Bliven. "I imagine he was just trying to make them go away. But perhaps the power got to him, after all. He always did have a short fuse."

Their excitement grew as the *Constitution* loomed larger and higher, the closer they approached. They knew her instantly from her figurehead of a club-wielding Hercules, a full seven feet tall—an oddly appropriate guardian of the ship, notwithstanding one usually thought of figureheads as feminine totems. This vessel's size and strength pled a masculine case. She rode high in the water, empty yet, showing two feet of new copper plating above the waterline.

They ascended the gangplank and took a few steps onto the spar deck.

"Stop," said Bliven. He did not need to add that he wanted a moment to take in the majesty of this new surrounding, for his gaze carried far up into the white oak masts.

"God Almighty," whispered Sam. There were massive fighting tops on all three masts, perched directly above the courses, fifty feet above the deck. Ratlines ascended from both port and starboard railings to the fighting tops, which were broad enough that more ratlines extended up another thirty feet from there to the tiny perches at the fore and main tops. And yet above that she was rigged for topgallants and royals, and skypoles yet above those on the fore and main masts.

"Two hundred twenty feet," said a cultured, high-pitched voice behind them.

Sam and Bliven lowered their gaze. "Beg pardon?"

"The mainmast is two hundred twenty feet tall." The man was obviously an officer but somewhat informally dressed, and he pointed an index finger at his right temple. "I thought you must be wondering." He held out his hand in greeting. "Edward Cutbush, ship's surgeon." He turned around suddenly. "You, there! You two fellows, take these sea bags below to the wardroom, if you please."

Cutbush seemed to be in his early thirties and a picture of health, fastidiously clean, with an energetic face that seemed small only because his head was so large. Sam and Bliven introduced themselves. Bliven was amused that the surgeon should open their acquaintance in such a way. "You actually know the dimensions?"

"Two hundred seven feet from Hercules up there back to taffrail, plus another hundred feet for the bowsprit. Just under sixteen hundred tons. She sets almost an acre of sail, just over an acre when the stuns'ls are set. Come, let me show you to your berths." Before they reached the ladder he added, "She is forty-three feet in the beam and draws twenty-two feet on average. Not a great sailer, though; she rolls like the very devil, and she's a wet ship forward; more than one man's been given a shower-bath while crapping in the head."

Twin ladders sank down from the ship's waist. Bliven looked up again; an acre of sail, it must be like being driven by a cloud. He took in the neat ranks of eighteen-pounders before descending, and on the gun deck, the equally tidy ranks of twenty-fours before Cutbush led them farther down to the berth deck, thence aft to the wardroom, which was separated from the chaos of the berth deck by a wooden screen. "Pray be seated," he said, and he indicated a long mahogany dining table with a dozen chairs around which the wardroom was organized. "It is morning yet, will you take coffee?"

Bliven and Sam exchanged looks of astonishment before accepting. Their sea bags lay against the far bulkhead.

Cutbush approached a sideboard of mahogany matching the table and removed three china cups, white, handsomely patterned in red and blue, from a tray. He opened the lid of a generous urn of chased silver, and on seeing it still part full, and steam rising, he held each cup in turn under the spigot. He set the cups before them, then returned with his own, and a small pitcher. "Here is milk, if you like"—he leaned down the table and scooted toward them a porcelain bowl that matched the cups—"and sugar."

Both took a little milk; Sam added a spoon of sugar. "My word," said Sam. "If this is fighting a war, include me, I pray you."

"Ha!" Cutbush was unexpectedly merry, for a surgeon. "There is less luxury during action, I can assure you." That might be, thought Bliven, but it would not seem so to the sailors outside. The top half of the wooden screen that segregated officers from men was a row of lathe-turned wooden spindles, decorative to be sure, yet allowing the officers to keep an eye on what might be transpiring down the more than hundred feet of hammocks. They also provided a window for the men to look in, at the mahogany furniture and sideboard and paintings and carafes of drink that were sure not to be watery grog. Considering the origins of most of those sailors, there was little wonder why officers so often resorted to the lash.

Lining the wardroom both port and starboard were a series of doors, with not more than two feet between each one, as though it were a file of closets. "Those are the officers' berths." Cutbush pointed. "Line officers, lieutenants, and warrant officers, behind you." He indicated behind himself. "Staff officers—surgeon, chaplain, purser, and the like—on this side. Mine is just there." He pointed to the door most forward, next to the open space of the berth deck. "Officers' head through there." He indicated a door in the port corner of the bulkhead. "The clerk will be along to assign your berths."

"We have one each to himself?" Bliven asked in surprise.

"Hold your celebration until you see for yourself how tiny they are. You may be wishing for company before long."

"Not I," said Bliven. "I will accept any privacy, with thanks."

"Where are you boys from?" asked the doctor.

"I am from Connecticut. Mr. Bandy is from South Carolina."

"That represents quite a disparity."

"A gulf that we must occasionally bridge," said Sam.

"We served together on the *Enterprise*," said Bliven. "Quite a stroke of good fortune that we are assigned to the *Constitution* together."

Cutbush shook his head. "Not many accidents in the navy, my boy. Are you not the two midshipmen who helped take that pirate ship, what, near two years ago? Someone probably noticed how you served well together. Other factors being equal, they would want to keep you together."

"To reward us or punish us?" wondered Sam; he and Bliven smirked at each other.

"And you, Doctor?" asked Bliven. "Where are you from?"

"Philadelphia, although I am in the navy so long now I sometimes forget."

Bliven pointed to Cutbush's wedding ring. "You are married. Have you children?"

"Two, yes, and a third on the way."

Sam elbowed Bliven in the side. "My friend here has a young lady in Connecticut who is worried whether if they marry they will have any time together. It will be good news to her that you have been able to start a family."

"We manage." Cutbush smiled. "We manage. Then, too, we find that absence does help our hearts to grow fonder."

The ship's clerk, a tired-looking middle-aged officer named Johnson, arrived and introduced himself. He entered his small office, abaft the bulkhead on the starboard side, and emerged with two precut pieces of thin cardboard, carefully inked in handsome cursive: *Mr. Putnam* and *Mr. Bandy*. These he fitted into small wooden sleeves by the doors of the last two berths, port side. "I trust you will find these satisfactory. If you don't, you cannot do better, as they are all the same."

"Certainly they shall serve admirably," said Bliven.

"If I may suggest, stow your bags in your berths. The commodore will see you now."

Cutbush retired to his cabin. "When you return, I will give you the grand tour."

Johnson led them up the after ladder; the gun deck was better lit that the berth deck, for the hatches were open up to the spar deck. The commodore's cabin at the stern was the brightest space belowdecks, illumined by the bank of enormous windows that mark the stern shear of any frigate. Johnson knocked twice rapidly on the cabin's door.

"Enter!" a gruff voice called from within. Johnson opened the door and the light came flooding into the after section of the gun deck.

"Lieutenants Bandy and Putnam reporting, sir."

"Show them in."

By the time they entered, Preble had risen and come around his desk. "Gentlemen." They exchanged salutes.

Bliven noted that he stood with his feet wider apart than his shoulders, the sure mark of a man accustomed to keeping his balance in a seaway; often he forgot to assume a less abrupt posture when it wasn't needed. "Good morning, Commodore."

Preble reassumed his chair gingerly, as though he were in pain, and motioned them to take two mate's chairs opposite his desk. He was in his early forties, stocky but muscular, his hair short and brown with a tint of red. He was balding from the forehead back, which he masked somewhat by combing his hair forward. "Are you settling in well?"

"Yes, sir, Dr. Cutbush has made us feel quite at home," said Bliven. He noticed that as Preble listened, he cocked his head to the right side, presenting his left ear. He assumed that it must be because Preble was hard of hearing in his right ear, but it gave him the appearance of doubting what he was being told.

"Ah, Cutbush," Preble said in an approving way. "Treat him well; he is the best man in this ship's company. He won't tell you this himself, but when the navy was reduced after the Quasi-War, he was one of only four full surgeons retained in the service. He is indispensable. Most of the ships get by with surgeons' mates and barbers and meat cutters."

"Our surgeon's mate in the *Enterprise* was most attentive in the performance of his duties," said Sam.

Preble waved it off impatiently. "No doubt, no doubt. But they have not the learning, the reading, the experience. The men in the navy deserve doctors, not apprentices. Cutbush is a first-class physician. I marvel at why he is even in the service—he could be making four or five times the money in private practice."

"Patriotism, perhaps," said Sam.

Preble looked at him sharply, at which Sam took alarm until he said, "Well spoken, young man." And they realized that Preble's small, dark eyes above his big nose, eyes that betrayed quickness and intelligence, would seem to look sharply wherever they looked. "Where are you from?"

"South Carolina, sir."

"Where exactly?"

"My family owns a plantation, in the Abbeville District. It is in the upper part of the state, near the Georgia line."

"Plantation, eh?"

"Yes, sir, we grow cotton, indigo, rice, and other crops."

"Slaves?"

"Yes, sir."

Preble's fleshy lips pursed. "I don't like slavery."

"No, sir. Well, you are hardly alone in that sentiment."

"And you, Mr. Putnam, you are from New England, I understand."

"Yes, sir, my parents are from Boston. They lost everything to the British in the Revolution and moved to Connecticut."

"They lost all in the war?"

"Yes, sir."

"Well"—Preble nodded—"we have that in common. I am from Falmouth. The British burned my family's house with the rest of the town." Sam and Bliven felt his passion rising. "There was no need for it. I shall never forget that arrogant officer in his red coat with his hateful accent saying he did not care, the entire town should burn to the ground. To this day it requires all my forbearance not to sink any English ship I come across. And now they say we are at peace." Preble huffed. "Peace! Who do you think it was went to the Berbers in North Africa and whispered in the bashaws' ears that their tribute no longer covered our ships? Peace! They have never accepted losing the colonies; mark my word, we shall have to fight them again, sooner than later."

"I wish my father were here to hear you say that," ventured Bliven. "He expresses an identical opinion, quite often."

"Does he, now? What does he do, your father?"

"We have a farm, at Litchfield."

A dissatisfied noise issued from Preble's throat. "Mmph. I don't like farming much. Takes too long to see anything happen. When I give an order, I expect it to be obeyed that instant. You can't order a good crop. You're too much at God's mercy, and even then you can't count on anything until the crop is harvested and safely stored."

"Yes, sir, that is very true. My father offsets the risk—he operates a drayage and livery stable in the town, and he does good business in cider."

"Wise man." Preble's tone lightened. "Well, have you seen the ship? What do you make of her?"

"We are undone," said Bliven. "She is magnificent. I am sure that Mr. Bandy and I both are thrilled to have been assigned to your command. Yet there is one thing that puzzles me. I am curious how I came by this assignment, for I have never handled guns of this size."

"I know," growled Preble, "but lieutenants who are experienced with heavy guns are suddenly in short supply. After what Morris—" He stopped himself, aware that in his wonted directness of conversation he was about to criticize a fellow captain, which he must not do, both for manners' sake and because it could, months or even years hence, result in a challenge to a duel. "Belay that," he muttered. "After the navy's experience of last year, we have hope that the government intends to finally"—he heaved a sigh for emphasis—"at *last*, deal with these barbarians as we should have from the beginning. Larger vessels are coming back into commission, not just *Constitution*, but *Chesapeake*, *John Adams*, and others. The officers who have experience with twenty-fours and eighteens, even twelve-pounders, are already spread too thin. And look here, even past that, our people are negotiating with the Sicilians to lend us gunboats and bomb scows, and I'll have to divert more men to them once we get over there. So we are snatching you up, and others who have, say, an aptitude for guns, and depend upon it that you can learn on the job. We have the twenty-fours on the gun deck and eighteens on the spar deck, but you will also see twelve-pounders on the quarterdeck. They will be your assignment."

Quickly Bliven figured sums in his head. The *Constitution* was rated a forty-four-gun frigate, but what he had seen was at least ten more than that. He knew that in every navy a ship's rating was flexible, and varied with the judgment of the captain, his personal preferences, and his expectation of what kind of action to expect on his next cruise. Those who preferred close fighting would want carronades that could be double-shotted with chain to clear an enemy's decks; others preferred a bank of long twenty-fours to engage at a distance. Preble wanted them all. That must be the key to understanding him.

"Well, what say you? Do you boys think you can sail with me?"

"Eagerly, sir," Bliven responded. "Right eagerly."

"And I," Sam added.

"Mr. Bandy, the scores on your navigational exam recommend you as much as Mr. Sterett's endorsement. When we're out there"— he pointed in the direction out of the harbor—"and I ask you where in hell we are, I will expect you to point to a map and show me, at any hour."

"Well understood, sir."

The commodore rose, and Sam and Bliven were instantly on their feet. "Your duties will not be heavy for now; we cannot sail for several weeks, and even then it depends on getting a crew. We placed notices in the newspaper two weeks ago, and but a dozen men have signed on. Universal problem, I know, but you will excuse my partiality in believing *Constitution* the finest ship in the fleet. Lack of enthusiasm in others can make me disagreeable—"

"Indeed, we quite understand," said Sam.

"—as I am sure you must have heard." He walked them to his cabin door. "Mr. Putnam, I have heard that you are a reader. Is this true?"

"Yes, sir, it is."

"Did you bring books on board with you?"

"What I could carry, yes, sir."

"What do you read?"

"History and geography, mostly, sir."

Preble crossed his arms. "Capital! Do you ever lend them?"

"To you, sir? Readily."

"Good man."

"I did have the experience in the *Enterprise*," Bliven added cautiously, "one of the lieutenants asked to borrow a book. Being only a midshipman, I did not feel at liberty to refuse. That was well enough, until I found the book later in the officers' head with half the pages torn out." Bliven still remembered the incident bitterly; it took no imagination to know what use those missing pages had come to.

Preble harrumphed. "Well, be assured your little library will come under my personal protection. The other junior officers can either give in to their jealousy or profit by your example. If they are wise, they will choose the latter."

"Yes, sir."

"Do you have Moore's *New Practical Navigator*?"

"The 1801 edition, on the very top of the stack, yes, sir."

"As do I," said Sam.

"Excellent." Preble nodded. "Different chapters will apply to your different duties. It is well for Mr. Bandy to have his own set of navigational tables; Mr. Putnam, by first gunnery practice I expect you to have memorized the firing sequence of heavy guns without further reference to the text."

"Yes, sir. We followed the manual on the *Enterprise*, but most certainly I will refresh my memory before we exercise the guns."

"Very well. You are dismissed." They saluted and Preble returned it. Sam preceded Bliven down the after ladder, and their eyes had to adjust again to the dimness of the lantern-lit berth deck. "Doesn't like slavery, indeed," fumed Sam. "Who does he think cut the live oak for this hull? Look down, you are walking on Georgia pitch pine. Does he imagine some Massachusetts gentleman sweated himself to saw it?"

They reached the wardroom and Bliven patted him on the shoulder. "Yes, well, console yourself. Apparently he does not think much better of farmers." Being from New England, Bliven knew as well as anyone that, in fact, Joshua Humphreys the builder had indeed sent carpenters to the South to cut and saw the ship's timbers, but he saw no profit in raising the issue with Sam.

"You're back!" They heard Dr. Cutbush's voice from within his berth, the door of which stood open.

"We will be with you presently," Bliven answered. They poured themselves glasses of water from a pitcher on the sideboard, then went by turns to the officers' head before presenting themselves again at Cutbush's door.

"Let us begin at the bottom and work up, shall we?" he asked, adding, "Well, what do you make of the commodore?"

"I believe the appropriate expression would be 'force of nature,'" answered Bliven.

"Ha!" exploded Cutbush. "I believe you have got him there. You've got him." They descended, but not by the after ladder. Cutbush produced a key and unlocked a hatch in the very floor of the wardroom, which he raised, and led them down into a very gloomy space indeed. It was on the level of the orlop deck but separated from it, a cramped space that seemed eerie for being nearly entirely empty, and it resembled nothing so much as a chamber in a cave, for its height was less than five feet from the planking to the top of the live oak knees that supported the berth deck above. Cutbush led them yet farther down a ladder of similar height to the orlop deck, into the very hold at the bottom of the ship.

"This is the ammunition magazine," said Cutbush.

Bliven assessed the racks of round iron shot, twenty-four and eighteen pounds, and the twelves that he would be responsible for seemed insignificant next to them. There were racks of bar shot and canisters of grape; Bliven could hardly fathom how much it all must weigh, so ballasting the ship that she probably could not have foundered in any circumstance. "How large is the crew?"

"Counting marines, four hundred and fifty," Cutbush answered.

"How many boys?"

"Thirty, in full complement."

"Great heavens!" Bliven exclaimed. "Thirty boys! Do they not collide with one another down in this darkness?"

Cutbush laughed. "They have some method to avoid it. Also there is a second magazine forward. The ship is too large and there are too many guns to be adequately served by only one magazine." They reached a bulkhead in which there was an opening covered with a heavy felt curtain. "In there is the filling room. As the cartridges are wanted, the men in there hand them through this portal. So you see, your powder monkeys have further to scramble to get your cartridges than on your schooner. Come, we can go in."

Cutbush ducked and crouched to half his height to fit through a low hatch, and Sam and Bliven followed. "This box contains the felt slippers the men have to wear, and having any iron implements in hand or clothing is strictly forbidden. What little illumination you see comes from a lantern beyond that sealed glass window in the light room. In here they make up the cartridges for the different-size guns; when they are finished they pass them through these openings."

"My word," said Sam. "They take every precaution."

"Yes," said Cutbush. "We can go on. In here is the powder magazine." He ducked through another tiny hatch into an even closer compartment in which not only was standing upright impossible, but it seemed that the only possible form of locomotion was to lie prone and push oneself with one's feet. They were lying against the very curve of the stern, which was lined with copper; indeed, the entire space was lined with copper, to keep the dank air from spoiling the powder or any outside fire from reaching it.

"This is the last place where enemy fire could penetrate," said Cutbush. "If it ever did, the ship would be blown to splinters."

Bliven nodded. They were directly beneath the wardroom, and above that, the captain's and commodore's cabins. If such a calamity did occur, there seemed a certain justice to the fact that the officers would be the first to blow sky high.

"I gather," said Sam, "we won't be repairing down here to enjoy a smoke."

Cutbush shook his head. "One incautious moment down here could cost the life of every man on board. Reflect on that. Look what happened to the *New York* just a couple of months ago."

"We have heard about that," said Bliven.

"They were damned lucky it didn't reach the powder magazine itself. Let us go back up," said Cutbush. "I dislike this place."

They ascended the two short ladders back to the wardroom, and they watched as Cutbush lowered, latched, and locked the hatch. "On we go," he said. They left the wardroom and descended the regular after ladder to the orlop deck, which seemed if anything even more eerie than the magazines they had just left, for they could look forward the entire length of the ship, in a deck less than five feet high.

"Forward there"—Bliven pointed to their unobstructed view of the hold, keel and ribs dimly visible—"that's for freshwater casks and the like?"

"Exactly," said Cutbush. "Come, I will show you my battle station, the cockpit. These right here are bread rooms." Bliven surveyed the warren of storage areas, which when they sailed would hold tons, and tons more, of rocklike biscuit. Cutbush led them forward, ducking under the oaken beams that supported the berth deck, to the area around the mizzenmast's footing. "Now, in most large ships this would be the place for the cockpit, but starboard there you see quarters for the surgeon's mates."

"God, they live down here?" asked Sam.

Even in the dim of the battle lanterns, they could descry the twinkle in the surgeon's eye. "Shh. They won't know better if you don't tell them. But I had rather that they not billet right next to such nasty business, so I moved the cockpit forward, as you will see."

Bliven pointed to matching compartments on the opposite side, to one of which the door was not only closed but barred and padlocked. "What is this to port? The brig?"

"Worse," said Cutbush. "Commodore's private stores. Preble likes to set a fine table; no one knows how he does it. That is his chef's berth next to it."

"His what!" Bliven exclaimed.

"He only comes down here to sleep, has the run of the commodore's cabin at other times. Doesn't mix much with the rest of us, don't know a thing about him. But when Preble convenes a captain's table, you will see something."

"Great heavens." Bliven pulled at the padlock on the bar.

"Rattle that lock when the chef is sleeping and you will see something, too. Preble is a cultured man, but he knows very well the kind of men they recruit for sailors. Just try to break into his private stores and hear this, he will resurrect keelhauling as a legal punishment. Not even I could save your life after such an offense."

They moved on forward, as Sam looked over his shoulder. "My word."

"Just there you see the cable tier, and the main hold beyond that. If you look all the way forward, you see a bulkhead beyond the foremast footing. If you go beyond that, you have the armorer's and master's storerooms, and the sail room, to starboard, and the gunner's and bosun's storerooms to port."

He led them just beyond the foremast, which passed on below and was anchored to the very keel. "In a battle, this is the most steady and quiet part of the ship, so this is where I try to put poor blighters back together." He opened a cabinet and lifted the lid on his chest of implements—scalpels, probes, tourniquets, and, most prominently, a bone saw. "It doesn't take much, really. It is surprising how little."

They returned to the berth deck. "The wardroom you have seen," said Cutbush. "Just forward of here are the midshipmen's quarters."

"How many of them?" asked Bliven.

"Twelve or thirteen."

"Good Lord, they might as well open a school with that many to train."

"Beyond that you see that hammock space for the crew. They sleep in shifts, of course, to maintain the watches." They ascended to the gun deck and its tidy rank of twenty-fours. "Down there you see the galley and the camboose, and the sick bay past there, that is my daily office."

"Next to the galley," observed Sam. "Let us hope that is no comment upon the food."

"Ha. Not really. I hold sick call every morning, and since all the men are present for breakfast, it is the most convenient place. Usually I hang sheets up to separate the sick bay from the rest. Gives us a little privacy."

"Is your cook a good one?" asked Bliven.

"Navy fare is navy fare," the doctor sighed. "He does the best he can, he makes better use of the steep tub than most, so the meat doesn't taste like a mouthful of salt. And he is probably more generous with the plum duff than others. Nevertheless, there is little difference between the biscuits on this vessel and on any other. Thank God, we officers manage better than the seamen, our purser stays well supplied and we can buy special items from him—chocolate for a hot drink, or brandied cherries even, and such like."

"That is good to know," said Bliven. "We had few luxuries on the *Enterprise*."

ON THE LAST DAY OF JUNE, Sam crashed into Bliven's cabin without knocking, causing him to leap clean to his feet. "What in hell?" demanded Bliven.

"Did you hear the news? We are ordered out!"

Bliven's annoyance dissipated in an instant. "Is it true?"

"The navy is relieving Morris of command; Rodgers will be in charge until Preble can take the new squadron over."

Bliven wiped the sleep from his eyes. "What happened?"

Sam fell back heavily on the mattress and Bliven sat by him. "Apparently, everything that Todd told us about," said Sam. "Get dressed. We are to go into town and hammer these broadsides wherever we think useful."

"How is that our job? Can't they find two seamen to do this?"

"Do you imagine we would ever see them again?"

"Oh. Yes. Let me see one."

Sam handed him the top sheet of a stack an inch high. "The Frigate *Constitution*," Bliven read sleepily. "To all able-bodied and patriotic seamen who are willing to serve their country and support its cause"—his voice trailed off into a mumble—"The President of the United States, having ordered the captain and commander of the good Frigate *Constitution*, of forty-four guns, now riding in the harbor of Boston, to employ the most vigorous exertions to put said ship in a position to sail at the shortest command"—until he said loudly and clearly, "Two months wages in advance!"

Sam smiled sardonically. "You think that will find us a crew?"

9.

FIFTY-SIX GUNS

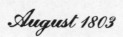

August 1803

liven leaned easily on the spar deck's rail, looking down with satisfaction at the *Constitution*'s ample tumble home. This added beam made her a stable shooting platform and allowed for the enormously thick hull—dense and perhaps impenetrable live oak between layers of white oak, an outer shell to absorb shot and an inner one to cushion from splinters—without sacrificing interior space. She had the breadth and gravity of a ship of the line, in fact. Preble meant to carry fifty-six guns instead of the forty-four for which she was rated. The challenge was her buoyancy, however. With such a broad beam and lacking the weight of a third gun deck, she needed to carry at least ten or twelve tons of kentledge, and beyond that they depended on her massive diagonal timber riders, which the designer counted on to prevent her hogging. Bliven smiled at Cutbush's remark that she was known as a wet ship forward in a seaway, with crewmen doused while relieving themselves at the head—an unpleasant circumstance, as the officers conceded, but a powerful disincentive for them to loiter there. Sam drew up beside him.

Bliven's attention was drawn up into the harbor as the *Nautilus* glided by, putting out to sea with her twelve guns. "Dale may be gone," he said, "but at least they're following his advice." Indeed, where the *Enterprise* had been the only small ship acting in concert with Dale's squadron, now there were four more schooners and brigs.

"Who is in command of her?" asked Sam.

"Somers."

"Oh, God." Sam shook his head.

"Well spoken," said Bliven. "Oh, God, indeed." He pressed his palms together and looked skyward soulfully, in the best manner of an El Greco painting. "If God favor the devout, Somers should have a brilliant cruise."

Sam laughed. "Well, thank God I don't have to serve with him. I can't bear that much piety in one human being."

Proud *Philadelphia* with her thirty-eight guns was next to depart; Barron had taken ill and Bainbridge replaced him—an excellent choice, Bliven thought. Bainbridge knew the ship, knew the waters, and knew his enemy all too well. Having once been humiliated by the dey of Algiers, he was sure not to compromise his country's honor again.

Then *Siren* and *Argus* sailed, each with sixteen guns, and *Vixen* with her fourteen, and *Enterprise*, her dozen six-pounders augmented by two more, with Isaac Hull commanding in replacement of the insulted Sterett. Word spread that the frigates *New York*, now repaired, and *John Adams* would be retained in the Mediterranean. When the *Constitution* finally sailed on August 14, 1803, less than two days after a full crew was aboard, it was rightly said that the United States had never deployed such a fleet.

Hardly was she clear of Boston Harbor when the lieutenants assembled all hands and began sorting out which men had experience with guns, and of what weight. The main battery, the twenty-fours on the gun deck, got first choice of men for gun captains, the eighteens second. Bliven's tertiary battery of a dozen twelve-pounders was allotted forty-eight men, half of whom had handled guns before, and he assigned them two experienced and two inexperienced men per gun, selected crew captains, and bade them gather around him for further instructions when their other business was concluded.

The lieutenants then apportioned general berth areas to the men, based on proximity to their guns. One day it might prove essential, in a sudden beat to quarters, to have them in the location, and using the hatches nearest their action stations. The hammocks of Bliven's crews would all swing in the after portion of the berth deck, for all the twelves were on the quarterdeck. This space they would share with the after crews of the larger guns.

The enlisted men noisily engaged in the ritual of dividing into three messes. In one of the rare democratic processes in the navy, the men were allowed to determine among themselves whom they wished to share their meals with, share their labors, and fight with.

Once this was accomplished, Bliven cupped his hands to his mouth. "Twelve-pounder gun captains to the after hatch!" he shouted and repeated. Once he counted his dozen, he said, "Let us go up out of the confusion. Mind, you will be on the quarterdeck, so watch your manners, please."

They ascended the after ladder. Bliven saluted the watch officer and explained their business, drawing a nod in assent. He led them silently to the last gun aft on the starboard side. "Boys, I don't know all your names yet, but I shall endeavor to do so as quickly as I can. You are the most experienced men allowed to me, and we will have our first gun drill in the morning. Therefore at various times during the day, I want you each to bring your crew up, show them their gun, and explain its parts and the essentials of firing. Is there any man here who does not feel he can do this?"

They looked around among one another and shook their heads. Most had fought through the Quasi-War with the French and could handle guns competently.

"Very well. I shall number you one to six port and one to six starboard and write down your names. Each of you report to me during the day the names of the other three men in your crew. Is that understood?"

They all nodded. "Yes, sir."

"Very well. Now each of you call below at the filling room. You will be given a horn of priming powder. This is an essential part of your uniform when we beat to quarters; do not on any account come to your action station without it."

Below in the wardroom he transferred their names to a master crew list, with three empty lines between the gun captains' names.

"Excuse me, sir?"

Bliven looked up and saw one of their thirteen midshipmen.

"May I speak with you, sir?"

Bliven leaned back in his Windsor chair and looked up expectantly. "What is it?"

"With a dozen twelve-pounders you will need someone to assist you in their operation. I would like to be considered for this." He was tall to the point of ungainly, his eyes large and liquid brown, carrying a permanent expression of inquisitiveness, his hair dark brown and very curly.

"What is your name?"

"Israel, sir."

"Israel?"

"Joseph Israel, sir."

"How long have you been in the service, Mr. Israel?"

"Five years, sir. I fought through the Quasi-War with the French."

"Five years and still a midshipman? That is a long time to serve with no advancement."

The midshipman looked down at his feet. "Yes, sir, it is."

"Can you tell me how this has come to be?"

The young man shifted uncomfortably. "May I speak freely, sir?"

"Please do."

"I believe I have performed my duties adequately. But, in all truth, sir, men of my faith are allowed to serve in the navy, yet we are never preferred for advancement. I am sorry if that sounds as though I am making an excuse, but that is the truth as I see it."

Bliven considered his name. "You are a Jew?"

"Yes, sir." When Bliven was quiet for several seconds, Israel continued, "My position with the other lieutenants has become fixed. When I saw you forming up your gun crews I resolved to come to you and hope for a chance to prove myself."

"Have you ever discussed these matters with the commodore?"

"No, sir. He is new to the command. If I were perceived to be trying to seek an advantage through him by circumventing the junior officers, my position with them must become untenable."

"Quite right." Bliven folded his hands in his lap. "Where are you from?"

"New York, sir."

"Why came you to sea?"

"Well. I suppose I should say 'for adventure.' But in truth, I am from a large family and I have few prospects. The navy seemed a field where I may distinguish myself, but then I learned too late that I would be specially marked for chastisement, whether earned or otherwise."

It was inherent in Bliven's openhearted nature to want to befriend this youth, but he quickly realized that their difference in rank made that inadvisable, even impossible. Israel might even be older than he by perhaps two years. Had they met on Litchfield Green, he would have gladly hailed him as well met. In fact, he was curious, for he knew almost nothing of Jews, and Israel did not look anything like the caricatures he had seen in books. Indeed, Israel was a startlingly attractive boy. It would have been interesting to witness how he would have navigated the Episcopalians and the Congregationalists competing for his soul, to say nothing of the extremes to which the young ladies of Miss Pierce's School would go to overlook his religion and encourage his attentions.

But out here he must show no partiality beyond what initiative and success merited; there was no need for the youth to know how fresh his own memories were of being savaged for the pleasure of the junior officers. "Mr. Israel, I am disposed to believe you. Always deal with me frankly and we shall do well together. I will speak to the commodore and see if I can grant your request. No one else has shown that initiative. You will face no hostility from me on account of your religion."

Israel took a noticeably deep breath. "Thank you, sir. I had determined, if I found you of the same mind as the others, to resign my commission at the next opportunity and make my way home. You have given me a reason to keep trying."

"Hm. Well, one moment." Bliven rose and reached into his tiny cabin and plucked a book from his mattress. He had already committed the necessary parts to memory. "Here." He handed him his *Exercise of the Great Guns*. "Guard this book with your life. The pages are marked. Learn them as well as you can; we have our first gun drill in the morning. You need not memorize it, you need only be familiar. The other midshipmen will be turned out to observe. Whatever I command the port crew, I will look at you, and you will repeat the command to the starboard crew. Some of them have fired guns before, and the most experienced I have made captains of their gun crews."

SIX BELLS OF the morning watch found Preble surveying the quarterdeck, satisfied that all was ready. "Reef your courses, Mr. Dawson. Helm, mind the pennants and keep us straight before the wind."

The officer of the watch relayed the order with a bellow to the bosun: "Reef your courses!" At the bosun's bark crewmen began scaling the ratlines, the experienced ones nimble as spiders, the unsure ones each careful to catch each line at the heel of his shoe, a few plainly terrified of their mortality fifty feet above the hard deck of Georgia pine. The ship slowed perceptibly as the mainsail sheets were loosed and the sails then furled and made fast to the yards. With the operation finished the officers had a clear view of the eighteen-pounders ranged down the spar deck as well as the twelve-pounders on the quarterdeck.

Preble turned to the marine lieutenant. "Beat to quarters."

"Aye, sir. Beat to quarters!" As the tattoo began, crewmen boiled up from below, carrying their hammocks, which they jammed into the netting along the rails.

Bliven watched as the new men among his twelve-pounder crews imitated the actions of the more experienced as best they could. "No!" he called out. He strode quickly to the port side. "Stow your hammocks with the coiled side down, like this." He set one into the netting on its end, like a picquet. "This way they will afford you some cover from enemy snipers, when we are in action. Do you understand?" Over his shoulder he called, "Starboard guns, do you hear? Hammocks to stow on their rolled ends!"

He looked forward to see lieutenants batten down the fore and waist hatches; his own after hatch must remain open for passing cartridges. Near midships the carpenter had rigged pumps, readied shot plugs, and otherwise prepared to contain any damage as though they were about to engage an enemy. The bosun had stoppered the topsail sheets and had marlinespikes ready to repair rigging. Three match tubs of water half full were set at intervals on the quarterdeck, each one sprouting four smoldering linstock matches tucked into notches around the tub, one match for each gun. The garland behind each gun was quickly and in turn supplied with a ball and charge of powder.

The wind whipped lively over the taffrail, singing in the lines and creaking the masts, which still bore the pull of topsails and topgallants. All else was quiet.

"Mr. Putnam," said Preble, "this will be a live fire exercise, with shot, firing each gun individually by turn. The navy has bought powder of a new supplier, and I wish to test it before we might depend upon it. We can mark the strength of our powder and judge the range of the guns at their normal elevation."

"I understand, sir. Sir, Midshipman Israel has volunteered to assist in my direction of the twelve-pounders. Subject to your permission, I have granted his request. It is the same post as I began my service on the *Enterprise*."

"Very well." Preble regarded Joseph Israel among the starboard gun crews, inconspicuous for the moment and trying not to show hope.

"That is very well; you have the deck." Preble nodded himself out of the way.

"Thank you, sir." He saluted. "Mr. Israel," he addressed to the line of midshipmen, "take your post at the starboard battery." Turning to the port crews, he bellowed, "Silence!" To an outsider it would have sounded silly, for no one was speaking, but all knew this was the first order in the drill, and did not just command quiet but initiated the sequence. He surveyed the layout of each crew to ascertain that they had correctly performed the tasks of beating to quarters.

"Good," he said to his six gun captains. "Mr. Israel?" He nodded to his midshipman at the starboard guns.

"Silence!" shouted Israel to his crews. He looked over the starboard guns and crews to see that they were arranged similarly.

"Mr. Israel, is all in order?"

"I believe so, sir."

"It is not in order," said Bliven starkly. "Number Five starboard gun, why have you removed the apron from your touchhole?"

"To be ready for priming, sir."

"We are not ready for priming. Put it back." Loudly, for all to hear, he continued, "Touchholes are to remain covered until the very moment they are primed, and covered again after they are primed. Do you understand?"

"Yes, sir."

"Very well." Bliven surveyed his port crews. "Port battery, cast loose your guns!" At the order, the crews loosed and coiled the muzzle lashings, threading one end through the eyebolts above the gunports. The crews removed each gun's ramrod, sponge, swab, crow, quoin, and handspike from their hooks and laid them neatly at the side. A man from each crew dipped his swab into the nearest match tub and wet the deck for several feet on either side and around his gun.

Bliven waited until the flurry of activity had ceased. "Number Three port gun," he shouted, "why have you not swabbed your deck?"

"I am sorry, sir," the gun crew's captain groaned. One of the men yanked up the swab and plunged it into the match tub, then thoroughly spread a thin sheen of water from halfway to Number Two, to halfway to Number Four, and for fifteen feet behind the gun.

"What is your name?" Bliven required of the crew captain.

"Garrison, sir."

"Well, Garrison, do you feel the wind behind us? When we prime the guns, this wind must blow some of the powder from the pans, which will land upon the deck. Do you want dry powder lying on the dry deck once the firing commences and sparks fly everywhere?"

"No, sir. It won't happen again, sir."

"Very well." Bliven paused for quiet. "Level your guns!" With a heavy creaking of wheels and grunting of crews the twelve-pounders were rolled in and the barrels unlashed and limbered, the breeches crowed up from their beds and the quoins so placed beneath them that the side sights were level, and then lashed down. Bliven saw the starboard battery taking this in, and nodded to Israel, who repeated the steps. This time, two starboard crew captains caught mistakes and corrected them without any delay.

"Take out your tompions!" shouted Bliven. One of each crew worked the wooden plug out of his gun's mouth that kept salt and weather out of the barrel and let it dangle by its lanyard. Again the starboard battery repeated.

"Load with cartridge!" Each gunner took the three-pound cloth cartridge of powder from the box, placed it in the muzzle, then the wadding, and the rammer pushed it deep into the barrel. The crew captain was waiting at the breech, probing with the priming wire until he felt the cartridge reach the breech, and cried out, "Home!"

"Shot your guns!" The gunners heaved the twelve-pound iron balls to the muzzles, as the rammers followed with a second wadding and gently but firmly rammed them home.

"Prime!" Each gun captain removed the limp, heavy apron from his gun's touchhole, unslung his hollowed and polished cow's horn, and removed the plug at the narrow end. He probed the touchhole again with the priming wire, this time piercing the cloth of the cartridge. The priming powder was of double the fineness of the gunpowder in the cartridge. The more fine particles that could be gotten into the touchholes, the greater certainty of the fire penetrating the cartridge for a good discharge. Having filled the touchholes, they poured an amount extra of powder into the shallow pan next to it, shielding it from the wind as they first stoppered their horn, and then bruised the exposed powder with the rounded end of the horn—not too harshly lest the whole charge go off prematurely. This was one operation that could be trusted only to the experienced gun captains. Having done it, they laid the aprons back over the touchholes and pans to keep wind off them.

"Point your guns!" Again the breeches were crowed up and the quoins removed, allowing the guns to nest down in their natural ten degrees of elevation. All four of the crew took up the ropes that had been threaded through the tackle anchored in the railing, and in heaving together ran the gun out until the fore of the carriage butted against the frame of the gunport. Three of the crew cast the lines out straight behind the gun so they wouldn't become fouled in the snap of its recoil, and all stood well aside, for the unstoppable recoil of a three-thousand-pound gun would knock a man to midships, injury certain, death quite possible. At the same time the gunner snatched his linstock from its notch on the tub and crouched near the breech, downwind and interposing his body between the gun and the match, puffing on it gently to keep the fire fresh and blow away any ash.

With the wind and swell coming from astern, the ship rolled very little; it would not be difficult to judge the range of a shot.

"Number One port gun, fire!" bellowed Bliven as he moved several steps toward the stern so the smoke would not obscure his vision of where the ball landed.

The gunner spun around smartly, touching his match to the pan. There was a small whoosh of flame, which as it entered the touchhole became a fountain of sparks shooting a foot into the air, some falling, glowing until they expired in the thin sheen of water on the deck. When the fire reached home in the cartridge, the report hit them like someone slapping them on both ears simultaneously. There was a sheet of flame, and smoke jetted from the muzzle for more than twenty feet before slowing and spreading out, leaving a perfect round smoke ring to hang lazily in the air. The ropes spun through the tackles as the gun and carriage backed six feet out of the port in less than a second.

"Mark it!" said Preble excitedly, and all eyes scanned the waves. A second later there rose a shower of water as the ball clipped the top of a swell and then splashed thrice more, like a pebble skipping across a pond.

"I make it eight hundred yards, sir," said Bliven.

"I agree." Preble nodded. That was exactly the range prescribed for a twelve-pounder at normal elevation; the powder in that cartridge, at least, was satisfactory. "That is very well."

"Sponge your gun," ordered Bliven, and then nodded at Israel, who tried to infuse his voice with as much authority as he could. "Number One starboard gun, fire!"

Bliven well knew that when they were in a zone of action, they would be cruising with the guns already loaded. The sequence would be somewhat different, and the gun captains would have to satisfy themselves that the cartridges already in the guns were dry and usable. They repeated the drill for each gun in the twelve-pounder battery, leaving Preble satisfied that they were ready for action.

"Mr. Israel," said Preble, once the tompions were replaced and the guns secured.

"Sir?"

"Please convey my compliments to Lieutenant Young, and tell him we are ready for him to exercise the eighteen-pounders."

"Aye, sir."

"Mr. Putnam."

"Sir?"

"That was very well. I want you to reposition your aft two guns as stern chasers. I will send you the carpenter, he will do everything necessary to the taffrail—eyebolts, all that."

"Very good, sir."

"Then rejoin us for the remainder of the drill. I want to work you up to competency on the large guns as well."

"Aye, sir, thank you."

They repeated the drill through the waist of the spar deck, with the differences that each gun required a crew of six to handle, and had a range of a thousand yards. They repeated the drill yet again with the long twenty-fours on the gun deck, each of which needed a crew of ten to heave the four-ton assembly of gun and carriage, and a lookout in the maintop to see the balls splash a full twelve hundred yards from the ship. The entire morning left Bliven's ears ringing; no wonder, he thought, that so many old sailors were hard of hearing. When all was done, Preble pronounced his satisfaction on the quarterdeck and said, "Captain's table this evening, gentlemen. Mr. Putnam"—he pulled him a little aside—"I wonder if you will supply me with a book."

"Gladly, sir, if I have anything that will interest you."

"History, perhaps, but something not tedious?"

10.

PREBLE'S BOYS

September 1803

I t was immediately after the second dog watch, the time when the majority of the crew spread their tarpaulins on the berth deck and tucked into their main meal, which this day included cheese, which was fresh, for they were just out of port, and rice and peas, which were dried but had had no chance to mold or spoil, that the lieutenants gathered in the wardroom in their dress uniforms, joined by Dr. Cutbush and the purser, whom they had quickly learned to rely on to supply not just cocoa and brandy but needles and thread to repair their uniforms, precious soap, and even swatches of lambskin with the wool attached, for their use in the officers' privy. None of the junior officers had seen his storeroom on the orlop deck, the key to which was a carefully guarded treasure that never left his possession, but they all determined that when the captain is a gentleman, his purser must learn every resource to supply him, and that was to their benefit as well. There was no charity in it, however, for the purser daily compared accounts with the clerk; everything the officers required, they paid for, or it was deducted from their pay.

And there was the ship's chaplain, an old Dutchman named Henninger with white hair and a deeply lined face, a large, tall man who proved to have a kind heart and a deep, soft voice that seemed to impart comfort even in casual conversation. Most of the younger officers tended to glide, not obviously, to whatever portion of the room where Henninger was not, so Bliven had him virtually to himself for a few moments. He proved to be of the Congregationalist faith, but Bliven quickly ascertained that he had seen too much of the world to be as doctrinaire and cocksure of himself as the Reverend Beecher of Long Island. Still, it would be well to be able to write Clarity that he had made a friend of the ship's cleric, who was of her faith. And he could not escape the intrusion into the back of his mind the thought that, should he fall in a coming battle, the letter of condolence back home to her, and his family, would be of a more heartfelt nature than what was more usually and generically written.

At length the door opened from the commodore's great sea cabin, and his cook, whose praises Cutbush had sung, said, "Gentlemen, if you please."

The great cabin was set for dinner, with walnut furniture, a Brussels carpet, and a cut-glass decanter and glasses on a sideboard. The only reminders present that they were aboard a man-of-war was the low ceiling with its thick beams of white oak and the butt end of a long twenty-four, its lanyards neatly coiled, the gun port sealed from the weather by a canvas shroud. When it came to a fight, even this most luxurious refuge of the ship fought, too.

Preble stood at the far end of the cabin, and standing with him was a tall man with long, thinning hair, gaunt but not sick-looking, and standing by him was a young woman, slender, not particularly pretty, as Bliven noted, but the bloom of youth could make up for some of that, and she appeared to be not much older than Clarity.

"Gentlemen," said Preble, "we shall have guests on our voyage; they will be with us until we call at Algiers. May I present Mr. Tobias Lear, our newly accredited consul to that state, and Mrs. Lear, who by way of introduction she may not object if I point her out as a niece of Mrs. President Washington."

She nodded in acknowledgment. "Gentlemen," said Lear, to nods and slight bows around the cabin.

Bliven had heard of him, that he had served many years as General Washington's private secretary, that he was present at Washington's death, that Washington had relied on him unreservedly in his last years and was crestfallen to learn that Lear had stolen tenants' rent from him, but had restored him to favor upon an abject enough apology. Bliven knew that almost no one trusted him, and there had been talk, not specific, that Jefferson kept him in government service in consideration of certain letters that Jefferson had sent to Washington, which Lear held in safekeeping, that would not reflect well on Jefferson or some others if they were made public. After Lear's first wife died, he married first a niece of General Washington's, and when she died he married a niece of Mrs. Washington's.

"Lieutenant," Lear said to Bliven, when his turn came for conversation, "that was quite a noisy time you gave us this morning. I understand it was your guns that were directly over our heads."

"Yes, sir. Exercising the guns is indeed quite a noisy business."

"I trust you will be equally lively if it comes to engaging the Moors at sea."

"A good deal more so, I daresay."

Lear laughed and nodded; that was Bliven's signal that he was being dismissed from the conversation, but he did not realize it until Lear turned his attention to Sam, and then the next one. Lear was a man in his full maturity, easily old enough to be his wife's father. Perhaps it was the sardonic arch of his eyebrows, or the long nose down which he looked at people, or the constant faint smile even when there was nothing apparent to smile at, but everything about his gaze seemed to not just be appraising a situation, but assessing what personal gain it might hold. And what is there to trust in a man who is so desperate to cement his association with an illustrious family that he marries their young women one after another? Instinctively, Bliven did not like him, but there was little time to dwell on it before they were seated for dinner.

The captain's cook, whom no one called by name and was never introduced, served them while wearing a white apron. He set before them portions of an excellent turkey *en croute* with carrots, peas, and potatoes; a side of Boston beans baked in molasses and whiskey; and thick slices of warm brown bread; and poured them glasses of Madeira wine, which Bliven had never tasted before. He was too inexperienced with wines to appreciate their subtleties, but he gathered from the comments around the table that it must be very fine. At the end he served them preserved pears over hot gingerbread, and small cups of hot chocolate.

The *Constitution*, Bliven calculated, had a crew of 450 men, 434 of whom would never have a prayer of sampling a meal such as they had eaten. The ship had two cooks, one for the captain and one for everyone else. There must be an art, he thought, not just for cooking the food and sharing the same camboose as the man who cooked the regular seamen's mess, but an art to carrying the captain's fare back to his cabin and not being murdered on that long passage down the berth deck for a taste of what he was bearing. Of all the advantages of rank that officers held over the enlisted seamen, this must be the most cruel.

"Well, gentlemen." Preble got their attention, trying to seem jocular. "You have eaten at my table and therefore are in my debt. So I am going to tell you a little of what I expect of you in the coming months. I shall speak politely, but you are to regard everything I say as having come down from the mount of Sinai.

"Now. You well know that our Congress did not declare war on the Barbary states, but they did recognize that hostilities exist and untied our hands in terms of taking prizes, engaging with initiative, and so on. I wish to say that I have no doubt in my mind that we will engage these pirates, and further, I believe that we will find them a more formidable opponent than many now suppose. We face an enemy who believe themselves to be superior beings, who feel commissioned by God to act as they have done, and who have no feeling for the lives or suffering of others. It is true that they have not heretofore shown themselves capable in battle, but when we invade their harbors and bombard their cities, we must expect a greater spirit than they have shown in capturing unarmed merchantmen and taking women and children for slaves."

There was a murmur of approval around the table.

"When we join the squadron in Gibraltar, I expect every man to fulfill his duty, but beyond that, we must act in unity, in good faith and reliance upon one another. By which I mean there is to be no fighting, and positively no dueling, among the officers or crew. Any quarrels among you will be nipped in the bud and settled. The navy secretary has asked me to register his most particular concern in this matter, and I absolutely order you to be diligent in its observance.

THE SHORES *of* TRIPOLI

"To those of you who have not sailed with me before, I say this. Make a mistake and you will be disciplined and encouraged to do better. But defy me, deliberately disobey me, subvert my authority in any way whatever, and I will make you wish you had never been born. Now, gentlemen, we are the officers of a great ship, sailing in the service of a great nation. There cannot conceivably be any quarrel among you great enough to override that. My door is always open to those who may need counsel. Do we understand each other?"

The "Yes, sir" that passed around the table was more emphatic than a murmur, and left Preble satisfied that he had made the necessary impression. "Very well, gentlemen, a good evening to you. You are dismissed."

Most had departed when he added suddenly, "Mr. Putnam, a moment more." When the others had left he added, "Have you something for me?"

"Yes, sir. I was afraid you had forgotten." He had been balancing a book on his thigh all during dinner, and handed it to him. "It is Dr. Thomson's new translation of *The Lives of the Caesars*, by Suetonius. Nothing tedious about them, to be sure."

"M-hm." Preble ran his fingers down the ridged leather binding.

"If you have already read it, I can select another."

"I have not read it, this will do very well. Do you recommend it?"

"It is fascinating to read," said Bliven, "but some of what they did was truly and epically horrible. I fear I have not succeeded in puzzling out why they often acted as they did."

"Power, unless I miss my guess. Power makes some men go mad." Preble held the book up in the air. "We shall see! I thank you."

"You are most welcome, sir. Good evening to you."

That night Bliven's sleep was enhanced by the Madeira, and by the

Constitution's roll in a moderately heavy sea. Her reputation was that she rolled deep, but easy, and she always recovered in a stately manner. It was not enough to make him sick, he reckoned, nor to keep him awake. Indeed, he slept soundly, until he was jarred awake by the staccato drumroll of a beat to quarters. Instinctively, he was in his shoes and pulling on his coat and sword, his head clearing of the Madeira only slowly, as he opened his cabin door to witness the other lieutenants and midshipmen in equal disarray. Then they heard the bosun's voice echoing down the berth deck: "All hands on deck to witness punishment!"

Sam encountered Bliven just outside his own cabin. "What in hell?" he asked.

Bliven shook his head. "I've no idea."

On the quarterdeck they found Preble fully in uniform; he looked as though he had been awake for hours. At the waist of the spar deck a square of marines surrounded a hapless-looking and unkempt seaman, with Dr. Cutbush, the bosun, the master at arms, and the cook in attendance. All four hundred fifty of the crew on the spar deck created a crush of men; Preble stepped to the front of the officers and pointed a finger at the luckless sailor. "All hands," he said loudly, "hear me now. This man was apprehended sleeping at his post. Men, we are sailing into a war. Such dereliction cannot and will not be tolerated. The safety of this ship and every man on it depends utterly on every man being diligent in his duty. Completely diligent. Now, for this crew it is a first occurrence, and for this man a first offense. Therefore I shall be lenient, this one time. But do not mistake my leniency for weakness. If you do, I swear to you, you will regret it." Preble swept his arm across the assembled crew. "The navy accords every man of you four hours in each twenty-four to sleep. That is enough to sustain any man to perform his duty. What seeks more comes of indolence, and indolence is intolerable!"

Somewhere in the back of Bliven's still-sleepy mind the question occurred to him, if four hours' sleep was sufficient for the crew, why were officers accorded eight hours? But it was not a question to pursue at the moment. He and the other lieutenants, and the midshipmen in front of them, saw the sailor's unbuttoned shirt stripped down from his shoulders, his hands lashed over his head to a hatch grate, which was then leaned against the rail of the spar deck. Preble surveyed the company and saw that all was ready. "Six lashes," he said flatly.

The offending sailor was not one that Bliven had had any contact with, and he did not look terribly afraid. The cook raised a dipper of water to his lips before it commenced, not especially because he was thirsty but because it was part of the ritual, as Bliven was to learn. The bosun handed the cat to the master at arms, who shook it out gently to separate its strands, as Dr. Cutbush stood by.

Every time Bliven saw a cat o' nine tails he was surprised that it was not larger, for it was less than a yard in length. It had a leather grip from which a plaited rope issued, that divided into three strands, and each of those three into three, the nine each knotted at the end to prevent further unraveling.

The master at arms looked up to the commodore for the order. Preble snugged his hat down on his head. "Commence punishment."

The sting of the hemp knots cutting into his flesh took the complacent sailor by surprise. He let out a sharp scream, very brief, before he controlled himself, clenched his teeth, and took the remaining five with grunts that issued from his throat, his entire body quivering by the time he was untied. Each tail had either raised a welt or cut the skin, the blood visible but not openly running. As he was still on the grate, Cutbush soaked a cloth in seawater and washed the wounds, a necessary first step in preventing infection, but the salt caused the sailor to gasp in a further and different pain. Cutbush then helped him up and led him below, where he daubed the open cuts with honey and applied bandages.

Preble strode sternly to the after ladder, telling the officer of the deck, "You may dismiss the company."

"So," said Sam as they went below, "Preble is not one to resort to the lash, is he?"

"Well, either Mr. Todd was sparing us too great alarm, or the commodore meant this only to get a grip on the crew."

"Yes, it was only six, after all," said Sam. "That can't have done any real harm."

They served themselves coffee in the wardroom. "Do you ever whip your slaves?"

Sam spun around on him, a dark chemistry of emotion in his face—surprise, anger, injury. "No, never!"

Bliven was surprised by the damage that the question had wrought. "I am sorry, Sam, if I were more awake I should not have asked."

"But you would have thought it, all the same."

The officers' steward set eggs and toasted bread before them, which Bliven acknowledged with a nod. "No, I should have wondered it, but I would not think that of you without asking you about it. There are so many stories that one hears of the South."

"Yes, stories. Putnam, suppose you yourself laid out the better part of a year's income on something, or somebody, to make your farm more profitable. Would you turn around and abuse him, risk his injury or death and lose that investment? I doubt it. Neither would I."

"No, of course you would not. I am sorry I raised the question, and more sorry to have upset you, truly."

Only twice more in the crossing were lashes resorted to, relating to the same incident, twelve lashes for a sailor who broke into the grog tub and within a few moments ingested so much that he got both drunk and sick together, and a dozen for the marine who abandoned his guard of the grog tub to run on deck and vomit over the side from seasickness. After only one heave a lieutenant angrily ordered him forward to the head, for retching over the side would never hit the water but spatter down the tumble home. It caused his absence of several minutes, during which the tempted sailor broke into the grog.

They were not yet within sight of land, but knew they were passing south of Cape St. Vincent, when a cry came down from the maintop: "Sail ho! Sail! Ho!"

Preble was on the deck within seconds with his glass. "Where away?"

"Off the port bow, heading south!"

"Can you make her out?"

"Not yet, sir!" the call came down. "Large sail, possibly a frigate!" They had been hauling close in a northerly wind; she would be upon them quickly.

Preble patted the large end of the glass into this left hand, thinking. Tripolitans don't have frigates; she might belong to any of the European powers. Still. He strode over to the officer of the deck, a freckled lieutenant named Edwards. "Beat to quarters, but do not roll out the guns, and keep the ports closed. Let us seem friendly unless we must act otherwise."

"Very good, sir." Edwards relayed the order to the marines and the stark tattoo of the drum began; once the men were on deck, the gunnery officers were summoned to the quarterdeck to learn the particulars. Preble was satisfied that all was ready; the guns needed only to be rolled out.

By the time this was done another call floated down from the maintop. "Sir! Her flag is green! She is Moroccan! A large sloop or light frigate!"

"Mm," grunted Preble. "Mr. Israel!"

"Sir?"

"Go below, give my compliments to Mr. Lear and ask him to join us, if you please, and bring up my speaking trumpet."

"Aye, sir."

On their present course she must pass ahead of them. "Mr. Edwards, steer southeast, if you please, to intercept her, and shorten sail. We will go with the wind and let her catch up, and see if she has anything to say."

Israel returned to his station at the starboard twelve-pounders, where Bliven joined him. *Constitution* began a gentle starboard turn, and Bliven understood that if there was action, his port guns would engage first. He made certain that the matches were lit, and the lanyards threaded through the eyebolts, ready to run out on an instant's command. "How are you faring, Mr. Israel? Are you keen for your first action—I suppose since the French?"

"I am ready for what comes, Mr. Putnam, but in truth, no one has ever told me how one is supposed to feel before an action."

Bliven laughed quietly. "Quite right. They leave that out of the manual, don't they?"

It took an hour for the Moroccan to come up on their port side; she could easily have kept her distance but seemed quite ready to speak.

She appeared to mount about thirty guns, about the same size as the *Essex* but of lighter build.

Bliven joined Commodore Preble, who continued to eye her suspiciously. "She seems friendly enough, but I don't know."

"Yes, sir," Bliven answered. "I am just remembering the deceptions of the *Tripoli* a couple of years ago. Anything is possible."

The Moroccan shortened sail just as she came abeam, duplicating *Constitution's* course. On her quarterdeck an officer in a black tunic with gold cording waved a speaking trumpet in the air. Preble raised his own trumpet to his lips. "I am Commodore Edward Preble, United States Frigate *Constitution*. What ship is that?"

The reply came readily. "Good afternoon, Commodore. I am Sidi Mehmet, captain of His Imperial Majesty's frigate *Maimona*."

"Well," Preble said aside to Lear, "at least they speak English."

"Yes," Lear agreed, "the English have dominated these waters for so long, nearly all the ships have at least one officer who is fluent."

Preble raised the trumpet again. "You are sailing in a war zone. Where are you bound?"

"Yes. We are sailing from Lisbon, bound for Salé. We have a passport from your consul, Mr. Simpson."

"I am suspicious of the look of it," said Lear. "He seems cooperative, and we are at peace with Morocco—but Salé and Mogador, those are the two ports that pirates use when they sally into the Atlantic."

"Commodore!" the Moroccan captain hailed them. "If you will please to send a boat, you will be welcome to inspect our papers."

Preble shifted his weight. "What do you think, Mr. Lear?"

"I should go. I know Simpson and his handwriting. If they bear a passport we must let them go on, whatever our suspicions."

"Very well, I will send some marines with you." Again Preble raised his trumpet. "Thank you, we will lower a boat. Let us shorten sail."

"As you wish, Commodore." No sooner had he spoken than a boarding ladder rolled down the Moroccan's side, and men went aloft to furl her mainsails.

"Mr. Edwards, have the bosun reef the courses, form up a detail of marines, and get the cutter into the water."

From the quarterdeck Bliven and the others watched the tall, thin Lear sitting awkwardly in his black formal coat as he was pulled over to the *Maimona*; luckily, the seas were only running about two feet, so there was little to go wrong in boarding her. He was on board for half an hour before he returned and reported.

"Well?" asked Preble.

"She is most certainly on a war footing; she seems ready for anything. I estimate she has thirty guns. But I have to say their passport seems valid in every respect. It was written in Simpson's hand."

Preble pursed his lips, almost physically chewing his thoughts. "My gut tells me she is up to no good, but we are approaching his shores, he is not approaching ours. He has every right to be here, whatever mischief I might suspect in his mission. Our first job is to remedy Commodore Morris's missteps, not repeat them."

"I have to agree on all points," said Lear, almost sadly. "*Maimona* is the Emperor's biggest ship, and it is tempting to take her off the board."

"Yes," Preble grumbled, "but we cannot, and we will not." He raised the trumpet. "Captain Mehmet, thank you for your cooperation. You are free to go. Fair sailing to you."

"Thank you, Commodore, the same to you." *Maimona*'s mainsails were quickly set and she diminished toward the south.

"Mr. Edwards," said Preble almost tiredly, "set all sail, resume course for Gibraltar, stand down from action stations." He went below with a scowl.

Bliven secured the twelve-pounders until they were wanted again, and found himself wondering exactly how much of warfare was feint and false alarm. On his first cruise he had fought desperately, but by the calendar most of their time had been taken up in the ennui of blockade. But this was different, the prospect of action held out and then withdrawn. He found he did not care for it, and hoped that either Lear would negotiate a quick end without a fight or Preble would lead them into a sharp, decisive action to force a peace on terms favorable to the national honor.

Before going below Bliven scanned the quarterdeck once more and then down the spar deck. At least, he thought, fighting on a frigate, he could fight with cannons and leave his sword in its sheath. That would be a good thing.

Bliven's relief, however, transformed into Preble's frustration, for nature seemed to set her face against them. What winds there were turned light, and often they were becalmed altogether. If there was one thing that maddened Preble it was inaction, the requirement to wait, and officers and crew learned the truth that he was a man devoid of patience. Their encounter with the *Maimona* had taken place on September 6 off Cape St. Vincent, and eight days' sailing had brought them only near Cádiz, a crawl of movement almost too slow to measure that found Preble striding his quarterdeck during his waking hours, huffing and growling.

Preble's favor toward Bliven, doubtless fed by the exchange of books, drew the notice of other officers that the commodore accepted bad news from Bliven that others would have feared to tell him. As the hazy light faded on September 14, they found themselves on a glass-calm sea, the sails hanging slack from their yards, with Preble pacing and huffing. Sam and another lieutenant approached Bliven. "We wonder, Mr. Putnam, if you might suggest it to the commodore, that if he directed some of his wind into the sails we might be under way again."

Bliven was still trying to think of an appropriate witticism in response when the cry came from the lookout, "Sail ho!"

"Where away?" shouted Preble.

"Starboard bow! At least I think it's a sail. It's hard to tell in this blasted light." By the time they beat to quarters the dark had come over them, moonless. Bliven stood by the quarterdeck twelve-pounders port, and Israel the starboard battery; the fog turned so thick they could only with difficulty make out the eighteens down the spar deck. The men stood silently at the ready, wondering if the lookout had truly seen a sail, or merely seen a patch of light reflected in the dimming haze.

"Shh!" Preble hissed, which was passed down the decks. Moments ticked by, until they heard the faint but familiar groan of rigging off their starboard bow.

Preble took up his trumpet and assumed the exaggerated clarity of speaking a ship. "Ahoy the ship!" he called. "What ship is that?"

The night afforded no answer, for so long that they began to feel foolish for speaking into the empty darkness. Preble started to put the trumpet to his lips again when a call came back. "What ship is that?"

The officers exchanged confounded looks. "This is the United States frigate *Constitution*," said Preble loudly. "What ship is that?"

Again they waited, the silence broken only by a groaning line or creaking beam. At last there was a response. "What ship is that?"

The others on the quarterdeck had sensed Preble's temper building.

"I am now going to hail you for the last time," he roared. "If a proper answer is not received, I will fire a shot into you."

There was no pause this time. "If you fire a shot, I will return a broadside."

The voice was in that accent that Preble loathed. "What ship is that?" he bellowed.

"This is His Britannic Majesty's ship *Donegal*, eighty-four guns, Sir Richard Strachan, an English commodore. Send your boat on board."

Steadying himself on a shroud, Preble launched up into the nettings and raised the trumpet to his lips. "This is the United States ship *Constitution*, forty-four guns, Edward Preble, an American commodore, who will be damned before he sends his boat on board any vessel!" He surveyed his quarterdeck guns, making out the dimly burning fuses lying in their coils. "Blow your matches, boys!"

The silence was pregnant, and remained so, until faintly they could hear the small splashes of oars, dipping in unison. Slowly they began to make out an approaching longboat, from which a voice issued, "Ahoy the ship!"

"Who are you?" Preble shot back.

"British officer of H.M.S. *Maidstone*, requesting permission to board." A boarding ladder unfurled noisily down the side and a blue-coated Royal Navy lieutenant swung a black-shoed, daintily stockinged foot over the rail.

He was no sooner upright than he was hustled to the quarterdeck. "My captain's compliments"—he saluted Preble—"and he begs pardon for our little game of charades. We are blockading Cádiz, as you may know. You quite surprised us, and we needed time to get to quarters. We did not know but what you were a French man-of-war, ready to open up on us."

"Must have been my accent," said Preble sourly. "What part of France did you think I was from?"

"Really, sir, we apologize, but false flags and false hailing are quite the going currency in these waters."

Preble pursed his lips. "That is true. But with eighty-four guns, I should think you would be rearing for action."

"Yes, well." The British lieutenant cleared his throat. "Actually, *Maidstone* is a frigate of thirty-four guns. We can't be too careful, with French ships of the line all about."

"Yes," Preble agreed drolly, "all about, thick as the Spanish Armada." Before the young Englishman could respond he added, "Well, will you come below and have some refreshment?"

Bliven stood close enough that he could see the man's mortification that after engaging in such a ruse, the British captain sent this man and did not come himself. "I thank you, no, we have been too long delayed in joining our squadron." He stepped back and saluted, which Preble returned. As the longboat pulled away, a tar halfway down the spar deck leaned on his eighteen-pounder. "D'ye see that, boys? The commodore give 'em what for thinkin' it was an eighty-four! How's that for sand? We're Preble's boys now, ain't we, men? Three cheers for the commodore! Hip, hip?"

Bliven joined officers and crew alike in lifting his hat to Preble, whose sourness evaporated. Clearly he enjoyed the cheers, and lifted his bicorne in acknowledgment—but even more clearly enjoyed the fact that after all these weeks, he had won the loyalty of his crew. If he had had any doubt, he knew now they would fight for him.

With the guns secured the officers filed below; Bliven took a cup of tea into his cabin and closed the door, reflecting. If he aspired to command, he should remember this night. This was how you led men.

11.

THE EMPEROR

October 1803

Preble may have enjoyed his triumph in winning over the men, but when a wind finally came, the lightest of zephyrs, it blew in their faces from the northwest. "Damn!" spat Preble. "Damn, damn!" Eight days it took them to cover the one hundred fifty miles from Cape St. Vincent to Cádiz; it was ridiculous.

He stormed below, passing Sam Bandy, who was sitting at table in the wardroom, working over the figures from his last sighting. Throughout the crossing, he had secondary command of the after half of the starboard twenty-fours, but for his main duty he fixed their position, hourly and faithfully. Preble had not asked it of him, but every evening Sam handed him a complete report of their hourly positions for the logbook.

"Mr. Lear!" Preble called out even as he pushed through the door to his great cabin, and found his diplomat and wife taking their ease. "Mr. Lear, the wind is simply against us and there is no help for it. But if we haul close we can make for Tangier. Tell me, is it absolutely necessary for you to call at Gibraltar before dealing with this emperor of yours?"

Lear leaned back in his chair and crossed his legs. "No, I would not call it absolutely necessary. We have our instructions, to pacify him if we can, aided with a show of force as needed. The necessity is, we cannot attack Tripoli after leaving a hostile Morocco in our rear. Of course, if we do not call at Gibraltar we will not have the benefit of the latest intelligence. But in all honesty, the commerce between Tangier and Gibraltar is so constant we may learn of any important developments from other ships in the harbor."

Preble had never stopped pacing. "Well, then, Tangier it is. I simply cannot sit out here any longer." He opened the door to his private cabin and emerged with a chart that he spread out on the table. Lear inspected it and discovered it was of the whole vicinity of the straits, with swatches of the Spanish and Moroccan coasts as they approached the narrows. Again Preble yanked open the door of the great cabin. "Mr. Bandy, will you come in, please?"

Sam entered; thinking that his latest information was needed, he took his papers with him and saw the chart. "Where are we?" asked Preble.

Sam took up a pencil, referred to their latest latitude and longitude, regarded the scale of the map, and set the point down carefully. "Here, sir."

All leaned over the table. Over a space of thirty miles the southern coast of Spain formed a great convex bulge, leading up the far side to Gibraltar Bay. The African coast by contrast formed a great convex indentation of equal size, with Tangier lying at the western end. As the opening narrowed from the westward approach, they saw seamounts and shoals clustered on the Spanish side; all the ships favored toward the African shore until hewing to the very middle channel through the straits themselves. "Can we make Tangier by morning?" asked Preble anxiously.

"How is the wind?" asked Sam.

"Still light, northwesterly."

"I should guess mid-morning, sir," said Sam, "A bit sooner if it picks up and doesn't change."

"Excellent. Excellent, excuse me." Preble strode through the wardroom and ascended the after ladder with more than his customary energy.

It was nearing the end of the first dog watch, and Bliven had the deck, distantly and unobtrusively supervising a tall young midshipman named Jerrell at the wheel.

"Mr. Jerrell, how are you faring?" asked Preble.

"Good afternoon, sir, very well."

"Mm." He glanced over at Bliven, who approached.

"A new course, Mr. Jerrell, south by east, we'll use this little wind instead of fighting it."

"That will take us toward Tangier, sir," said Bliven.

"Exactly. Aeolus has barred us from Gibraltar for the time being, but as our next business must be in Tangier anyway, we will proceed there directly. Well, bring her around smartly, Mr. Jerrell, carry on."

The dog watches having but two hours' duration, Bliven at its conclusion went belowdecks hungry but knowing that dinner was still two hours distant. He clattered quickly down the ladder to the gun deck, and he glanced further down into the berth deck; it occurred to him how easily had he accustomed himself to the proportions of a frigate. Those who inhabited his world in Litchfield would become dizzy from this enclosed and relentlessly efficient space, but to him it was palatial, and the tiny *Enterprise* seemed a lifetime away.

Finding the wardroom empty for the moment, he went forward to the galley for a cup of tea over which to read. In passing down the berth deck, some of the sailors just coming off their watch were preparing the remains of their morning biscuit for a snack. They had removed their neckerchiefs, wrapped biscuits in them, and, taking turns with a hammer, broke them into small pieces to soak in their tea. The racket in the closed deck was frightful, yet that third of the crew then trying to take their four hours of sleep lay so exhausted that they roused in their hammocks only slightly.

"Mr. Putnam, good afternoon."

He recognized the ship's surgeon's raspy, high-pitched voice before he had taken cognizance of him. "Good afternoon, Dr. Cutbush."

"I was preparing tea. Let me pour you some."

"Precisely why I came, thank you."

It had already brewed, and the second cup was instantly filled. "Lemon?"

"Thank you, no."

Cutbush paused in his motions. "You do not care for lemon?"

"It is not my habit."

"Don't see many lemons in Connecticut, I'll wager."

"Not often, no."

"Never tried it? Let me urge it upon you. Use lemon in your tea, and you will never be touched with the scurvy."

"Truly?"

"What the British discovered with limes is equally true of lemons, I am sure of it. I prescribe it."

"Very well, lemon, then. I shall adapt."

"Ah, good. You only wanted for encouragement." He handed Bliven the cup.

He thanked him and started back to the wardroom, but Cutbush interrupted him. "Come, keep me company." He inclined his head farther forward, toward the sick bay. Bliven saw for himself that indeed, as Cutbush had earlier described, he had hung sheets forward of the galley that morning and left them up after sick call, to screen himself off from the constant commotion of the gun deck.

Apart from Preble's friendliness on account of his books, Bliven was unused to such familiarity from a superior, but then Cutbush was not a line officer.

Cutbush seated himself at his small desk and motioned Bliven to the other chair as he closed several books, marking his places by closing them on each other at their open pages. Although he had become familiar with the interior spaces, it seemed to Bliven that the spare accommodation of the sick bay revealed the ship in a way that the other areas did not. The massive spaced ribs protruded within, thicker even than the thirty-inch oak hull, making plainly visible the ships' famous resilient strength, which sheltered the sick and the injured within. It seemed appropriate, in an odd way, that just as the prostrate seamen revealed their inmost bodies in the sick bay, so too the very skeleton of the ship stretched about them.

"You seem to have no patients today," Bliven ventured.

"I try to keep a healthy ship," said Cutbush as he arranged himself. "I am certain that the most prevalent disease I treat is malingering. I must write a treatise about it. Ha! Trick is to diagnose something so terrible that a day of excused duty can't be worth the treatment."

Bliven grinned. "Do you invent names for new diseases?"

"Constantly." Cutbush gestured to the empty berths in the sick bay. "As you see, it works!"

"May I ask? Cutbush is an unusual name. Does it have a particular history?"

"I have wondered that myself." As Cutbush relaxed, Bliven could detect no accent in his Pennsylvania speech. "I have no idea."

"Cutbush," said Bliven. "Perhaps it was a name for foresters, or gamekeepers."

"My father was a sculptor and woodworker."

"Indeed?"

"Oh, yes, his best commissions were figureheads for ships. A number of the navy's first ships had his figureheads on their prows."

"Ah. So, you have done him one better."

"How do you mean?" Cutbush asked.

"Well, carving upon live people instead of wooden ones, you see."

As Cutbush smiled Bliven continued, "I've been wanting to ask you, the commodore is often unwell. Is it serious? Should he even be out here?"

Cutbush's eyebrows rose. "He is a hard man to keep down. He has ulcers of the stomach, painful, but not fatal if controlled. And how are you? Have you any complaints or maladies?"

"None, sir, I thank you. I am very well."

"Well." Cutbush rose and stood over him. "Look up into the light." He cupped one hand behind Bliven's head and the other under his chin, looking into his eyes. "Open your mouth, stick out your tongue."

Bliven did as he was bidden. "Do you suspect something? Is something going around?"

"Not at all. I am pleased to see so strapping a specimen when I chance across him." He tested Bliven's shoulders for any weakness but found none. "The sea affects different men differently, you see. Some men thrive on it, others begin their decline the day they leave port. You, I am inclined to believe, are one of the former. Have you any tendency to seasickness?"

"No, sir, I am happy to say."

"Good, but let me caution you." Cutbush sat back down and took a sip of tea. "Lads come to sea thinking they are invincible. They think that mundane injuries only happen to older seamen, and mostly they do. But always carry it in the back of your mind, when you are about any activity that is strenuous, keep your mind on it. Mind your footing aloft, lift burdens carefully and not from an awkward position. Nothing can cut short a man's usefulness more than to wrench his back or give himself a hernia—and that does not happen just to old men; you can be struck down at any age."

Bliven thought suddenly of Todd back in Boston. "Or lose a leg in battle."

"Yes, I should be very sorry to see you lying in pieces on my table."

"You showed me your cockpit before, a dingy place to exit this world, I must say. This is much nicer. Is that your pharmacy?" He looked more closely at the open chest and saw supplies of castor oil, calomel, and ipecac syrup, just as he would see at home.

"Yes, one must make do with remarkably little," Cutbush said wistfully. "Emetics, purgatives, astringents—mostly they aim to help the body heal itself. I wish I could do more in the way of real intervention. I do have Peruvian bark for a fever, acidulated wine to relieve the effects of consumption, but of course once that sets in there is little to be done. Mercury ointment, of course, for the men who have been with loose women. But it is not much of an arsenal." Cutbush shook his head. "Not much at all."

"One of the seamen who was flogged said you treated his wounds with honey?"

"Ha! A little secret from the ancient Romans. Galen wrote about it, that and many other things. I believe we share an interest in what can be learned from the past, do we not?"

"Indeed we do," said Bliven. "I have never read Galen. Do you have that book?"

"He wrote several books, actually, but sadly, no, I do not have them on board. Much of what he wrote is outdated, of course, but when I did read it, I was struck by how much we should perhaps revisit in a more modern way. That honey kills infection is beyond question; the Romans used it for centuries."

"My word."

"Did you know"—Cutbush paused and smiled—"Galen believed that most diseases of the mind could be cured by talking with a wise old man who was trained to tease out the distempered passions? And once uncovered, he believed the patient would be free of them."

"Oh, my."

"Nowadays we just lock madmen up in asylums, or hang them if they kill or steal. If you ask me, there are many lessons in the past that deserve a new hearing. But now look, I have kept you too long. Be off with you, I am glad to find you so well." He reached for his stack of books and began opening them to the pages he had marked.

Bliven refreshed his tea in the galley and squeezed the last drops from the remains of the lemon that the doctor had left on the cutting board. Lemons were similar to limes, to be sure; he could believe in their efficacy against scurvy. But poor Cutbush, he reflected, how lonely he must get for lively and educated company.

. . .

TANGIER LAY ON THE NORTH SHORE of Morocco, but like the ports within the Mediterranean, the harbor faced east into its bay, embraced by two long breakwaters. The wind had picked up during the night; it was still bright morning when Preble eased the *Constitution* into the harbor and dropped anchor. Lear knew the town, and he pointed out the Medina to their right, on the Atlantic shore, the casbah above it, the emperor's palace to their left with a view of the bay. Through the glass Lear and then Preble spied out the diplomatic missions with their flags fluttering above them—British, French, Spanish, Portuguese, Sicilian— but on peering where he knew the American mission to be, there was no flag.

"Why don't you fire a gun?" Lear asked. "That is the commonly understood signal to bring the consul out. Simpson should be here."

"Yes," said Preble. "I agree." He summoned Bliven, who fetched one crew. They had traveled with the guns loaded, and screwing out the wadding and coaxing out the ball would take time, so they simply fired a twelve-pounder into the emptiness of the bay, where the ball fell harmlessly. The report of the gun echoed back from the city, loud enough that they were certain it was well heard.

After half an hour passed Lear began to frown. "This is not well," he muttered, and repeated himself at intervals. After an hour and a half he was certain. "Something is very much amiss," he told Preble, and gestured up at the rigging. "Can you make for Gibraltar?"

The advancing day brought a fair wind from the south, off the desert. "Yes, we can be there this afternoon."

"Then let us away. Nothing good awaits us here."

Preble nodded grimly; Edwards had the deck. "Weigh anchor, Mr. Edwards, get us out of here, make course for Gibraltar."

"Very good, sir."

THEY REACHED GIBRALTAR late in the afternoon, and Preble was pleased to see the *Philadelphia* sunning herself at anchor, and even more pleased to spy Consul Gavino on his way out to them before they reached their anchorage, and saw a gentleman in the boat with him, wearing a black tunic with a gold-corded front. They reached the *Constitution* at virtually the same instant as Bainbridge, in the *Philadelphia's* jolly boat. Preble's first action was to send his chef ashore with silver to round up a suitable dinner, for during their weeks at sea even the commodore's stores had begun to wear thin, and the chef was increasingly challenged to keep a respectable table set.

Preble received them in his great cabin, as Bainbridge introduced Gavino to the commodore, and Gavino in turn stood aside. "Commodore, may I present His Excellency, General Sir Thomas Trigge, the governor of Gibraltar."

"An honor, sir." Preble saluted. "You are acquainted with Mr. Lear?"

"Yes, very well. How are you, Mr. Lear?" They shook hands warmly.

"Commodore," said Lear, "let me add by way of introduction that it was General Trigge who withstood the four years' Great Siege of Gibraltar twenty years ago, and before that he served on our own soil— and on our side, I am happy to say—in the French and Indian War."

"Indeed!" exclaimed Preble, and he regarded Trigge afresh. He was past sixty but looked much older, sunken and pasty but quite plump, showing the worse for his many years of cares. The only thing taut about him was his tunic, glinting with all the gold filigree of a British royal governor. "We are very honored to have you aboard, sir. Shall we be seated?"

"Sir," began Bainbridge, "we need to bring you abreast of the latest developments with Morocco, which are numerous as well as . . . thorny."

"Are we at war?" asked Preble.

"No, sir, but close to it."

"What of our consul, Mr. Simpson?" asked Lear.

Trigge lifted his glass of wine just off the table. "He is safe, but he is in arrest and under guard, albeit in his own house. If I may go on?"

"Please." Preble gestured openly.

"His Majesty's government is distressed by this turn of events, not only for the cause of peace generally, but, of more immediate moment, at this season Gibraltar relies almost entirely on Morocco for fresh foodstuffs. Now, I am sensible of the fact that you cannot allow Morocco to seize your commercial vessels, but if you then go about taking their ships in turn, the supply of our victuals must dry up. We are aware that your primary mission to Emperor Slimane is diplomatic, so if you will permit me, let me urge you to expend every effort to reach an accord with him. And if there is any service that His Majesty's government can perform to help you in this endeavor, you may rely on our help."

Preble took this in quietly, realizing that this recitation must be the reason Trigge had come. "And what is this emperor's bearing toward us at this moment?"

Trigge measured his words. "Suspicious, almost hostile. He will say that he took your ships only because you took his, and he will question your cause for doing so."

"Ha!" puffed Bainbridge. "I took the *Meshuda* red-handed, smuggling arms into Tripoli, I don't care whose flag she was flying. *Mirboka* was in piratical possession of the *Celia*, for God's sake."

Preble held up his hand. "Wait, wait, wait. I know nothing of these events. Have you a report?"

"Oh, yes, sir, sorry." Bainbridge dug inside his coat and produced a folded sheaf of papers. "Briefly, several weeks ago, Rodgers was patrolling off Tripoli in the *John Adams* and overhauled a ship trying to break the blockade. She proved to be the *Meshuda*, operating as a merchantman. You remember she had been a Tripolitan brig that Barron had bottled up in Gibraltar, then she changed flags to Morocco and we had to let her go. Her master said they were carrying provisions, but Rodgers's inspection found a cargo of arms and ammunition. He took her as a prize to Malta. And then not a week ago I was cruising off the Cabo de Gata, and I came on the Moroccan *Mirboka* with an American brig, the *Celia*, in tow. Naturally, I announced myself, took her as a prize, and recovered the *Celia*. It seems our Moroccans have been very partial neutrals indeed, sir."

"Yes, but the emperor can disclaim knowledge of these things," said Trigge calmly. "Sometimes in diplomacy, it is best not to keep accounts too strictly. In all friendship, I urge you to accept that the future must weigh more than the past. That keen American sense of right and wrong is well known, and respected, but you must consider what you need of the emperor: you cannot fight Tripoli unless you first make peace with him."

"Yes," said Lear, "Slimane is a Moorish potentate, no less than the dey of Algiers or the bashaws of Tunis and Tripoli, perhaps a bit more haughty—he has been in power longer and killed more people to get there. But we must do what we must do, to take him off the board."

Preble nodded. "I understand. But for success, an effort at peace must be made from strength. Bainbridge, will you come back to Tangiers with me in the *Philadelphia*? Two ships will make double the impression as one."

Bainbridge smiled. "It's better than that, sir. Rodgers is expected at any moment with his squadron. If you can wait for them, we should mount four or five sail, not two."

"A hundred and fifty guns, more or less, that should do the trick, then," said Preble. "The more guns behind us, the friendlier we can be, eh? What do you say, Lear?"

"I agree, but I beg you, leave the diplomatic business to me."

MORNING FOUND PREBLE breakfasting alone in his cabin, on fresh eggs and ham, and milk, that his cook had found in the town, followed by a rich and satisfying custard; it all made Bainbridge's report of his activities even more enjoyable than it otherwise would have been. Bainbridge and Rodgers, operating free of Morris, who was always in port and at parties, had exceeded expectations at making the Moors pay a price for their piracy. The morning improved still more as Preble observed the *Vixen* glide up and anchor behind him.

He was further glad to see the tall *New York*, showing no evidence of her previous fire, join them in the afternoon, but she bore a problem as well, for she carried Richard Morris and his family. As far as Morris knew, he was to hand the *New York* over to Rodgers and come home as a passenger on the next likely vessel, probably the *Adams* at the end of her rotation. Preble's presence surprised him, as he knew it would Rodgers, and he quickly surmised that there would be friction between them—even as he realized what a mean consideration that was, for he himself was out of the game and would never be allowed back in it. Exulting in the discord between others was pointless if there was nothing in it for him.

Preble hosted them at dinner that evening, and even the cook's roast duck and savory rice did not make the evening less painful. It was obvious that Morris felt his shame very deeply, and his wife even more so, reproaching herself that his downfall must in part have been her fault. Preble found it awkward to condole in good manners with a man whom he considered deserving in every particular to be broken from the service, or even with his wife, who in her remorse still evinced too clear a pride in carrying herself at the side of a commodore. They did not stay late, for which Preble was grateful, and he watched them being rowed back to the *New York*. They could stay there until Rodgers claimed her, then they could stay at the consulate, or they would have no difficulty renting rooms, for Morris was known to be wealthy.

The next day his squadron grew even as his thicket of etiquette closed about him, for the *Adams* and *John Adams* came in together under John Rodgers. What genius in the Navy Department, Preble wondered, ever conceived of having two frigates of nearly identical design named *Adams* and *John Adams*? It must necessarily be a source of confusion, both then and in the future, for everyone not intimately concerned with naval affairs.

Of greater concern was Rodgers's pennant. Rodgers had learned from Bainbridge that the Mediterranean was shortly to host two American commodores, and he was vociferous in his displeasure. He was younger than Preble, but had been in the service longer, and he made it clear that by navy seniority he ought to be retained in command.

Preparing his ground, Preble had his clerk draw up a copy of his orders giving him command of all the ships, orders that neither Rodgers nor anyone could question, and then laid over it a delicate letter to Rodgers, expressing the highest admiration for his abilities and conduct of the blockade and protesting his determination not to deprive Rodgers of any consideration due him. "The Moors," he wrote, "are a deep designing, artfull, treacherous sett of Villains, and nothing will keep them so quiet as a respectable naval force near them."

As soon as Rodgers dropped anchor, Preble sent his jolly boat over with this packet, and it returned a half-hour later with a respectful note from Rodgers asking a quick meeting. This he granted, and they readily agreed that the Moroccan issue took precedence over all others. As though he were sailing into an action, Preble was organized and addressed the factors in turn. They agreed that they should await the *Siren* and the *Argus* before returning to Tangier. All their ships would go: *Constitution, Philadelphia, New York, Adams,* and *John Adams,* plus the brigs and schooners. They would not send word beforehand, they would simply materialize on the emperor's doorstep, which must cause something between consternation and panic, after which Lear's peace proposals should get an attentive hearing. Once a peace was signed, *Adams* would return to Gibraltar and take the disgraced Morris home. Rodgers would take the *John Adams* and *New York* for independent cruising and convoying, still in his rank of commodore; Bainbridge would take the *Philadelphia* and one of the schooners to begin the blockade of Tripoli; Preble would take the *Constitution* to Algiers to deposit Lear and see what could be done about Barnes and his daughter, and then to Naples to finalize the agreement with the Sicilies to supply gunboats and bomb scows to begin reducing the city of Tripoli itself.

By nightfall Preble was feeling much more confident of his position, but it was a busy schedule of activity, and all must begin with Tangier. If only it had proven so simple. Word came in that the emperor was not in Tangier but in Mogador, hundreds of miles to the south. As delays went this was not a bad one, for by it they could ascribe knowledge to Slimane of the presence there of the *Hannah*, another American merchantman lately taken by his corsairs. Preble set out once, but was waylaid to tow a distressed and dismasted British frigate into Ceuta. To seamen a distress signal plays trump over any other duty, and while Preble disliked the English intensely, the benefit to relations between the two countries was clear from the notes of thanks and compliments that made their way higher in the departments.

It required a few more weeks of loitering in Gibraltar, waiting for other vessels to arrive, seeking clearer instructions, for the stars to align in such a way that Preble and the *Constitution* could lead his large squadron—augmented now by the *Nautilus* and the *Enterprise*—boldly into Tangier Bay in early October. They were too many to jam within the breakwaters, and therefore they lay out of range, but that also arranged itself well. Nearly two miles out, the emperor would not feel such an immediate threat, which would make Lear's peace proposals sound more sincere, but they also had space to anchor all of them showing their broadsides to the fort and the city, leaving no doubt about what they could do.

Through his glass Preble assayed the layout of the fort—in truth, the decaying remains of an ancient castle that had guns placed between the crenellations, but could not stand an hour's punishment—and the directions of the guns, and he selected places in the harbor where his ships could anchor and not all be fired on at once. Then he went below to wait for Lear to finish preparing.

There came two raps at the door of the great cabin. "Enter," said Preble. "Ah, Mr. Putnam, your arrival is timely. Mr. Lear and I are shortly to be granted an audience with the emperor of Morocco. I desire you to come with us."

"Me?" Bliven was genuinely perplexed.

"I am making you my adjutant. In our weeks at sea you have been diligent in your duties, as have the other junior officers. But it has also become apparent to me that the crew respect you, the midshipmen look up to you, perhaps because you don't abuse them. But beyond that you have evinced a curiosity about the world, and an ability to deal outside your sphere, in a way that I think makes you a candidate for greater responsibilities. All of my lieutenants can fight, I expect them to. But not all of them care for learning, or can hold an intelligent conversation. So I am going to start exposing you to a broader world." All this he said very rapidly, as though he had rehearsed it, and Bliven knew well enough that Preble was not comfortable bestowing compliments.

Bliven blushed. "Commodore, I thank you for—"

"Stow it, you can be grateful later. For now, we're off to see the emperor. Pssh!" he huffed suddenly. "Emperor! Of this place! Emperor of scorpions, maybe."

"Underestimate him at your peril," warned Lear as he emerged from his compartment. "When his father died, four brothers fought for the throne, each one as cunning and cruel as the next. It was Slimane who emerged victorious."

"So he is a fratricide as well as a pirate."

"Thrice a fratricide. That is the world from which he comes," answered Lear. "And besides that, he is the sovereign over multiple nationalities—Arabs, Tuaregs, Berbers—so to be perfectly correct, he is in fact an emperor. Well, we mustn't be late."

Preble nodded. "Putnam, round up the bosun, have him lower the longboat, and have him find some clean clothes for the rowers."

The palace lay on the south side of the harbor and very near the waterfront, a section from which the common people were cordoned off. Halfway there they spied an honor guard of spotlessly uniformed janissaries forming between the wharf and the palace entry. "Well," said Preble, "come here with one ship and they turn their backs on you. Come with a fleet and it's quite different, eh?"

A chamberlain met them at the door and conducted them through a courtyard and a reception hall and into a throne room that was well populated with courtiers. Emperor Slimane was a hard-looking man, small eyes, high cheekbones, medium dark skin. He sat upon a dais, on a settee piled with brightly colored silken cushions. Extending to his left was a padded bench on which sat his divan, his cabinet of advisers, all looking at the Americans expectantly as soon as they entered. Also eyeing them was a leopard weighing perhaps eighty pounds, who lay at the foot of the dais in a jeweled collar on a leash held by an attendant.

Consul Simpson joined them as they entered the chamber, and Lear shook hands with him. "Are you all right?"

"Yes. I have not been jailed, only held in house arrest."

The chamberlain led them to the foot of the dais and announced them, then peered at them expectantly for the better part of a minute before he said with evident annoyance, "You are to kneel in the presence of the emperor, until he bids you to rise."

"American officers do not kneel, sir," said Preble curtly.

"It is but a courtesy. He will quickly bid you to rise."

Preble widened his stance. "Nevertheless."

"It is custom!" spat the chamberlain.

"Not for American officers, sir!"

From his silken dais Slimane observed the exchange without expression, except it was impossible for Bliven not to notice that the emperor's mustache and beard were trimmed well clear of his mouth and seemed to exaggerate a peculiarly cruel turning down at the corners. Slimane posed a single question in Arabic to the chamberlain and resumed his repose of apparent disinterest.

"Do you not fear to be detained for such an insult?" he asked Preble.

"No, sir, we do not."

"How not?"

"Because, sir"—Preble folded his arms on his chest—"in the event that we are detained, I have left positive orders that no attempt is to be made to negotiate our release, ransom us, or in any other way attempt to recover us. If I, my aide, Mr. Lear, or Mr. Simpson are harmed or in any way impeded, or the honor of our country compromised, my frigates will before your plain view open fire on your fort and continue firing until it lies in ruins. While they are thus engaged, my brigs and schooners will fire on your palace until it is also in ruins. After this, all the ships will open fire upon the city, starting with the Medina, until there is nothing left, save piles of stones."

As the chamberlain translated, Bliven saw the fires kindle in Slimane's eyes and grow brighter until the exposition was concluded.

"That is true, sire," volunteered Lear. "I have copies of his orders to forward to my government—"

Slimane interrupted him with a sharp question to his chamberlain, and then turned to two uniformed officers of his divan. Each spoke in turn as the emperor's expression turned increasingly sour. It became apparent that they were explaining to him the number and disposition of Preble's ships, their positions relative to the harbor's defenses, and the likelihood that he could indeed reduce the city to rubble.

"Mr. Lear," said the chamberlain, "it is you who represent your government. How can we demonstrate our continued friendly regard for the United States?"

"Commodore," said Lear quietly to Preble, "I urge you, let me guide the discussion henceforward."

Preble nodded.

"Sire, our great desire is to renew the bonds of friendship which have until recently prevailed between our two countries."

As suddenly as shutters being thrown open, Slimane's countenance lightened, but he lost none of his imperial hauteur. "We wish this also," he declared through the chamberlain. "We are glad that you bear in mind that after your revolution, Morocco was the first country to recognize your independence."

"No great idealism there," snapped Preble. "That only meant you were the first to recognize that British tribute no longer covered our ships, and you were the first to capture our vessels on the high seas and demand ransom."

"Commodore, please," purred Lear, "these are diplomatic issues.

"Sire," Lear continued, "it pains us to have to point out that you have captured and now hold for ransom an American merchant ship and crew, in clear violation of the convention between our two countries. Your Majesty was lately in Mogador and would have seen her, the *Hannah*."

"That ship," said the chamberlain flatly, "was taken in retaliation for your capture of two of His Majesty's warships, which first violated our treaty."

Lear nodded. "The first ship was taken without orders—albeit she had just captured another American merchantman, which was recovered—and will be returned in exchange for the American merchantman. The second ship was the *Meshuda*, lately under Tripolitan flag."

"But now under our flag," said the chamberlain angrily. "We are neutral in your war with Tripoli; you have seen her papers."

"Yes," said Lear, "and the *Meshuda* under your flag was taken while smuggling ammunition into Tripoli, violating the blockade we declared against Tripoli several months ago, a declaration of which you were given full notice. She was seized in the act and there can be no dispute about this."

"We deny your right to any such blockade," declared the chamberlain.

"Oh, please," Preble sighed.

Without warning Slimane stood, casting silence over the room as the counselors of his divan rose as one man and bowed deeply. "Mr. Lear," he said in heavily accented English, "I have information that our ships acted under orders of our governor of Tangier, without our knowledge. It is easily undone. We desire to continue as the friends of the United States. May I suggest the terms, that all property shall be restored to both sides, and our treaty of 1786 shall be renewed in all its terms. Surely nothing more than this is required."

"Your Majesty's wisdom," soothed Lear, "calms all discord with a quiet word."

"Come back tomorrow and apply to my chamberlain. My prime minister and my admiral will be awaiting you, you may negotiate the details with them, and I will sign it when you are finished." Slimane descended the dais, looked Preble down and up, and then looked into Lear's eyes. "In my country, Mr. Lear, when a military inferior speaks rudely and out of turn, we cut . . . out . . . his . . . tongue."

"Undoubtedly, Majesty," Lear said, bowing, "there are many points on which my country could learn from yours."

Slimane's lips screwed up into something like a smirk, and without further regard of the officers he gathered his robes about him and exited, followed by his suite, and the leopard, as he said something almost wistfully to the one nearest him.

Lear, Preble, and Bliven walked, accompanied by Simpson, back down to the quay between the files of janissaries. "What was that last that he said, as he was leaving?" asked Preble.

"Ah." Lear smiled. "He said that a man like you is a worthy enemy, and therefore better kept as a friend."

"Did he," muttered Preble with some satisfaction. "By God."

"Better than having your tongue cut out, sir," ventured Bliven.

"Hmph!"

"Well, we got what we came for," said Lear. "Morocco will be out of the war. It is worth it to give him his ships back; he'll keep them out of the way. You can be sure, if he thought he could beat us, we would be on our way to the bagnio at this moment."

Preble stooped to step from the quay into the longboat, but stopped with a jerk and grabbed at his stomach. "Shit!" he hissed through gritted teeth.

Bliven stepped forward to help. "Sir?"

"You go first, lad, help me down."

Bliven stepped off, then took a secure grip on Preble's hand and arm and eased him to a seat. "Oh." Preble breathed heavily at last. "Thank'ee."

Bliven marveled. He had long since left off counting damns and hells as profanity, and this was the first really abhorrent word he had heard the commodore utter. He marveled further that for all the nerve Preble had shown in the face of this bloody-handed despot, his ulcer told another story. How much his outer resolves must cost him through the hole in his stomach. "Are you all right, sir?"

Preble nodded. Lear paused to take a farewell of Simpson, as they arranged their next meeting to set down terms for the emperor, then joined them in the longboat, which the bosun's mate pushed off and ordered oars down.

"Sir," said Bliven, "I know I am new to all this, but still it did seem to me that you more than held your own against him."

"Heh!" grumped Preble, happy to get the moment behind him. "You know, I remember I was a little shaver, it was before the war so I must have been about eight. I had been behaving badly, until my father said he was disowning me. He said he had sent for a big Turk to come carry me away in a sack. I thought nothing of it and I carried on. I had no idea that he went down to the docks and made some arrangements. That evening before supper, the front door crashed in and there came this huge Mussulman in a turban, just as black as night, and he was carrying a big burlap sack with an open drawstring. 'Where is he?' he says. 'Where is he?' My parents were sitting in their chairs, never moved a muscle.

"Right away I grabbed up the tongs and snatched a coal out of the fire and thrust it at him. 'I'm not afraid of you,' I says. 'I am not afraid of you.' Right there my parents laughed out loud, and the Turk burst out laughing, they all laughed till the tears ran. And I was standing there with a coal in my tongs ready to brand whoever came near."

"Oh, God." Bliven laughed.

"And, young man, if I was not afraid of these people when I was eight years old, I am goddamned sure not afraid of them now."

Tobias Lear looked toward the ship as it grew closer, a smile creasing his gaunt face.

"Mr. Lear, sir," said Bliven, "this has all been very interesting and

I am grateful to have had a part in it, but I am not certain how you arrived at a satisfactory conclusion."

"Ah." Lear raised a finger. "When dealing with a potential adversary, never present him only with a threat or only with an offer. Best to provide both, first making certain that you can make good on both the threat and the offer. In this case, the commodore was the threat, I was the offer. The result was as you saw. Your enemy will almost always take the offer."

They made fast to the *Constitution*'s boarding ladder. "You go on up, Putnam," said Preble. "I'll be along." Bliven scampered up the angle of the ship's broad tumble home, and made it his first business to search out Preble's cook, and had him prepare an egg and milk, which he took in just as the commodore was settling himself in his cabin.

"Thank'ee," Preble sighed. It was not a full measure of thanks, which could have been taken to admit the growing seriousness of his infirmity. It was a contracted thanks in the new English fashion, that acknowledged the service yet lightened the moment.

For the next several days, Lear shuttled back and forth to Simpson, haggling terms with a deputation of the emperor's divan. At length Preble's wonted impatience began to take him over, nightly asking Lear what was taking so long.

"You must remember, Commodore, we are dealing with Arabs. Terms are almost never final with them. Every new occurrence can raise new obstacles, and everything is negotiable, and renewably negotiable. It is their culture."

"Can I help?" Preble pressed. "How can I help?"

"Be here," Lear assured him. "The presence of your ships here, silent, steady pressure, not too threatening, not too far, lends the weight I need."

. . .

IT TOOK NEARLY TWO WEEKS before Lear boarded the ship with the renewed treaty bearing the emperor's seal and tughra; he related that it had been signed with almost no ceremony at all, as though they were happy to be done with it.

"Thank God!" bellowed Preble. That very afternoon he and Lear wrote out the necessary letters, forwarding the treaty to the government for ratification, Preble outlining his situation, and suggesting that an occasional friendly letter from President Jefferson to the emperor could have its own salutary effect. He summoned Charles Stewart over from the *Siren*, loaded him down with the documents, and dispatched him to Gibraltar.

Preble made ready to sail the next day, but was startled by the arrival of two lighters, loaded to the rails with bullocks, sheep, and fowl, gifts from the emperor. They had lost the light by the time they divided the stock among the ships; morning brought the sight of an assembly gathering along the breakwater, the royal band playing such an exotic air as Bliven had never heard, hundreds of the emperor's lancers sitting on their horses, and they estimated five to six thousand foot soldiers waving in farewell.

As capstans turned and sails dropped, the Tangier fortress saluted them with twenty-one guns, which Bliven was detailed to answer, firing his twelves all around the quarterdeck and reloading and firing nine. Peace, he concluded, provided a much finer pageant than war. Preble lifted his hat in salute as they sailed slowly by as if in review. "What a pretty send-off," Bliven said to Lear as the passed.

"You think that, do you?" said Lear. "You know what that is? That is a show of force. Slimane is telling us, 'You have the sea, but I have the land.' He is saying, 'Good-bye, nice to have seen you, don't push your luck again.'"

Bliven looked again to see if they would seem different with this knowledge, and in a way, they did. He did not wish to be naïve, but neither did he wish to see the world with Lear's cynicism, even when he was right. Knowing him was instructive, but he would be glad to leave him in Algiers.

Less than four hours in a following wind brought them to Gibraltar, where their first sign of trouble was the *Siren*'s pinnace, circling in the harbor until they saw where *Constitution* would anchor, then coming straight for them. Lieutenant Stewart scampered up the boarding ladder as soon as it was dropped.

Preble received him in his sea cabin and instantly perceived Stewart's distress. "Stewart, what is amiss?"

"Sir, I am sorry to report three of my men either deserted when they were onshore or were taken by the British."

"What do you mean 'taken'?"

"Press-ganged, sir. I believe they were taken by force to serve on that big bastard seventy-four you see over there."

"Have you applied to her captain to interview the men?"

Stewart snorted. "He has given us no satisfaction. Unctuous, arrogant, self-important blow of snot."

"Have you applied to Governor Trigge?"

"He will not receive me."

"Well, by God, he will receive me. When did this happen?"

"Last night."

Preble sat and scratched out a note. "Take this to him and wait for a reply."

Stewart returned in an hour and a quarter and handed Preble a folded paper.

Commodore, I regret that I am in possession of no facts relevant to the disappearance, or desertion, of the three seamen from the Siren. You are at liberty to call on H.E. Captain Lord Kington, commanding H.M. ship Hector, now in harbour, and see if you can advance your case there.

Very resp'y.,
Your obedient servant,
Trigge

"Well, fine. Do you have a trumpet in your boat, Stewart?"

"No, sir."

Preble yanked open a cabinet and removed his brass speaking trumpet and followed Stewart out. The pinnace sliced smartly across the harbor to the looming seventy-four, her guns spread over three decks, her bow bearing a grotesque of a massive muscled human figure with the head of a bull. The boarding ladder offered a dizzying climb up to the spar deck, whence they were led down to the great cabin at the stern of the second gun deck, and then into the presence of Captain Lord Arthur Kington, R.N. He was a tall man, an angular man, wearing a powdered wig, though they were falling from fashion, which in Preble's mind lent him a resemblance to the pictures he had seen of Captain Cook.

He heard Preble out placidly, looking down a stunningly long, aquiline nose. "I am sorry, gentlemen," he said at last, "I know nothing of a third man, but two of your men approached one of my officers, claiming that they are subjects of His Majesty and desiring to be brought into my crew. I have done so, according to our regulations, and I regret that I cannot make them available."

There was a smugness in it that Preble mistrusted, as deeply as he mistrusted all English officers. "Why in thunder not? I just want to talk to them."

"That is why we promulgated regulations, to spare our seamen such intimidation."

"Or to prevent them regaining their liberty," swelled Preble. "I want to hear from them that this was their choice, and if it was, so be it."

Kington rose. "I am sorry, I cannot help you. Good day. Bosun!" The door opened. "Conduct these gentlemen back to their boat, if you please."

"Your admiralty will be hearing from our Navy Secretary. I will tell him that you acknowledge having two of the men on board under sequestration and denied a request to interview them. You have not heard the last of this."

Kington smiled. "Again, good day."

The pinnace bore them back to the *Constitution* in silence, until Preble growled, "Goddamned English sons of bitches."

"Sir," said Stewart, "why would not Governor Trigge help you?"

"I don't know. Perhaps he is scared to cross the navy. Did you know well the missing men? Were they the kind to desert?"

"No, sir. Two ordinary seamen and one able. I have had few difficulties with any of the crew."

"Well, I will initiate an investigation, but I hope our men did in fact choose this course for themselves, because if they did not it will likely be years before we can recover them. Damn haughty English bastards."

"Do you want me to go see Trigge?" Lear asked Preble when he came back aboard.

Preble considered it. "No, I thank you. If he was willing or able to help us, he would have responded better to my note. I do not think you would find the English as susceptible to your administration of pressure as was the Moroccan emperor."

"Oh, I can assure you, providing us with enough guns, they would be."

Preble looked at him and saw he was not joking.

"I believe we are unsettling our English cousins," Lear continued, "now that we can deploy squadrons as capable as their own. Give us a few ships of the line, we would unsettle them even more."

"We are only here to fight the damned pirates. You'd think they would be grateful, since they haven't found the masculinity to do it themselves."

"Yes, but the British, like all diplomats, are looking more moves into the future. I think they sense trouble from a truly powerful American navy."

"Good," Preble snorted. "But, hell, now we must get you to Algiers. You should have been there a month ago."

With the emperor's bullocks chewing their cud in a pen rigged on the quarterdeck, and sheep and fowls below, there was no need to top off provisions and they put to sea early in the morning. Desiring to preserve what was left of their good will, Preble as he exited their bay saluted the fort thirteen guns, and was happy to hear them returned.

12.

THE LION'S MOUTH

————◆————

October 1803

A s soon as they were free of the harbor, Preble released the parts of the squadron to the points of the compass for the assignments long agreed upon. From Tangier they passed through the straits; Bliven watched the great white rock as they cruised by, and he was persuaded he could never tire of the sight. Perhaps one day he could show it to Clarity.

It was some five hundred miles due east to Algiers, which with a decent wind they covered in three days at just under eight knots. Lear had already prepared letters to send ashore requesting an audience, and information concerning Joseph Barnes and his daughter. Preble decided to forbear saluting the fort until he knew how they should be received; having not himself been to Algiers before, he could not be certain that the firing would not be taken as hostile.

He need not have worried, for Lear returned to the ship with a summons to an audience at two that afternoon. Preble was not pleased to see the dey's palace high on the hill in the casbah; he was not ill but did not relish such a climb. He straightened his clothes and then had a sudden hope. He leaned out the cabin door. "Mr. Putnam."

"Sir?"

"I do not expect such good luck, but I suppose it might just be possible that Mr. Barnes and his daughter will be released to us today. Ask Mr. Bandy to get dressed and come with us. They are Southerners, as he is. The girl may be helped by having someone who sounds like he is from home."

"Right away, sir."

"Lieutenant Bandy," said Lear when he joined them, "part of the protocol of presenting my credentials is to give the dey some presents. Could you carry this little chest for me?"

"Certainly, sir, yes." Bandy took from him a small, latched mahogany chest the size of a letter box.

They were all in their best as they landed at the foot of the mole, met by a platoon of janissaries and the dey's black chamberlain. "Mr. Jonah, good afternoon."

"Good afternoon, Mr. Lear. How are you?"

"Very well, thank you. May I introduce Commodore Preble, and Lieutenants Bandy and Putnam?"

"Gentlemen, welcome to Algiers. My name is Jonah. I have the honor to serve as chamberlain to His Highness the Dey Mustapha the Sixth ibn Ibrahim."

"Good Lord, you're an American!" exclaimed Sam.

Jonah sagged with a smile and looked away, recognizing the deep Southern accent and what Sam's preconceived notions of him must have been.

"Now, now," said Lear, "Mr. Jonah hears that from almost every American who lands. We really can't ask him to repeat his biography for everybody. It is a long walk, Mr. Jonah. Shall we be off?"

They passed down the arches of the bagnios, the cells emptied for the day's labor, but they all knew what they were, and they entered the warren of rising and turning streets. Sam made his way to Jonah's side. "Forgive me, but do you think you could bear to repeat the story one more time? I am beside myself with curiosity how you came to be here."

"We will turn left at the next corner, gentlemen," Jonah said before turning to look at Sam. "I can tell from your voice you are from deep in the South, is that correct?"

"Yes," said Sam. "From South Carolina."

"Ah." He paused to frame his words. "I and my family were taken by Arab slave traders when I was a small boy. My village was south beyond Timbuktu; they were Moslem, we were not. They took us to the coast and put us on a ship for America, a ship that was more terrible than anything else I can remember. They took us to Virginia, where we were sold. My mother and my brothers and sister were all sold to others, I do not know what became of them. I did not go to a plantation. My master was a ship captain who needed a servant, and I became his cabin boy."

"I am so sorry," interjected Bliven. "That was very wrong and should not have happened to you. We do not all believe in slavery."

Jonah turned and looked at him full in the face. "Thank you, Mr. Putnam, but you may spare me your self-righteousness. The ship that took me to America was from Boston."

Sam shot Bliven a look that should have expressed vindication, but managed only shock.

"At any rate, I sailed with my master; we were taken by the Algerines. The owner of my master's ship failed to ransom him, and he worked as a laborer for seven years before he died in the bagnio."

"So," said Sam, "he became a slave also."

"Life does occasionally mete out a measure of justice, yes. Some men in the palace took pity on my situation. They educated me, and when it was found that I had an aptitude for learning, and I learned to speak Arabic, I was placed in the service of the dey. I rose through his departments. With the greater number of English and Americans at court, my usefulness increased. I became his translator, and now I am his chamberlain."

"Oh, my." Sam began to find himself short of breath, not so much from the climb as from the scope of Jonah's story. "Do you still miss your home?"

"I remember very little of my home."

"What of your home in America?"

Jonah stopped suddenly. "Why ever would I consider America home?" he said and began to walk on.

"Ah." Sam was quiet as they turned to ascend another street before asking, "Do you ever think of escaping?"

"Why would I?"

"Despite your station, you are a still a slave, are you not?"

Jonah stopped again, surprised. "Mr."—suddenly reaching to remember his name—"Mr. Bandy, yes, the one who bandies words, now I can remember. Mr. Bandy, slavery here is a different condition. I saw how the plantation workers lived in Virginia. 'Hoe the corn, yes, Massa.' 'Pick the cotton, yes, Massa.' 'Fried po'k and cornbread, thank you, Massa.' Here, I have a servant, I have a woman, I live in the palace. It has much to recommend it even as a chosen profession." He turned away and led them on.

"Mr. Bandy," said Lear, "at this rate we will never get there. Surely Mr. Jonah has gratified your curiosity."

"Yes," said Sam. "Yes."

And given him much to think about, thought Bliven.

They entered the confused maze of the casbah, and Bliven wondered briefly how he should ever find his way here again without an escort, but as they entered the square before the palace he realized that all the little streets radiated from it. Coming from the harbor, as long as one kept ascending up, one would arrive here, for it was at the top of the hill. Jonah conducted them through the chicane into the cool of the interior and up the marble staircase, and opened twin mahogany doors into a well-appointed and quite Western-looking drawing room. "Gentlemen," said Jonah, "if you will wait here, I will let His Highness know that you are here."

Preble waited until he was gone. "Look here, Lear, we're not going to go through this kneeling business again, are we?"

"Ha. No, the protocol in a dey's court is less severe than with the emperor. Now, mind you, old Mustapha knows his station, and he guards his prerogatives. In fact, it will not surprise me to learn that he feels himself underpaid. Of all the Berber lords, he is the oldest, he's been on his throne the longest. He is not as grand as the emperor, nor as violent as the bashaw in Tripoli, but let me assure you he does not regard himself as their inferior in any respect."

A pitcher of water and glasses reposed on a sideboard, to which they helped themselves, for they were thirsty from the climb and, in truth, nervous of the pending audience. The double doors swung open again and Jonah appeared. "Gentlemen, if you please, His Highness will receive you in the courtyard."

October had begun to tame the heat of the Barbary Coast, and the sunlight in the courtyard was brilliant but not oppressively hot. Led by Jonah, they advanced to the dais in pairs, Preble and Lear followed by Bliven and Sam. Jonah mounted the dais, and at their introduction all the officers snapped to attention and saluted, which the dey acknowledged with an inclination of his head, and then spoke aside to Jonah. "You are welcome, gentlemen. But, tell me, what happened to the commodore from two years ago, Mr. Dale?"

Preble stepped forward. "Mr. Dale is retired, Your Highness, and he lives quietly with his family."

"Ah. A state much to be envied."

Bliven was struck by his age, and his being completely swathed in white cotton. Such simple dress made it the more surprising when he noticed that four of the wrinkled fingers bore magnificent rings. Following the introductions, a motion from Jonah brought another white man to mount the dais, from the rear.

"Mr. Barnes?" said Lear, too soft and cautious for an exclamation, but in great surprise. He appeared well kept, his clothes laundered and pressed, his face shaven and his hair tidy. "Are you all right?"

"Yes, thank you. I am well treated."

"I am Tobias Lear, newly accredited consul to Algiers."

"I am glad you have come. I gather, then, that my letters have reached the right places, and our needs are known, to get on our way to Sicily?"

"Indeed, they have. Your government is undertaking every effort to gain your release."

He saw the dey relate something to Jonah. "Is this not interesting? Algiers finds itself honored with the presence of two American consuls."

"One of whom," Lear rejoined instantly, "I hope will soon be on his way to freedom, and I am here to present my credentials to Your Highness as your new American consul, at your service."

He handed his packet to Jonah, who held it out to the dey, who reached out and touched it. "We are pleased to welcome the new consul of the United States."

"Mr. Bandy?" Lear reached out and took the small mahogany chest from him. "It is my pleasure to present to you these small tokens of the esteem in which my country holds Your Highness, and the friendship of Algiers."

Jonah took it and opened its contents for the dey's inspection, and he glanced inside. "We thank you for these . . . very small tokens indeed, but this is not the tribute that has been long expected."

"Highness?" Lear was surprised that the dey got to the heart of the matter so soon.

"Your last payment of tribute was two years ago. Patiently we have been waiting, relying on our friendship with your country, that you would meet this obligation, to which you previously agreed. Our brother princes of North Africa have not hesitated to take what is due them, from your ships, but we have waited in friendship. May I believe that you have brought this tribute, and it awaits in your beautiful ship that anchors in our harbor?"

Even for a diplomat, Lear was taken aback at his abruptness. "Highness, it is my government's hope to reach a better understanding between our two countries, one that will include the benefits of culture and commerce, and not be dependent upon acts of illegal piracy."

"Mr. Lear, this is not a good beginning. Piracy is an honorable practice of the faithful, that we are permitted to carry out against infidels, to do with them as we choose. We have made this clear many times. We are willing to listen to proposals of a new arrangement, but because you have kept us waiting two years without payment, we now require an additional surety of your good faith."

"What has Your Highness in mind?"

"Some years ago your government accorded to us a frigate as your annual tribute. As I am recognized as the overlord of Tunis and Tripoli, I will be satisfied to be presented with another. He held up his hand suddenly. "Not even one so large and fine as you arrived in, but a serviceable, and equipped, frigate."

Lear swallowed, and Preble bit his lip. "Of course, Your Highness. I do not have the power to grant this request, but I can assure you, I will make your exact desires known to my government."

The dey dropped his head tiredly, flattening his long white beard against his wraps. "Yes, all must begin anew. But we urge upon you, being two years tardy, to act with haste. I am known as a temperate man, but there is an end to my patience."

"I shall be happy to meet with Your Highness's ministers and set down an exact accounting of what would satisfy your requirements, and how we may resume the friendly relations between our countries. But now touching upon the state of Mr. Barnes, and his daughter, who are held hostages . . ."

"We think of them as our guests, Mr. Lear."

"I beg Your Highness to understand that all the usages of international law accord safe passage to diplomats, who are the necessary emissaries who represent their government to another government. Their function is indispensable, and their safety must be guaranteed."

The dey seemed wholly unimpressed. "Mr. Lear, I have learned that in your country you have a principle of business that I believe is a good one. If you begin a course of action that may be dangerous, you can make sure that your affairs will not suffer by paying a sum of money to a man who will bear the risk for you. You call this insurance. The English have been doing this for many years. Are you familiar with what I speak?"

"Very well, sire, yes."

"There was a time when our relations were regular, and friendly. But your country has set us so much in doubt—you have taken the ships of my brother princes, you have compelled a treaty against the interest of my sovereign, the emperor, your warships prowl the sea like lions looking for prey. If I undertake a new round of talks with you, I must have some surety that you are not merely buying time, to bring more warships and do myself and my people harm. Surely this is not beyond your understanding."

Lear stood a little straighter. "Will my continued presence here in Your Highness's court not be insurance enough of our good faith?"

"I have better already," said the dey with a tone of triumph. "I have Mr. Barnes." He gestured behind him, to the top floor of the palace, which featured an overhanging, screened wooden balcony. "And I have his daughter."

Lear flushed. "Your Highness, my government takes the gravest possible exception to threatening innocent civilians—"

"Please. We do not threaten them. As I said, they are our guests, but they shall remain here at our pleasure until we are satisfied of your intentions. We do not single you out for this method. We assure you, if the French or the British behaved in such a threatening manner as you have, sending an entire navy to our waters, we would resort to the same . . . surety."

Without meaning to, Bliven drew in his breath. He was no diplomat, but he had been around enough tough-minded men to know when a situation was taking on a dangerous tint. He leaned forward and said right into Preble's ear, "Well, if he finally arouses the British lion where nobody else has been able to, he may well be sorry for it later."

"What?" The dey held up his hand and brought all else to a close until Jonah told him what the young officer had said, and smiled when he understood.

When the dey finally spoke up on his own accord, addressing them directly, more audibly, his voice was old and soft, and somewhat effeminate. When he looked at Bliven there was a tenderness in his eyes that in a different circumstance one might have seen as possessive. Bliven felt certain that it was his physical qualities that were being appraised, not his bearing, but there was confidence in the old dey's voice. As with the emperor, they learned that he understood more English than he had let on. "You speak very certainly of lions. Have you ever, yourself, seen a lion? Do you know lions, what they can do?"

Bliven had been speaking metaphorically, but had to smile in appreciation that the dey had caught him blustering on a subject that he really knew nothing about. "No. Tell His Highness that I have never, myself, actually seen a lion."

The dey caught him smiling and smirked back. "Would you like to see a lion?"

The American officers looked around among themselves, then to Preble. Any offer of hospitality must surely be a good thing. Preble nodded his assent. "Yes," said Bliven finally. "Yes, we should like that very much."

The dey summoned Jonah closer and whispered privately to him for some minutes, occasionally laughing softly. At length Jonah stepped back and bowed, and the dey made them a gracious gesture to dismiss them.

"There is a menagerie beyond the garden," said Jonah, "if you will come this way."

Thinking that he might not see this ancient courtyard again, Bliven looked around and then up. They were already standing on the second level of the palace, and he saw an outdoor stone stair ascending to the third story, one side of which was an open arcade from which there must be a view down to the city. In front of them, the third story divided, and projecting above it was a kind of mezzanine, not fully a fourth story, with no exterior entry. It had a wooden front and an evident balcony that looked down into the court from a wooden screen, decoratively pierced. As it arrested his eye one of its screens opened on hinges and he realized they were shutters. A veiled woman in red silk looked down on him, and when briefly she lowered her veil he saw she was white, with brown hair that fell about her shoulders. She was large, but quite pretty in the face, and when she was sure that his eyes had met hers, she nodded to him and he made a small bow. Again she lifted her veil and closed the shutter.

"Lieutenant?" It was Jonah's voice. "This way."

He led them to the stone stairway at the side of the courtyard, which they discovered had a mate beneath it that took them back to the first floor. At the bottom a short corridor led to what Bliven took for a banqueting hall, for there were long, low tables, too low to match any chairs, set with silver trays, but he saw rows of cushions set down each side and understood this must be how they dined. This hall opened onto a fine stone veranda enclosed by iron grilles, with a gate that led to a garden of greater tropical splendor of ferns and cycads than he could have imagined. Only after they entered did Bliven notice the wandering presence of small hoofed stock that he took for antelope, browsing in perfect serenity. Moslems, he had come to learn, shared a belief in the Garden of Eden; perhaps this was their representation of it.

"Excuse me one moment, gentlemen." Jonah unlocked and entered what looked like a storehouse. When he emerged he was bearing a short lance, impaled on the end of which was a joint of animal flesh— he could not discern what joint—weighing about twenty pounds. Jonah handed it to Bliven. "Come. Would you care to serve the first course, Lieutenant?"

At the far end of the garden, but screened by greenery so they could not see it, were four large cages, each housing an enormous maned male lion.

The one they approached had been lying on one side, but with his head up, watching their every move with amber eyes that moved hardly at all, but as they came near he pushed easily to his feet with a growl that seemed to make the very gravel dance on the path. Bliven had never heard a sound so low, so ominous. The floor of the lion's cage was a yard above the ground, so that when he stood his belly was at their eyes' level, and Bliven found himself looking up at his dark brown mane as he shook it. The mane extended down to a straight dark brown fringe under his belly, flecked with straw. When they were fifteen feet away he roared once, briefly but unnerving, and so deep that Bliven felt it as much as he heard it. The lion faced them, stock-still, as they came up to the bars.

"If you please, Mr. Putnam," said Jonah. "He is hungry."

Swallowing, Bliven inched nearer, selecting a point not nearest the lion but to his front, and, standing well back, slipped the meat through the bars on the point of the lance. In the flash of half a second the lion lashed out, its tawny paw opening out to the size of a dinner plate, extending claws the size and shape of the dagger he now kept in his cabin, and raked the meat from the end of the spear. In reflex Bliven started back and gasped. With a satisfied grunt the lion seized the flesh in his jaws, exposing straight yellow teeth that could have bitten into a man as easily as a doll. He circled to the back of his cage and lay down, and leisurely tore strips from the mass of meat.

Jonah gestured to the caged monster. "Well, Lieutenant Putnam, now you have seen a lion. What do you think?"

Bliven shook his head. "I am undone. He is magnificent. I had no idea, the size and power of such a beast. Part of me is sorry to see him caged up like this, but my God, what a terror he would be if he were free."

"I am glad to hear you say so," said Jonah. "Because you see, gentlemen officers, there are in this world some beasts that you don't want to let loose into the world. It is best to keep them fed, to keep them . . . pacified. I will wager that your commodore and your consul take my meaning, even if it escapes you."

"We understand perfectly," Preble said sharply.

"Very well, gentlemen officers, and we hope you will continue to bear in mind that the British lion is not the only one to be feared in this world. Now"—he led them to a wooden gate in the wall that he pulled up on a latch and swung open—"if you turn right down this street you will come to the palace square, and you can find your way down from there. Mr. Lear, no doubt you will want to go back to the ship and collect your things. Next time you come, we can help you find someone to get your consulate in order and you can move in. Good day to you."

He closed the gate behind them, leaving them alone to ponder the day's events and how they might best proceed.

13.

NAPLES

———◆———

1803–1804

Back on the *Constitution*, Preble poured them all glasses of sherry and indicated seats around his table. "Well, Lear, what are you going to do?"

Lear shook his head. "There is nothing I can do for poor Barnes, at the moment. But his is one case where time can be on our side. It always takes at least two months to send a letter home and receive a reply. And I can stall a few weeks longer, I can haggle for a couple of weeks just over their initial demands, so each step of the process can take three months. For all we know, you could sweep the sea clean in three months."

Preble pressed his lips together. "Don't think I won't try."

"A clean defeat would solve everything."

"Well, first we have to square things with the Sicilians. I know they're supposed to be putting together supplies and gunboats for us. Bandy, go find us a chart. How long do you think till we can get to Palermo?"

"Actually, Commodore," said Lear, "Palermo is out of it. The Bonapartists have suffered a defeat, and the king has moved his court back to Naples. But"—he shook his head and shrugged uncertainly—"by the time you get there, who knows? Naples has traded hands twice already. You might stop at Palermo on your way there and get the information before you go all the way to Naples."

"Indeed?" Preble held up the bottle of wine to offer more; Lear nodded and scooted his glass over. "Besides, if your cook has a use for marsala wine, that is a capital place to lay in a stock of it."

"What about you, Lear? You think you will be safe here?"

Lear made a dismissive "Pah!" with his lips. "I think so. He certainly won't harm me as long as he has a chance to make a new fortune. He'll be expecting presents—a chest of gold and silver, a nice gilt coach." He pointed a finger playfully at Preble. "A new frigate."

"Over my rotting body," said Preble darkly.

"Besides, I can work my way back into the diplomatic corps here. We all look out for each other, just as they have all been protesting Barnes's detention, although they have taken no action. Anything too outrageous would complicate his ties to the other countries. So in sum, yes, I think I will be fine."

Bliven marveled again at the calculating Lear. Seemingly he could summarize in an instant who was involved and what their stake was, what moves they might possibly make or why they would not, what possibilities had already been exhausted and what remained. If he ever acted without an honorable motive, he could be a terrible force for ill.

"And what of Mrs. Lear? Shall you keep her here?"

"Oh, yes, I have no doubt she will be welcomed into the diplomatic community."

"Where is Mrs. Lear?" asked Preble. "I've not seen her since we returned."

"Resting in her cabin. She sends her greetings."

"Is she game for all this?"

"Very much so," Lear said. "She is a spirited young lady."

Yes, thought Bliven. Lear could use her Washington name to knot himself into the good opinion of the other consuls and depend on her presence to possibly shield him from the worst that the old dey could do. Yes, she could be very useful to him. God, he thought, now he's got me thinking like him.

Preble poured himself another glass of sherry. "What do you know of the American consul to the Sicilies? I guess he's had to stay over indefinitely while Barnes"—he slapped his hand down on the cork to secure it in the bottle—"has been corked up."

Lear appreciated the play. "Ha! Yes, David Barton, he's a good man, everybody likes him. I admit there are intrigues within the diplomatic service"—he looked up dubiously over the rims of his spectacles—"but no more so than in the navy."

"Psh!" huffed Preble. "It's a nest of snakes then."

Lear smiled briefly. "But Barton is very intelligent, very attentive to his duties, and he is a real, what the French call a bon vivant. You will guess this when you meet him, for he weighs at least twenty-five stone—the more noticeable because he is not very tall. He and his wife, Susan, are well matched, for she has the same appearance, but they appear healthy and are widely known to be kind and hospitable. This has helped us, for his nature coincides exactly with the king, who has made him a particular favorite. We owe Barton a great deal, for it is he who secured the king's permission to borrow those gunboats and bomb scows you so covet to use against Tripoli."

As he spoke, Preble began unconsciously to rock just a little forward and back. His stomach hurt, and he knew he must drink no more wine that night. "That is very useful to know. I shall know exactly how to proceed with him."

Bandy returned from the chart room with maps of the central Mediterranean, of Sicily and the west coast of Italy, with an inset for the Bay of Naples. They picked up their glasses and he spread them out. After several seconds Preble said, "Well, Bandy, what do you make of it?"

"With a decent wind, four days to Palermo, if we stop there, and from there"—he looked at the chart again—"a day and a half north to Naples."

"Well, either or both," said Preble. "Better than going via Messina, eh, Putnam? Hard straits to pass."

"Yes, sir." There was no need to add that they were the origin of the myth of Scylla and Charybdis, the crashing rocks and the whirlpool of *The Odyssey*, almost as treacherous to navigate in modern times as ancient.

"Well, Lear, I suppose you and your lady had best pack. We'll put you ashore in the morning, and we'll leave with the first usable wind."

They raised Capo Boeo on the evening of the third day, and anchored the night at Marsala so as not to run afoul of the Egadi Islands that pepper the west coast of Sicily by running them at night. It should have been an easy day on to Palermo fifty miles to the east, but fighting stiff north winds, it was a hard haul instead of two and a half days. They learned in Marsala that the royal court had indeed settled itself in Naples, but put into Palermo anyway for shelter, for there was no fighting this wind, which in the north-northeast heading required for Naples would have been a half-gale dead in their faces. Like the ports of North Africa, Palermo was on its north coast but its sheltered bay faced the east, a perfect location to lay to and await a favorable wind.

In their two days there, Preble was able to learn no details of the aid that was to be forthcoming from the Sicilian government—number and types of boats and ordnance. He obtained a translator and was able to find the district naval office, but he had no hard facts, only that he had heard the flotilla being lent the Americans was to assemble not in Palermo but in Syracuse. This was a minor problem, for the navy office agreed to send American vessels on to join him if they showed up there. He also learned which were the finest merchants for wines and cheeses, and he learned that the Italians have a weakness for preserved meats and sausages. He expended thirty-five dollars of his own money on a selection.

He held the basket of delicacies firmly in his lap as he was being rowed back to the ship, and it was a hard job, for though sheltered, the bay was choppy. He would have his chef dress it all up nicely as a present for their consul and his wife.

But damn, he thought, he would have to traverse the Strait of Messina after all. In a moment he consoled himself: Syracuse was closer to striking at Tripoli, and that was the most important thing.

It took two more days for a southerly morning wind to push briskly off the island and into the Tyrrhenian Sea. Naples lay two hundred miles north-northeast. This wind might push them at seven knots; if they weighed anchor without delay, they would be in Naples by noon the next day.

Bliven had seen drawings of the Bay of Naples in geography books, so he had a previous idea how things must generally look. As they approached he saw a capacious, trapezoidal basin fifteen miles along the coast, with the great Mount Vesuvius in the center of it. In the northern, obtuse angle lay Naples, and in the southern, acute angle lay the ancient city of Pompeii. People had been digging there for forty years, writing about it incessantly, how it was preserved in a moment of time. Bliven was ravenous with curiosity about it; surely God could not be so cruel as to let him come this close and not feast his eyes on the place. The actual sight of the bay exceeded his expectations beyond measure; he thought it the most beautiful prospect of a coast he had ever seen. And this, he thought, this is where Pliny anchored when he described the destruction of Vesuvius in the first century.

"What do you think, Putnam?" Preble's voice surprised him from behind and he realized his reverie must have been obvious.

"I am amazed."

"I see you are. But pray come back to the present long enough to lower a ladder for that boat you have not seen approaching."

"Yes, sir. I'm so sorry." He saluted and tended to it before he could be reproached further.

"I will be in my cabin."

Twenty minutes later Bliven knocked on his door and presented the Bartons' steward with an invitation to dinner. If they could be on the wharf by six, he said, there would be a carriage for them. Preble accepted with gusto and sent the steward away with the basket he prepared at Palermo.

The interjection of a carriage into the invitation complicated things. Edwards was his first lieutenant, but since making Bliven his aide that line had blurred, not in duties but in preference. A carriage meant four spaces, and he wished to give the surgeon and the chaplain a time ashore. He could not take Edwards and Bliven both, but as his aide he chose the latter and determined to make it up to Edwards in some other way.

The consulate proved to be a solid large house in a fashionable district, something on the order of a small villa. The palaces of Tangier and Algiers were grander, but this was the finest residence built in the Western mode of architecture that Bliven had ever found himself in. The casement windows had marble sills and surrounds, the staircase was of marble, the floors, where not carpeted, were delicately inlaid.

Consul Barton, rather than waiting for them to be announced, greeted them at the door in the heartiest manner. He was wearing white knee breeches of the old fashion, a red-violet waistcoat, and a dress coat of straw yellow, which caused Bliven to wonder if his intention was to draw people's attention away from his girth by his colorful attire. "Hello, sir! You are the commodore? Delighted. You sent that basket of comestibles with your compliments, for which we are highly, highly grateful. So grateful, in fact, that you shall sample them straightaway!"

"I thank you, sir," protested Preble, "but I brought those for your use and enjoyment!"

Barton laid a hand on his back and conducted him into the drawing room. "Yes, I know, but listen, you have caught me in a little subterfuge. We are going to serve you a real Italian dinner, and that begins with what they call antipasto—cold meats, olives, and the like—and your arrival caught us with the pantry embarrassed. So you see, your arrival was perfectly timed!"

All this he said in such a disarming manner that Preble laughed—it occurred to Bliven that although the commodore could smile, and joke, and tell a funny story, he had never seen him laugh—and held his hands up helplessly. "You have me, sir. We shall eat of them with mighty curiosity, for much is new to me."

"That I do not believe." Barton smiled roundly. "Every officer who visits has remarked on the fine table you set, and the magic which you sometimes employ to do it."

Preble looked aside. "Yes. Well, then, much will be new to them, eh?" Never had Bliven seen him so disarmed and put at ease.

Mrs. Barton entered wearing a gown of deep blue silk, trimmed with white lace, and a parure of small sapphires to match, sparkling at a distance, but the stones small enough that Bliven felt assured they must be genuine. Of Mrs. Barton, Bliven judged that her figure, ample as described, was one that benefitted from previous fashions, for skirt hoops were so broad that all Susan had to do was wear a smaller one. With the flowing new Empire gowns, she could no longer blend right in. Still, her seamstress had lowered that high new bustline so she was gaming the eye.

The introductions made, Barton had begun steering them all into the dining room when they were interrupted by a knock at the door. Bliven turned and saw a maid answer, and beyond the door he saw a footman in the most astonishingly formal livery. The maid curtsied as she took a letter, which Susan opened, and caught her breath twice quickly. "Well, gentlemen, it seems that your ship's arrival was noticed from the royal palace. Get hold of yourselves, the king and queen will be joining us. Please continue your conversation in the drawing room while we reset the table."

"Are they staying for dinner?" asked Barton.

"You know them, they come and go at a whim. Best to be prepared to serve them."

"Quite right, quite right."

To Bliven the visit was a blur. The footman must have stepped straight off the carriage, for the Bartons greeted the couple in the hall not two minutes later. Susan had mastered a full court curtsy, and both king and queen kissed her on both cheeks; Barton, in his turn, bowed deeply, after which the king shook his hand as vigorously as a commoner.

They sat to dinner, the king eating heartily of the antipasto, the quality of which he enthusiastically endorsed.

"It is from the commodore, Your Majesty. He brought it to us from Palermo."

"So"—the king nodded and determined to try his limited English on them—"you, waste no time, to find what is good, no?"

"I try, sir, I try. Life is too short not to enjoy a good table."

That was a little beyond him, but Barton translated. *"Ah, molto bene!"* said the king. *"Molto bene!"* He also downed a large portion of the beef main course, while the queen, although she evinced an eager appetite, ate with a practiced daintiness.

After the beef the king's hands flew up. "Ah! *Ci scusiamo!* I fear, we must leave you now." All rose with him, although he waited no ceremony and allowed the queen only time to again accept Susan's curtsy and kiss her before they vanished as suddenly as they had come.

It was Barton who broke the silence: "So you will understand why some people refer to him as Il Signor Mistral. He blows in and out like a storm," and they resumed their dinner with a laugh.

The subject of pirates did not broach itself until then. "Well, Commodore," said Barton, "I understand you are finally going to rid us all of this pirate menace."

"I am going to try my level best, sir. Our country has finally given us the means to do it, and the sooner done, the less expense."

"Quite right," said Barton. "And it is about time."

"Yes," said Preble. "A worthy point, because what I have trouble understanding is why this situation has been tolerated for two hundred years or more. These are pirates! Hang 'em, don't buy them off!"

"You know," said Barton, "I'm not sure you appreciate that piracy here is an ancient thing. And piracy here has a different, well, meaning here, much different. Now, we're Americans, when we think of pirates, we think of Blackbeard, and skull and crossbones, and all that, outlaws on the run. It's nothing like that here. Here, it goes back at least as far as ancient Rome. Julius Caesar was captured by Cilician pirates and had to be ransomed."

Bliven suddenly held up a finger. "And Caesar told them he was insulted that they didn't demand a bigger ransom, did he not?"

"He did," Barton said approvingly. "I am glad you know that story. Piracy here is ancient, and then when Mohammedanism came along, the Moslems consider it their right to enslave anyone who doesn't belong to their religion. Do you know how many hundreds of thousands of white European Christians have been abducted, either at sea or in coastal raids? They had to be ransomed, or else they were sold into slavery, or worked to death. Good heavens, the Catholic Church even started a holy order—the Mathurins, they're called—whose only job was to raise money for their release. And the women—well, sailing on the Mediterranean has always been a risk. That Mozart fellow even wrote an opera about that, *The Abduction from the Seraglio*—that's a fancy name for a harem."

Bliven's mind went back to the palace in Algiers and the wooden shutters.

Barton continued, "Now, the main reason it goes on is the European countries discovered it was cheaper to pay the Moors to leave their ships alone than to fight them. So piracy has become an accepted state policy for generations. I think people in the future will look back on this and wonder how they had so little character."

"Well, I'm a simple sailor," said Preble, "but when I look at a map, I see one color from the Bosporus through the Levant down into Arabia and across North Africa." His hand made the sweep of the map in the air. "The map says Ottoman Empire, and if that's the case, why not carry the issue straight to the source? Why not send a fleet to Constantinople and deal with the sultan as we dealt with that so-called emperor in Tangier?"

Barton waved his glass expansively. "That would do you no good. The Ottoman Empire is but loosely put together. It has many component parts, and each one has a good deal of autonomy. Those four states of the Barbary Coast pretty well do as they please. As long as they send their taxes and tributes to the sultan in Constantinople, he lets them run their own shows, and everyone remains too polite to mention that the central government is too weak to enforce its will on them in any case."

"So the empire is crumbling?" asked Preble.

"Well, no, or if it is, it has been crumbling for centuries. I think it would be more accurate to say that everyone accepts a certain amount of chaos in the provinces as the price they pay to be able to continue calling it an empire."

"Who is the head man?"

"Now the sultan himself, Selim the Third. He is not a bad man, truth be told. He is a poet and a musician, he reads philosophy. And he is a reformer. He has opened Western-style training schools for army and navy officers, and modernized the civil administration. He wants to bring his country into the nineteenth century, but he's got powerful opposition, and he has to keep them placated."

"Who?" asked Bliven.

"His clergy, for one. For the Mohammedan mullahs, the clock stopped a thousand years ago. They feel threatened by anything modern. But it's his own elite troops, the janissaries, who are much more dangerous. They have their own sources of taxes and influence; they hate the new military organization and refuse to give in to it, and above all else, they form the palace guard, so the Sultan has to keep them satisfied or he can lose his own head. Janissaries killed his grandfather, as they have killed a number of sultans over the years."

Preble nodded. "There would seem to be precedents for that in this part of the world. Look how many caesars were killed by their own Praetorian Guard." The commodore's sideways glance at Bliven sufficed as thanks for the loan of Suetonius, and Bliven had the good sense to keep quiet.

"Very similar," Barton said. "A very similar circumstance, indeed. You are a student of history, Commodore Preble?"

"Somewhat."

"Perhaps you will have time to visit the excavation at Pompeii. Something new comes out of the ground every day, seems like. Some of it quite shocking." Bliven noticed Susan smile and turn away with a blush. Barton wiggled his fingers. "Fertility gods," he said quietly, "that kind of thing."

"Regrettably, I think not," said Preble as he began to tire. "Perhaps one day when we don't have a war to fight." Bliven's heart sank.

BAY OF NAPLES
OCTOBER 23RD, 1804

My dear Miss Marsh,

With matters between us having advanced so far by the time I last departed Litchfield, I daily feel myself blessed so far above other young men, perhaps equally deserving, that I sometimes worry whether my good fortune and happiness have come at the expense of some other. Is

there but some finite amount of happiness in the world, I wonder, and
does one man's excess of joy decree a greater sadness for another?

Such a subject is perhaps fitted to explore in your novel. I have not
forgotten your novel, nor your original commission to relate to you
such adventures as I have had that may bear upon it. I feel that I may
properly address myself to you under this proviso tonight, for I have
dined with a king!

Our passage from Boston to Europe was uneventful, in that we
suffered no calamities, but I should rather say that our crossing itself
was an event. O, that you could see our frigate when she is under full
sail, crushing the swells beneath us, the topgallants and royals so high
above us they should as well be clouds that had caught on the spars.
The commodore has made himself a hero to the men, for in a night fog
off Cádiz he was challenged by a British vessel and ordered to heave to
and send a boat. Instead, he swore them out in the most seamanlike
fashion and made ready to fire, causing them to relent and send a boat
instead. The gun crews gave him three cheers and now I am certain
would follow him anywhere. They call themselves "Preble's boys" and
glory in it—a very large lesson, if my opinion is consulted, in how to
command men.

Our first business was in Tangier, with the object of pacifying
that state to simplify dealing with the others. There the emperor of
Morocco (he calls himself emperor although it appears a preciously
poor country to boast an emperor) dealt very highly with the
commodore and the consul, but the presence of our whole squadron in
force in his harbor caused him to tune his fiddle to a friendlier key. In
negotiating the treaty, their prime minister began by wanting money,
ships, even jewels and delicacies of food as part of the consideration.
I do not know how much of this Mr. Lear conceded, or what

inducements he did employ, but the emperor took himself out of the war straightaway and demanded no more tribute. As it is Morocco that commands the Atlantic coast of Africa, our commerce should be safe in that sphere, as long as His Imperial Majesty believes that our ships have the capacity to reduce his ports to rubble—and as long as we take care that in fact we can do so.

Cannons were fired as we left Tangier—but only as we exchanged salutes in friendship. I think we must all have felt invincible—

You will be surprised to learn that among the lieutenant officers now aboard the Constitution, I am the oldest but for two. The navy stands in such terrible need of men that they will accept almost anyone. When the commodore saw that some of his officers were ancient fossils of fifteen years, he muttered such oaths and spells that you might doubt his religion. I feel quite certain that the secretary of the navy will hear of his displeasure. Yet do I perceive that here, in the coming months, do I but modestly distinguish myself in the coming operations, I may come home a lieutenant commandant, at eighteen! We shall see!

We called at Algiers to deposit the new consul there, Mr. Lear, late personal secretary to President Washington, and we surveyed conditions at Tunis and Tripoli. There we were informed of the willingness of the Two Sicilies to contribute to the war—gunboats, supplies, men—but we had to come to Naples to fetch them.

A boat came out to us from the American consul, a Mr. Barton, and his wife, inviting the officers to dinner. I know this gave some pause to the commodore, for when the last squadron was here under Morris, they did little else but attend dinner parties, and Mr. Preble is anxious to leave a better mark. But I do not believe that Mr. Preble's reputation could be made to suffer by indulging in some society, certainly not after his being praised by Nelson himself. Our party was the commodore, the surgeon, the chaplain, and myself. I went in my capacity as the commodore's aide, but by seniority he should have taken his first lieutenant, so I hope it causes no resentment.

The consul's house we would not call a palace, but it is very grand by our standards, steps of marble, floors of wood laid in the most imaginative parquet, and most brilliantly colored rugs. We had almost commenced with the first course (for society here is so polite that they eat in stages) when a messenger pounded on the door, with the intelligence that we were about to be honored with an informal visit from Their Majesties, thus dinner was delayed a few moments. The king is a great lover of ships and the sea—he had seen our frigate enter the harbor and anchor, and lost no time to gratify his curiosity. So they dined with us most readily.

The queen is Maria Carolina, poor, unhappy woman, the sister of the Austrian emperor. How strange to think of a queen as unhappy, for not everyone will feel sorry for a queen. After Their Majesties retired, Mrs. Barton related to us that it is well known that the king and queen do not love each other, and that she married him out of a sense of duty, her brother desiring an alliance with the Sicilies. One suspects that this duty must not be altogether disagreeable, for indeed she has given him eighteen children. Half of them have died before the age of five, as related by Mrs. Barton, so that does excite a great natural pity for her.

Her sister was Marie Antoinette, who lost her head in Paris a number of years ago. Therefore the queen despises anything French, and anywhere two or more people can be found plotting against Napoleon, there will she be, in spirit if not in person (but, I hear, often in person). That she finances many schemes herself I do not doubt, for *even though she and her husband have waged a ruinously expensive war against the Bonapartes, they maintain themselves in a luxury that you would find fantastical, and of which I hope your stout New England sensibility would disapprove. To dinner the queen wore a necklace of diamonds and rubies, the smallest of which were the size of cooked beans, all cleverly cut, and they flashed like fire. I think, Miss Marsh, of your own inclination toward charity, and I wonder, if the queen shortened her necklace by two inches, if she could feed the poor of Naples for—what—a year?*

And then there is her husband. The Sicilian king, called Ferdinand III, is a disreputable sneak of an old man who invades Naples to get his throne back every time the French are defeated, and flees every time they win a victory. The last time he ran away it was his good fortune to have Lord Nelson in the harbor, and the whole royal family escaped smoothly on the Vanguard, 74 guns. Also he is the most famously ugly man—set aside king—on the continent, and his nose is of such a dimension that when he sneezes, it must be heard from Gela to Palermo, and probably sets Mount Aetna into eruption.

Curiously, this awful man made us feel perfectly at home. You see, according to Mr. Barton, he was never meant to be king, for he was a third son. But the old king's eldest son became imbecile, the second son left to become king of Spain, and that left poor Ferdinand, whose education had been neglected. He had been left to grow up on the wharves with the fishermen and their wives. He learned to love hunting and fishing and gambling, and, let us say, other sports—in Connecticut he could not be elected alderman. Yet he became king at the age of eight, and his prime minister, a man whose cleverness never bent toward virtue, further ignored the king's education to keep power in his own hands. The queen bye and bye got rid of him because, as

*she thought, if anyone was to control the king, it must be she—ah!
Such a nest of intrigues you never saw, and how it makes me thank
God for our own revolution, that we threw off kings and their
trappings. And just think if our cause had failed, what we would
have, King George being now famously lunatic.*

*But I lost my story—that will not help you get published. The king
made us feel welcome, because he grew up having no royal manners.
The people call him by two names: One is Il Nasone (for the obvious
reason), and the other is Il Lazzarone, because he spent his youth
among Neapolitan peasants. So his manner is thoroughly hearty, and
so lacking in court etiquette—and thus does not require it of others—
that you would think him a boor even at one of Miss Pierce's socials.
His humor is crude but warm-hearted; he belches and he swears. And
forgive my telling you this, but I must, for Mr. Barton nearly fell out of
his chair trying to relate it—when hosting guests in the royal palace,
if the king farts, he then scolds his dogs. He has done this for so long
that now, whenever he breaks wind, the poor dogs run under chairs,
thinking they have done something wrong, and guests in the room
actually believe that one of the dogs has done the thing—or else are
wise enough to pretend it.*

*There. Now I fear I have done it, pray do not be offended. The only
way to refine such a letter to be suitable for a young lady's eyes would
be to leave out those things that give shape and edge and blood to the
world. I do not perceive that you are cut from that cloth, nor that this
is what you would want of me. Am I wrong? If I am wrong, I do not
fear that you will be too shy to tell me so.*

*Also at this dinner we learned somewhat of the enemy we are to
fight, the bashaw of Tripoli, and against such a heathen prince it
would thrill any Christian sailor to give battle. We have seen to our*

business in Tangiers and Algiers and Tunis, which leaves our principal
foe, Tripoli, to face us alone. It may take some time to teach this
beastly miscreant a lesson. Therefore, if you agree to respond to this,
as I warmly hope you will, you may address it to me in care of the
United States Consul in Naples.

We ourselves make for Syracuse in the morning—the king,
whatever criticisms one may otherwise level at him, is proving a great
friend, and supplying us with gunboats, mortars, powder, &c., to aid
in the fight. He does not keep his main naval strength in Naples, as
there is too much danger from Bonaparte, but he declares we shall
find all ready for us in Syracuse—ah, that famous ancient city, my
anticipation at seeing it, after so much reading about it, is such that I
fear I shall wander the streets searching out the house of Archimedes,
when of course it must have crumbled to dust centuries ago! One hears
that there is little left of the city, which indeed is why the commodore
chose it. Palermo or Messina have many more comforts, but he equates
this with distractions for officers and crew, and he prefers that our
thoughts stay constant upon our duty.

This letter is sent with the best wishes for your health and
happiness, from

> Your very affectionate servant,
> Bliven Putnam, Lieut.,
> U.S.N.

THEY STOOD OUT FOR SYRACUSE the next morning, south-southeast
under full sail; the sun was setting just as they raised Stromboli, which
was a stroke of luck, for the dull glow that issued from its crater

warned them clear as effectively as a lighthouse. Preble began to shorten sail, as he wanted to approach the Strait of Messina at least an hour after sunup. Messina the city and the harbor lay some miles beyond the most treacherous obstacles, so he could not put in for a pilot. He accepted that the danger and the responsibility were his.

He put Bandy at the wheel as they approached, and Bliven offered to go aloft and spot for them. "By God, thank you, Mr. Putnam, I am relieved. But be warned. Boys, the wind is with us, and as we get close it may increase perhaps threefold, for it is being forced between the mountains. Be careful up there. Mr. Bandy, you must hold this course. If the whirlpool is running you will see it come up on the port bow. Putnam will call down to you when he sees it."

"Yes, sir, I will."

"But you must keep this course until you could piss your pants. Once the straits open up on your right, you must make a starboard turn and come due west until you are further instructed.

"Look lively now, Putnam."

Going aloft was not Bliven's favorite thing. He did not have the deadly dread of heights that some men have, but the combination of height and roll and the sight of men reduced to the size of monkeys on the deck was an ill combination in his mind. But he must not think about it. He mounted the netting and climbed the ratlines, carefully and one at a time but not in a frightened way, to the fighting foretop, then out to the side and up the second ratline to the tiny swaying masthead. In it he found a ruddy young sailor whom he barely knew. "Well, we could be in for quite a ride the next hour," he said.

"Yes, sir, Lieutenant, that's what I hear."

"You game for it?"

"I am if you are, sir."

"Good man." *Good man, indeed,* thought Bliven. He was not about to admit how glad he was for company up here. Alone he might lose his nerve, but he had learned never to do so in front of the men. "What is your name?"

"Harrison, sir."

"Well, Harrison, here we go."

With his sharpest observation, Bliven could barely make out the tree line on the Calabrian coast dead ahead, when he discerned turbulence well ahead off the port bow. He raised his glass, and only in the magnification did he see it, a great spinning black hole in the sea, and he saw it just as he felt the ship lurch ahead in the compression of wind and current behind them. Of all the things he had seen since he had gone to sea, this was the only one that truly frightened him, truly turned his bowels to water as he witnessed the mighty power of the ocean. Gripping the handrail, he shouted down, "Whirlpool! Two points off the port bow!"

"How far?" shouted Preble.

"A mile and a half!" At least he hoped it was that far. He looked to his right, praying to see the Sicilian coast open away and give them room to turn. He could see it ahead, but a turn now would ground them.

"A point to starboard, Mr. Bandy," said Preble. "We can give it a little more room."

"One point to starboard, aye, sir."

A minute and a half later they heard Bliven shout down again. "Turbulent water, one thousand yards off the port bow." Bliven looked pleadingly at the Sicilian coast and saw it recede, showing blue water off the starboard bow. He spun back to his left; he needed no glass now to see the black whirlpool sucking an endless spin of water down into its depths. "Whirlpool! One mile off the port bow!"

"Start your turn, Mr. Bandy, gently."

"Aye, sir." Sam's expression never betrayed any emotion, yet he gave himself away.

"I said gently, Mr. Bandy, you'll have us on the rocks."

"Aye, sir." He stopped the wheel in a fifteen-degree starboard turn, squeezing the blood from his fingers before he would turn any sharper.

Sam had determined not to look but could not help himself. Even without the benefit of being aloft, he could see it, heaving piles of foam for more than a thousand yards before the whirl sucked them down.

"Steady, Mr. Bandy."

"Aye, sir."

Preble watched the Sicilian shore recede. "Very well, thirty degrees starboard turn, Mr. Bandy, come to due west."

"Thank Christ, sir!"

It took Preble so by surprise that he bellowed out laughing and couldn't stop, until at length he coughed and grabbed his stomach. "Mr. Putnam, come down from there!"

"Aye, sir! Well, Harrison, I thank you for your company." Only then did he notice the sailor's eyes shut tight, his knees shaking, his very white hands gripping the handrail. "Harrison!"

"Sir?"

"It's all right, we're through." Suddenly Bliven was glad that Lieutenant Sterett was no longer around. He would probably have hanged the boy.

On his way to gunboats being gathered in Syracuse, Preble had little desire to stop in Messina, but put in long enough to see if any of his ships happened to be there and was surprised to see *Nautilus* undergoing minor repairs. He sent word to Somers to follow him to Syracuse when he was able, and pressed on. It was seventy miles, and propelled by the shooting winds through the strait and four-knot current, they reached it by dusk, discovering the *Enterprise* already there. Bliven took great pleasure in seeing her again, now under Isaac Hull, but was glad to be serving where he now was.

He had made it a habit to be on deck whenever they entered a port that was new to him, and as they passed over the breakwater into the harbor of Syracuse, he squinted into the sunset and tried to imagine where the fortress would have been, from where Archimedes beamed his deadly mirrors down on the Roman fleet. Fitting, he thought, that he should ponder this while shielding his eyes from such a glare. He retired early, for he had drawn the next day's morning watch, and he did not see *Nautilus* follow them into the harbor and anchor next to *Enterprise*.

THEY WERE NOW WELL INTO AUTUMN, and the chill was pronounced. Bliven was on the quarterdeck, coffee already within him—gratefully, for the cold made him sleepy—to start his watch. At six bells, the sun just rising over a still Ionian Sea, the quiet was shattered by two pistol shots that echoed across the bay. He judged the general direction, pulled out his glass, and saw six men on the shore, just outside the city walls. He made out a navy cutter pulled up onto the beach, and he no sooner determined that they must be fighting a duel than Preble came boiling up from below.

"Give me that." He yanked the glass from Bliven's hand and peered through it intently. Even as he squinted, the morning quiet was split by the cracks of two more shots, and he saw one of them fall. "God damn it, I knew it, I knew it!" He spun around. "Bosun!"

"Sir?"

"Get the longboat and rowers into the water. Mark over there by the city wall? Bring those officers to me without delay. If one of them is dead, bring me his body! Take the lieutenant of marines with you and disarm them."

Bliven was relieved for the forenoon watch but stayed on deck as the longboat returned and he lowered the boarding ladder for them. Stephen Decatur, who now commanded the *Enterprise*, came up first, then others; last among them was the famously devout Richard Somers from the *Nautilus*. There was a bloodstained patch at his right hip, on which he limped heavily, and a large bloody bandage compressed his upper right arm. Johnson, the commodore's clerk, saw them coming and rapped on the sea cabin door to announce them; they filed in without pausing.

All Bliven heard for the next quarter-hour was the thunder of Preble's rage: "God damn it, Somers, you were going to fight them all? You epic idiot, you prince of fools! Were you not aware that Decatur is the best shot with a pistol in the navy?"

"Apparently not that good, sir. It was Lieutenant Decatur that wounded me in the hip; he hit nothing vital."

"Why, you goddamned gull, that is his signature! Every man he has ever dueled he has shot in the ass! And you, Decatur, remove the smile from your dainty face or I will do it for you! Decatur, you of all people, sir! Your first tour was cut short when we had to send you home after your little altercation with that British officer. Damn you, you are a good fighter and you can be a good officer, sir, but your lack of self-control is costing us your services!"

"If I may, sir." Decatur reached into a waistcoat pocket. "A copy of my letter to Lieutenant Somers, attesting my regard for him, apologizing for any words that were meant only in fun, and urging him to reconsider his determination to fight me, or the gentlemen who had moved him to think it proper to challenge them all."

He laid the letter on Preble's desk, but the commodore did not pick it up. "Nevertheless, you fought him! And you, Somers, why was this not good enough for you?"

"A man can only be pushed so far," swelled Somers. "Their abuse had—"

"Oh, shut up!" shouted Preble. "Anything you can say I have heard fifty times before from others. God damn ye! The enemy is out there, not in here! I tell you, if this incident is ever, ever repeated, I care not who is at fault, or who challenges, who accepts, who the seconds are, all involved will be dismissed from the service and cast off in the nearest port, so help me God. Do you hear me!"

Bliven heard an echo of "Yes, sir."

"Each of you is fined one month's pay. Now, get this man below and see what Cutbush can do for him."

They filed out, neglecting to close the cabin door. "God!" Bliven heard Preble explode within. "God! Why do I suffer these people?"

14.

PILLARS OF FIRE

———◦———

Autumn 1804–Spring 1805

A mid the fury of his berating the lieutenants over their duel-fest, Preble did not notice Decatur lay a sheaf of papers on his desk. It was only after relieving himself from the stern walk, sending for a glass of milk, and gathering himself for a few moments that he organized the weeks of dispatches.

The most troubling was from Oliver Hazard Perry, a lieutenant on the *Adams* when she called at Gibraltar to transport Richard Morris and his family home. A British sloop, the *Phaedra*, anchored only a hundred yards off her bow, and during the course of the night enticed five of *Adams*'s crew to jump overboard, desert, and swim to the British vessel. None were recovered, and once again the civilian authorities in Gibraltar were either powerless to affect the situation or were in sympathy with it. In any case, the question had to be posed whether such harassment was a new British policy, and how that would affect America's conduct of the war.

Preble stood over his general overview map of the Mediterranean.

He was in Syracuse, because that was where the Sicilians had bivouacked their gunboats and bomb scows to fit out. His own base of operations he had planned for Malta, which was more than two hundred miles closer to his enemy than he was. American ships had never been hindered there, but the warmth of the greeting that American ships received in any British colonies seemed to depend on the individual eccentricity or temper of the local authority. It made ensconcing themselves in a friendly port, like Syracuse, seem preferable to a neutral port that might turn on them.

"Mr. Johnson!" Preble called loudly, and at once his clerk entered from his office.

"Send out a dispatch to all consulates, naval stations, and ships that henceforward all squadron communications will be directed to this place, and all ships will consider this their home port while in the Mediterranean."

"Very good, sir."

"Where is Mr. Putnam?"

"He had the morning watch, sir. I believe he is resting."

"Send him in to me, if you please."

Johnson's knock on Bliven's cabin door produced no answer, but Bliven heard the knock from the chaplain's cabin, where he had been having coffee with Reverend Henninger, and came out into the wardroom.

"The commodore wishes to see you, Mr. Putnam."

"Excuse me, Reverend. I'll return if I can."

"A good bargain. If you return I gain your company. If you don't, I gain your coffee."

Bliven knocked on the frame of the open door. "Commodore?"

"Mr. Putnam, come in. I am stewing over some matters. If you look across the harbor, you see what I take to be our gunboats and bomb scows. I want you to go over there and learn how long they think it will take to have them ready to sail. Then I want you to recommend some method that we can keep up that fitting out, but also free us to get to hell out there and fight a little. My responsibilities to fleet operation require the bulk of our time here, but this is the best fighting ship in the Mediterranean and I can't keep her bottled up in Syracuse. I could oversee the work here from a damned fishing ketch."

His jealousy was intensified two days later, when Bainbridge brought in the *Philadelphia*. Preble watched her enter. His own *Constitution* was half a class heavier and more powerful, but *Philadelphia*'s matchless lines made her in his mind the most beautiful ship afloat. She let go her anchor a hundred yards off the *Constitution*'s starboard beam, and it seemed like Bainbridge had a boat down and on his way over before the chains stopped running. In Preble's sea cabin they saluted and shook hands quickly, and the commodore motioned him to a chair.

"Well, Captain, what have you been up to these two months?"

"My report, Commodore." He handed over a thick fold of paper. "I have operated agreeably to your orders of September thirteenth, convoying American commerce, staying in any port no longer than twenty-four hours."

"Very well." Preble nodded. "Very well. But now it is time to carry the fight to Tripoli itself. Look across the bay there. Sicily is providing us with a large augmentation of firepower, enough to attack the city and end their nonsense. You, Mr. Bainbridge, will have the honor of being our first caller there. I am sending you out in consort with the *Vixen*, to operate a close blockade of their port."

"Excellent," enthused Bainbridge. "Capital."

"Now, those are damned tricky waters. You know well there are shoals near the coast, and reefs offshore, and only a narrow slot between them to get into the harbor. You keep the *Philadelphia* in deep water, let the *Vixen* flush out the targets that try to snug in where you can't go. Don't do it all yourself."

"No, sir, I understand."

"I will be down there in a few weeks with the *Constitution*, probably with *Argus* and *Nautilus*. Maybe five ships in his harbor might lead old Yusuf Karamanlis to his senses, where two ships did not."

Bainbridge smiled with confidence. "Sir, I cannot confess to any sense of optimism on that score, but I am looking forward to the next few months. It will be an honor to operate in tandem with you."

"Well, go load up everything you need. The Sicilians have been proving themselves to be allies in every sense. Then Godspeed and good hunting to you."

AS NOVEMBER NEARED ITS MIDDLE, Preble could stand sitting in Syracuse no longer. *New York* and *John Adams* were actively patrolling and convoying merchantmen; the *Philadelphia* and the *Vixen* were off Tripoli. The preparation of his ancillary vessels was well in hand. If ever there was a time when an extra show of force might turn the trick on the bashaw of Tripoli without further violence, this might be it.

He ordered the *Constitution* to make ready to sail, escorted by *Argus* and *Nautilus*. They sortied on November 12, and two days later were hailed at sea. "This is His Majesty's frigate *Amazon*, Captain Mountjoy. Are you the *Constitution*?"

"We are," boomed Preble in response. "Edward Preble, commodore."

"It is my duty to relay to you. Have you heard about the *Phila-delphia?*"

"Heard what? We have no news."

"I am sorry to tell you the *Philadelphia* has run aground at Tripoli. She has been captured; Captain Bainbridge and his crew are held prisoner. The Berbers have remounted her as a gun platform."

It was Sam Bandy who was standing the watch. "If that is a joke," Preble grumbled to him, "it's in damned poor taste."

"Are you sure?" Preble called back to the *Amazon.*

"I am sorry, the information is confirmed. There are dispatches for you in Malta. Good luck to you." The *Amazon* plowed ahead on her course, leaving Preble in shock. He wanted to return to Syracuse, round up all his ships, and attack in fury. But he could not. *Philadelphia* in Tripolitan hands must be neutralized before thinking of any kind of attack.

"Mr. Bandy, maintain your course for Tripoli. We will find the *Vixen* and get to the bottom of this."

They raised Tripoli the following midday. *Vixen* was nowhere to be seen, but through his glass Preble certainly made out the silhouette of the *Philadelphia.* "God, it's true." He turned away sickly, handing his glass to Bliven. He raised it to his own eye, and beheld in the magnified circle the *Philadelphia's* clean, raked lines, seeming in perfect order except maimed by the presence of a stump where her foremast should have been, the red and yellow stripes of Tripoli fluttering above the captive Stars and Stripes. All her eighteens and twenty-fours were rolled out, expecting to repel an American attack.

Bliven stared at her long and unblinking. So this was what defeat felt like, and he did not care for it. At least it was defeat with the prospect of vengeance, and he felt the instinct for a fight rise within him.

"Mr. Bandy," said Preble quietly.

"Sir?"

"Mr. Putnam will take the wheel. Get below, find a chart, set us a course for Malta. Perhaps we can learn something definite there."

"Right away, sir."

When he returned they set their course, north by east, four hundred miles to Malta, and Bliven realized that he must live a while with the bitter taste of disaster unrighted.

What they found at the American consulate in Valletta was a report from Bainbridge, written from his captivity. He had sent the *Vixen* to Lampedusa on information that there was a Tripolitan there she could capture. Nine days after she sped off, Bainbridge saw a lateen sail racing west, skimming the coast, obviously running his blockade. Bainbridge made all sail, including stuns'ls, and pursued her for two hours, eventually close enough to fire her bow chasers, but his quarry pulled away. Deep in Tripoli harbor, Bainbridge put about and began tacking his way back. He had studied the chart and believed he was safely back in deep water, when they were thrown off their feet as the ship shuddered to a dead stop.

Within moments they could see Tripolitan gunboats, trapped in port for weeks, begin making sail, now that they had the beast caged and wounded. Before they could get to him Bainbridge tried everything to lighten his bow and get moving again. The stiff wind was from the east, so he backed sail. Still not moving, he cut loose all three bow anchors, and still not moving, and seeing Tripoli's gunboat fleet bearing down on him, he began rolling his guns over the side, and when that did not lighten him enough, he set men to chopping down the foremast and heaving that over the side—anything to lighten the bow. He kept his after guns to hammer out a battle with the gunboats, but once it became obvious that the Tripolitans could simply maneuver to where he could not shoot at him and pound him to pieces, he did something that is the nightmare of any American naval commander: He surrendered.

Preble read this report with increasing pain in his stomach. Bainbridge's report was the very model of the answer to the question on the lieutenant's examination of how to get your ship off a bank. But the fact that he could recite, indeed perform, these steps mitigated nothing of his responsibility for having grounded his vessel in the first place. Preble had told him to stay the hell out of shallow water, and he didn't do it.

Nor did it help Preble to feel better, to remember that Bainbridge was one of the few commanders who had lost a fight with the French in the Quasi-War, when he surrendered the *Retaliation* late in 1798. And now he had lost the *Philadelphia*, and his temper rose as he noted, lost her in a dangerous pursuit that he should have reserved for the *Vixen* and never undertaken himself. How could he have been so stupid? If he had aught to say in the matter, he would court-martial the strutting little cock.

Returning to Syracuse was a bitter duty, made the worse by fighting an opposing and nearly opposing wind. Losing a thirty-six-gun frigate to the enemy, three hundred men taken prisoner, was a calamity in itself. But there was also danger far in his rear, for there were those in the navy, those who coveted his pennant, who could make it out that he was responsible, for the commander is always responsible, even for the stupidity and disobedience of a subordinate.

Worse news awaited him back in Syracuse, a dispatch and confirmation that the Tripolitans had recovered and remounted the *Philadelphia*'s guns, making an assault on the city next to impossible, and in fact had refloated her. If she was seaworthy, which was still to be determined after grounding, and if they repaired her foremast, she would be a formidable opponent on the open sea, for she was built as tough as the *Constitution* and mounted only three guns fewer on the broadside. And even if she was lame, moored within the reefs known only to his enemy, she could check any attack on Tripoli itself. Further dispatches confirmed that Yusuf Pasha knew he had taken an advantage, for he had laughed at the Danish consul, whom the American government requested to negotiate terms for the release of Bainbridge and his crew, and laid down such terms as no nation would consent to. Now the crew of the *Philadelphia* were set to the most bestial slave labor and made to suffer in such a way as to taunt the United States.

With *Philadelphia* gone and the other frigates convoying merchant vessels, it became vital for Preble to take the *Constitution* back down to Tripoli and let the bashaw know that America's eye was still on him. Two weeks before Christmas he sortied with the *Enterprise* under Decatur; it was a dangerous mission, for the prevailing winter winds were strong northerlies that could easily trap them on the African coast. But almost immediately upon reaching their station they had luck.

Preble sighted a small ketch with Tripolitan rigging and decided to show English colors to see what would happen. The ketch made for them right willingly, and Preble sent Decatur out to snatch her. She proved to be the *Mastico*, bearing a cargo of slaves for the sultan in Constantinople, as well as passengers who proved to be high-ranking courtiers, including the bashaw's physician. Preble treated them generously, shared his table with them, making it less onerous that they were now his prisoners, and prisoners of such stature that he might be able to bargain for the release of Bainbridge and some of his crew.

Back in Syracuse, Preble certified the captured ketch as a prize of war, renamed her the United States Ship *Intrepid*, and began fitting her out for American service. She was only sixty feet long, but he might usably employ her as one of his gunboats.

Decatur obtained an interview with Preble and broached a plan that was at once stunning in its audacity but also made him think that Bainbridge was not the only strutting cock he had to manage. But in good manners he heard Decatur out, then leaned back in his chair and crossed his arms on his stomach. "Let me understand you." He glowered at Decatur. "You want to take that captured ketch. You want me to give you enough men to storm and take a fully armed frigate. You propose to sail them across the Mediterranean in that sixty-foot ketch that I would not trust a day's fishing in. You think you can sneak her at night into the enemy's well-guarded harbor, and you expect to gull the enemy crew into letting you tie up to her, after which you will all spring on board her, kill or drive off her crew, assess whether she can be got away, and burn her if she cannot. Do I understand you?"

Decatur grinned. "Yes, sir."

Preble continued to stare at him. "On the other hand, it will be at night, the ketch is rigged as a Tripolitan, and you will be disguised and have the Italian pilot doing the talking for you." He broke his gaze and looked down at the papers on his desk. "Well, God love a man who thinks like a fighter. *Philadelphia* must be recaptured or destroyed; my ending this war is a near impossibility without it. It cannot be done without risk. It is likely that you and many of your men will be killed, but if you succeed, your reputation must become imperishable."

Decatur closed his eyes and nodded. "I will not deny that has occurred to me."

"And if you are killed, you will become a legend."

The look on Decatur's face was the first that showed he knew what the odds were. "I should hope so."

"Then you shall have your chance. I will send a schooner with you to cover your withdrawal, or take on your crew if you founder on the way, which you well may."

Not an hour after Decatur left, Preble heard a knock at the door of his sea cabin. "Enter!"

"Commodore? I am Midshipman Israel. May I have a moment?"

Preble pushed back from the papers he had been hunched over. "I know your name, Mr. Israel. Damn, do you think I am so high and removed I don't know your name?"

"I am sorry, sir."

"Well, what can I do for you?"

"Sir, the word is that Lieutenant Decatur is going to take a boat to Tripoli and try to recapture or burn the *Philadelphia*. I would like to be considered for this duty, sir."

"Why?"

"Well, sir," he stammered, surprised that it should require explaining. "I want to contribute something toward our victory, sir."

"More than you can with your duties here?"

"That would seem a fair prospect, sir."

"M-hm." Preble rose and, clasping his hands behind his back, paced to his stern windows. He looked out across the harbor of Syracuse, to the workyards where his bomb scows and gunboats were being fitted out. "Well, Mr. Israel, your request is denied."

Preble heard no acknowledgment, turned, and saw Israel standing with his head down. "Yes, you have a question?"

"May I know a reason, sir, why I am turned down?"

"Young man, commodores do not in ordinary circumstances explain their decisions to midshipmen."

Israel seemed even more downcast. "No, sir." He could not help thinking that it was for the same reason he had been denied both advancement and the opportunity for it for years past.

"But look there," said Preble. "See out there, a whole squadron of gunboats and mortar boats. The king of Sicily is putting them at our disposal. But I must find a way to man them. Every one of them must have some semblance of an officer to command, and I will be cleaning out my ranks of midshipmen to fill that order. Now, Mr. Decatur is going to Tripoli to either steal a ship or start a fire, he is not going to shoot anybody. And if he must, he knows how to use guns. Your duty there would be wasted. You see?"

"Yes, sir," he answered glumly.

"Now look here. Mr. Putnam has told me of your particular circumstances in regard to your assignments and lack of recognition. You will not find that I hold you back unjustly. In fact, if Mr. Decatur is successful, I will take this squadron and attack Tripoli myself, and you shall have command of one of the gunboats."

Israel's relief was tempered with embarrassment. "My thoughts about this were unjust, sir. I apologize."

"Very well. By the way, Mr. Israel, how did you come to learn of Mr. Decatur's pending mission?"

"From Mr. Decatur himself, sir."

"M-hm. Where is he?"

"Gone back to the *Enterprise*, sir."

"Well, find the bosun and take our jolly boat over to the *Enterprise*. Ask Mr. Decatur, from me, how successful he thinks his mission will be if he finds the Tripolinos waiting for him with guns loaded and trained." Preble's voice began to rise and he ended by shouting, "Because word of his mission leaked out because he didn't know enough to keep his own goddam mouth shut?"

Israel had to smile. "May I relay the message in your words, sir?"

"No, be respectful, but convey my full meaning."

"Yes, sir." Israel saluted and left, even as Bliven entered.

"Yes, Mr. Putnam?"

"I assume that Israel wanted to go down to Tripoli with the *Intrepid*."

"He did."

"But he will not?"

"No."

"Sir, what if I wanted to go?" Bliven shifted from foot to foot hopefully.

"I would rather you did not."

"Sir, you won't even be close to sailing again before we get back."

"Do you believe you will get back?"

Preble sank into his chair and looked almost like he was sulking, but he was not, he was reflecting on his own youth, and his memory that young men must and will stand their turn at danger or corrode from not getting it out of their systems. He knew that he could not be seen to favor Bliven or keep him out of harm's way. Finally, he flung his hands up in the air. "Go!"

Early in the morning of February 5, 1805, Decatur, late of the *Enterprise* but now the *Intrepid*, and Stewart of the *Siren*, gathered in Preble's sea cabin. For more than a week sailors on the *Constitution* had watched the lucky volunteers gradually become decked out in costumes as Italian fishermen or peasants as more and more discarded clothes were rounded up from local families.

There was a man in the cabin they did not know, but Preble was eager to introduce them. "Gentlemen, I would like to present to you Salvatore Catalano of Palermo. He knows the harbor of Tripoli intimately, he speaks Maltese and fluent Arabic with an Italian accent, and he has volunteered to get you next to the *Philadelphia*. Finding him was the special favor of the Italian commandant at Syracuse, and I believe he has done us a capital service."

The last things that *Intrepid* took on board were the combustibles that would be used to torch the *Philadelphia* if, as they believed, they found her not seaworthy. Riding the northerlies, it took only four days for *Intrepid* and *Siren* to reach the waters off Tripoli. With seventy-four men in a forty-ton boat, none could call it pleasant, especially after they discovered that their meat was foul. But they anchored that night off the Tripoli reef, and sent a small boat to reconnoiter the western entrance to the harbor, which Catalano pronounced impassable in that wind and tide.

And truly they had lost their chance, for from nowhere blew a gale that cost the *Siren* her anchor and forced both vessels clear enough of the coast to ride out the storm, in which they tossed for four pitching and yawing days. By the time the wind abated, most of them vowed that a death in battle would be preferable to what they had been enduring.

With *Siren* standing off on the night of the sixteenth, Catalano took the *Intrepid* into the harbor flying British colors, coasting in the lightest breeze toward the *Philadelphia*. The only sound was the harbor chop as it slapped against their bow as the single sail of their ketch edged them closer into the unknown. A quarter of a mile in, no alarm had been raised that they could determine; there was a good chance they had not yet been seen. To the west the lights of the city became clearer, and to the south, the lanterns of the Tripolitan ships could be seen intermittently twinkling.

Bliven stood next to Decatur on the quarterdeck, his spine tingling, the hair standing up on his neck. The wind was light and chill, but he knew that was not why he was shivering—it was the consciousness that this dark was like that of the jungle, that death could await them where they could not see it and come from a quarter they did not expect. At least in a sea battle, he thought, you could see your enemy, know how to prepare and respond. But this—he was certain that this night's dark was *the* most complete in which he had ever been immersed. He took a deep breath. Who knew from where a cry might pierce, or muzzle flashes illumine the night? Yes, he thought, give him his fight with the *Tripoli* any day, over this.

Well into the harbor, Catalano nudged the wheel to starboard in a broad turn, placing themselves between the enemy fleet and the *Philadelphia*, which lay nearer the north mole. Bliven was much surprised to discover that the night could not have been as dark as he'd imagined, for as they neared the captive frigate she loomed even darker, her lanterns showing much higher and only suggesting her dimensions. A bit nearer and he realized that she rode on an even keel, and he shook his head. If only Bainbridge had held out a bit longer, as he surely had the men and the guns to do, the tide itself would have floated him free. But he had hastened them into trouble and then hastened to conclude that all was lost. That was what made Bliven angry; had *Philadelphia* sailed under a prudent commander, none of this would have happened, and his life and the lives about him would not be at hazard.

Yet Bainbridge was lionized. The nation had had its fill of prudence, and the last person with whom Bliven could share his doubts was Decatur. Cloaked as a Sicilian merchant, he stood by Catalano, to all appearances relishing everything that Bliven found not unnerving, for he was in possession of his nerves, but stupidly dangerous. Decatur was, he judged, another Bainbridge, younger and even more reckless.

Two hundred yards from the frigate, Decatur sent Bliven forward to light the lantern on their bow, lighting one hanging from the stern at the same moment. Then he walked the bare ten yards to the opening of the hatch. "All right, boys, this is it," he rasped. "Have your guns ready, but don't use them unless you have to; have your grappling hooks ready to throw. Once we hail them, there's no turning back, you understand? Even if we are discovered, we can take them. Boys, some sailors serve their whole lives and never have a chance for such glory as this. Are you with me?"

Excitedly whispered agreement issued from the hold.

When challenged from the *Philadelphia*'s deck, Catalano opened his act, performing piteously in Arabic that they had lost their anchor in the storm, asking to make fast to them until morning. After minimal convincing the Tripolitans passed a hawser down for the ketch to tie up, and she was almost secure by the time those on the frigate spied *Intrepid*'s anchor on her far side and raised an alarm. Decatur already had found footing on the *Philadelphia*'s chain plates and bellowed the order to board.

Bliven's part was to lead a squadron up the larboard netting, cutlass in his right hand as he pulled himself up with his left. Through the netting he peered onto the deck, making certain that no blade was raised to hack them down as they topped the railing. He waved his sword above those behind him. "All right, boys, over we go!" They came over the railing in a swarm, gaining the spar deck in so many places that the light guard retreated and formed themselves in a defensive line behind the hatch, unsure what to do next.

Knowing better than to discharge guns and awaken the harbor, Decatur led a charge with drawn swords. The Tripolitans' deck guard numbered no more than a dozen, and having lost to surprise and momentum and numbers, broke and ran for the starboard rail, launching themselves into thin air, hitting the water with terrific splashes, and began swimming to shore. Other splashes that Bliven heard but didn't see let him know that other Moors belowdecks were shimmying out the twenty-fours' gun ports and making the same escape.

The ship was secure within a very few minutes, and the men began fanning out to the tasks that they had had many days to verbally rehearse as the gale blew them about. Bliven's task was on the berth deck. Torch in hand, he dragged a pile of bedding forward to the galley and, finding live coals in the camboose, raked them out onto the blankets. He upended the coal bucket on them and cast a lit battle lantern down hard upon them, making enough of a blaze to illuminate the deck, well enough to see that it, too, was deserted.

He descended the forward ladder to the orlop deck. By torchlight he discovered the sail room and, taking an armful of canvas patches, rushed lower still to the paint stores in the very lowest curve of the bow. Knowing that fires were burning above him, he felt for the first time the tightness in his chest of being in a tight, cramped space—an awful place to be trapped and burnt to death. Quickly he piled the canvas against buckets of paint and held the torch beneath them until they caught fire. Back up to the orlop deck he set fire to the canvas in the sail room; flames were already licking about the hatch from above on the berth deck. He shielded his face from them, but felt the heat pressing close as he regained the gun deck and greedily sucked in the cool night air on the open spar deck. Other teams torched the wardroom, the cockpit, the after storage areas, steerage—all the blazes quickly became self-sustaining, and it was astonishing how fast and how completely the ship took light. Perhaps, he thought, it was the hundreds of tons of long-dried wood, perhaps it was the tar that sealed the gaps, but the ship was full engulfed as the men began descending the netting back to their ketch. Wary eyes kept on the flotilla of gunboats deep in the harbor detected no movement whatever.

Last on the *Philadelphia*'s deck was Decatur himself. Illuminated by the fiery lace of burning rigging, he seemed almost to stroll amid the destruction, peering up contentedly as flames licked higher up the masts and spread out in the yards, engulfing the main and mizzen tops and turning them into balls of fire twenty feet wide and thirty feet long. At these great pillars of fire Decatur gazed, almost as a painter looks upon his masterpiece. Bliven waited, bobbing with the others at the foot of the boarding ladder, anxious to pull well away from the hulk before the blaze worked its way down to the magazine. At last Decatur swung a leg leisurely over the rail and descended, dropping finally into his *Intrepid*. Bliven was the first to see the look in his eyes; satiety, like a predator who had fed. Such a countenance, such weirdness in a man, perhaps madness, is not to be looked upon without emotion. Perhaps that was why the Berber sailors had broken their line and run until they launched themselves overboard. Not that they feared the marines' charge, but perhaps, he thought, Mohammedans feared Satan as much as Christians did, and they saw that look in Decatur's eyes.

As they exited the harbor the dying *Philadelphia* herself saluted them, for her double-shotted guns began discharging in the heat of the fire, the port guns sending balls skipping among the gunboats swinging at anchor, the starboard guns leveling house and shop walls somewhere in the city.

. . .

PREBLE WAS DELIGHTED TO HEAR of Decatur's success in the *Intrepid*, and equally pleased to have Bliven back aboard the *Constitution* as his right hand. Preble spent much of the spring writing letters to the bashaw of Tripoli, now stripped of his captured frigate, with increasingly attractive offers of peace, including large sums of money. Yusuf Pasha responded to each one, sometimes truculently, sometimes with a hint of interest in restoring calm, until it became clear that he was leveraging each letter to get still better offers. The year 1804 offered a stifling hot summer at Syracuse, as Preble's impatience to strike at Tripoli was repeatedly frustrated. Difficulties of supply kept his Sicilian auxiliaries from being ready; he could not assemble sufficient firepower of his own because American commercial traffic kept his own vessels out to escort them. During these long months Bliven learned how much of a junior officer's energy was drained away as he changed into a bored, impatient secretary.

By the end of July, Preble had had enough waiting, strung his Sicilian auxiliaries, totaling now six gunboats and two bomb scows together, and sailed to assault Tripoli itself. Escorting *Constitution*, he assembled *Enterprise*, *Argus*, and *Siren*, and another Tripolitan capture that he weighed down with no fewer than sixteen six-pounders and named the *Scourge*. Upon raising Tripoli they discovered that Yusuf Pasha had used the intervening months well to prepare, and he deployed twenty-two gunboats to defend his harbor and city.

On the morning of August 3 Preble attacked in full fury. The *Constitution* did not risk the shallow harbor waters, but stood off, and Bliven supported the schooners with longer-range fire from his eighteens and twenty-fours. When action was broken off they had sunk three of the

Tripolitan vessels and rendered five more ineffective for want of crew left alive, against an American cost of one dead and a dozen wounded. That one death, however, was grievous. Stephen Decatur's brother, James, in command of a gunboat, boarded a Tripolitan after she surrendered, and her captain shot him through the head as she resumed the fight. When Bliven heard it he remembered Lieutenant Sterett and the *Tripoli*, and marked these people down as having truly no honor.

After this action the Tripolitans could not be brought to battle again, and after the *Constitution* silenced the fortress's batteries things reached a stalemate, for Preble had no force with which to land in the city.

Stephen Decatur's wild success in torching the *Philadelphia* reached even the ears of Lord Nelson, who pronounced it the most daring act of their time. It also led Preble's other junior officers into conceiving other, equally chimerical schemes, so that their luster would not pale next to Decatur's. Only one of them made sense to the commodore, however.

Yusuf's wounded flotilla of gunboats would not attack, but they took up a strong defensive position that could equally not be attacked without grievous loss. Then it was the praying Somers who proposed to improve the odds. Somers proposed sacrificing the tiny *Intrepid* as a bomb ship. Load her with tons of explosives, set her course into the Tripolitan fleet, let her crew light her fuses and escape in a small boat. Such a devastating explosion could destroy the greater number of enemy ships at one blow.

It was risky, but Preble agreed. Volunteers were called for, and once again, few were chosen from the number who stepped forward. *Intrepid* was loaded with a hundred thirteen-inch mortar shells from his bomb scows, fifty nine-inch shells, and five tons of black powder.

Somers picked a crew of a dozen, the bare minimum needed to handle the vessel, and they tied a longboat to her stern.

Just as she made ready for the mission, Preble ran up signal flags for her to wait as he scratched out additional orders. He looked in the wardroom and saw Joseph Israel was the only one present.

"Mr. Israel!"

The chair scooted back noisily as he leapt to his feet. "Sir?"

"Get a boat, take these over to *Intrepid*, quickly, as she is ready to sail."

"Yes, sir."

Several minutes later the jolly boat sidled up to the *Constitution's* boarding ladder, landing one oarsman before rounding under the stern shear to be hoisted back up to its davits. The sailor reported to the watch officer, who sent him below to report to Bliven, who was now reading in the wardroom. "Sir?" said the sailor uncertainly.

Bliven looked up and returned his salute. "Yes?"

"Sir—um—Mr. Israel did not return from the *Intrepid*."

Bliven sat back in his chair. "What do you mean, he did not return?" The sailor, a redheaded Irish boy named Keegan, related the more complete story.

Bliven exhaled mightily, fearing the storm to come, but then rapped twice in quick succession on the door of Preble's sea cabin, paused, and rapped a third time, a short code that they worked out so the commodore would know who was knocking. "Enter," came Preble's reply.

"Beg pardon, sir." Now it truly was too late, he noticed, for Preble was standing at his stern windows, watching the little *Intrepid* bob and slap her way into the west pass of Tripoli harbor, with the *Siren* close alee and behind. Unlike her abortive attempt the night before, this time the wind stayed behind her and she scooted between the reefs and under the guns of the fort, toward the Tripolitan fleet. "Sir, I have to inform you that Midshipman Israel did not return from the *Intrepid*."

"What!" Preble spun around. "What in hell do you mean, 'did not return'?"

"Sir, obeying your command, he carried your last orders over to her. He noted the full hold of powder, and the two guns she mounts with which to defend herself, if necessary. He asked who was experienced to handle them safely in proximity of so much powder; he volunteered to stay aboard as their gunner, and positively refused to leave."

Preble's eyes grew wide. "Somers allowed this?"

Bliven looked out the window. "Apparently so, sir." He smiled sardonically. "Maybe he thinks to convert him to his own faith."

The look of ferocity in Preble's eyes faded and lightened until, to Bliven's amazement, he began to laugh. "That clever little Jew boy has taken the weather gauge on me. I wonder if he knows."

"Knows what, sir?"

"That I once did the same thing myself." Preble grasped his chair and sat gently. "When I first became a captain, in seventeen and ninety-nine, they gave me command of the *Essex*, and orders to the Pacific to escort a convoy of East Indiamen home. We sailed with the *Congress* under Captain Sever. He was senior, he was a pompous old hen, and I did not like taking orders from him. *Essex* was new from the yard, and her rigging was set in cold weather; we got near the equator and the rigging slackened so I could not sail her hard at all. Then one night we hit contrary winds and I gradually worked away. In the morning the *Congress* was nowhere to be seen. So I rounded the Cape of Good Hope and crossed the Indian Ocean to Batavia. Brought the Indiamen home safe, too, and loaded with dishes and silks and spices. My stock was high with the Boston merchants after that, let me tell you."

"Oh, look, sir, two alarm guns firing from the fort. They must have seen *Intrepid* coming in. Well, I wonder that you were not court-martialed, sir."

"What could they do? Sever and I had agreed that if we became separated we would proceed independently and rendezvous in Cape Town. When I got there the harbor was empty but for a British squadron of four sail, so I victualed and watered and sailed on. I followed my orders to the letter—as far as anyone knew. Heh!"

"My!" was all Bliven could manage, finding himself awash in astonishment, and at being trusted with such a confidence.

"If you ever repeat that story I will hang you."

"Never, sir."

"I paid for it, though," said Preble. "I tell you, Putnam, the food in those islands"—he shook his head. "They have spices so hot that no white Christian has any business to eat them. Burn a hole right through your stomach, and don't I know it? That is where I got my ulcers, and I carry them to this day." He stopped and sighed. "Well, our Mr. Israel has gone on his own hook from here into Tripoli, which is an offense surely less egregious than going from Boston to the Indies. Now, if he were running from a fight, I would have them overtaken and I would hang him in front of the whole squadron. But he is running to the fight, and such alacrity is wanted. If he survives, I shall reprimand him, and then by God I shall see him promoted."

Bliven nodded. "The Bible carries a high admiration of the Israelites at war. Perhaps his example will inspire more of his race to join the service."

Preble looked up, his eyes wide. "I had not thought of that."

"Yes, sir. You look uncomfortable. Is there anything I can get you?"

"Yes, as you mention it, go below and find my cook, have him send up an egg and milk to take the edge off, if you can spare a moment."

"Of course, right away. GOD!"

A flash of light, brighter than the sun, suddenly lit up the harbor, rising, spreading, diffusing, and eventually burning itself out as it rose hundreds of feet in the air. The next they knew, three of the *Constitution's* stern windows blew in from the concussion of the explosion, showering them with glass.

Preble could barely breathe. "Too soon! That was too soon! Do you think they made it all the way in?"

Bliven shook his head. "I don't see how. I don't."

WITH MORNING CAME CONFIRMATION from the neutral consulates that the *Intrepid* had blown up some half a mile from the Tripolitan gunboats. Unidentifiable body parts rained down on the waterfront; there were not, nor could there be, any survivors. Somers was gone, and Israel, and eleven brave sailors.

Sam found Bliven alone in his cabin, lying in his berth, his eyes staring ahead without expression. "May I come in?"

Bliven nodded and pointed toward the chair. Sam seated himself. "You've heard?"

"Yes." Neither knew what to say, and finally Bliven shook his head. "It was very wrong of me to make fun of Somers and his religion. If he had known, he should have forced me to fight him with the others."

"You meant nothing by it," said Sam. "Neither of us did."

"If Somers had not been goaded into it, he would not have undertaken such a hopeless and chimerical venture, trying to show that he was the bravest of all."

"Well, he must have succeeded, because now that is how he will be remembered. But I know you took a particular watch over Midshipman Israel. Oh, Bliven, you must feel worst of all about him."

Indeed, Sam had struck the wound for which there was no balm. Bliven squinted and grimaced, and choked when he tried to speak. It took several seconds to govern himself again. "He could not help it that he was born Jewish. He was a good fellow, honest and sincere. There was nothing about him of what they say Jews are. But you could tell, in his bearing, in his speech and his expectations, he always knew he was being looked down upon."

"And you were the only one who tried to help him. God saw that."

"Gentlemen."

Bliven and Sam leapt to their feet at Preble's voice outside, and joined him in the wardroom. "Gentlemen," said the commodore, "as you saw, our gambit with the *Intrepid* was not a success. Our gunboats can hold off their gunboats, but we are the most powerful vessel in the harbor, and I am compelled now to do something to make the bashaw feel the weight of American power. I will take us in as close as is prudent, and Mr. Putnam, you will undertake to bombard the city."

Bliven swallowed. "Yes, sir. That will likely cause civilian casualties."

"I know that," said Preble solemnly. "But this bastard has been taking and enslaving Western civilians for decades."

"Might he not harm or kill Bainbridge and his crew?" asked Sam.

"It is possible, but I doubt it. He knows that there is a ransom for them sometime, somewhere. Come."

They ascended to the quarterdeck, where they saw their fleet of

Sicilian gunboats forming up between them and the Tripolitans. "We will come in as far to the north as we can. Mr. Bandy, you will make a slow pass southward, we will be about a mile from their waterfront. Mr. Putnam, you will quoin up your starboard twenty-fours to maximum range and fire on the city as rapidly as you can. Your port guns will stay ready to engage in case any of their gunboats break through. Target first the buildings that are flying flags; we may assume them to have some official function."

They saluted together. "Aye, sir." Before descending to take command of the gun deck, Bliven raised his glass to his eye and observed the waterfront, of shops and warehouses, of merchants whipping along small donkeys laden with fruit, of idlers taking in the sun. He tucked the glass under his arm and scampered down the ladder, having determined not to use the glass once he began firing. After marking his first target, he did not care to see where the balls struck.

Preble stood aside, hands clasped behind him, as the *Constitution* beat to quarters; Sam shortened sail to topgallants only, just leaving them steerage, and below, Bliven commanded the gun crews in crowing up the twenty-fours, removing the quoins, and nesting the breeches down into their carriages. He surveyed the gun deck; it was mopped and wet, match tubs in place, extra cartridges and balls in their boxes. If it was an impression they wished to make, he decided to fire a full broadside at first, and then allow each crew to fire at will.

At Preble's nod Sam made a slow turn to port. Preble strode to the after ladder and saw Bliven at the foot of it. "You may commence firing as you bear, Mr. Putnam."

"Aye, sir." He saluted back up. Bliven spared a pitying thought for the unsuspecting merchants and their donkeys. "Starboard broadside at the ready!" he shouted as he strode quickly down the gun deck, and the crew captains blew their matches. Down the first gun he sighted what he took to be a customshouse and then a warehouse, waiting until he judged that the ship's length had passed so that every ball would strike something. "Fire!"

Jets of fire and powder smoke roared beneath Preble's feet, followed by an audible cheer from the crews. "Independent," roared Bliven, "fire at will! Now is your chance, boys! Remember the *Philadelphia*, and the *Intrepid*! Come on, now, give 'em their own back!"

From the gun deck the twenty-fours boomed fast and regular, and Preble saw columns of dust rise where waterfront buildings were holed and then stove in and collapsed. It took ten minutes for the *Constitution* to pass the length of Tripoli's quay, when Bliven ordered a cease of fire and ran up to the quarterdeck, saluting Preble. "Have you further orders, Commodore?"

He returned the salute lazily. "Yes, that was very well, we will come around for a second pass before we retire."

"Aye, sir." Bliven returned below, and as they continued the bombardment the irony struck him that he of all people should be laying waste an ancient and historic city before ever even visiting it—but ultimately it mattered little, for whatever damage they caused, the bashaw's white Christian slaves would only be set to work the next day to repair.

On the quarterdeck Preble was compelled to the same conclusion, that it was having little effect on either the city or the attitude of the bashaw. It was necessary, of course, to be able to report that he had bombarded and reduced the city, but that afternoon Preble stood out of Tripoli harbor and anchored in the bay, alert lest any of their gunboats venture some suicidal attack on his squadron. This was not beyond possibility, for surely the Tripolitans could see as well as he could his ships starting to ride high and top-heavy from the sheer expenditure of so much shot into the city.

No sooner had he anchored than the *Argus* entered the bay, sidling up to the *Constitution* and lowering a boat, sending over dispatches in the care of a distinguished-looking middle-aged man in the uniform of an American army general officer. For his age he came nimbly up their sea ladder; Johnson the purser conducted him into Preble's sea cabin and closed the door after him, and they remained there undisturbed for nearly an hour before Preble ordered signal flags run up. Soon all the vessels had boats in the water to attend a captain's conference in the *Constitution*'s wardroom. The compartment was crowded; Preble sat centrally at his table and motioned Bliven to a chair at the side.

"Gentlemen," began the commodore, "it is time for our campaign against the Tripolitans to enter a new phase. We have cleared the sea lanes of their corsairs, and that is very well, but our indefinite continued presence will be required to maintain that security. Our bombardment has hurt the town considerably, but we cannot say that Tripoli is defeated. They are punished, but not defeated, and as soon as we withdraw, we must expect that the old situation will establish itself again. And of course, Bainbridge and his crew are still held as slaves. I fear that all we have done is prove the truth of an ancient maxim, that a land power, or a primarily land power, cannot be completely beaten by naval power alone. The United States, I hardly need tell you, does not have the capacity to place a large army on the shores of Africa to compel Tripoli to our will.

"Now, gentlemen, you see sitting at my side General Eaton, who is an experienced consul to the North African states. There is probably no one who has a more intimate knowledge of their character and their way of life than he. After his term as United States consul to Tripoli, and after the outbreak of hostilities, he went home to lobby for the hypothesis I just presented. After much"—Preble hesitated—"consideration"—Bliven saw the corners of Eaton's mouth twitch up into a little smile, and he understood that terrible battles must have been waged over the course of action about to be presented—"the government has returned him to the theater of action, empowered to raise a native army to engage in the land campaign that can bring this war to a successful conclusion. So I will let him explain to you the particulars of how he intends to proceed. General Eaton?"

William Eaton stood, his uniform almost blinding in its newness, its crispness. Some of the officers knew his name from his four years in North Africa, that he had served in the Revolution but in no rank so grand as a general. He must have gained such a commission especially for the venture he would explain.

"Gentlemen," said Eaton, "the Arabs have a famous expression, that the enemy of my enemy is my friend." He let that register for a moment. "Our enemy in Tripoli is the bashaw, Yusuf Karamanlis. I am going to tell you about another enemy of his, whom most of you do not know about." He continued, explaining that Yusuf was not the rightful bashaw; that title, in fact, had belonged to his elder brother, Hamet Karamanlis, whom Yusuf had overthrown and exiled, and whose wife and children Yusuf still held in captivity in his fortress in Tripoli. "Now," said Eaton, "the remarkable fact about the overthrow of Hamet Pasha is that Yusuf let him live—this was an unusual mercy in a culture known for fratricide as a means to power. But"—Eaton raised a finger—"this was a mercy that we mean for Yusuf to regret."

Eaton went on to explain that Hamet Pasha had established a new life for himself in Egypt, gained a general's billet in the Mameluke army, and was at that moment suppressing a rebellion near the upper Nile. American spies had contacted him, and he had agreed to lead a native force under American officers to engage his brother's forces in Libya. Moreover, Eaton explained, he would hold the element of surprise, for he intended to attack Tripoli from the east, striking from out of the Libyan Desert, which many believed could not be crossed. And again, moreover, he related to the officers that there were minorities within the Ottoman Empire, peoples of whom perhaps they had not even heard, who had long chafed under Moslem domination and who would supply soldiers. Many of them, he said, were Christians, not just Coptic Christians from Egypt, but Maronites from the Levant and Orthodox from Greece and Cyprus. Best of all, said Eaton, he had brought money to pay them—not promissory notes, or bonds, or other printed paper, but a chest with twenty thousand dollars in gold and silver, a universal currency understood by all soldiers of fortune. He would raise his army in Alexandria, drawing supplies and money from the ships that would shadow his movements as he marched west. When he reached Tripoli, a flotilla of American frigates would give the fortress and city such a pounding as they had never endured, even as his native army poured through its streets. With Hamet Pasha restored to this throne, America would have won not just the war but the peace.

"I know that many officers have their doubts whether this plan will succeed," Eaton concluded. "But I am happy to say that many men in the government have given their support, beginning with President Jefferson. Here in the area, I am happy to say that our consuls, Mr. Gavino in Gibraltar and Mr. Tobias Lear in Algiers, have forwarded the plan as a speedier way to bring the war to a conclusion."

Bliven had sat at the side of the gathering, and felt his hackles rise at the mention of Lear's name, recalling all his discomfort and mistrust of his oily nature. If Lear supported this plan, it was likely for reasons of his own, which he would reveal only in his own time.

The gathered officers exchanged a whole language of looks around the crowded wardroom, a few impressed with the probity of the plan they had heard, most disbelieving that Eaton or anyone else could bring such a scheme to fruition, and a couple, Preble was convinced, perceiving a menace to their own ambitions if a land attack should cut short the naval campaign.

Preble rose. "That is all, gentlemen, thank you. I will keep you abreast of plans as they develop." The officers in the cabin began to disperse. "Mr. Putnam, will you stay?" When they were alone he added, "Please close the door." He sat again, heavily, looking older than his years, and Bliven realized how much he had aged during their long months at sea.

"Can I get you something, sir?"

"No, I thank you. Please sit down. For once we will dispense with ceremony. Besides, I don't feel like looking up at you."

Bliven seated himself across the table where he would be in easiest vision.

"I have one thing to tell you, Putnam, and one thing to ask you."

"Yes, sir?"

"What I have to tell you is General Eaton brought me the news that I am being relieved of my command."

If there was one sound foreign to Bliven's lungs it was a wheeze, but he wheezed. "What? Why?"

"Officially, for my health. The Navy Department is suddenly so solicitous of my suffering from the ulcers that I must go home and recuperate."

"Well, pending a less kindly reason, that does not sound unreasonable."

"The unofficial reason is my conduct of the war is found wanting. Specifically, I am blamed for losing the *Philadelphia*."

Bliven shot to his feet, his fists clenched. "That is outrageous. That was Bainbridge's mistakes, from first to last. You have even spoken of court-martialing him, if we ever get him back."

"I know. I even drew up charges. But it has become apparent that Bainbridge is intended to be a hero. The country's mind is made up, and I would only make myself ridiculous by protesting." Preble pointed Bliven back to his chair. "Take your seat. A captain is responsible for everything on his ship, even so a commodore is responsible for everything in his squadron."

"Surely you can fight it, sir."

Preble shook his head. "No, I would not care to do that. Lieutenant, you and I serve our country at our country's pleasure, and our country's gratitude, when it is bestowed, is not always, let us say, equitably distributed. I am not the first officer to be turned out to pasture, nor will I be the last."

"Still, it is an outrage."

"Nor do I forget that I was given this command over the claims of senior captains. At some point they must be satisfied."

"So they have been ever busy managing your recall?"

Preble shook his head. "I did not say that, and even if I believed it, I also consider that I have a wife at home, and a little boy who hardly knows what I look like." He saw Bliven look glumly down at the table. "That is something you will have to think about one day."

"Yes, sir."

"And it is true that I am not well. I do not know how long the Almighty will vouchsafe me continued breath, but I do not believe I shall make old bones." He sighed. "In fact, if it were not for the mischief that I believe underlies this, I would judge that they have done me a favor."

"Is there anything I can do, sir?"

"You will satisfy me best by continuing to develop as the kind of officer you have launched yourself to be. But, I adjure you, take up no weapons for my sake, if that is what you have in mind."

Bliven nodded, not in agreement but in understanding. "Who is replacing you, sir?"

"Sam Barron. Good man, had nothing to do with my dismissal, as near as I can tell."

Barron, thought Bliven. That was a good kernel in a very sour pudding.

"Now, Barron is coming in the *President* and will arrive any day, which leads me to what I wish to ask you."

"Anything that is in my power, sir."

"I would not feel right ordering you to do this, but I want to assign you to Eaton, as his naval attaché. That means, more particularly, as my spy. From everything that has reached me, his proposal to hire Arab and Levantine mercenaries caused almost as much a war in Washington as we have out here. The army was all for it—they would be, because the navy costs far more money to maintain than the army and they are tired of seeing all that money sucked away from them. The navy, for the opposite reason, is adamantly opposed to it. Barron is known to be particularly hostile to Eaton's mission.

"Would not Commodore Barron prefer to name his own attaché once he arrives?"

"No doubt he would, but if I can spring you out of here quick enough, you and Eaton will be in the Libyan Desert and pretty well beyond recall. And Jefferson's and Eaton's plan will be in effect, and neither Barron nor anyone else can do anything to subvert it, and will have to support you. It will be difficult and dangerous. You will likely have only a platoon of marines to protect you until Eaton raises his army. If you detect anything afoot to cut the ground out from under Eaton, you get word to me, and I will set it straight."

"Where will you be?"

"I?" Preble smiled wanly. "I am going to make my way back to Naples. There I shall enjoy some very good food, some very good wine, and my intention is to be, let us say, too ill to manage the trip home for a few months."

"But you will be no longer in command. What can you do in Naples?"

"I will have the consul's ear. Barton is an intelligent man; he knows there are those in the navy who are out for their own glory. If some officers try to thwart the president's policy, he will know how to act." Preble's tone turned abruptly serious. "Mark me, now, once Barron has taken command, use all your resourcefulness to assist Eaton in his object, unless he receives a direct order to stand down, which is unlikely because he came here under instructions from President Jefferson himself."

"He believes in Eaton's plan?"

"The president is willing to gamble on Eaton to end the war. He would do anything for the government to stop hemorrhaging money on the navy. He recognizes that we have ended piracy on the sea, but it will begin again as soon as our backs are turned, unless we throttle these Berber warlords as they should be. Now, I will not order you to this service, but I want you to volunteer for it. Will you?"

Instinctively, Bliven knew this was not a moment to hesitate. "Yes, sir, willingly."

Preble sighed. "Good man. And just think, you will be perhaps the only naval officer in the country who will win part of his glory in desert sands. Heh! Let others be jealous. Now, get your things packed. I want you over on the *Argus* tonight; you and Eaton will sail with the tide in the morning."

15.

SEA OF WATER, SEA OF SAND

March–April 1805

The last thing Bliven heard before boarding the *Argus* with Eaton, bound for Egypt, was that Samuel Barron had arrived in Malta, so Preble had dispatched him just in time. Preble still seemed certain that Barron had had no hand in his downfall, which made his authority tolerable. But to the great preponderance of sailors who did not care who was in charge, sailors who could barely tell one from another, Barron stood out. Barron was a legend. The tale had raced through the fleet, during the Quasi-War with France a few years since, how as a third lieutenant he had saved the frigate *United States*. Her rigging had been set in Boston in the crisp of winter, but then in breathless summer, finding herself cruising the West Indies in search of French prizes, her rigging had slackened to the point where a sudden gale threatened to dismast her. The American navy was slow to learn this lesson; Preble and the *Essex* had only narrowly escaped such a fate, and the *Congress* was not so lucky, for she lost not only her masts but her bowsprit as well, and it required the closest management to limp her home for expensive and time-consuming repairs. Seeing the danger, Barron obtained the captain's leave to command a crew and reset the rigging, which by pulling together timed to the gusts and the roll, they succeeded in doing. That Barron was a daring leader of men was established just that early in his career.

Bliven had served on the *Constitution* so long now, he had almost forgotten how confining, how claustrophobic, the interior of a schooner can be. He almost felt as if his cabin were a coffin, but he knew he must make the best of it, for his *Rollins Geography* told him it was a thousand miles, more or less, from Tripoli to Alexandria. With a strong following wind they could do it in five days, but it was more likely to take two weeks. At least it was not as crowded as he remembered from the *Enterprise*, for *Argus* carried only a platoon of marines instead of the company they had squeezed into the ship on his first cruise. And as Eaton's adjutant he would have no duties except as Eaton gave him. It was in the *Argus's* diminutive wardroom that they took each other's measure for the first time.

"Mr. Putnam." General Eaton looked at him as though he were appraising a needed but too-expensive utensil. Eaton was a large man just emerging from the prime of his life, with enormous blue eyes set beneath a prominent brow ridge, above which his forehead sloped back severely. No one could call him handsome, but he sat rod-straight, and even seated in his too-small chair he wore his uniform exceptionally well.

"At your service, sir." Bliven knew that his accent would give him away, and the accustomed ritual would have to be repeated.

"Of the Connecticut Putnams, I'll wager," said Eaton.

Only to himself did he sigh. "Yes, sir. General Israel Putnam was my great-uncle."

"Well, then." Eaton's countenance lightened, and his large blue eyes seemed as peaceable as a summer sky. "I feel myself in familiar company, then. I am from Mansfield."

"Truly?" Bliven relaxed a degree at what he regarded as an offer of amiable superiority, which he did not mistake for familiarity. "My family know Mansfield well. In my grandfather's time we lived in Putnam, but my father moved to Litchfield after he lost everything in the Revolution."

Eaton nodded. "And I was born in Woodstock, which is even closer to Putnam. We moved west when I was ten, although not so far west as your family." He held up a hand for just a second. "Now let me finish reading." He returned to Bliven's orders, dual orders, competing orders, one from Preble and one from Barron.

At length he rapped the edges of the papers on his camp desk to align them before setting them aside; he looked up and said, "Well." His voice expressed a complete lack of commitment, but his eyes looked Bliven down and up, then sought out his eyes for any hint of temerity.

"I hope you will not think me too young for the duty I have been assigned."

"Young man, I almost missed the Revolution. Had to run away from home when I was sixteen to join up, that was in seventeen and eighty. Made sergeant by the end of it. In no wise will you find me prejudiced solely on account of your youth. Carry out my orders promptly and well, and you will find me a just sponsor to add to what Commodore Barron writes of your gallantry in taking the *Tripoli*, and what Commodore Preble writes of your service to him."

"Thank you, General Eaton."

"But mark me: Falter, and you will wish we had not met this night."

"I hope I shall give you no cause for such censure."

"Very well, then. You are detailed to me, personally, as my adjutant. The marine detachment outside there have Lieutenant O'Bannon in command, but you will answer only to me. Now, Barron remarks particularly on your skill as a gunner. Do you feel that confidence is justified?"

"Well, making allowance for one or two lucky shots, yes, sir."

Eaton evinced a wry smile for just a second before it disappeared. "There are four field pieces in transit from the squadron, with powder and shot. When they arrive, they will be under your command. Some of our Greek mercenaries say they have experience with artillery. You are to ascertain the fact of their proficiency, allow for some training, and do so with the absolute minimum expenditure of powder."

"I understand, sir. If I may ask, where are we going?"

"Why do you ask?"

"Sir, I understood that we were going to Alexandria, and I heard officers remarking earlier upon seeing traffic bound there and departing. We seem to have passed it."

"Ah. First we are going to meet one of my informants in the village of Rosetta, east of there, on one of the outlets of the Nile."

"I understand. Thank you, sir. Will that be all?"

"Yes, Mr. Putnam. Good night to you."

Bliven returned to his cramped cabin, with that one word echoing and rattling around in his mind: the Nile. How often had he read about it? Would he see it, or would he be denied, as he had been at Pompeii?

Dawn answered his questions as the *Argus* dropped anchor in the mouth of a river whose banks were a hundred yards apart. They entered the discharge enough to escape the sea swells, but, lacking a chart, they anchored when the sounding shallowed to eighteen feet. They lowered a boat, and with eight rowers pulling against the sluggish current, Eaton and Bliven reached Rashid—it was the French who renamed it Rosetta during their brief occupation—in forty minutes.

The city was fronted by a sand beach along the river, which the cutter coasted up to and was hauled a few feet up onto the ground. Bliven had not read of it, but he was astonished by its size, its activity, the abundance and intricacy of its architecture. Eaton knew it better, and explained that after the Ottoman conquest they had favored Rashid with its river traffic as a commercial center over the more ancient Alexandria, which was allowed to languish and fall into decay.

The Napoleonic contests in Egypt had made such an impact that their Western uniforms drew little notice. Eaton seemed certain of where they were going, and Bliven felt very much in tow as they entered a principal square and then a shop in which Eaton ordered them cups of coffee—tiny cups, the coffee brutally strong but of a curiously sweet taste. He indicated a table well into the interior, which Bliven took to mean that Eaton did not wish them to draw undue attention to themselves.

"*Salaam!*" Eaton rose and was greeted by a wizened old Arab, whom he allowed to embrace him although he was only tolerant of it. "*Salaam!*"

The entire exchange took less than ten minutes before they were on their way back to the boat. "I had no idea you spoke the language, sir," said an amazed Bliven.

"Well enough," said Eaton.

"Did you find out what you need to know?"

"Yes, Hamet Pasha is on his way down. I thought he might meet us here, but he prefers Alexandria."

"But if this is the larger town, wouldn't you have better luck raising an army here than in Alexandria?"

"I would think so, but I'm sure he has his reasons. It is forty miles closer to begin the march, but knowing him, there is always another game afoot."

They were back on the *Argus* by one o'clock and standing out to sea, beating to westward but making slow progress. The sea was easy, and Eaton had them put into a small bay and lower the boat. "I don't know if this will interest you," he told Bliven, "but come with me anyway."

They jumped from the boat onto the hard-packed sand and strode inland guided by the sight, on the rise, of a wrecked cart with one wheel off. It was all in a rush that Bliven became aware of the bones—a horse's bones at first, at the front of the cart, but then nearby descried what he knew to be a human rib cage, partly buried in the sand. With his eye drawn down and then slowly looking in larger circles, he realized they had walked into a great field of bones, more ribs seeming to claw their way out of the sand, long bones and pelvises, skulls and parts of skulls. Whether once buried and slowly surfacing, or never buried and only slowly sinking, their empty eye sockets seemed loath to give up the light and the air. And all was silence but the rhythmic pounding of the surf and the rare cry of a gull.

General Eaton leaned against the gate of a wagon half buried in the sand. "Well, Mr. Putnam, what do you make of it?"

"What place is this?"

"Abukir. Terrible battles were fought here."

Bliven shook his head, unsure how he should answer. "I'm sorry, sir, I've heard of it, but I don't know that history."

"Napoleon defeated an army of British and Turks here in 1799; he lost about a thousand men, the Turks lost about eight thousand. After Napoleon left, the British retook it four years ago, as a preface to taking Alexandria. And all that happened after the sea battle out there in the bay—the French lost two frigates and eleven ships of the line to Admiral Nelson."

"Yes, sir," said Bliven. "That's the battle I heard of." Extraordinary, he thought, that the French could lose eleven ships of the battle line in one action, and we had not a single one in commission, yet we aspired to be a respected power.

"Indeed." Eaton nodded. "Tell me, did you know your great-uncle, General Putnam?"

"They tell me that he saw me and held me a few times, and wished a glorious career for me. I was but two years old when he died; I do not remember him."

"Do you find war glorious, Mr. Putnam?"

"I—I might have done, but I killed two men when we took the *Tripoli*. I felt frightened, and then I felt sad, and sorry." Oddly, at that moment, what he most remembered was how carefully he had tried not to step in their blood.

"Ah, but when you returned home, and you and your shipmates were all welcomed as heroes and were given bounty pay and shore leave, and everyone knew who you were—did you not enjoy that acclamation?"

"I did, yes," admitted Bliven.

"That was well," said Eaton, "for you deserved it. You served honorably and returned victorious in the service of your country. But I mean war itself, battle—glorious?" Eaton pushed himself away from the derelict wagon, searching the sand for a moment before he picked up a bleached skull, holding it away from him to let the sand drain out a great jagged wound at the back that was likely the cause of death. "Here." He handed it out to Bliven, who took it. "That man had a name, and joys and prospects that were cut off. Perhaps he had a wife, and children, who never saw him again, parents who grieved for him. Tell me, how many people live in your Litchfield?"

"About four thousand, General."

"Well, eight thousand died on this beach in the Battles of Abukir. Imagine two of your entire towns consigned to violent death here. Imagine what this place looked like then. What it smelled like. That is what real war is like, and not many men can make a career of it."

"No, sir. But many must stand ready to, to protect what we have won already. Is that not true, sir?"

"It is. It is." Eaton looked around bleakly and then squarely at Bliven. "I just wanted to satisfy myself that you are not one of those who enjoy it."

"Sir?"

They walked, leaving deep divots in the dry sand, back down to the boat. "Some men," said Eaton, "are born to spread death and destruction. If you must have a war, it is lucky to have them on your side. But such are the men who start wars, too. You can probably look around among the commanders of your own ships and identify such men, could you not?"

Bliven found himself somewhat alarmed. "Sir, I could not name them without impugning their patriotism."

"Well said, Lieutenant. It is not important for you to name them, only to recognize them, and be on your guard against letting them influence you."

THE WIND WAS still almost against them and it was a hard two days to make the twenty miles through the mole into Alexandria. Bliven was on deck to assay as much of the city as he could see, and indeed, it made a poor comparison to Rashid. Yet plainly it was very old; he regarded the Fortress of Qaitbay at the entrance of the harbor, at the extremity of the island of Pharos, which he had read was built from stones of the great lighthouse after it fell, indeed erected on the very foundation of the lighthouse that was one of the Wonders of the Ancient World. Though they passed within easy view, Bliven raised his spyglass to see it in detail. Its construction was a mishmash of stones, white and cream and brown, seemingly both limestone and sandstone, the fifteenth-century stones sharp-cut, other stones ancient and very worn. Its curtain wall and central keep seemed of the same vintage as European castles, and cannon now jutted from the crenellations that once sheltered archers. In his mind's eye, though, it was easy to superimpose the ancient lighthouse, more than three hundred feet high.

Somewhere probably within his sight, Cleopatra seduced Julius Caesar, and later, after Marc Antony's death, ascended to her tomb and let the asp bite her. Bliven had been at sea long enough to know that his passion for history had made him the butt of jokes, but here in this ancient place, it exasperated him how the past could be so alive to him, or he to it, that it almost spoke to him, and others heard nothing.

"Lieutenant Putnam?"

He shook from his reverie. "General Eaton." He saluted.

"It is nearly time. We and the marines will make a camp near the beach east of the city. Hamet Pasha will know to join us there."

"Yes, sir."

"We will hire pack animals, so there is no need to travel too lightly. Pack some changes of clothes and things you will need. We will assemble on the spar deck and leave in an hour."

"Yes, sir." In his cabin Bliven packed his sea bag as though he were going home; he had left most of his books with Preble on the *Constitu-*

tion, but one item did catch his eye, the large jambia dagger that he had snatched from the pile of weapons on the *Tripoli* before they were thrown overboard. He pulled it out of its worked leather sheath and regarded the gleaming blade before replacing it. He almost stuffed it into the bag, but then thrust it through his belt, the way it was meant to be carried.

When he reached the spar deck, Lieutenant O'Bannon, tall, black hair, gray eyes, and intensely earnest, had already assembled his marines, and the bosun's crew were getting the *Argus*'s cutter over the side. In the bottom of the cutter he saw that Eaton had procured two tents, one for himself and one for the two lieutenants; the marines would sleep out, or have an open tarpaulin of sailcloth to keep them dry, in the unlikely event of rain. Even as they set up camp, a dozen rough-looking riders galloped into their camp and identified themselves as having been sent by Hamet Pasha to find Eaton. They were Maronite mercenaries from the Levant; one was sent back to guide Hamet to the camp as the others made their camp, apart but within sight of Eaton's.

Before sunset they had organized a camp and prepared a dinner— rations from the *Argus*, he noted, salt beef, peas, and bread, and as they ate he noticed one thing amiss. "General Eaton, sir?"

"Mr. Putnam?"

"Excuse me, sir, but today is Wednesday, and navy regulations specify pork and rice on Wednesdays. Are you quite certain this is permitted to have beef on a Wednesday?"

Eaton smiled tightly. "For our purposes, yes, but I am glad you mention it. The Arabs loathe pork, they detest pork, consider it unclean, and I made certain to bring none. It would make a very bad impression for us to be seen eating pork. Take care you acquire none, and pass that on to O'Bannon and the marines. Do you understand?"

"Yes, sir, I will." At least, he thought, if pork was such an abomination, there was not much likelihood of their being tempted by it in this country.

After dinner Eaton made a show of his relaxed leadership by taking Bliven, O'Bannon, his corporal, and three marines, joined by a few of the Maronites, to seek some refreshment in the city. In a culture with no alcohol, coffee and tea were the alternatives, and they settled on a shop a couple hundred yards down a well-traveled thoroughfare.

If it had a name they could not discern it, but plainly it was a place of entertainment: it had an arcade open to the street; exotic music issued from it; crowds of local men drank tea and coffee, and smoked from water pipes an herb that Bliven learned was called hashish.

The American marines felt much put upon that there was no alcohol to drink, there or in any other gathering place, but their disappointment was dispelled by the appearance of a succession of girls in the most gossamer garments they had ever seen, and they performed a shocking sort of dance, swaying their outlined hips, shimmying their naked bellies, all the while keeping time with tiny cymbals slipped onto their thumbs and fingers. Each wore a kind of black kohl about her eyes, accentuated out from the corners like ancient Egyptian drawings, and lipstick the shining reddish purple of dark cherries. Bliven was quick to notice that when, in dancing, one of the girls caught the eye of a man she began to play up to him, smiling at him, teasing him, dancing toward him in a way that could not be taken as other than seductive.

Between the music and the crowd it was too noisy for whispering, but Eaton leaned over and said into Bliven's ear, "Open a place like this in Boston, eh?"

Bliven shook his head. "Look at them. They're what? Ten years old? Eleven? I don't know what to say!" He was not exaggerating, for although they wore shallowly conical felt brassieres, it was apparent that their breasts, had they come yet at all, still had much developing to do.

"They're expected to marry at twelve. Single and fourteen is considered a disgrace."

Together they watched a lithe young girl in a costume green as limes swirl and twirl and shake her way toward a middle-aged local man, better dressed than most, fully bearded, a profusion of gray hair issuing from his ears and nose. She turned at the last instant and backed toward him, like a ewe anxious to be bred. Suddenly the man rose, took her by the hand, and led her through a curtain of threaded beads into a back hall that they had not noticed before. "So that's what is afoot," said Bliven.

"Not our place to judge," said Eaton. "Not our country, Putnam, not our people, not our customs, nor laws, nor history. Don't forget, we are the outsiders here. We're the ones being judged."

They saw a second girl, in yellow, lead away one of their Levantine mercenaries.

Seeing Eaton and Bliven in their uniforms, the apparent proprietor seated himself at their table. "Gentlemen," he spoke in English. "You are the Americans? Welcome."

"Thank you, sir. I am General William Eaton; this is my aide, Lieutenant Putnam."

"Welcome," he repeated. "Do you enjoy yourselves?"

"Yes, sir, thank you," said Eaton.

"Your girls are very pretty," said Bliven. "And very young."

"Thank you, young effendi. You are the leaders, of your men?"

"I am," said Eaton.

"Ah. Therefore, you will not . . . visit? . . . with the dancers?"

"No, I thank you."

"Then may I ask, do you permit it, for your men?"

Eaton shrugged. "If they wish it, I will not prevent them."

"Ah." The man opened his hands in gratitude. "They will praise your goodness. Let me send you coffee, with my compliments."

Eaton nodded to him. "You are very kind, sir."

A carafe of coffee arrived, thick and dark, and stronger than any Bliven had ever tasted, even as they watched a girl in crimson make an approach to O'Bannon's corporal. The local men had taken their exertions in stride, but by the time this thin girl got close enough to mesmerize the corporal with her eyes, like a leopard swaying before a peacock, he was beside himself. He got to his feet, and she took his hand and led him through the beaded curtains.

Five minutes later a shout of apparent disgust issued from the rear and he returned, disheveled, and rejoined the marines with such a blasted look on his face that Eaton called him over. "Pugsley!"

He took small steps to come over. "Sir?"

"What happened, Pugsley? Was she not to your liking?"

"Well, sir, she"—he wrung his hands—"she—"

"Speak up, man, what is it?"

"Sir, she isn't a she, sir."

It took a few seconds for his meaning to become clear, at which Eaton threw his head back and roared in laughter. "Very well. Maybe you boys should pay your bill and return to the camp."

"Yes, sir." He hesitated to leave. "General Eaton, sir?"

"Yes?"

"I didn't—that is, I mean I would never—"

"No, no, of course you wouldn't. No one would think it."

"I mean, she, *he*, could have fooled anyone!"

"Corporal, give it no more thought. Compose yourself, now, and get your men back to the camp."

"Yes, sir."

When Eaton turned back to his table he found Bliven with a hand cupped over his open mouth. The general fished in his small leather purse and placed a silver and three copper coins on their table. "Come, Mr. Putnam, we should go with them. Safety in numbers, you know, our uniforms could make us targets, just the two of us."

They and the platoon drew stares as they made the short walk back to the waterfront, and they were alone as the paved quay gave way to the beach, and their camp in the dunes. Eaton plopped heavily on his stool before his tent. "What is it, Mr. Putnam? Something has been working into you like a wood borer. What is it?"

Suddenly Bliven wished he had a cup of grog. "'Sir, here we are, in Alexandria." He tried his hand at the native: "*El Iskandaria!* The lighthouse! The library! Cleopatra! Second city of the Roman Empire! So much history, so much to see and to learn!" He leaned forward almost in an accusatory way. "And what have we done? We visited a . . . a den, that specializes in the, well, procurement of little boys. Is that the best we could do?"

Eaton managed to check another round of mirth. "Ah, poor Mr. Putnam. You seem to have made a mistake. You joined the . . . *navy* . . . when apparently you meant to join the Royal Geographical Society."

"Yes, sir." He felt vaguely insulted but was compelled to admit the truth in it.

"Now, look here. There are officers and gentlemen who can appreciate your bent for knowledge and learning. I am one of them. But look out there." He pointed out to the marines gathered by their fire, and the camp of the mercenaries beyond. "They could not give a flying gull's cry about Cleopatra, or the library, or your flaming lighthouse. If you can't learn to come down to their level now and then, you're going to have a very lonely life. To say nothing of very dismal commands."

Bliven considered it. "Yes, sir. Good night."

DAWN CRASHED UPON HIM WITH GUNFIRE, a chorus of ululant whooping, more gunfire, and the thunder of a hundred horses racing up to the Maronite camp. Bliven was in his boots and outside his tent at the same instant that Eaton emerged from his. They barely had time to do up their waistcoats when six of the new arrivals cantered over, one a length ahead of the others, all horses and riders magnificently appointed. Bliven studied them intently, for Clarity would want him to record this minutely.

Eaton held his arms wide in greeting. "Hamet Pasha, it has been too long."

They embraced quickly and tightly. "Are you well, Eaton Pasha?"

"I am very well, and very happy to see you. Will you stay and have some coffee?"

"Ah, Eaton Pasha." Hamet raised his hands and looked aside. "You are my friend, we have much to talk about, but I remember your coffee tasting like river water."

Eaton laughed heartily.

"Let us arrange our camp, put up our tents, and rest, and we will speak of all things tonight. You come to us. Our tents are bigger, and we have real coffee."

"As you wish, my friend," said Eaton.

Eaton had intended to spend the day renewing contacts in the city, arranging to hire camels and drivers, but the arrival of Hamet Pasha accelerated that process as merchants arrived in a steady stream all day, calling on Hamet first, most retiring quietly, some few—enough— entering the American camp and offering their services. After witnessing Eaton engage in much haggling with them, Bliven came to understand that in this culture, such hectoring negotiation and renegotiation was expected, and to not engage in it was considered rude. They and Eaton eventually settled on a rate of eleven dollars per head of each animal for the duration of the expedition, payable in silver, a princely sum—breathtaking, even—but to hear the camel drivers describe it, a rate on which their children would starve.

Each was keen to demonstrate the superiority of his animals; Bliven had seen camels before, in every African port they had called in, but he had never mounted one until now, and it was unlike anything he had imagined—how an animal so graceful in movement could be so cruelly ungainly in lying down. The first time one lowered for him to dismount, he was so surprised by the forward lurch as it went to its knees that he was thrown completely off, somersaulting into the sand, to hysterical laughter from the drivers and even a disgusted bawl from the animal itself.

In a flash he was on his feet with a broad smile, and held up a finger and said, "Again. Show me how." This won him some respect, and they pantomimed how, when the camel plunged forward to its knees, he must compensate by leaning far back on his saddle, and then come forward as the animal settled down onto its haunches. The second time he did it perfectly, to a round of applause.

In Alexandria word spread like the wind of what was afoot. Hamet

Pasha's men worked the Greek quarter of the city, and before break-fast was even over, Bliven was putting together a roster of mercenaries who sought them out with their offer to fight. He tried not to reflect that in America's own revolution, Hessian mercenaries were univer-sally reviled, and now Americans were resorting to the same tactic. He persuaded his conscience, however, that if the Ottoman government was deserving of any loyalty, volunteers would not be lining up.

In the evening Eaton and Bliven washed and put on their best be-fore entering Hamet Pasha's camp, which was a thicket of tents in the midst of his followers' camps, all seeming surprisingly organized and permanent for having been put up in less than a day.

Hamet Pasha greeted them before his own tent, within scent but not sight of aromatic food cooking. He greeted Eaton again with a full embrace. "You honor me with your visit."

"Highness," Eaton said, saluting before returning the embrace. May I present my aide, Lieutenant Putnam? He was commended for gal-lantry when the *Enterprise* captured the *Tripoli*."

"Ah." Hamet Pasha nodded. "You are that young man."

"You have heard of the engagement?" asked Bliven.

"Of course. And also"—Hamet Pasha laughed—"of the fate of my brother's admiral. Come inside and be welcome."

Within the tent they arranged themselves around a great brass tray, which was presently laden with rice, lamb, onions, and flatbread. "You mean that renegade Scotsman?" Bliven continued.

"Scotsman, yes, so he was."

"What happened to him?" asked Bliven. "I've never heard."

"Ah." Hamet Pasha sighed. "After the fight, the ship—or, as much ship as was left after the fight—was able to reach Malta. It was better repaired, and returned to Tripoli. When my brother learned what had happened, Admiral Rous was arrested and bound. He was mounted backwards upon an ass, and to show what kind of bravery he had, he was hung all about with the entrails of a sheep." There was a ripple of laughter in the pasha's entourage. "From there, he was ridden on this ass to the square, where he was laid down and tied to a scaffold. His legs were lifted into the air, and he was whipped, five hundred lashes on the soles of his bare feet."

Bliven flinched. "That hardly seems just."

"He lost the battle," said Hamet Pasha in a hard way.

"He did not fight skillfully, but he fought hard, both honorably and—well—not so honorably."

Hamet's eyes became as hard as glass. "The only dishonor in battle is to lose," he said loudly, and Bliven knew this was for the benefit of his retinue. "If any man think otherwise, he may not fight for me." There was a hauteur to him, an inbred sense of title, and Bliven thought, yes, he could see how simple tribesmen would follow him.

"Yes, sir," Bliven said. "I understand."

Hamet Pasha held up a hand. "Ah, but the five hundred bastinadoes that he suffered was not the joke. The joke was that my brother intended this punishment as an example, to inspire the sailors he had assembled in Tripoli to man his ships. But these men were not inspired to fight, they were inspired to steal away. The next morning their camp was empty. Now my foolish brother has ships, but no one to sail them. He is helpless before your navy."

General Eaton smiled in a cautionary way. "Not so helpless. His fortress still mounts one hundred fifteen heavy guns. No fleet could defeat that; the ships would be blown to splinters."

"That is true. But you have no need to engage his heavy guns. He now has no navy to challenge your blockade. No supplies can reach him by sea, and once we take Derna"—Hamet Pasha tapped his finger emphatically at the place on the map—"nothing can be sent him by land."

Bliven looked at the map and saw that Derna was hundreds of miles to the east of Tripoli, beyond the Gulf of Sidra. "Why Derna, particularly, when it is so far away?" asked Bliven.

Hamet Pasha leaned forward, tracing his finger west from Alexandria. "Regard this. These places we shall pass—El Alamein, Sidi Barrani, Tobruk, Bomba—they are mud huts in the desert. But Derna"—he tapped his finger again—"Derna lies between the sea and a mountain. It is a paradise of fruit and sheep, and fields of grain. My brother sits in Tripoli, that is his capital. But Derna is his storehouse, his granary, his treasury. If he lose Derna, and your ships blockade him from the sea, Tripoli must fall in time, as the ripe date falls from the tree."

Eaton also tapped on the map. "But my friend, there is no need to fight a battle there. We can put you on our ship and transport you with ease; you can meet your army in Tripoli and only have to fight once."

Hamet Pasha shook his head. "No, no, this cannot be. No army would stay together for so long. An army follows its leader, and if the leader desert them, the army dries up, like a wadi in summer. I must ride with them to lead them, and you must ride with me. On this point there can be no dispute. It must be so."

After fierce but fruitless argument Eaton gave way, resigning Bliven and himself to weeks of uncertain saddle travel in the Libyan Desert, even as Preble had foretold. They rose to excuse themselves, but Hamet Pasha delayed them for a moment longer.

"Lieutenant." He pointed to the dagger in Bliven's belt. "How do you come to have a jambia of the Wahidi? May I see it?"

"Of course." Bliven sucked in his stomach and withdrew the dagger from his belt.

Hamet Pasha examined it closely. "I know this tribe. How do you come to have it?"

"Highness, when I was a midshipman on the *Enterprise*, the man who wore it tried to kill my friend."

"He was on the ship you fought?"

"Yes, Highness."

"And you killed him?"

"Yes." It was an embellishment, but harmless, he judged.

"Very well, you came by it honorably." He handed it back. "Let lions tremble at your approach."

As they walked back to their own camp, Bliven resisted the urge to look back over his shoulder.

"General, do you really trust him?"

Eaton shrugged. "I don't need to trust him. I trust that he wants his throne back, and he trusts that I can give it to him. Now, granted, I would feel better if he were with us and we were all back on the *Argus*, making for Tripoli. But he has a point. He doesn't trust his men to cross the desert without him, and they don't trust him to be there if they got there."

"Then what holds it all together?"

"In a word, Putnam? Greed. That chest of gold and silver that I have on the ship. That magical box holds the power to make all this happen." Eaton laughed, with a cynical edge. "Trust him, you ask? I trust him to be an Arab. They are the most self-serving and duplicitous people on earth. Never believe you have made a friend of an Arab, Mr. Putnam. If you do, it will be your death."

Bliven found himself remembering that effusive exchange of faith and trust and affection when Eaton and Hamet Pasha had parted. "I am sorry to hear that. I believed differently from all that swearing and hugging."

"Do you know why he threw in with us?" Eaton stopped walking and looked down at him. "We have promised him the throne, and we have a squadron of warships off the coast and twenty thousand dollars in coin to raise an army, to make that happen. But I tell you, if his brother offered him thirty thousand to stay away, our throats would be cut tonight and our bodies never found."

Bliven looked on with wide eyes. "Why doesn't he do it, then?"

"Well, happily for us, Hamet knows his brother would promise him the money, and after the deed was done, his brother would say, 'What money? We never spoke of money.'"

"They are that deceitful?"

"Remember, I was still in Tripoli when Hamet was exiled. Do you know how it happened? After Yusuf deposed Hamet he said he was content to be in power; he offered to patch things up between them, and offered Hamet a provincial governorship, which he accepted. Hamet loaded up a caravan with his wives and children and all his household and led them out of Tripoli. As soon as he passed through the city gate, it was slammed shut behind him, wives and children and possessions still inside. That was his weakness, he trusted his own brother. That was when he came to Egypt, alone."

"Good God." Bliven looked back at the camp where they had met and realized he had understood nothing.

"And that business with the camels?" Eaton went on. "Do you think it was an accident that he appointed that particular man to help us acquire camels? I can assure you, that man has at least six relatives and dependents who are camel drivers. Each one will make his hardest bargain, and whoever negotiates the highest payment, they will all demand that rate or simply not go."

"Good God," Bliven repeated.

Eaton lowered his head and laughed quietly. "And that's before they get us stuck out in the desert and more in their power. It is a good thing that we will have most of that twenty thousand dollars safe on the ship, or it would not last a week. And we must always keep something in reserve, to make it worth their while not to leave us to die of thirst in the desert."

At length they reached their own tents. "Sir, I am sorry to be so thick about things. It is all very strange to me."

"Lieutenant, I pray you do not misunderstand me about the Arabs. They come from a great civilization. My God, they made mighty advances in science, and medicine, and mathematics, and art, and poetry—when Europe was in the deepest part of the Dark Ages. I don't know when they became such a thieving and conniving people. Perhaps it was the desert did it to them. It would be hard to make a living out there. I don't know, but understand that I have a deep respect for Arab people, but would I trust my life to one? Never!"

"And yet," said Bliven, "we are, aren't we? Ten of us, hundreds of them."

Eaton smiled sardonically. "I do believe that God's principal amusement is irony."

"Ha!"

"We'll get *Argus* to unload your field guns tomorrow. That will have a good effect; they will see a gun battery and know we're serious, you can start putting together crews to work them. Best of all, I can show their leaders the money and make a down payment to the camel drivers and the mercenaries. They will know that there's gold and I'm not just lying to them, but they will know they won't get paid in full until Tripoli is taken."

Bliven selected sixteen of the Greeks for his gunners, based on the advice of one to whom they deferred as a leader and who spoke English with passable fluency. After pantomiming the basics numerous times, he ran them through the gunnery drill three times with live powder so they got accustomed to the sound.

To Eaton he pronounced them as ready as he thought they could be, and they set off westward into the desert on March 6. Bliven had noticed that in the Arab world, their religion forbade them portraits or artistic representations of the natural world, for some reason he could not fathom, but in compensation they had raised calligraphy, with quotations from their Holy Book, to a level of art he could not have imagined. Their banners of green, yellow, red, and dark bright blue were held out straight by yards; the personal finery of Hamet Pasha and his retainers, the very trappings of their horses, the peculiar ululant whooping of their women camp followers, and the discharge of musket, he realized, would take him an entire evening by a fire with Clarity to even describe.

Yet once they were in the desert, it was astonishing how fast it fell away into drudgery and bickering. In ten days the camel drivers revolted at Massouah Castle, which was the first Eaton learned that, while he had hired them at eleven dollars per animal for the duration, the drivers had gone to Hamet Pasha and got him to agree that the eleven dollars would pay them only to this point.

Three weeks into the journey, they found themselves riding along the top of a ridge, with the Mediterranean visible far to their right, and a rocky, beige-brown depression on their left, studded with reddish-black boulders. The waste extended as far as their vision into the interior, the horizon indistinct in the shimmer of heat both beating down and rising up.

Bliven pulled off to his left and reined in his horse; Hamet Pasha joined him. Bliven pointed into the distant haze. "Highness, how far does this extend? Is there anything out there at all?"

"If you live to ride for a week," answered Hamet Pasha, "Siwa. It is an oasis, with water and date trees."

"Siwa!" exclaimed Bliven. "Where Alexander the Great was proclaimed a god."

Hamet Pasha's eyes widened. "You know of al Iskandar?"

Bliven leaned onto his pommel. "Yes, a bit."

"Why are you sad, young effendi?"

"Because I won't see it. We have come all this way, and I won't get to see anything of interest. Have you heard of Pompeii?"

"Yes, of course."

"We were so close I could have ridden out and seen it in an afternoon, but we went back to the ship." Bliven heard a camel bawl as their supply train passed behind them. What a thought that he, a lieutenant in the United States Navy, was riding in the footsteps of Alexander. "Alexander," he whispered, almost to himself. What an ancient country this was.

"And others came later," said Hamet Pasha. "And more will come after us."

After a month of what seemed almost imperceptible progress westward across the desert, their rations were reduced to rice and perhaps chickpeas that they were able to buy in mud-walled villages. The camel drivers began demanding more, and more immediately, on pain of stranding the infidel commanders where they stood. No degree of

Eaton's insistence could induce them to admit that they had ever agreed on a price, and the majestic certitude of their lying left Bliven shaking his head.

By the time they reached Bomba things had become mutinous. At least Eaton had arranged to rendezvous with his small support squadron there, and Bliven and an Arab rider were dispatched north to the coast. Topping a crest, they looked across the beach and Bliven heaved a sigh of relief to spy the *Nautilus* lying to, with *Argus* and *Hornet* not far off, and a boat quickly in the water and rowing toward shore. Aboard the *Nautilus* he found Oliver Hazard Perry in command, Barron's man, he knew, and himself a reckless glory seeker, another Bainbridge waiting to happen.

Bliven was alert for any hint of criticism of Eaton or his mission, and even wondered how he might get a letter to Consul Barton in Naples if he detected a scheme afoot. Perry, though, expressed his admiration at Eaton's accomplishment in crossing the Libyan Desert, and readily gave Bliven access to the chest of coin to buy off the camel drivers. He selected only three gold coins, for Eaton to flash about, and then counted out five hundred dollars in silver. That would quiet the camel drivers and also give Eaton the chance to tell them they had not proven themselves trustworthy to have gold in the camp.

"Rendezvous with us again at Derna," Bliven told Perry. "We will light a signal fire on the morning we mean to attack. When you enter the harbor, you may open up on the fortress and reduce it if you can, but certainly keep them occupied. We will attack once we see that your fire has had an effect."

"We will be there," said Perry. "Count on us."

As the launch approached the beach, Bliven leapt out a moment early, into the surf, where a four-foot breaker soaked him up to his chest. He buried his face in the next one and shook the salt water out of his hair. The refreshment of it was wonderful. With his heavy purse of silver securely around his neck he found his Arab companion sitting on the sand, holding their horses' reins—when suddenly his blood ran cold with the realization that he was carrying five hundred dollars in silver and was alone with an Arab who fought for the highest bidder. As they mounted, Bliven gestured ahead. "I do not remember the trail well. Will you lead?" From what he had seen, he was not about to ride with his back to this armed brigand.

Eaton welcomed Bliven and the silver back into camp, for Eaton was even then at the beginning of another terse confrontation with the camel drivers. By then his patience with them was ended, and had they made another row he was prepared to shoot some of them.

They resumed their march, and three days past Bomba their flankers came back and halted the line. Eaton, with Hamet Pasha, O'Bannon, and Bliven, advanced on foot up a rise, crouching lower as they neared the summit, finally lying flat on a ledge of limestone to peer over the edge. Below them spread a small city as white as Algiers, girdled with fields and orchards. Beyond lay the blue crescent of a bay, with a single spidery limb of a mole, and three small vessels with Arab rigging in the harbor. "Derna, at last," said Hamet Pasha.

"I did not realize we were so close," said Bliven quietly. "They must know they are at war. Why have they no lookouts posted?"

Hamet Pasha continued to peer through his glass. "And why should they think that an army would cross the desert? They have sentries, but they are looking out to sea."

Each of the four surveyed the city through his glass, O'Bannon looking down frequently to sketch out a rough map of the city, the harbor, and the fortress. Each one came to rest his gaze on the white, castellated fortress, with its file of eight black guns, seemingly twelve-pounders—French, by the look of the carriages. Probably accepted as tribute at some time, they were pointing into the bay, with no apparent provision to be able to turn around upon the countryside.

Eaton tapped Bliven on the shoulder. "Look down there to your right. You see that break in the hillside, that patch of forest?"

"Yes, sir."

"Before we attack, you set up your battery in the cover of those trees. See if you can breach the walls near the fortress. They don't look all that substantial."

"Neither do the guns, sir."

Eaton chuckled. "Well, true enough, but you will be within range to keep them occupied. If they think we're going to attack the fort, that will tie men down there while Hamet's mounted force storms the city through the residential streets. The squadron will arrive tomorrow; they will support us from the sea as well."

"So we just need to lie low until then," said O'Bannon.

"Right. Send men back up the road a few miles. Seize anyone on it. No one enters, no one leaves. We should be able to conceal our presence just long enough. And have a couple of your men pile up a great stack of brush right here for a fire to signal the squadron when we are ready to open the fight."

"Yes, sir." O'Bannon crouched away and then trotted down the hill.

"You seem troubled, young effendi," Hamet Pasha said to Bliven. "I think you are not afraid of the battle tomorrow, for we know you have the heart of a young lion. What troubles you?"

"Thank you, Highness. I am not afraid of the battle. But what I do mind," said Bliven, "is that if I fall, my fiancée at home will not know how, or where. She may not know for months even that I am dead."

"Ah. You have, what is it you call, a sweetheart."

"Yes."

"Ah, young effendi, do not be downcast," said Hamet Pasha. "If you die, I will hire many women to weep for you."

Somehow that did not strike Bliven as an equivalent substitute. "Thank you, but I would not want to be any trouble."

Hamet Pasha shrugged. "It is our custom."

They made their way back down to Eaton's tent, where O'Bannon and the general stood at a small table, pointing at his map. "Your Highness," Eaton said as they approached, "I recommend that before dawn you take your Arab force to the west side of the city. You can follow the cover of this wadi that goes around it to the south. When you hear our ships open fire, wait a few minutes and lead your men in, clear the streets. When the defenders' attention is divided between the ships and you, I will lead my marines and the Greeks against this side of the city. Mr. Putnam will open fire on the wall just as soon as the ships begin firing, and see if he can make an opening for us."

"That is good."

"In honor, I must first give the governor of the city the chance to surrender and save blood being spilled."

Hamet Pasha looked impatient. "Do you suppose that he does not know by now who it is he faces?"

"Perhaps he does," said Eaton calmly, "but the usage of war is to avoid the battle if possible. If I send in a message, do you think he will respect a flag of truce?"

"Yes, but send it with one of my men."

Eaton pulled paper from his writing box and seated himself, penning the next day's date: April 27, 1805.

HIS EXCELLENCY MUSTIFA BEY
GOVERNOR OF DERNA

Sir,

I want no territory. Advancing with me is the legitimate sovereign of your country. Give us a passage through your city, and for the supplies of which we shall have need, you shall have fair compensation. Let no difference of religion induce us to shed the blood of harmless men who think little and know nothing. If you are a man of liberal mind you will not balance on the propositions I offer. Hamet Pasha pledges himself to me that you shall remain established in your government.

Eaton

He had hardly begun writing when the camp was disrupted by a dusty clot of a dozen Berbers who thundered in on magnificent horses. Their leader dismounted and made his obeisance to Hamet Pasha, who embraced him and motioned for them to join his army. A second contingent of a similar size arrived before he had finished.

Well, Eaton thought to himself, *so much for surprise,* but the added strength was good recompense. "Hamet Pasha, who are these men?"

"Local chiefs. They have come to swear their allegiance to me, and to fight for me. Others are coming. They tell me that the city is divided. Many in the city are for me, but they cannot say so, for fear of their lives. Mustifa Bey is Yusuf's dog. Once he is brought down, the city will come over to us—except for those who have licked his hand. For them, justice will come."

Eaton thought it would be indelicate to point out that Hamet Pasha had mangled his metaphor—that if Mustifa Bey was a dog, he would have no hand to lick. His meaning was clear enough, however.

Bliven slept soundly that night, hardly disturbed by the dozen more bands of riders who arrived to join Hamet's army. Upon being awakened shortly after four, it was the work only of a moment to be done up in his waistcoat and coat, his navy cutlass dangling from his left, and his belt threaded through the jambia's scabbard. Eaton joined him and the marines as they breakfasted on lamb and rice.

Just before first light, O'Bannon sent one of his marines to the hilltop overlooking the city, and he reported back almost immediately. "Well?" asked Eaton.

The marine saluted. "I only saw one ship, lying to, northeast of the city."

Eaton scowled. It was too early in the day for things to start going wrong. "Are you sure?"

"Quite sure, sir."

"Mr. Putnam, take my glass, get to the top of the hill. See what you make of it."

"Yes, sir."

"Take this fellow back up with you. We can attack with the cover of one ship, if needs be. Your brush pile is ready to light?"

"It is, sir," said the marine.

"Well, do not light it except upon my order. Let us give Mustifa Bey his one chance to stop the battle." He handed his letter to Hamet Pasha, who handed it to a rider, wonderfully mounted and bearing a large white flag instead of one of their brilliant silk banners inscribed with verses from the Koran. He spurred away at a gallop and they waited.

Bliven trotted back down the hill. "Well?" Eaton looked up expectantly.

"Sir, it is the *Nautilus* lying close by. I could see *Argus* and *Hornet*, but they are several miles removed. I am certain they will bear in once they see the signal, but they cannot reach the harbor before noon.

In an hour and a half, Hamet's rider clattered back into camp, and Eaton unfolded the same piece of paper, with one line appended to the bottom, crudely, in English: *My head or yours. Mustifa.*

"Very well," he said to himself, and handed the paper to Hamet Pasha. "We shall fight. Your Highness, you should gather your men on the west side of the city, but you may have to wait a while before you hear the cannons. Who knows, the first ship may open up before the others arrive, but be in position to attack when you hear the guns."

"*Insh' Allah,*" said Hamet Pasha. As God wills. In the preceding days, the latecomers drawn by the scent of plunder had swelled his following of horsemen to more than a thousand, leaving Bliven to wonder if that truly was God's will—especially since it was not infidels, but other Moslems, whom they were about to pillage.

"Well," said Eaton quietly, "let us begin. Light the signal, right away."

Hamet and his riders galloped down the slope to the wadi that circled the city around its south wall, using its cover to thread their way to the west side. The sky was cloudless, and Eaton waited with Bliven in the motte of trees as the marines and Greeks rolled their small field guns from the camp to the edge of the forest.

"Mr. O'Bannon," said Eaton, "have your man stay up on the hill until he can report what action the squadron is taking."

"Yes, sir."

Eaton pointed with his saber. "You see the fortress there, Mr. Putnam? Its walls seem quite substantial, but just on the landward side of that, do you see?"

"Yes, sir," said Bliven.

"The wall looks like it thins to a curtain. Concentrate your fire about a hundred yards south of the fortress. It looks that there is a bit of a square behind it, and some buildings that will give us cover once we're inside."

"Yes, sir." Bliven began carefully sighting his guns on the same spot, midway between two slender buttresses.

Hamet Pasha and his horde should have been halfway to the west side of the city, waiting on the thunder of the cannon. "Mr. O'Bannon, are you clear on the order of battle? Once the squadron engages the fortress with a few salvos, Mr. Putnam will fire on the wall to make us an opening. The sound of the heavy guns will signal Hamet Pasha to open the assault with his cavalry from the west. Then I will lead you and the marines and the Greeks from this side."

"Yes, sir."

O'Bannon's marine returned from the signal fire, which was shooting flames twenty feet into the air. "Sir, our other two ships are moving in, but Mr. Putnam is right, it will be afternoon before they can get here."

"Damn." Eaton sighed. "Well, Mr. Putnam, you must feel rather at home."

"How so, sir?"

"A desperate battle about to begin, and all must wait on the favor of the winds and the currents."

Bliven smiled tightly and briefly. "Yes, sir. I mark the similarity."

"No wonder the ancients put their faith in sea gods and wind gods, and probably gods of every accident that can happen."

"How efficient we are to roll them all up into one, eh?"

"Are you boys still hungry? Have you eaten sufficient?"

Bliven and O'Bannon allowed that they had.

"Well, let us have some more coffee. That is one commodity that this land seems to have in plenty. And we wait."

THUS NOON CAME AND PASSED, and the officers ate some of the Berbers' aromatic unleavened bread. "Lookout, sir," Bliven remarked suddenly, about one-thirty.

"Well?"

The marine saluted. "All three ships have joined together and have formed a line to enter the harbor. They should be there in about half an hour."

"Very well. Gentlemen, if you are praying men, pray now, for there will be no time very shortly."

The water within the mole lay still as glass as the American ships stood in on the fresh landward breeze they had been waiting for. Eaton and O'Bannon formed their men at the top of their hill, and Bliven from his motte of trees observed the scurry of men on the walls of the fortress, limbering and quoining up their guns as others scampered out of fortified doorways with cartridges of powder.

The bearing of the coast angled gently from west-northwest to east-southeast, with the thin mole stretching its spider arm straight to the east, giving the ships a westward direction into the harbor, straight into the muzzles of the fort's guns. *Hornet* and *Nautilus* dropped anchor and opened their gunports within a hundred yards of them, content to engage in a contest of twelve-pounders. *Argus* was last in line and dropped her anchor just south of them, positioned to turn her big twenty-fours into the city itself.

There was no exploratory or ranging fire; their bombardment commenced at two o'clock with full, crushing, almost simultaneous broadsides. Bliven watched intensely for the effects and saw chunks of limestone gouged from low in the fort's wall, with chunks and chips flying far out into the water, as marked by their splashes.

Tongues of orange fire, eight of them, spurted from between the crenellations, followed by the slap of their concussion and their reports—somewhat shallower than that from the ships. The cartridges should have been of a standard size, he thought; perhaps their powder was inferior. That suspicion he confirmed when he saw that the first return fire fell short, some fell far short, but two splashes overshot the ships, which made him think that the quality of their powder must be inconsistent; that would be a great advantage.

The first salvo from *Nautilus* and *Hornet*, while they hit the fort, seemed to cause no damaging effect. There was no guessing how thick those walls were. They must have elevated the guns, for the second salvo struck much higher, one ball shattering a crenellation next to one of the Arabs' guns, the stone chips like musket balls striking down half the gun's crew, who spun around, arms flung over their heads, and lay still. Unless there were more men able to work the guns, their eight just became seven. The third salvo knocked a second gun from its carriage.

"Mr. Putnam!" Eaton called down. "You may begin firing."

"Yes, sir. Battery! Prime your guns!"

The Greek and Cypriot gunners looked at him dumbly. "Prime your guns!" he shouted again.

"We have done that," protested the one, named Demetriou, who spoke English.

Eaton saw Bliven's shoulders sag and laughed. "It's all right, Lieutenant," he shouted. "Just have them get on with it."

"Yes, sir. Battery, fire!"

The four howitzers roared to life, and he was satisfied that he had aimed well; he saw the balls strike within fifty feet of each other near the base of the wall, only one having struck the ground first.

"Reload!" As the crews swabbed and rammed home cartridges and balls and wadding, Bliven sprinted to the two guns on the outside and shifted their aim a degree toward the middle. He judged their elevation adequate, for it was more useful to weaken the wall at its base and bring the whole thing down than merely create a elevated gap that must be scaled.

Bliven looked up to his left and saw the forces closing tight behind the general, O'Bannon and the eight marines right behind him, the corporal bearing the colors. Behind them were three dozen Greeks under two pretended Greek lieutenants, and two dozen Levantines adding their mass to the force but with no command, and some few Arabs who, lacking horses, could not ride with Hamet Pasha.

It was not much of a force with which to attack a city wall, and he prayed that this volley would breach it. "Battery, fire!"

When the balls struck, a thin slice of the curtain of the wall wobbled and fell, revealing the construction rubble of its interior. "Reload!"

"General," Bliven called up to him, "I believe one more salvo will give you an entry, if you want to start down."

"Very well," said Eaton, and he raised his sword. "Forward men, quick march, and let's be on 'em!"

"Battery!" Bliven glanced over at the nearest cannon, just as one of

the Greeks—or Cypriots or Levantines, he could not tell them apart—
touched his match to the pan—the same instant that Bliven saw with
horror the ramrod still jutting from the barrel. "Stop!" he screamed.
"Don't!"

There was a spray of fire from the pan that then spouted from the
touchhole. Bliven fell flat, his feet toward the gun, and covered his
head in the case it should explode. For that second the thought made
him sick of having to gather up the parts of their bodies, and resolved
even in that second he would not do it, but would make the other
Greeks do it.

The boom rolled over him, but he felt no injury and heard no scat-
ter of debris to tell him that the gun had shattered. When he looked
up he saw the gun crew, leaning forward from their cover, gesturing
angrily and hurling insults at the city. The gun was intact, but its ramrod was nowhere to be seen. The crew looked at him, astonished and
a little disgusted that he had sought cover from the shot; they were
utterly oblivious to the risk they had run.

"Idiots!" Bliven shrieked at them. "Simpering, blithering idiots!" He
pounded his head with his open palms and tugged at his hair but did
not pull it out. They could not be worth pulling out his hair. "How
could you be so stupid!"

He ran over to them and inspected the gun, which seemed undam-
aged. Then, in the simplest English and vigorous pantomime, he made
them understand that the ramrod was to be withdrawn before the gun
was fired. The first crew were laughingly happy to have been corrected
from their mistake. Bliven had shouted his warning in time for the
other three guns to hold their fire, and the crews shrugged the incident off, content that no real harm had been done. "You other guns"—
Bliven raised his hand and flung it down—"fire!" This last salvo struck

home on Derna's curtain wall, punching a hole through it almost at ground level; the mound of rubble at its base could not have been more than four feet high to have to scale up and over.

Bliven ceased their fire after that salvo, as Eaton and his men were halfway up the wall and running downslope. Throughout these moments his eardrums had regularly throbbed from the concussion of *Nautilus* and *Hornet* reducing the fortress, gun by gun, until the opposing fire ceased. But as he saw Eaton and his men two-thirds of the way to the collapsed wall, he also beheld the fortress's defenders, with their cannons now useless, streaming out of it and taking up positions in houses near it, ready to let loose on Eaton as they clambered through the wall. There must have been three hundred; it was shocking that the fort could have held so many, and they came boiling out like ants out of a mound. His anxiety only increased as he saw musket barrels begin to protrude from loopholes in their cut stone walls.

Bliven's helplessness turned to a cheer as he saw *Argus* open up with her big twenty-fours on the houses. They were beyond the range of Perry's twelve-pounders, but a single ball from a twenty-four would bring a whole façade of stone crashing down, killing or at minimum destroying the cover of those within. *Argus* was only barely large enough to mount twenty-fours; he was not aware whose idea it was to rearm her in such a way, but at this moment it was proving brilliant. At her third deeply rolling salvo, two more houses near the fort collapsed, and the retreat of those soldiers loyal to Mustifa Bey and Yusuf Pasha who had lately streamed out of the fortress now streamed back in.

Through his glass Bliven observed Eaton mount the rubble, his sword aloft, encouraging O'Bannon and the marines. Old man he may have been, but there was no doubting his courage. They followed him through, fanning out into a small, sparsely shaded square, taking cover behind tree trunks and corners of buildings; then the Greek and Levantine mercenaries, taking cover behind the marines.

Then suddenly he saw the eruption of musket smoke into the little square from loopholes in the facing houses. By the time the popping rattle of the volley made its way up the hillside, two of the Greeks had toppled over, and one of the marines, caught in sprinting from one sliver of cover to another, flew backward in mid-stride and lay stock still, having never known what hit him.

He could hear *Nautilus* and *Hornet* keeping up a lively fire on the fortress, so Mustifa Bey's soldiers there would be too engaged to pay Eaton any attention. The danger was from those in the houses facing the square, and the execution they could work on Eaton's little force, firing from their loopholes before *Argus* could sight them and root them out.

For the next moments Eaton was pinned down, and he had too few men to cope with the emergency. With a metallic scrape Bliven withdrew his cutlass from its scabbard and turned to his gunners. He started down the hill, circling the sword over his head as he turned to his gunners. "Come on, boys! Forward! We are needed!"

He dashed on, and in twenty yards he looked back and saw no one following. Demetriou, the one who spoke English, said, "We shoot cannons. We don't do that."

"Well, you rot in hell!" Bliven screamed back. It was a calculation that took a fraction of a second—he could not go back for them. They would not fight, and there were sixteen of them to his one. If he forced them to follow him, one might cut him down before he ever reached the wall; if he threatened them, it would have been a simple matter for them to kill him, return down the road they had come, and melt back into the mishmash of a culture they came from. But from that moment Bliven settled on it that not one of them would be paid a single copper lepton if he had any sway in the matter.

He did not fear turning his back on them, for they had no firearms, and he dashed down the slope, each footstep adjusting as it landed on rocks and tufts of grass. At least, he thought, there is no fire coming outside the walls now. He studied through the breach as he approached it, and saw Eaton and most of his men take refuge in a substantial house on the south side of the square; reaching that door became the immediate goal.

He was through the breach before realizing that he himself had no firearm, but the marine lying dead between him and the door had fallen with one. He altered his direction and flung himself flat on the ground behind the body, scooting the musket out of the way as he worked the man's belt to remove his packet of cartridges and balls. Of all the puffs of smoke directed at the house where Eaton was sheltered, two came directly at him, and it was almost unnerving to feel the body shudder as the balls struck it; apparently, the Berbers thought they might pass through the corpse to dispatch him as well, but thus far he was fortunate.

The worst moment was to find himself flat on the ground after those balls struck, face-to-face with the marine. He had seen the bodies of Berbers shattered on board the *Tripoli*, but this was the first time he had encountered a visage similar to his own, and looked into eyes as blue as his own, and realized that they did not see him in return.

When he finally was able to pull the packet off the man's belt, with only his right ear and eye exposed above the corpse's chest, Bliven observed until it seemed like most of the Berbers facing them must be reloading, and he dashed as he never had before, leaping headlong through the door and rolling on the floor.

"Putnam!" shouted Eaton. "Good man!"

"General." Bliven arranged himself. "What do we do now? How do we proceed?"

"It is dire, it is dire," said Eaton with agitation. "Look you, O'Bannon, come here!" They peered through a window of the house, exposing as little of themselves as they could. "There may be a dozen of them in that house, but see, there are scores more giving them a flanking cover from that garden wall on the right, and a couple of hundred more in the houses beyond that. *Argus* is taking down the houses one at a time, but they don't know where we are; they are as like to strike us as the enemy. They will not cease fire until they see our colors on the fort, so that must be our object."

"Yes," said Bliven, "I see." He was dubious, and saw that they all were dubious, even Eaton. Equally he saw that in making such a reckless charge, the reports and future generations would extol their valor, when in truth this was their only hope to avoid annihilation.

"Look you." Eaton pointed again. "Most of the loopholes in that house are on the side facing us. When we run, let us run hard around to the front of the house, before they can reposition how to shoot, and the house itself will screen us from most of the garden wall. Do you see?"

"Yes, sir," said Bliven, and O'Bannon echoed him.

"When we have done that, if we live, we will repeat the action on the fort. The walls there are too thick for loopholes. We must storm right through the gate so fast that they cannot take us all. But first this house.

"All right, everyone, hear me, now. Everyone load and prime your muskets, but do not fire until you enter the house, and then shoot the first thing that moves. We may just see the better side of this."

They heard the crack of a musket as stone chips scattered from the wall behind them. "Load and prime muskets," ordered O'Bannon, indicating to Eaton when they were ready.

Eaton crouched by the door, his saber sheathed and musket in his right hand. "All right?" All the marines and a few of the mercenaries nodded. "Go!"

Eaton was first out the door, wanting nothing in speed to stay ahead of the younger men behind him. They flew across the courtyard as on their left a volley erupted from house and garden wall together. One of the marines cried out as he was struck and thrown down onto his side in the dirt. Three of the Greeks were similarly struck in the same instant, two attempting to crawl out of harm's way, the third lying still.

Once they were across from the front of the house, Eaton's cry of "Charge!" became more a primal bellow of rage, kept up for several seconds, and taken up by all the rest as they surged toward the house, shouting as though mad to keep their courage up.

A half-dozen musket reports flashed from the door and windows; Bliven was running immediately behind Eaton when he heard a ball strike; Eaton cried out and dropped his musket as his left hand was thrown down to his side, a bloody hole in his wrist that immediately began draining blood.

"General!" cried Bliven.

"Go on! Go on! I'm all right!" With his good right hand Eaton pulled his saber from its scabbard even as his men surged around him, and he took up the charge again. O'Bannon and the marines were all through the door, virtually together, and Bliven braced himself for the explosions of musket shots indoors, but there was nothing.

He heard doors being kicked open, but heard the marines repeating,

"Nothing. Nothing." They burst through a door to the rear room of the house, and out the window beheld the Berbers leaping like athletes over the garden wall, and they and the others there disappearing at full run into the warren of narrow streets beyond.

Eaton reached the door, his saber ready and his left arm limp at his side, but O'Bannon met him at the entry. "General, the house is ours. They have fled."

"Very well! Very well! Your muskets are still ready?"

"All of them, yes, sir."

"Then we must be on the fort, there is not a moment to lose."

"General, your wound!" Bliven saw a cloth lying on a table that he ripped into a strip and bound Eaton's wrist as tightly as he could, noting the blood, but also noting that there was no spurting or voluminous discharge, so the vessels must be intact.

"Thank you, Mr. Putnam. Thank you."

"General Eaton, sir," O'Bannon called from the front door, "come look at this!"

From there they had an oblique view of the back of the fortress, from which they saw what must have been the entirety of the garrison flooding out in a full run, fleeing to refuge in the hive of the city.

"Well, that is understandable," said Eaton. "Their cannons have been knocked out. They have no stomach for close combat."

A few seconds after what seemed the last of them dashed out, Eaton said, "Men, we must assume there are still some remaining within. We will charge them in close order, just as we did the house. If the inside is ours, find the staircase up to the parapet as fast as you can and hoist our colors. Then we can have some sailors land and see to our needs and our wounded."

From the quarterdeck of the *Nautilus*, Perry had been watching the fort intently. He had ceased his fire once he was certain that he had put all its guns out of action, and had heard the rattle of musketry, punctuated by the deep booms of *Argus*'s twenty-fours; now it was a waiting game. He noted the time as four twenty-five in the afternoon when he saw the red and yellow stripes of Tripoli come jerking down the fort's flagpole, replaced seconds later by O'Bannon's large American flag.

Perry could not help himself, he doubled over and shrieked in triumph, followed by every man of the *Nautilus*'s gun crews, and almost simultaneously similar cheers erupted from *Argus* and *Hornet*.

Eaton could hear them plainly on the quay by the fort. Exhausted, he sat heavily on a large crate of he knew not what, and savored the sound of it, and the sight of the Stars and Stripes over the fort. Distantly they could hear the rattle of musketry rage in the unseen warren of streets—gunshots, occasionally a scream, and knew that the waterfront's defenders must have run into Hamet Pasha's advancing horsemen.

O'Bannon and his two uninjured marines emerged onto the quay, bearing first one, and then returned bearing the second bodies of their fallen comrades. Three others who had been wounded plopped themselves on the pavement, resting. Only distantly could they hear the Greeks and Levantines celebrating, as they gathered on the quay, ready to receive their pay, seeming heedless of their dead, who lay where they fell. Distantly in the city could they hear the pillaging. Well, thought Eaton, at least it was Mustifa's head and not his own.

General Eaton rose and approached his somber marines, sensing an imperative to comfort them, to tell them of the gravity of the moment. His bandaged wrist showed a growing red stain of blood. "Gentlemen," he said quietly, "this is a somber moment. Two of our comrades have fallen. They died bravely, displaying the gallantry that we know we can expect of American marines. They shall never be forgotten. Neither shall this moment ever be forgotten. This is an important moment. You marines, in planting the American flag on the shores of Tripoli, have raised our banner in triumph, on a foreign shore, for the first time in our history. Our nation does not aspire to be a feared tyrant in the world, but let the world take note of this, that neither will we be trod upon, and when our rights and honor are violated, we will have justice."

The marines did not cheer; they nodded sadly. They heard a horse cantering, drawing closer within the tangle of streets, until Hamet Pasha emerged on his Arabian charger. He drew to a halt ten feet from Eaton. "The city is ours. Allah be praised." He saw the bloodied sheets covering the two bodies. "You have suffered losses. The memory of these men shall be imperishable. The world will remember American bravery, and how happy we are, that we are allies."

He walked his horse to stand near General Eaton. "You are injured. We have a physician in the city."

"Thank you, Your Highness. The surgeons on our ships will tend to me shortly. You are very kind."

"You are not dangerously hurt?"

"No, I think not. But—his head or mine—what of Mustifa Bey?"

Hamet Pasha relaxed his reins and smirked, making a disgusted, dismissive sound as though he were sucking something from between his teeth. "He has taken sanctuary in the bashaw's palace."

"Wait." Eaton was working through some confusion. "Your brother has a residence here in Derna?"

"Of course."

Eaton thought for a moment longer. "But the palace is now yours."

"Yes."

"Then why do you not go in and get him?"

Hamet Pasha began making emphatic gestures. "Because the steward has extended him hospitality and the safety of the harem. He cannot be touched there."

"Well, by God," roared Eaton, "we will go get him!"

"No! It is the most sacred law we have. If he comes out, he will lose his head. If the steward betrays him, or if I seize him—we will become the detested of God." Hamet leaned far forward in his saddle toward Eaton. "No one of us will do such a thing!"

Hamet Pasha's charger spun a spirited circle before he regained control. "Besides, the palace is in a quarter of the city which is still in his power."

Eaton threw up his hands. "You just told me the city is ours!"

"Well, most of the city is ours. Where he is, he can do nothing, his people can do nothing. Only they must be watched for a while, until we decide what to do."

Eaton held his throbbing hand. Now one of the ships must be left behind to cow a dissident element, and he must find additional naval cover for his attack on Tripoli. And how could he feel secure with Derna in his rear with no American force left in it?

"Be not downcast, my friend," puffed Hamet. "We have won a great victory. And what now are our plans?"

"We will rest," said Eaton, "then one way or another we will march on Tripoli."

"Excellent. It is well. One thing more."

Eaton looked up. "Yes?"

"I wish for Lieutenant Putnam to accompany me a short while."

Eaton thought for a second. "We will have need of him here. How long?"

Hamet shrugged. "You may have him back on the day after to-morrow."

It might not be the best thing, Eaton considered, to deny an accommodation to the next ruler of Tripoli, when his friendship would be of such advantage to the United States, and the more so when that friendship was attested to by the blood, not yet wiped off, on the scimitars of his retainers.

"Very well." Eaton looked over his shoulder. "Mr. Putnam?"

Bliven stood. "Sir?"

"Would you be so good as to accompany Hamet Pasha and attend to whatever it is he requires of you?"

"Of course, sir."

Hamet barked in Arabic to his retainers, one of whom produced a saddled horse, holding the reins out to Bliven. "Ride to your camp and take up your bedding. Take no thought for food; we have food. Return quickly, it is a long ride."

16.

THE *DEFENDER*

May 1805

liven galloped first to the motte of woods where his guns were concealed and found his Greeks celebrating the sight of the American flag fluttering over the fortress, hoisting cups of a dark red, oily Greek wine. He had them hitch their teams and ordered them to haul them through the meadows into the city and down to the waterfront to turn the guns back over to the *Nautilus*.

There was only a sparse guard in the camp, where he stripped off his shirt and washed quickly, putting on a fresh shirt before his waistcoat and coat again. He quickly wrapped his kit and cantered back down to the city, where he found things exactly as he left them. "Ride by me," said Hamet Pasha. "Let us go."

With ten heavily armed men just behind them, they clattered noisily westward through Derna's torturous narrow streets, which made Bliven think of Algiers, except they were not ascending a height. They were halted as they entered a small square in the western reaches of the city. A crowd was gathered about two men whose hands were bound, and who each stood on a large swath of white canvas or sail-cloth. As Hamet Pasha reined in, one man who seemed to be in charge approached him with a bow and, with many gestures at the bound men and at the people and in different directions, blurted such a staccato of Arabic that even had Bliven acquired any facility with the language he could not have followed it.

What Bliven could see was a change in Hamet's countenance from the thoughtful man who could engage him in solicitous conversation to something else, a much harder man, a Berber prince called on for judgment. And that judgment came swiftly, as he snapped a very few syllables, gave half a wave of his hand, and turned his horse to continue their ride westward.

Bliven's gaze was torn between following Hamet, and the eruption from the mob as, in less time that it took before he could avert his eyes, the two bound men were forced to their knees. Each suffered one man to pull by his hair as another flashed downward with a thick-bladed scimitar, striking their heads from their bodies, which fell as limp as grain sacks.

What took him was the surprise of it; the violence and the gore—to his own shock—did not revolt him. He had seen worse when taking the *Tripoli*. Almost in a continuous motion the severed heads were cast upon the bodies, and men took up the corners of their canvas shrouds and bore them off before the ghastly effusion of blood could soak through the canvas.

When next he came abreast of Hamet Pasha he found his jaw set and his eyes hard. "Young effendi," Hamet said, "mercy is a virtuous thing, and beloved of God, for those who deserve it. These men did not deserve it. They were the servants of my brother who oppressed my people."

"Your Highness"—Bliven searched out some kind of phrase that Eaton or Lear would have found acceptable—"my country has every faith in your justice. Who am I to judge otherwise?"

At this Hamet Pasha searched him with a penetrating look, and the hardness began to pass from his countenance. "It is well, then. Forget what you have seen. Come!"

They left the city behind as the road west split into two, one that followed the edge of the sea and one that rose into the upland. Bliven judged it near the limit of the horses' capacity, alternately walking and cantering them until nearly sunset. Bliven used the long silences to judge the day's events. It had been more than three years since he first went to sea, but he had aged much more than that. He beheld himself harder, and sharper—*tempered* was the word he settled on. Yet the time passed was so brief that he could remember something like innocence, or callowness, and he was not so changed that he did not look back on that time with warmth.

They dismounted in a meadow of tuftgrass, and each of the Berbers produced a small carpet, which he spread upon the ground, and in unison they prostrated themselves to the east, praying. During this time Bliven made no move to eat or make himself comfortable, not knowing what might give offense. He pondered for a moment the incongruity that such a devout people could also be so cruel, but a quick wave of feeling superior was just as quickly defeated by the burden of the Crusades and the Reformation. They were not so different.

That night the tuftgrass beneath his blanket proved so soft he felt almost as though he were on a mattress; the morning mist was cool but not uncomfortable. They breakfasted on wonderfully strong, aromatic coffee and unleavened bread, and after the Berbers had prayed again they took up the westward ride.

As the sun reached well above the horizon the dirt of the track they were following grew thinner, and then their horses' hooves began clopping on bare rock. Bliven recognized in an instant that it was a white stone road, and in another mile it was edged with curbstones. The road began to rise, and Hamet Pasha suddenly galloped ahead to its high point. When Bliven joined him, Hamet pointed ahead and said, "Look."

What lay ahead of and below them was a sea of ruins—columns, curtain walls, streets, courtyards, small buildings almost intact. Bliven's jaw dropped before he recovered himself. "Why, it's a city!" He looked agape at Hamet Pasha and back. The road they were on splayed out into a grand avenue that passed the marble semicircle of an amphitheater and the roofless thick walls of what must have been rich houses. "It is a whole ancient city!"

Hamet Pasha was not smiling, but Bliven saw the satisfaction in his eyes. "Siwa," he said, "it was not possible to take you there. But al Iskandar was here also. Greeks, and then Romans, and then Jews and Christians, and then the faithful."

Bliven breathed so deep, he thought he must faint. "Please, may we go down?"

"Come." They eased their reins and the horses walked slowly, Hamet's retainers following well behind.

"What place is this?"

"It is called Cyrene."

"When was it abandoned?"

"I do not know."

The completeness of some of the buildings was unsettling, as though the inhabitants might appear at any second, but the silence of it was crushing; when they stopped their horses there was no sound but the wind. They passed on their right a marble wall twenty feet high, unbroken for at least a hundred yards, except in the very center there loomed a columned portal the whole height of the wall. Hamet turned his horse beneath the portal and said, "Come."

"What caused such a big city to be here?"

Hamet harrumphed and smiled. "There was an herb that grew here. Most excellent for lovemaking, but no babies would ever come. They sold it all over—Egypt, Palestine, Greece, Rome. The Romans paid its weight in silver."

"I should imagine. What was it?"

Hamet shrugged. "It no longer exists. They picked it all."

They dismounted and walked their horses across a vast courtyard. Just inside the tall curtain wall and several feet from it a ring of columns, many standing and as many fallen, surrounded the entire enclosure. Bliven estimated that it made at least six or eight of the town square in Litchfield. In the center, they approached the foundation of a rectangular building, and they sat on a step. "What happened in here?" asked Bliven.

"This is where they worshipped the emperors. The emperors said they were gods, and you see what it came to. Al Iskandar said he was a god, yet he ended also. There is only God, men should not reach so high." Hamet shook his head suddenly. "Why do you care about this?"

"I don't know. There is just so much to learn. General Eaton laughs at me."

"When I am bashaw again, in Tripoli, I will send scholars and learned men here, to dig and study, like at Pompeii you speak of. Come back," he said with sudden ebullience, "and I will tell you what they learned."

"Maybe they will find some more of that herb."

They mounted again. "Ha. I doubt it. People have been searching for centuries. Let us see a bit more, and then I must return you to your general."

WITH THE CITY CARRIED, Perry had anchored the *Nautilus* close in—closer in than he would have dared, lacking a trustworthy chart, making Bliven think that Hazard Perry was living true to his name and reputation. It was late in the evening when Bliven boarded and discovered his little field guns back on the ship. He found Perry on the quarterdeck and they traded smart salutes.

"Mr. Putnam," said Perry heartily, "I understand you have been taking an excursion with the new bashaw."

"Yes, sir. He took me to the ruins of an ancient city, a little west of here."

"Ah. Well, at last I have a chance to congratulate you on your part in taking the city. Not all the opposition has been quelled, of course, but the situation is quite under control."

"Thank you, sir. Your little field pieces actually did work some execution on the city walls and allowed General Eaton through."

"Excellent," said Perry. "How did your supplies last? Did you run out of ammunition?"

"No, we had plenty. I brought back the remainder."

"Really? I thought surely you must have fired all your shot. I heard that you were reduced to"—Perry could contain himself no longer and howled in laughter—"to firing your ramrods!" He doubled over and gasped for breath.

Well, fine, thought Bliven. Now he would be a laughingstock of the entire fleet, thanks to his damned Greeks, who had the gall to call themselves gunners. "Did you not hear?" he answered evenly, "that ramrod skewered the governor, right up the ass." There was nothing to do but join Perry in the laughter.

Perry cleared his throat and resumed a serious manner. "I do have orders to relay to you, in event of the successful capture of Derna."

"Indeed? I pray you, tell me."

"Prepare yourself," said Perry, "this may come as a shock. The war is over. A treaty was signed in Tripoli three weeks ago."

A slap in the face would have been less of a shock. "What! How?"

"I'm damned if I know. But now the war is over, someone has to go to Algiers and pick up that consul who has been held there, and his daughter, and any prisoners still held in the bagnios. The old dey has agreed to release them. You have been selected."

Only dimly did it register that Bliven was being given his first command, but that did not seem like the most important matter at the moment. "Does General Eaton know that we are done?"

"No. He is in the cockpit below, having his bandage changed. The news was just handed me."

"God." Bliven shook his head. "I pity the man who tells him."

"Pity yourself, then." Perry extracted folded papers from his coat and handed them over. "These are his new orders. He may leave Derna in the hands of Hamet Karamanlis, but he and you and all other Americans are to stand down. He is to abandon the march to Tripoli, join the commodore at the base in Naples, and await further instructions. You will join them there also, after you tend your errand in Algiers."

Bliven surveyed the shattered waterfront and up at the battered fortress, and thought of their two dead marines and the wounds borne by many others. "So all this was for nothing?"

Perry considered it. "Indeed, this action was fought after a peace was concluded, but I would not say it was for nothing. I can't imagine we would have agreed to a peace now unless it was on advantageous terms, and Eaton's army here created those conditions."

"But promises were made!" Bliven protested. "Promises were made that cannot now be abandoned."

"Well." Perry shrugged. "I am just a lieutenant in command of a two-hundred-ton schooner. Those questions are too large for me."

There was no sense postponing it. "I'd better go below and tell the general. Fish me out if he throws me overboard."

He found Eaton in the wardroom, his hand freshly bandaged, drinking a cup of coffee that the surgeon had spiked with rum. "Mr. Putnam," he acknowledged.

"General, how is your hand?"

"Well, I shall bear a scar, like the great Captain Cook, but it will not be any debility. How was your excursion?"

"Very educational, sir, and I am glad to see you better. Sir, I—"

"Have some coffee, Putnam."

"Thank you, sir, I will." He poured himself a cup, half wishing also for a shot of rum in it, but he did not ask. "Sir, I have just spoken with Lieutenant Perry; new orders have arrived."

"Bearing upon our mission?"

"Yes, sir."

"Well, let's see them. Are those the orders in your hand?"

"Yes, sir. I feel first I should say—"

"Nonsense, hand them to me."

Bliven did as he was bidden, unable to think how to soften the blow. He rose and paced the wardroom nervously as Eaton read slowly, and then a second time more slowly. Even in the dim lamps of the wardroom he saw the color drain from Eaton's face.

"No," murmured Eaton. "This cannot be." He looked up vacantly. "We are ordered to abandon the march to Tripoli. They have made a peace with Yusuf. Hamet Pasha they are cutting loose; he is to return to Egypt. This is impossible."

"Sir, who are the orders from?"

Eaton looked again at the last page. "Commodore Barron in Malta. The treaty was concluded by Tobias Lear. I do not understand; he was the one who cleared the way for us to make this expedition. This is impossible."

With a sick feeling Bliven remembered all that he sensed about Lear, and believed that he did understand, all too well.

Eaton began almost physically to swell. "This is outrageous. I spent a fortune. I made promises on the honor of the United States. I—"

Bliven could see his rage rising like magma in a volcano, and wished to stem it. "Sir, how will you ever tell Hamet Pasha?"

"Oh, good God. Do we still have people ashore? Tell Lieutenant Perry he must get them onto the ships at once. If any are still ashore when Hamet finds out he has been so foully double-crossed, they won't live for ten seconds."

"I will see to it at once." Bliven clattered up the ladder, thankful to be away from Eaton's stricken presence. "Mr. Perry"—Bliven found him still on the quarterdeck—"General Eaton urgently recommends that you recall any of our people who are still onshore. If they are there when the news breaks—"

"Thank you, Mr. Putnam. I have already sent a boat for them. This eventuality was mentioned in my own orders. It was foreseen that Hamet Pasha might receive word of this before we did ourselves."

"No"—Bliven shook his head—"he had not at the time I left him." He started suddenly. "Your own orders? From whom?"

Perry blinked in surprise. "Why, from Commodore Barron, of course."

Bliven nodded in slow recognition. So Barron was part of it. Well, once he picked up the consul and his daughter from Algiers, at least he must go to Naples. Preble would still be in Naples, and he could condole with him there.

Bliven returned to the wardroom, thinking that someone had considered this move and its ramifications very carefully, someone who could foresee likely consequences, and it was Tobias Lear's catlike smile in his mind's eye when he regained the wardroom. "All the Americans ashore are already being rounded up; they will be aboard shortly, General."

Bliven resumed his chair to offer his silent support, for truly there were no words to offer, when Eaton spoke suddenly. "I must write a letter to Hamet Pasha. Our lives would not be worth two pennies if he sees us again."

Bliven found Eaton's letter box in his baggage and set out paper and ink and pen for him. "Can you write, General?"

"Yes, yes, thank you. I can hold the pen adequately."

"What can you tell him?"

Eaton sighed deeply, chose careful and marked words, and spoke slowly. "Abandoning an ally, whom you have induced to rely on you, after he has set you in a place of advantage, is the oldest trick in Arab diplomacy. He will recognize it instantly. He will be shocked, only because he did not think us so sophisticated." His eyes met Bliven's with deep pain. "Nor did I. Nor did I."

Eaton had not yet dipped his pen in the well when both jumped as they felt the concussion and then heard cannon fire, not on this ship but close, six-pounders, by the sound of them, then a shouted order to beat to quarters, the drum tattoo and the thunder of men scrambling to their posts, unlashing and rolling out guns, men struggling up the ladder with tubs of water and linstock matches already lit.

Bliven and Eaton exchanged astonishment. "Maybe all was spoken too soon," said Eaton, and they hurried up the ladder to the quarter-deck. At once they saw the cause: The ships were obscured by the length of the mole, but they could tell from the rigging that raced by, a small brig flying Tripolitan red and yellow stripes, trying to run into the harbor, hotly engaged by the *Hornet* and with the *Argus* bearing down at her best speed.

Eaton and Bliven went straight to Perry. "She has no idea we're here," said Perry. There was no time to weigh the anchor, and he ordered it cut loose, and he commanded the bosun to set topsails and jibs. She gained some little steerage as soon as the sails filled, and they heard another exchange of broadsides from the other side of the mole.

Perry brought her about. "Mr. Andrews," he roared to his second lieutenant, "she will turn sharp into the harbor as soon as she's clear. Meet her with the port broadside before she knows we're here. Fire at my command when I turn."

"Aye, sir!"

Perry made eastward toward the end of the mole, and once he saw the Tripolitan's bowsprit become visible entering the harbor he made a sharp starboard turn, bringing his port guns to bear on her at a hundred yards before she could take any evasive action. "Fire!" *Nautilus*'s half-dozen port six-pounders roared to life, and at least two of her balls struck home, for a second later they saw chunks of wood fly into the air from the brig, but too far away to see how much damage they had wrought.

It hardly mattered. With two American schooners closing on his port quarter and now another on his starboard beam, and seeing an American flag flying from the Derna fortress, the Tripolitan collapsed his sails and ran up a white flag.

At first Bliven thought, *I've seen that before,* but this was a different circumstance from his encounter with the *Tripoli*. Further resistance here was not just futile but suicidal, and the question became moot when she dropped her anchor and her men appeared on deck with their hands in the air.

"Bosun, rig an anchor!"

"Already done, sir." They looked forward and saw a line secured through a clot of cast-iron kentledge brought up from the bilges. It would not hold in a strong tide, but it would do for now. The bosun had smartly prepared to drop it over the starboard side, out of the Tripolitans' view.

"Let go your anchor." It took out thirty feet of line before it slackened and they tied it off. The last question of their intentions was answered when Perry got his cutter down filled with marines, and at its approach every last one of the Tripolitan crew dove into the water and swam for the mole.

The marines boarded the ship cautiously, but after searching it minutely signaled that it was abandoned. They took command of a ghost ship; Perry went over with his bosun's mate and Bliven. They rounded her stern and saw her name, *Sameera*, painted in English and Arabic. "Mr. Putnam," said Perry, "it is my duty to send you to Algiers, and I cannot spare one of my own ships. As senior officer in command, I declare this ship a prize of war."

"But the war is over."

"They didn't know that. And they fired on us. I declare this ship a prize of war, I name her the United States Ship"—he thought for a moment—"*Defender*, and I place you in command. Sheffield, my bo-son's mate, will act as your bosun. You will accept volunteers for a prize crew. You may have one man in four from my crew and the crews of *Argus* and *Hornet*, when they join us. You will sail for Algiers as soon as possible, I would hope in the morning. Do you understand?"

"Aye-aye, sir."

They boarded the brig. Mr. Sheffield, acting bosun, was an extraor-dinarily tall and lanky Englishman with a heavy influence of Nordic from his mother's side. They inspected and found the damage inflicted was purely superficial. It was below, in the hold, where they found themselves shocked almost silent.

"There are enough arms here to start a revolution," breathed Bliven. Braces of muskets, kegs of powder, swords, all of the latest manufacture. How lucky that they had not landed damaging shots on her; she could have blown herself and them to atoms. "Do you wish to offload them, Mr. Perry?"

"No, take the cargo intact to the commodore in Naples. I will re-port its presence; they can decide what disposition to make of it."

Bliven had no trouble finding volunteers to go to Algiers, for with that assignment came the prospect of an earlier arrival at Naples, with light duty until their schooners could reclaim them, and who knew when that might be? He also took six marines under a corporal, a swarthy youth of nineteen named Jones.

From Derna it was eight hundred miles west by north just to round Cap Bon, and then another four hundred miles due west to Algiers. Much of it he fought ahead at about four knots in only a marginally favorably wind, and it took ten days to reach their destination. He felt more in command as these days passed, and lacking Sam's navigational skills, he was meticulous in skirting the hazards of Malta and Pantelleria, and the many islets and submerged rocks that spiked the capes of Tunis.

He felt not just relieved but accomplished when he stood into the bay of Algiers in a shimmering late afternoon, proceeding in until he could view the long stretch of arches of the bagnios, as he wanted to get an idea of the number of prisoners who left every morning for slave labor and returned stooped in the evenings. He considered firing a gun as a signal to bring the consul out, but at last report Lear was in Tripoli, working his dark magic.

He decided at length that it was just as well to call at the palace in the morning, present his orders in a businesslike manner, and fetch Barnes and his daughter, for all had been agreed already.

NEXT MORNING he was up before the sun, leaning on the rail, watching for signs of life in the bagnios, which when it came he counted about a hundred prisoners mustered and marched off. He thought of the nearly a year that Bainbridge and his crew had been held in Tripoli; they were now to taste freedom again, but these had surely been here longer.

The *Sameera*, now the *Defender*, had no craft larger than a jolly boat, which he had lowered, and it was rowed to the quay by the bagnios. He and Corporal Jones had made themselves as presentable as possible, and he decided to loiter a bit at the head of the quay to see if anyone came to meet them, for once they headed into the tangle of streets, of which no one seemed more important than another, they would be easier to miss than find. After twenty minutes and growing more anxious, he finally inclined his head to the corporal and they headed up toward the casbah and the palace. They saw few people in the streets, but he could not determine if that was significant.

When they reached the palace entrance they knew they had been noticed, for Jonah the black chamberlain was waiting for them at the portal. "Lieutenant—"

"Putnam." He saluted. "This is Corporal Jones, United States Marines."

"We were not expecting visitors," said Jonah. "Are there others coming?"

"No, we are the whole delegation, I'm afraid."

"I do not understand."

"Is Mr. Lear still in Tripoli?"

"He is," Jonah answered. "Your consulate is vacant at present."

"You are familiar with the terms of the general agreement between the United States and the Barbary powers?"

"Intimately."

"Then it will not surprise you that we have come for our consul to the Two Sicilies, Mr. Barnes, and his daughter, and any sundry American prisoners which you still hold. Your master agreed in this convention to release them."

"It is not in my power to let you have them."

"May we have an audience with the dey?"

"I doubt that he will see you."

Bliven folded his arms truculently, a posture unusual for him, but he had practiced it when alone in his cabin, with the added affect of cocking his head to one side. "Mr. Jonah, it is my duty to carry out the orders I have been assigned, and my government will take a very dim view indeed of obstacles being thrown in my way at this late date.

Now Tripoli and Derna are nearly destroyed, and that war is over. Do you really want the entire American fleet in your harbor to have to collect these few people? Does your master really want to look down the barrels of two hundred guns? If they come here, does he think they will not use them?"

It took several seconds, but they could see Jonah's resolve crumble. "Very well, follow me. I will see what I can do."

Bliven and Jones waited for a quarter of an hour in the drawing room with the mahogany furniture before Jonah came back for them. "His Highness has graciously consented to an audience, but I warn you, he is not pleased."

Jonah led them back to the limestone courtyard he remembered, overlooked from the fourth floor by the wooden lattice balcony that he knew now must be the dey's harem. Led into the dey's presence, they removed their hats and saluted.

"Am I of so little account now that they send a lieutenant and a corporal to speak to me?" demanded Mustapha. "I will not speak to less than a captain!"

"Your Highness," Bliven said, bowing slightly, "let me assure you that no disrespect was intended by detailing me to make this journey." He started to say that the senior officers were much occupied with the conduct of the war, but quickly realized that would make it sound like they were too busy for him, and it would make matters worse. "Perhaps they were aware that Your Highness seemed pleased with me on our last visit."

"My lions were pleased with you."

"Yes, sir. Your Highness, my government has sent me to recover Mr. Barnes and his daughter, and sundry other American prisoners that you may hold, as provided in the treaty lately agreed to by Your Highness."

"I see. And, Lieutenant, it has come to our notice that your government has agreed to pay my vassal, the bashaw of Tripoli, a sum of sixty thousands of dollars to end the war. As I am his superior, I have the honor to demand one hundred thousand dollars for the release of your citizens."

"Your Highness, I have no knowledge of such a provision in the treaty, but I was informed that the release of our consul and the others Your Highness has already agreed to."

The dey stood angrily. "Of course you have no knowledge, you are a mere lieutenant. Go back, tell them to send someone of authority to deal with me, someone who will agree to my terms—or, perhaps, appoint a new consul to the court of the Two Sicilies."

Though he was angry, it was impossible for Bliven not to notice the old man's frailty as he descended his dais and glared at him and Jones. "My chamberlain tells me that you threaten to bring your entire fleet if I do not meet your demands."

"Not our demands, sire, only the terms that you agreed to."

"Why are these two people so very important to you?" the dey demanded petulantly.

"Because that is our creed, sire, that no one should be unjustly imprisoned. As Americans we believe that every life has value, that God gives every man the freedom to pursue the best destiny he can make for himself. Perhaps that is the difference between our way of life and yours."

The dey's head snapped back, his eyes like dark embers framed in the voluminous white of his hair and beard, and Bliven realized he had said too much. He wondered if maybe now he and Jones would join those already in the bagnios.

"Ah, Lieutenant," the dey said at last with a sigh. "You have become as noisy as your superiors. And equally annoying." He turned his back and walked away, lifting a finger for the chamberlain to follow, but Jonah first shot them a look over his shoulder of such undifferentiated emotion that Bliven was left wondering what it was he meant to convey.

They were left to find their own way out, but without an escort they were free to talk, and cast about for a solution. Bliven's thoughts kept centering on their hold full of muskets and powder, and the hundred American prisoners in the bagnios. If they could find a way to liberate and arm the captives at night, perhaps they could storm the palace and free the consul and his daughter before the barracks could respond.

AT TEN THAT NIGHT, Bliven had lain down in his berth, wondering just as sleep stole over him whether the old dey was puzzling over what the Americans might do, if he felt vulnerable at all at this state of affairs. He started awake when he heard the watch shout a challenge, and he heard the small, hollow thump-thump of a small boat tying up to the boarding ladder. He was on his feet and in his boots before two sharp knocks rattled his door. "Enter." He smiled at himself, for he had said it like Preble, without meaning to.

"Lieutenant, sir"—it was one of the marines—"this Negro gentleman has come aboard and requests to speak to you."

"Have him come in."

Jonah entered, wrapped in a black cloak, shod in soft slippers. "Lieutenant Putnam, I hope you will forgive my intrusion."

"If you will forgive my surprise."

Jonah smiled tightly. "Understandable. Lieutenant, you spoke very boldly to my lord today. No one has ever said such things to him. He was furious."

"I realize I said too much. Won't you sit down? I did not mean to give offense."

Jonah stood by the chair but was plainly too nervous to sit. "But did you mean it?"

"Did I mean what?"

"What you believe, that all men deserve a chance to make their own way. That every life is important. Did you mean it?"

"I did, yes. We do not always live up to it, mind, but yes, that is the creed upon which our country was founded. It inspires us, even when we fail to achieve it."

Jonah unwound his cloak and Bliven saw that he was carrying a large bundle. "If I place myself in your hands, will you take me to America and deposit me in a place where there is no slavery?"

"I am sure that can be arranged, but that would seriously complicate our talks with your master, would it not?"

Jonah drew himself up. "He is no longer my master. Please listen." Now he sat, and motioned for Bliven to do the same. "Do you remember your first visit, the walled garden, and the gate through which you left?"

"Yes, very well."

"At this moment that gate is unlocked, as is the door to the banqueting hall. If you take that staircase all the way to the top, a corridor leads to the harem. Its door is always guarded by two eunuchs, and you would have to take care of them."

Bliven rose and opened the door of his cabin. "Corporal Jones, if you please," he called out.

He was quiet until Jones appeared. "Arouse your marines and tell them to get something to eat. Then come back here."

It took only a couple of minutes. "Jonah, you remember Corporal Jones."

"How do you do?"

"A pleasure, I'm sure, but what the hell are you doing here?"

"He is helping us effect an escape," said Bliven. "Now, how many guards are there over the bagnios at night?"

"Four."

"Who has the keys?"

"The chief of the watch stays in a sentry post at the far end."

"Jones, if your men can overpower those guards quietly, we can release and arm the prisoners. We have at least one gun and sword for each, do we not?"

"Yes. By God, sir, I like the way you think."

"Jonah, where does the consul stay?"

"His room is directly beneath the harem, on the third floor."

Bliven thought hard and fast. "There must be a palace guard. What of them?"

"Their barracks are against the fortress wall, on the other side of the palace. If you approach in secret and if you can avoid firing weapons, they may not respond at all."

"All right, Jones, get your marines ready, break out a hundred muskets and swords. The guards would see the jolly boat coming toward the quay—we'll have to go to the city waterfront and make our way around."

"Yes, I understand," said Jones, who saluted and disappeared.

With Jones gone, Bliven noticed the look of gravity on Jonah's face. "You have taken quite a step tonight, Jonah."

370

"This is the third time that I have faced the lion," he said, nodding.

"I do not know what you mean."

"When I was a child I was captured and taken to America, not knowing if I would live or die. As a young man I was captured by pirates, not knowing if I would live or die. And now you agree to take me to America, and I have no idea what fate awaits me there. When you face the unknown, you do not know how it will turn out. Or as we say, when you face the lion, you cannot know if he is hungry or not."

DURING HER BORING MONTHS in the harem of Dey Mustapha, Rebecca Barnes discovered that life actually was quite unregimented. She discovered that, contrary to Western perception, the harem was not just the retreat for the potentate's voluptuous interludes. In the Mohammedan world, all women lived sequestered, and the harem housed all his female relatives, who lived together, until one was wanted for a wife, and established a kind of pecking order like hens in a yard.

Rebecca quickly learned that, as she was consistently referred to as a guest, she could impose her wishes on others, for in the Islamic world, hospitality is an almost sacred responsibility. She learned to balance on that edge between requesting comforts for herself and making herself so obnoxious that they might actually throw her into a prison. It became her habit to sit up later in the women's common drawing room, snacking, for there were always trays of dates or figs or sweetmeats, or reading, for courtiers, especially the English consul, had managed to procure some English books for her.

Thus she was the only one awake to hear the commotion far down the staircase that lay outside the harem entrance. She knew better than to try to open the entrance door, which was barred and guarded, but as she heard the tumult grow louder, which was unprecedented for this time of night, some indefinable feeling warned her to be prepared. She was accustomed to going barefoot upon the carpets and stone floors of the harem, but as soon as she heard the commotion in the courtyard and looked down from the lattice shutters and saw American marines charging up the staircase, she ran to her chamber, found the shoes in which she had been captured, and put them on.

Hearing the same cacophony, the dey's wives and female relations began emerging from their bedrooms and opened a squealing, chattering retreat regarding what it was best to do. One who also saw armed men in the courtyard grabbed Rebecca by the wrist and sought to pull her into the stone bath chamber, but she shook her off; there were no weapons, but she seized a small alabaster box and raised it in a threatening manner. The oldest of the women stopped suddenly and shouted; during her months in residence Rebecca had come to understand enough Arabic to know she was saying they could overpower her.

She backed through their entry loggia toward the heavy oaken doors to the outside, when the shouts and footfalls of the marines became audible on their own floor. Two sudden gunshots outside the doors sent the other women scrambling back toward their interior recesses.

Bliven left ten of the armed prisoners by the staircase in the courtyard to prevent anyone from following them up as he and Jones led the marines in bounding up the stairs to the third floor, where two split off to find the consul, and two more marines followed them up to the fourth floor. There they saw as they were told two enormous guards flanking the door, wearing Zouave pantaloons held with broad red sashes and open vests, and they held broad scimitars that they had drawn from their sashes upon hearing, and seeing, the Americans approach. They were a sight never to be forgotten, like something out of the Arabian Nights, or painted Blackamoors in an English country house.

As they advanced with scimitars drawn, Jones stopped and commanded kneel and fire to the two marines behind him, followed an instant later by the bang-boom of the discharge of the muskets, igniting the main charges. Normally the sixty-caliber balls passed through their targets, but these men were so beefy that they fell dead with the lead inside them.

Bliven was the first to unbolt the door and spring through, alert for more opposition, but saw only Rebecca, who jumped back as the door crashed open.

"Miss Barnes?"

"Yes."

"We are attempting to break you out. Are there more guards up here?"

"No, never."

"Are there any more white women held here?"

"No, I am the only one. The other women have locked themselves in their rooms."

"Come, then, there is not a moment to lose."

The report of the muskets had finally alerted the barracks, and a commotion began to grow at the far quadrant of the palace. Bliven took her hand and all fairly flew down the stone steps. Consul Barnes and two other marines awaited them at the landing on the third floor. Further, they all descended to the limestone courtyard where the dey held his audiences.

As they rushed on down, Bliven just caught sight of the van of palace troops pouring into the court from the entrance portal. "Squadron!" he shouted to the armed prisoners, and they knelt and cocked the hammers. "Fire!" All ten muskets exploded simultaneously, eerily lighting the courtyard and the palace guards, who curled and fell into a ball or fell back and splayed spread-eagled on the paving stones. It bought them time, but only seconds. "Come on, boys!"

Bliven led them down, racing through the corridor, past the banqueting hall, and out into the garden. As they neared the gate, he could hear more troops storming down the staircase; they could not shoot them all.

He turned left and right in near panic as he saw Barnes and his daughter dart out the gate. "This is madness, this is madness," he repeated to himself as he lifted the latches on the lions' cages and opened their doors. He counted on the beasts' surprise to make them retreat before him; he flapped his arms shouting, "Ha! Ha!" With roars of alarm and confusion and defiance, he herded them down the walk toward the banquet hall door. Bliven slammed the gate shut behind him just as he saw the first of the troops reach the door at full run but then stop within two steps at the sight of four angry lions crowding their path.

Their shouts, a scream or two, Arabic babble, and the roaring of the lions faded into the distance as Bliven and the others raced downhill through the streets.

Sheffield the bosun's mate had the capstan turning to weigh anchor the moment he saw Bliven hustling his raiders and refugees down the quay. There were a number of small boats tied up along the waterfront, enough that all got safely onto the water without a return trip being necessary. As soon as the boats were tied on, he set the sails; the breeze was favorable but light, and they must make headway at once.

The crew cast each boat adrift as they pulled its people up the boarding ladder or over the netting; the last boat cast off as they nosed out of the harbor and into the open sea.

Through those first moments Bliven kept a suspicious eye on the fortress, expecting any moment the enormous guns to open up on them, but all there remained dark and silent.

17.

THE NEEDS OF DIPLOMACY

❖

July 1805

With the new consul and his daughter safely below and the liberated prisoners of the bagnio celebrating on deck, Bliven scooted out of Algiers as rapidly as the wind would carry them. He had his eight guns primed with matches burning, in case the old dey decided to send someone in pursuit, but two xebecs that rode in the harbor never stirred. Perhaps, as with Tripoli, it was from lack of crews, or perhaps the dey merely decided to let this chapter end itself. That Moorish fatalism that could lead these people into acts of stunning bravado, Bliven had come to realize, could just as unpredictably lead them into a nonchalant acceptance of something that they had tired of trying to master.

Within an hour they left the smell of the city behind, replaced by the bracing fresh salt sea air. With late morning the hot desert southerlies gave them a solid push toward Italy, for his Tripolitan brig's rigging made good use of it, running fast straight before the wind as only brigs can, not turning northeast until well out of sight of the coast.

Once under way and in a routine, Bliven was surprised to find that Barnes needed greater care than his daughter. For daily wear she cleaned and wore clothes that had been left by the pirates, and showed by her spirit that she regarded it, or had determined to regard it, as an adventure. Her father, however, kept to his cabin. He declined to go about dressed like a Moor, and he expressed the irony that he had fewer clothes now than he did when he was a prisoner, for in their flight he was compelled to leave all behind.

In such a small and foreign vessel the captain's cabin was more comfortable only for its stern windows, and it contained the rolls of charts that he needed time to open out and determine which ones he needed.

He thought at first to share the space with Barnes and give Rebecca the privacy of the second-best cabin, but no sooner were they at sea in this arrangement than he noticed Barnes drawing himself away into corners, his hands together at his chin, his eyes too grieved to show any thought.

The first time he saw him in this posture Bliven asked, "May I get you something?"

Barnes shook his head. "Thank you, no."

"Are you all right?"

It drew no response, and Bliven realized that though Barnes seemed physically sound, some injury more terrible than physical must have been done him. He made Barnes as comfortable as he could and he improved by degrees, washing his shirt in his cabin and wearing it wet on deck until it dried, eating more and gradually taking greater part in conversation.

Bliven put into Palermo long enough to learn the fleet's where-abouts, that the gunboats and mortar scows were returned to their base at Syracuse—*Oh,* he thought, shaking his head, *thank God I don't have to thread the whirlpool on my own*; never again did he want to experience that great, black, swirling hole in the sea. Instead, he headed northeast and eased the *Defender* into the Bay of Naples on the sixth of July, where he found the *Constitution* lying lazily at anchor in the shimmering Neapolitan heat, near the *Wasp* and *Nautilus.* Lacking pilot or charts other than those in Arabic, he dropped anchor as soon as he felt sheltered in the bay and before the water became dangerously shallow.

An inspection of the bosun's lockers had produced national flags and naval jacks of the United States, England, France, Spain, Portugal, Sweden, and the Sicilies, but the signal flags would have been recognized only among the Ottoman navies. A telling indication, Bliven thought, of the limits of the Tripolitans' abilities to deceive.

Before Bliven got *Defender's* jolly boat down, Preble had sent the *Constitution's* jolly boat over to fetch him and report. The day was windless, the bay still as glass in the summer heat, and Bliven stood to better enjoy his approach to the looming *Constitution's* familiar tumble home, so broad that the boarding ladder lay flat against it, no more difficult to ascend than the ladders within. After a week on his tiny brig the spar deck seemed enormous; a quick glance to his right revealed Preble on the quarterdeck, feet wide apart as always, hands knotted behind him, waiting.

"You were successful?" Preble asked even before quick salutes and the shaking of hands.

"Yes, sir. I have the new consul and his daughter on board. But, forgive my confusion, I understood that Commodore Barron was now in command."

"He is," Preble shot back, "but he is unwell. He is in his cabin." He lowered his voice. "In fact, he is most very unwell. He is so unwell that another change of command is being undertaken."

"Indeed?" Bliven gasped. "Back to you?"

"Oh, hardly. Rodgers again."

Bliven sagged. "Oh, no."

"Heh! Quite a pretty dance, eh? But I am the one alone on the quarterdeck for the moment. We've been waiting on you so we can go home."

"Well, I am beyond delighted. Now, the consul and his daughter are most anxious to get ashore, get into some new clothes, and have some decent food. And, contrary to all assurances, we found the Algerine bagnios crowded with American prisoners. I took it upon myself to fetch them home; I have a hundred and four on board, two died en route, just too weak. As you can imagine, our deck is very crowded, and they are almost crazy to get ashore. What shall we do with them?"

"Oh, God, I don't know, we can ask the consul. I suppose we could leave them here so they can await commercial passage, or I suppose we might have to bring some back with us. God, I hope not."

"The Barneses are my first concern, sir."

"Of course they are." Preble nodded. "Of course they are. Casualties? Did you lose anyone?"

"No, sir. I would characterize resistance in the city as token, at most."

"Well, I am not surprised," Preble concurred. "With Morocco out of it and Tripoli reduced, and Tunis has never been in play—I suppose the old bugger in Algiers had no heart to go on alone."

"We did have to shoot a few guards in getting the girl out of the harem. Some others chased us through the garden, but—well—the lions were very useful in keeping them well behind us."

"Ha! Your report should read like a novel. Do you have it?"

"Not yet, sir, no, I am sorry."

Preble crossed his arms and turned suddenly as exacting as he was with any other junior officer. "You've had a week, Putnam. Why not?"

"Well, sir, the young lady has been rather a handful."

"Indeed?"

"Yes, sir. I would have thought, considering we rescued her with nothing but the dress she was wearing, she would have kept close in her cabin. But she is a gruesome resourceful and managing young woman. No sooner was the ship in our power and we were under way, but she scoured through the vessel, picking out spare pantaloons and blouses. There was no cooking in the galley before she had thoroughly boiled the clothes and kitted out herself and her father with three complete suites, so they had the freedom of the ship. Were it not for their white skin you would take them for the purest brigands."

"Well, by God" was all Preble could say.

"And then she went through the bedrolls most systematically, finding in one of them a scimitar, which she now wears in her sash like Grace O'Malley herself."

"Well, now," breathed Preble; the approbation in his voice was plain.

"And what's more than that, she interested herself in every aspect of the sailing, and the navigation. She inquired of me the purpose and operation of every line and sheet, had me demonstrate the sextant, and inspected my calculations. And if I did not know better, I would swear she understood them."

"Ha! If I were not but three years married and my wife with a babe in arms, I would explore the possibilities with this young woman."

"And she is but sixteen, sir."

"Hm! So she is more within your range, then. Do you fancy her?"

"No, sir." He hesitated, and decided not to reveal more, as he and Clarity had agreed to keep their engagement secret. "I believe I have still fairer prospects at home. She is most genially sociable, though. I have tried to keep her pacified, but she was even after me to play at cards with her."

"I did not think you played at cards."

"I do not, sir."

"Ha! How has she found the cuisine on your vessel? Not happy with tea and biscuits, I'll wager."

"Actually, sir, we liberated some fresh provisions on our way back to the ship. I'll put it in my report."

"Which you will attend to presently."

"Yes, sir, right away. But to answer your question, Miss Barnes took command of the galley first day. She has done the bulk of the cooking, and she has done rather better than tea and biscuits. She did accept help when some of the men offered it—and she was offered a great deal of help."

Preble squinted. "I trust there has been no question of improper fraternizing?"

Bliven shrugged in a helpless sort of way. "I had to sleep sometime. But I cautioned the crew, and we did make a kind of latch lock for her cabin door. Otherwise, I believe she is most capable of defending herself."

"Heh! Scimitar and all that. Well," Preble sighed, "let's get them ashore—if you are not too tired?"

"I am fine, sir."

"Good. Take the jolly boat to the wharf. Get to the consulate and tell Barton of their arrival and their needs. I will send the cutter over to your ship to fetch them, and they will follow. Have Barton send his carriage down for them."

"Very good, sir."

"And then when you get back to your *Defender*, get your things together and come back over here."

"Oh." Bliven was unable to mask his disappointment.

Preble noted it. "Acquired a taste for command, have you?"

"Yes, sir, I confess that I have."

"Well, I have certified her as a prize, and you shall have a commandant's share of the proceeds, but I need to find her a permanent crew and I can't do without you here."

"Yes, sir. Thank you."

"You will have commands, Putnam, but be patient. I am recommending you for lieutenant commandant, so change your epaulette over when you have the opportunity."

Bliven backed up a step and saluted, but stopped even as he turned to go. "Oh, I almost forgot, sir. We also have that sort of court chamberlain from Algiers, you know, the former slave who is so well spoken? What shall we do with him?"

Preble's eyebrows flew upward. "He came willingly?"

"Indeed, sir. He stole away from the palace, unlocked gates, made arrangements to aid in the Barneses' escape. He is responsible for our success, and really he has nothing but the clothes on his back. Should we deposit him at the consulate as well?"

Preble considered it. "That—could be problematical. They are all Virginians. How do we know they would not take him back to work on a plantation?"

"I see your point, sir. I did promise him that we would take him to a place in the United States that was free soil."

"If they take him to the South, someone will surely claim he ran away from them. More like half a dozen people will claim him. He wouldn't have much of a chance."

"No, sir, he would not."

"Well, when you are through with everything else, bring him over here with you. At least if we take him to Boston he can make a living for himself, being so educated and all."

"Yes, sir. I am glad to hear you say it."

"Maybe we can berth him with Bandy. Heh! I would pay money to watch that arrangement for a month." Preble saluted quickly. "All right, be off with you."

"Aye, sir."

Constitution's jolly boat took him into the quay, and from there Bliven well remembered the direction to the American consulate. He received no answer when he knocked on the consulate door, but, passing around to the rear garden, he surprised Susan, cultivating flowers on her hands and knees. She wore a very plain blue printed smock, her hair in a ruffled cap, her shoes old and very scuffed. She looked up as she heard footsteps approaching. "Great heavens, Lieutenant Putnam!" She got to her feet and found her balance after a few seconds' vertigo. "You know, if you had put forth a little effort, you might have caught me in an even less elegant moment."

"I apologize to have taken you so by surprise. Mrs. Barton, you are looking very well, and your garden is beautiful."

"Well"—she surveyed the tidy parterres—"the early ones are blooming, but we must plant now to keep some color on into the fall. You must have only just arrived; we've had no word of it."

"Yes, ma'am. We dropped our anchor not two hours ago."

"And may I hope that congratulations are in order, that you had a successful mission?"

"Happily so, ma'am. That is why I am here. I have the new consul to the Two Sicilies, Mr. Barnes and his daughter, on board."

"Oh!" Her hands flew to her lips. "That means we can go home." There was an ardor and a longing in her voice that he never suspected might lurk there.

"They are rather the worse for wear from their many months of captivity. They want clothes and are much in need of decent food and rest. May we entrust them to your care?"

"Of course, yes! Did they come away with no things?"

"No, ma'am. My understanding is that they had the use of their trunks during their captivity, but the nature of our escape was such, they really brought nothing with them."

"When are they coming?"

"They are on their way now, in fact."

"Heavens! Walk with me."

The villa's carriage house and stable lay on the far side, giving Bliven an unexpected transit through a part of the garden he had not seen before, lower and shaded by poplar trees. "Does it not grieve you to be leaving all this?" he asked.

Susan stopped, surprised. "Yes, but rather no. We have enjoyed our years here, but in truth, the thought of going home, to Virginia, and family—if a ship sailed tomorrow I would try to find a way to be on it. But the fact is there is much business to attend to, we probably can't leave for some weeks. Now I have to think about what size clothes for the girl. Tell me about her."

"She is sixteen," said Bliven, "well grown for her age. In fact, if you have a spare dress or two to lend her, that should suffice until you can take her to a milliner."

"Excellent. What about him?"

"Well, he is about my breadth, perhaps four inches taller—that's a different case. I don't think Mr. Barton's clothes would fit him."

"No." Susan laughed. "Mr. Barton wears a size all his own. But what you describe is about the size of the English consul. I will arrange something."

"Luigi!" Susan called their driver out of his room at the rear of the carriage house. "Hitch up the carriage and take Lieutenant Putnam down to the wharf. Wait there for a man named Barnes and his daughter; bring them back here."

"*Sì, signora.*" As he harnessed the team, Susan started suddenly. "Oh, I nearly forgot, come with me." She led him into the villa through its kitchen door in the rear, down a passage, and through a paneled door into the public area of the house. From a table in the entry hall she handed him a large parcel of letters. "The post arrived this morning; these are addressed to men on various of your ships, through the care of the consulate. Could you take these and see them safely delivered?"

"Gladly, yes, of course."

Susan saw him up into the carriage. "Bring your commodore back for dinner at eight. Mr. Barron has important dispatches for him."

"I understand that Mr. Barron is quite unwell."

She nodded. "And has been for some time. Mr. Preble has been acting in his place, and he is always welcome."

That having the ring more of a summons than an invitation, Bliven directed the jolly boat back to the frigate to alert Preble, then over to the *Defender* to collect his things. He found the *Constitution*'s cutter already there, with Barnes and his daughter preparing to disembark.

The captain's cabin on a Tripolitan schooner was no palatial accommodation; still, it was an island of privacy that he had come to enjoy, and he looked about for a last time.

Back on the frigate he deposited his sea bag in his former berth, inspected his books, and spied Sam Bandy taking his leisure in the wardroom as soon as he emerged. "Sam!"

"Oh, my goodness—" He shot out of his chair and they took hands. "Welcome back. I assume you wearied of riding your camel?"

"Lord, I think I still have sand in my shoes."

"And I hear you founded a whole new school of gunnery—firing ramrods, was it not?"

"Oh, don't you start. Beware of Greeks who say they can fire cannons. But look here, Mrs. Barton gave me this pile of letters for the squadron. Can you take a minute to help me sort them by ship?"

They divided the bundle, and ten letters down from the top of Bliven's stack, his heart leapt as he saw his name elegantly written on the outside of a thick letter, returnable to Miss C. Marsh, Litchfield, Connecticut. Deftly it went into his pocket. He would not read it now; he would savor the anticipation as it built all evening. Five letters further down he handed one to Sam. "This one is for you."

Bliven just had time to unpack, and obtain a needle and thread from the purser to cut the epaulette from the left shoulder of his coat and sew it—he could hardly think how clumsily he must be doing it—to the right.

David Barton met them on the porch of the consulate as they approached, round-faced and good-natured as Bliven remembered, and conducted them inside, where they discovered Barnes and Rebecca in much better appearance—Barnes in a suit borrowed of the British consul, and Rebecca in a dark blue dress that he assumed was Susan's.

He was also surprised to find General Eaton, who said he had come up on the *Nautilus* after his having been summarily disengaged after capturing Derna.

"Commodore, a word privately for a moment," said Barton, "if you all will excuse us." Susan conducted the rest into the drawing room until they returned, with Preble having not quite finished searching out pockets in which to tuck a wealth of dispatches.

After the dishes were cleared away from dinner, Barton announced that he had received a copy of the terms on which peace had been reached with Tripoli. He unfolded several sheets of paper with close-packed writing.

"Some of it I'm sure we can guess," said Eaton. "The United States is going to continue to recognize Yusuf the Usurper as bashaw of Tripoli?"

Barton paused to judge what he might say to reflect his greatest sympathy. "Yes, General, that is one of the provisions. Howbeit, I know it is a consideration unpleasing to you, and to which you are not reconciled."

It was obvious that Eaton had more to say on the subject, but clenched his teeth to prevent it. "What else," he said at last.

"The first clause is that we assume the status of most favored nations with respect to mutual trade, the second provides for an exchange of prisoners. Now, it also provides that since we are holding about one hundred prisoners, and they are holding about three hundred Americans—"

"That will be Bainbridge and his crew," said Preble.

"Yes, since they hold three times as many prisoners as we do, we will pay them sixty thousand dollars for their return."

"What?" the color drained from Eaton's and Barnes's faces simultaneously. Eaton held his hand out to Barton. "That cannot be. May I see?"

Eaton perused the paper. "This is"—he took a deep breath—"this is so. We fought a war! Americans died, to win the freedom of the sea, to not pay ransom—and the first thing we do in making peace is . . . pay them ransom? It is inconceivable! It is outrageous!"

"May I see?" asked Barnes. He read the page quietly; he did not sob or in any way alter his tone of voice, but all could see tears spilling out of his eyes. "So all that we have been through, and yes, all that—I—have suffered, is of no account. No justice, no vindication, no reparation for their evil conduct, we just call it all off and agree to play together henceforward like nice children. This is dishonorable to a degree that I cannot fathom. I cannot believe that my country could strike such a heinous bargain as this."

He looked at the last page and read softly, "Done at Tripoli in Barbary, the fourth day of June, in the year one thousand eight hundred and five, corresponding with the first day of the sixth month of Rabia, twelve hundred twenty." Signed for the United States, by Tobias Lear. Quietly he handed the paper back to Barton; Susan looked helplessly upon these men who purportedly held some station of trust with their government, now reduced to such shock.

"I should have stayed another week," said Preble, "and reduced Tripoli to cinders."

"By God, I do not accept this," hissed Eaton. "I am not done with this. Lear!"

"General Eaton?" Bliven's tone of voice showed the greatest sympathy and solicitude. "I venture to say this only because we served such a long adventure together, and you can have no doubt of the high—very high—esteem in which I hold you."

"What is it, Putnam? Speak freely."

"When I was with Mr. Lear in Tangier, and Algiers, he said some things to me that I shall probably never forget. One was that the object in politics, whatever that object is, is always distinct from the means, that when you wish to bend another to your will, you should present him both a threat and an offer. If your enemy knows you can deliver on both, he will likely take the offer, at which time the threat becomes expendable. It seems to me that in his making peace with Tripoli, you and Hamet Pasha were the threat, which by your skills and determination you made a very real and present threat. And so Yusuf Karamanlis took the offer."

"And so General Eaton's service is expendable," said Barnes bitterly.

Bliven looked up at Eaton and found his large blue eyes staring at him coldly. He dabbed his lips with his napkin, slowly; his hands were shaking and it was apparent from his ironclad self control that he was so angry he could barely form words. "Tell me, young Mr. Putnam, when Mr. Tobias Lear was so sagely giving you his tutorial in statecraft and diplomacy, what, may we know, did he say of the national honor?"

Bliven felt Eaton's stare run him through like a saber, and he looked almost in fright down at the table. "General Eaton, sir, I never heard Mr. Lear speak of honor."

"Ah." Eaton looked around the table. "Thank you. There I will rest my case, for the evening. But in future I shall take this matter to the government, and I will see to it that it sticks to them like a blister!"

"All of this is well spoken," erupted Preble. "But it is not what weighs most heavily on my mind." When all eyes were on him he continued, "We went to war with these people because they were taking our ships and cargoes, and enslaving our citizens, even as they have done to Europeans for centuries. They say freely that their religion gives them the right to do this. I greatly fear that simple defeat"—he pointed at the treaty—"even if this could be called a defeat, will not answer the case. They should have been reduced, utterly, perhaps even destroyed. If this is where we leave it, we will have to fight them, again and again. I fear that his agreement is but a larger case of General Eaton's camel drivers. No price is final with these people. When circumstances improve, they will demand more."

"Gentlemen"—Barton shook his head—"gentlemen. I respect all the sentiments expressed here, and I feel myself honored to sit here in company with men who have carried themselves with gallantry and honor. Yet I feel bound to risk saying, there were other factors at play in making the peace that you may not be aware of."

The look that Eaton shot him was itself a challenge. "Such as?"

Barton nodded. "His Majesty King Ferdinand has forbidden any further supply of munitions to our ships. If you had marched on Tripoli itself the squadron could not have supported you, and you could not take Tripoli without them. Were you aware of this?"

Eaton's stare bore a hole through him. "I was not. Why has he done this?"

"It was not from lack of friendship to us, but his own defenses were becoming depleted in the face of the continuing threat from Bonaparte. He has been chased out of Naples before and he does not care to repeat the flight to Palermo." Barton let this register for a moment. "And moreover, young Mr. Putnam has a point. Yusuf the Usurper"— he paused in amusement at his unintended alliteration—"has been suing for peace for a couple of months. The feeling in the American government is that you have administered enough of a lesson for its effect to last. And, as long as they leave our ships and people alone, it is not worth more American treasure, let alone one single additional American life, to punish them just for the sake of grinding them beneath our heels. This is their part of the world and they have their way of life, and so long as they respect the international laws of nations, then the United States will have no more quarrel with them."

Eaton was crumbling but only slowly. "And what of the sixty thousands in ransom paid to recover Bainbridge and his crew? Is that honorable?"

"General Eaton," Barton asked, "do you come from a large family?"

Eaton was both dismounted by the change of subject and cognizant that his anger had come to dominate the evening. He was willing to speak of more pleasant things. "Yes, sir, I have twelve brothers and sisters, and with my dear wife I have two sons, three daughters, a stepson, and a stepdaughter."

"And may I gather that you are, say, about forty years old?"

"I am forty-one."

"Then you are yet in the prime of your life, and have a future. I am well past mine, although I live well and happily, but if I were young and had much to live for, I think I would try to put such a monstrous injustice behind me, and enjoy the remaining years God gave me, especially if I knew that vindication was uncertain, and even if it was obtainable at all would take years of more anger to achieve."

Eaton gave him the same glacial stare.

"Forgive me if I speak out of turn, General."

"No, I appreciate your sentiments. However, what has not yet entered the discussion is that the twenty thousand dollars in gold and silver that I expended in Egypt and Libya was my twenty thousand dollars, which I placed at the government's disposal on the promise that it should be paid back."

Barton had been taking a sip of wine but set his glass down, wide-eyed.

Eaton continued, "If the government wishes to use me so ill as to merely scare the bashaw into making a treaty—which he won't keep, by the way, but never mind—very well. But they needn't think that I will contribute twenty thousand dollars to that cause. Sir, I mean to have it back!"

"Speaking as the new consul here," Barnes spoke up, "I will support you in that cause."

"And speaking as the old consul here"—Barton held up a hand defensively—"let us pause to take stock. There is nothing in the treaty that touches upon General Eaton's contribution to the war. He may find the government as willing to repay his twenty thousand as they were willing to hand over sixty thousand to the tyrant in Tripoli. Is it not so?"

"May it be so," nodded Eaton, still angry.

"Now, Mr. Jefferson's secretary of state is an extraordinarily crafty man," Barton continued. "Let us remember that Mr. Madison opposed the Jay Treaty some years ago, and he has the Quasi-War with France to point to as the result of not taking his advice. I have every confidence in Madison's sense of honor, but one must never forget that his primary goal is to further the interests of the United States, to increase its power and prestige before the rest of the world. And he can act as pragmatically as a situation requires to achieve that, even at the cost of his personal opinions. And he requires no less of his ministers and consuls representing the country in courts abroad. Mr. Barnes, you have suffered a great deal of injury, which you may now be called upon to set aside. I can assure you from my own correspondence that Mr. Madison has viewed your situation with the greatest solicitude, but if it has rendered you unable to support the government's positions, whatever they may be, he will not spare you."

The silence around the table let Barton know that his admonition was not taken lightly, and that it was time to lighten the air as he always sought. "But look, now," he said more brightly, "there is no guarantee that the treaty will even be ratified, is there? It may hover around and be debated for a year or so, and we'll be right back where we were. And there is also no bar to Mr. Barnes pursuing a private indemnity, if he wishes, against the Algerine government."

There was no need to add that with a peace having just been concluded with the bashaw of Tripoli, and with quiet now settled over the whole of the southern Mediterranean, the chances of the United States raising any trouble to vindicate Barnes's imprisonment were very small. Barnes sat, motionless and sullen.

"For us, gentlemen," Barton gestured grandly, "we must play our parts gamely, each according to his station—which I am happy to say will include attending the opera, three nights from tonight. It is an opportunity for our commodore to thank the king for his indispensable aid, which, you will tell him"—Barton made sure to catch Preble's eye—"yes? You will tell him, made the difference between victory and a prolonged and indecisive conflict, a sentiment that our new consul will second."

Preble had looked weary all evening. "Very well. What time?"

"Our carriage will pick you up on the wharf at seven."

"With Mr. Putnam," said Susan. "I particularly wish his company."

When all had departed, Susan Barton went downstairs to lock away the silver. Since hiring Rafaela at a good wage to oversee the kitchen and scullery, she no longer counted the silver herself, but her eye was practiced enough to know at a glance before closing the chest of flatware, and from the arrangement of trays and chargers in the silver closet, that all was as it should be.

It was always labor to ascend the stairs, but she had never lost her satisfaction in hearing her footfalls on stone steps. In even the best homes in Virginia the staircases were of wood, and she would have to accustom herself to that again. Marble bespoke a station, a permanence and an order that, as far as she could forecast, the United States would likely never achieve. The corridor that led past the file of bedrooms had runners of cut-pile Aubusson, half an inch thick, and she made almost no sound as she walked toward their suite at the rear of the house, overlooking the garden.

She paused a moment at the door of Rebecca's room, thinking that if she heard her still awake she would knock and say good night, but to her astonishment she detected a muffled sob within. Disbelieving, she waited until she heard another. Susan rapped lightly and rapidly with her fingernails. "Rebecca?"

No answer came, and she clicked upon the latch and peered in. "Rebecca?"

She saw her sitting on the side of the bed in her nightclothes, her face buried in a handkerchief, but at the sight of Susan's face at the door, amiable and solicitous, she beckoned her inside. She sat next to Rebecca, so close that their combined weight made a single deep depression in the feathers of the mattress. "My dear, my dear, what is it?"

With comfort at hand, Rebecca tried to toss it off. "Oh," she said, "oh, it's nothing, and it's everything." She looked into Susan's eyes, light blue, clear as aquamarines, and the kindest, she thought, that she had ever encountered.

"My poor child." Susan put her arm around her.

"I am close on a whole year older, a year when I should have been here, a year that I cannot have back again."

"I know."

"And nine months in that, that place! Oh, God, how did I live through it?"

"Oh, my dear." Susan shook her head slowly in condolence and squeezed about her shoulders. "It is beyond me to even imagine the horrors you must have experienced, imprisoned in a Moorish harem for nine months. It must have been—the men must have been— brutish."

"No, no!" cried Rebecca. "You don't understand! Nobody touched me!" The looks on their faces met, and Susan's utter amazement confronted Rebecca's deep wounding at so profound a rejection that not even her jailers would have her. Rebecca took Susan's shock as confirmation of the injustice of her plight, the humiliation she had suffered, and a single heaving gasp escaped her lips before she composed herself again. "Nobody wanted . . . me." She sniffed. "Nothing interesting is ever going to happen to me."

"Oh, I see," Susan whispered.

"Jailed up in there eating those awful olives and dates. And I shall never be able to eat lamb again."

"Well," ventured Susan, "I promise we won't serve you any lamb while you are here." They laughed. "But this other—"

"No one will ever want me. Look at me, I am plain. Do people think I don't know this? Who will ever look at me?"

"Nonsense, girl. Look at me, we were cast from the same mold, yet I have a good husband and a good life. I have servants, and featherbeds, and watered silk."

"But you are pretty."

"No, I know how to make myself look pretty, and that makes all the difference. We can do the same for you."

Rebecca broke her gaze and looked at the floor. "You are kind to say so."

"It is true, and we will start, right now. The first tactic is to change one's outlook. No one can be pretty when she is cross, or self-pitying, no matter her justification in feeling so. Beauty begins in being kind to people, taking an interest in them, helping them when you can. If you do that, the beauty inside rises to the surface, and it shows. Really, I promise you, people can see it."

Rebecca looked at her once more. "I do not wonder that Mr. Barton loves you."

Susan smiled. "Mr. Barton and I are not young anymore. And when we are together, that way, well, let us say no artist would be moved to carve statues of us." They laughed. "But we do love each other, and respect each other." She sighed. "Still, being pretty is no guarantee that a man whom you want to notice you will do so. But God did not make us capable women to no purpose. We just need now to set our minds to making something happen for you."

"Then you don't think me terrible?"

Susan framed Rebecca's face in her hands, looking deeply at her. "Brown hair, brown eyes," she said. "That is to your advantage. Blue eyes convey transparency, but distance. Brown eyes convey mystery and passion, and that is what is wanted. My hairdresser is coming in the morning. Why don't you come to my room after you wash up, and we'll see if we can't help nature just a little bit."

"I shall never forget your befriending me."

"Well, let us think. You can't have met anyone here that you fancy, there hasn't been time. We cannot leave immediately. I shall think up a list and see to whom I can introduce you."

In such a consideration demureness seemed pointless, but Rebecca attempted it anyway. "Well, that gentlemanly Lieutenant Putnam and I became rather good friends after he rescued me. We had several lovely visits while we were on his ship."

"Perhaps he was not aware of your interest. Is he spoken for? Did he mention a sweetheart back home?"

"He did not."

"Well, let's see. Three nights hence is the opera—oh, my dear, you will get to meet the king! Not many American girls get to do that, do they? Can you curtsy?"

"Of course."

"Not a little social pop-down, dear, but a full court curtsy. Never mind, I'll show you. The king won't really notice if you curtsy correctly, he'll be looking down your dress."

Rebecca erupted in a short, sharp laugh, her first in a long time.

"Mr. Barton and I, and you and your father, will be there, and so will some of the American officers. Let me work on it. I'll see to it that you meet someone."

PREBLE WAS QUIET THE WHOLE TIME the jolly boat rowed them back out to the *Constitution*. He swayed idly with it as they were rigged to the davits and hoisted up. He steadied himself with the bosun's hand as he stepped over the taffrail onto the quarterdeck, and turned around to Bliven. "Mr. Putnam, a word with you in my cabin, if you please."

The commodore's return was long expected; the lanterns were lit, the chef had seen them coming and materialized with a cup of cool milk. Preble waited until they were alone and the door was shut, and he pointed Bliven to a chair. "Mr. Putnam, I expect word of this will get around soon enough, but until then, this is in confidence."

"I understand, sir."

"The other Barron sailed from Gibraltar some days ago. He is putting into Port Mahon to take on supplies; he should be here in a bit over a week. He will assume command of the Mediterranean squadron at that time. Our days here are numbered—you have known that this would happen for some time."

"Yes, sir, but I still don't like how you have been treated. When—"

"Barton told me first thing we got to the consulate this evening."

"Ah, that's when he took you aside into his—"

"Yes."

Bliven shook his head. "It still smells of intrigue, and it is unworthy."

"Well, I thank you for your indignation. Heh!" Preble laughed so seldom that Bliven was always shocked by it. "Tell me, Mr. Putnam, what did you think of old Mr. Barton's giving of advice this evening—about counting up the cost of fighting for your vindication, and being able finally to just say, 'Oh, to hell with it'?"

"To General Eaton, you mean?"

"Did you think he was speaking only to Eaton?"

Preble's meaning sunk in slowly. "He was speaking to you as well, sir, wasn't he?"

"Yes. He knows that I am somewhat pricklish over the whole matter. Happily, I am better situated to take his advice than General Eaton, poor bastard. He was very badly used, I fear. You have your old berth, next to Mr. Bandy?"

"Yes, sir."

"Good. Good night."

Bliven stood to go. "Sir, I am very glad to be sailing home with you."

"Thank you. And—your Algiers report, end of day tomorrow."

"Without fail, sir." From the wardroom Bliven took a lit lantern into his berth; he already had one in there, but all night he had carried the letter from Clarity in his breast pocket, and he wanted good light. He took off his shoes and stretched out, taking care that a lantern was hanging over each shoulder.

LITCHFIELD, CONNECTICUT
8TH MAY, 1805

My Dear Lieutenant Putnam,

Or perhaps, if your forecast has been verified, you are now Lieutenant Commandant Putnam. Your kind favor of three months ago came to hand only two days since.

It is true that I did encourage you to write me of your adventures, and indeed, your account of meeting the old king of Naples, and of his manners, and we now know of the firing of the gallant Philadelphia and the bombardment of Tripoli are all quite thrilling. You must not be surprised if you read of them in my novels one day.

However, touching upon this other incident you relate, that of the Sicilian king scolding his dogs after himself committing an unpardonable social faux pas in releasing nature's vapors, I must confess that I am perplexed utterly, how to incorporate it into any book—even a novel. For my own part, you need have no fear for the delicacy of my sensibilities. The true case is so much to the contrary, that when I read of the king, and of the dogs scurrying under chairs

*at the sound of his farting, knowing that they were to be blamed, it
reminded me of nothing so much as what I hear of Mr. President
Jefferson and the members of the current Congress. Whenever the man
commits some new act meriting opprobrium, even outrage, his
henchmen in the Congress scurry about like mad to search out
arguments to make it sound as though what he has done is not just
legal, but is somehow congruent with his political philosophy. I declare
that ancient Greece produced athletes of no greater flexibility.*

Bliven found himself laughing out loud, and decided he must share
such a feast. Racing out of his own berth, he rapped sharply twice on
Sam's door before opening it and entering without waiting upon an
answer. "Sam—"

Sam Bandy shot off his mattress with a gasp, by habit back into the
bulkhead and not upward, for there was barely room to stand. Bliven
saw on Sam's face not that he was startled, but a catastrophic shock,
deep and desperate sadness, his eyes red in the lamplight, his breath
shallow. A letter lay open on his table.

"Sam?"

He collapsed back onto his bunk, his head hanging loosely, his eyes
unfocused.

Bliven joined him on the bunk, taking his hand. "Sam, what is it?"

"My fa—" His voice caught, for he had never said such a thing before, and he swallowed, fearful of hearing it. "My father is dead."

"Oh my God, Sam," he whispered. For a moment they felt nothing
but the ship's slow rise and fall in the bay swells.

"Close the door, please."

"Of course." Bliven did so—naturally, Sam would not want the men
to see him in such a state—and then sat again. "How?"

"Yellow fever."

"Oh, no."

Bliven released his hand and reclined against the bulkhead. "What shall you do? Will you need to resign your commission and go home to manage the family's affairs?"

"No." He thought for a minute. "It wouldn't do much good to resign here, I'm halfway around the world. But no. There are my two brothers close at hand, they can help my mother make decisions, and she is strong. The overseer and our people will keep working as before. I wish I was there, but no, I am not needed, not really."

"When did all this happen?"

Sam looked again at the date on the letter and calculated back. "Just over two months ago."

"Well, the poor man is long past his pain. That is a blessing."

"Yes. But I would like to have said good-bye." He turned away and cried softly.

"Is there anything I can do for you?"

Even in port, only the captain could order the grog tank opened. "Galley, please—bring me a cup of tea? No one must see me like this."

"Of course." It was too early in the evening for the galley fire to have been banked. Some of the crew saw him coming forward through their hammocks and stood, until he raised a hand. "As you were, men." Willingly they dropped back down to their sail-canvas tarpaulins on which they were reclined, gambling or playing Going to Boston.

He reached the camboose, and as he prepared tea Bliven thought what he would do, if such a blow fell upon him. Indeed he would have to resign his commission, return home, and manage the farm and the business. His mother could not do it all, and they had never hired anyone other than seasonal harvesters. Through this he descried one advantage of the Southern system that they had never discussed, that plantations assumed something closer to lives of their own. He could not set it down as any merit of slavery, but indeed, such large operations need not cease with the death of any one person, even the master.

Sam was a little recovered by the time Bliven handed him the tea, and they sat together again. "My mother," said Sam, "ordered some furniture and mirrors from France. The merchant in Savannah wrote her that they had come. My father took some of our people and two wagons, and went down the river to fetch them. April in Savannah, it should have been too early in the year for the fever. But he had four of the darkies with him; there was no place for them to stay in the town, so he camped with them outside of town, by the river. And it had turned hot; there was a heavy mist on the river that night. Three days later he was dead." He shook his head hopelessly.

"Sam, I am so sorry."

"He could have gone into town and stayed there," he said, almost like he was protesting. "He could have written a letter explaining their business, and left the slaves there in the bottoms. They could show people the letter if they were questioned. But he didn't." He looked into Bliven's eyes. "He didn't want anyone molesting his people. He was not a cruel man." He began to weep again. "I can't bear for anyone to think he was a bad man."

"I do not think that. Certainly he was a good man, Sam."

Sam sipped his tea, very hot and sweet. "He was more than my father, really. My brothers are much older, they never had time for me. He was my friend and my teacher. There were not many neighbors, I had not many friends. I do not warm to people easily. I do not know what I shall do, knowing that he is gone."

"I also feel great tenderness for my father," said Bliven softly. "You have met him, you know why. And I have no idea how I shall respond to this calamity, Sam, when it happens to me, and it almost surely must, one day. But there is one thing about your present disaster for which you must feel comforted."

Sam looked at him searchingly.

Bliven wrapped his big, salt-roughened hand around Sam's. "You must never, not ever, believe yourself friendless."

Sam Bandy's body seized, a convulsion ruthlessly controlled, as tears poured from his eyes. Strange, thought Bliven, grief we can bear, it is comfort that overwhelms. In a moment Sam could speak, but he could not look up. "Indeed, I am not."

"We even had to swear it, did we not? What other two friends ever had to do that?"

Sam smiled through his agony. "True. Wait, what was it you wanted to tell me, when you came bursting in here?"

"Oh, it's of no consequence, Clarity wrote me a quite devastating assessment of President Jefferson that was too funny. It will keep for another time."

Sam nodded. "Yes, I must write to my mother. She does not know where I am, and she sent her letter through the Navy Department to forward to me." He smiled sadly. "She had the furniture sold in Savannah, she could not bear to look at it."

Bliven stood up. "I guess you will not feel like attending an opera tonight."

"Oh, no, I had forgotten. I can't possibly. Can you tell—"

"Leave it to me. It will be late when we return, but will you knock if you need me? Anything at all."

"I will, I thank you."

Bliven returned to his berth and closed the door behind him, shaking his head. What terrible detours Life can launch us upon. Our lives can change direction entirely, with no warning whatever. He could wash overboard in a storm; a gun could misfire and explode, he could lose his footing while aloft. His parents seemed healthy but who could really know? Clarity could take typhus. Suddenly it seemed a miracle that anyone ever reached old age.

18.

LIEUTENANT COMMANDANT

———◆———

August 1805

He sat, and returned to Clarity's letter. Ah, yes, she was discussing the intellectual malleability of Jefferson's lackeys in the Congress.

> *I have particularly in mind for this criticism his recent purchase, wholly illegal and unconstitutional, of French Louisiana from Bonaparte. Tell me, on what page of any national document does he find the authority to have done this?*
>
> *Nevertheless, he is reelected, and apparently with a greater popularity than in that terrible canvass of four years ago. Not I, nor many others hereabouts, have forgiven him the terrible calumnies that he caused to be published against Mr. President Adams at that time. We take some comfort, however, in learning that the unsavory printer whom Mr. Jefferson engaged to do that deed, has become disaffected from him, and turned his poisoned pen 'round upon Mr. Jefferson himself. One hears that the printer, as part of his payment for*

savaging Mr. Adams, desired the emolument of being made postmaster in Richmond. Mr. Jefferson, one supposes owing many political debts and favors in his native state, preferred another to the station. The printer therefore chose to take his revenge, and one reads everywhere now that Mr. Jefferson, who as we all know is long widowed and otherwise to be sympathized with, has for many years sought the favors of a slave on his plantation. Her name is Sally, and they seem to have several children together. The extraordinary thing is that Mr. Jefferson has not denied it, indeed he has made no reply whatever.

From this I conclude two things. The first is that there must be some truth behind it, for otherwise Mr. Jefferson would surely have the man in court facing a libel action—except, now as I think about it, Mr. Jefferson was returned to the presidency with the warm support of the South, where such things are thought less of, or perhaps even approved of. He has made a clever turn, to be sure, increasing the value of his property with new slaves while at the same time satisfying his passions on this hapless woman. My second conclusion is that, as censurable as Mr. Jefferson's conduct may be, it is a symptom of the illness, not the illness itself. If there were no slavery, such a relationship could not exist, except with the consent and affection of both parties.

And now, can I not see you smiling—there she goes, you are saying, back on slavery again. I do confess the evil of it vexes me as much as when we spoke. Perhaps even more so, for there is a new development of which I must tell you—and at least you cannot criticize me for slighting you with a short letter.

The learned Reverend, Mr. Beecher, now visits Litchfield nearly on a monthly basis. He is from New Haven, of course, so his own family connections could bring him back regularly from his church on Long

Island. Of late he has become imbued with the spirit of abolition; he
is afire with the wrongs of slavery, and is raising money to fight it.
It has become known in the community that the Pierce sisters have
increased their support for his efforts, and even my own father, who I
need not tell you takes a less strict approach to such matter as drink,
has subscribed donations to his church. So have many others of our
acquaintance.

Bliven lay the letter down to allow himself a few moments' disgust
about Reverend Beecher. The man should become a poultry farmer;
he surely did seem to be proving his skill at plucking prime chickens.
He took up the letter again.

On Sunday last he preached a sermon overflowing with conviction,
on the sure error of those at the South who believe that slavery is
sanctioned because it exists in the Bible, and because St. Paul advises
the slaves of his day to meekly obey their masters.

His countenance is goodly as well as godly, indeed one might call
him handsome, as you will remember. This does not bear upon his
intellect, but I believe that the average layman will hear a message
better from a comely person than from a homely one. He is only nine
and twenty years old, which I think a fine age to preach convictions.
He is old enough and educated to know many truths, and young
enough to preach them with passion—and when he preaches he seems
to be on fire. His skill in speaking is such that I am grateful he is in
the service of God and not politics, for he could convince anyone of the
rightness of his beliefs. I know that you and he did not warm to each
other upon first meeting. I pray that you and he will become friends, if
only for my sake.

Bliven stopped reading, disquieted for a moment, and then cast down altogether. Had he a rival, in only the second letter he received from her? Why was he nine and twenty, and no mention of his being married? If he had a wife, surely Clarity would have written of her. As his gloom deepened he finally realized what was happening with him—that if his feelings for her were no deeper than infatuation, he would not care, one way or the other. But he realized how much she had come to mean to him.

He admonished himself to leave this off, but dwelt on it in spite of himself. Clarity was educated, not just in the school subjects but in the graces that formed a large part of Miss Pierce's success at turning out young ladies ready to enter society. Clarity would never have praised this Beecher fellow if she thought her words would kindle jealousy. Therefore it was clear that, either her regard for the man was harmless, or things between them had changed. Perhaps, like the young lawyers from South Carolina, she also looked on him after all as the drayman's son, invited to a party out of kindness, but surely not cut from their cloth. It made him feel sad and small—and confirmed that if this was to be his luck with women, then he chose well a life at sea.

Oh, the time! Bliven realized he must attend the commodore, and get ashore for the opera. He quickly donned a clean shirt, then his waistcoat, coat, and sword, and regarded as much of himself as he could see by angling his sight down in the tiny mirror. Preble had given the other junior officers leave to explore their own amusements, and they had taken the cutter. He sought out the bosun's mate to select four rowers and prepare to lower the jolly boat before rapping on the commodore's cabin.

"Enter," called Preble.

Bliven made his quick salute. "The men are getting the jolly boat ready, sir."

"Very well. Where is Mr. Bandy?"

"Oh, you haven't heard. The post brought him a letter from home; his father has died. He's taking it rather hard and wants to be alone for a while."

"Oh?" Preble gave a sharp look outside into the wardroom, where he could see the closed door to Sam's cabin. "Damn. Damn, there is no good time for news like that. Is he all right?"

"He will be. He just needs to get over the shock."

"Should I speak to him?"

"That is most kind, sir, but I think not. Truly, I believe he wishes to recover himself before seeing anyone."

"Poor boy. Damned hard luck. Well, we had best be off." Up on the quarterdeck they swung over the taffrail and into the boat, whose rowers were already seated, holding their oars vertical. Once they hit the water Bliven took the tiller. At only sixteen feet long the jolly boat took a slapping from the chop in the bay, but they were not noticeably wet by the time they made out *Constitution*'s cutter tied up at the quay.

They found Consul Barton and his wife awaiting them in a carriage. "Boys"—Preble turned to the four oarsmen—"you may enjoy yourselves, but be moderate. When we return, I do not want to find you drunk, or beaten up, or in custody. Do you understand?"

There was a low chorus of agreement. "Well, go find your mates from the cutter and try to keep out of trouble."

David Barton descended from the carriage to greet them; they removed their bicornes as they stepped up into it, leaving Barton a moment's embarrassment in discerning how to pull up his own large bulk, eased when the driver dismounted and helped him.

"Commodore," Susan greeted Preble.

"Ma'am."

"Mr. Putnam, how nice to see you. Where is your friend Mr. Bandy?"

"He sends his regrets, ma'am," said Bliven. "The mail brought him the most dreadful news that he has lost his father. He is most terribly stricken, and begs to be excused."

"Oh!" The pain on Susan Barton's face seemed quite genuine. "I am heartily sorry to hear it. I shall have Rafaela prepare a supper basket for him and leave it in the hall. When we return from the opera, will you take it out to him?"

"Yes, gladly, how very kind."

Susan tapped the driver on the back. "Luigi, did you hear? Once you leave us at the theater, go back to the consulate and see to it, then come back and wait for us."

"*Molto bene, signora.*" The two horses walked on with a light tap of the reins on their backs.

"The theater has a supper room," said Barton. "Consul Barnes and his daughter are already there to meet the king. We will stop in there first to make our courtesies. Now, I would not load up a large plate, as we will go straight on to our box. The king, you know, is very modern and will want to shake hands, so take care not to be holding a plate if he does."

"The queen is Austrian," said Susan. "She's very fond of Mozart, so she will be there. She may speak to you to be courteous, but you mustn't speak to her unless she addresses you first."

"I have heard of operas," said Bliven, "but never attended one. What are we going to hear?"

"Ha!" laughed Barton. "The king is very proud of himself. He remembered that the theater did a production last year of *The Abduction from the Seraglio*. He thought it would be peculiarly appropriate, considering your late adventure in spiriting the Barneses out of Algiers, to command a repeat performance."

They settled into their box, and such music Bliven had never heard before. The rollicking overture, with its triangle and cymbals meant to effect a "Turkish" sound, its halting modulation in a minor key during which the mind's eye easily conjured an intruder, tiptoeing down a dark and dangerous corridor, its headlong rush to the safety of a double bar—all might well have been played to accompany his sortie into Algiers.

He spoke not a word of Italian, and even if he had the singing was so ornamented he could have followed none of it, but the plot was so transparent there was no need of language. All that he need do was enjoy his first exposure to such ravishing, pure music.

Susan reached over and tapped Bliven's arm with her fan. "I am so sorry to trouble you, but Miss Barnes is not feeling well. Could we possibly impose on you to take her back to the consulate?"

"Yes, certainly," he whispered. Of course, he must betray nothing of his grief at having this experience cut short. "But would her father not prefer to do it himself?"

"He would, but we need him to stay; the king may wish to speak to him later."

Bliven looked across the box at Rebecca, gowned in pale blue silk, her hair fashionably done up but looking wan and labored for all that. A moment's eye contact with Susan and he rose and crossed over to her. "Miss Barnes, would you like me to take you back?"

"Oh, would you? That would be most kind."

As they exited the box Bliven glanced over his shoulder, across to the royal box, and saw the king conducting the orchestra from his chair with evident delight, and the queen affecting not to notice, but clearly embarrassed. He judged that she had discussed such gauche behavior with him before, with no good effect. His and Rebecca's absence would not be noticed.

Once Rebecca was safely in the carriage, the fresh air seemed to revive her. "So, Lieutenant, once again you rescue me from a difficult situation."

Bliven smiled, mindful of her perfume. "Well, you seem rather better situated than when we first became acquainted."

She was quiet as they passed down the street to the consulate. When they stopped he helped her down and escorted her inside.

"Will you see me up?" she asked.

He hesitated, wondering at the necessity of that, but quickly acquiesced rather than make her feel awkward.

"You know, since I've been here, it's been hard not to think back, on Algiers, and the women that I lived with in the, well, harem."

"Yes?"

"Did you know that Arab women are often married by the age of twelve?"

"Indeed?"

"Most of them are grandmothers at twenty-five."

"It is a different way of living, without question."

"Do you know, the women bathe, every day?"

Bliven felt himself shying away from such an intimate subject. "Perhaps it is the climate."

"No, not at all." They reached the door of her chamber, which she opened, and led him inside by the hand. "They hold themselves in readiness for their men, if one of them should come and, well, desire her." She rubbed a hand idly at the bustline of her dress. "Oh, this is getting us nowhere." She drew close to him, pulled his head down, and kissed him, fully and sweetly, after which she lay her hands flat against his chest. "Do you know what to do? I can show you, if you need."

His heart pounded, his search for words fruitless until he found refuge in the stupid platitudes of gentlemanly conduct. "I can make you no promises!" he blurted.

Rebecca drew back. "Nor I you. But we have been through much these past months, in our own ways. Have we not each seen the uncertainties of life? You or I could take a fever and die tomorrow, or your ship sink. We have this place and this moment, and I want to know what love is while I am young. Don't you?"

He let her remove his coat, and then his waistcoat and shirt; he held her, wanting to reciprocate, but after a brief search realized he had no idea how her elaborate gown came off. "Let me," she said. "It gets complicated."

She pulled the rustling dress over her head as he removed his shoes, and in a moment they embraced bare-chested. She unfastened his breeches, even as he thought, of all incongruous thoughts to have, how much he disliked these uniforms and preferred the new and easier style of trousers.

When there was nothing more to remove she swept her hands down the breadth of his chest to his waist. "I have never seen a man before."

He swallowed. "Then how do you know so well what to do?"

She laughed quietly. "In truth? There are some novels. They are banned, but some of them are smuggled into the country. They are very clear on how it all works."

They lay on her bed, awkwardly, for it was a bed for one, and once uncorseted she proved larger than he anticipated. He kissed her throat as he stroked her breasts; they were large, as formable under his hands as udders, which he found did not kindle passion. Still, he knew to kiss and caress them. He inhaled deeply; the lieutenants whose coarse talk he had heard about women prepared him for odors unfamiliar and earthy, but there were none. They were dear and gentle with each other, and explored everything that was new to them.

When it was over and they had rested a few moments in each other's arms, Rebecca ran her fingers through the faint, downlike hair that was beginning to show on his chest. He opened his eyes as she said, "I don't want you to worry about this."

He looked at her for a moment, thinking. "It is no accident that the house is empty, is it?" he asked softly.

"I'm afraid you were 'set up,' as they say. You have been a perfect gentleman, you have incurred no obligation whatever. You have been very kind to a lonely girl. Whatever life I have in the future, I will never forget you."

"Nor I you." He didn't know what else to say.

"And now, you ought to wait downstairs. They will be coming back soon." She smiled and pushed against him gently. "Wouldn't do to have you found up here."

Rebecca watched him dress, thinking as he became more and more covered, that he was the most perfect young man, physically, she was likely ever to have—and she found herself oddly content with that, for if she once possessed such a man, she must be powerless to keep him. She would find someone closer to her station.

Bliven's shoes echoed down the marble steps to the first floor; such a large house, he thought, and so quiet. He took up the basket that had been prepared for Sam, and took a seat in the dim drawing room, trying to reflect not on what had just happened, but on what wonderful music he had heard. He had heard hymns in church, and fiddlers in taverns, and the gypsy music in Gibraltar that they called flamenco, but this Mozart—he realized that he lacked the vocabulary to even assess it, it was so new to him, except to think it was transporting and transformative. And now there would be weeks more at sea, returning home to a place where such music, and such cities and such food and such houses, were unknown. He fell asleep thinking how much growing America had yet to do.

The clatter of the carriage, and footsteps in the hall, shook him awake. There was a flurry of leave-taking; the part that registered most clearly was Preble acknowledging that the *Constitution* would sail for home in three days' time, and the Bartons pressing on them that they must attend a farewell party the following night. No wonder Morris made such a failure of his command, he thought groggily. If one had a bent for parties, one could find something going every night in port.

Susan slipped a sealed envelope among the bread and fruit and preserved meats, and placed it over Bliven's arm. "Please tell Mr. Bandy how sorry we are for his loss, and tell him we most earnestly hope he can come to our farewell tomorrow."

"He will be so grateful, thank you."

"How did you leave Rebecca?"

At mention of his daughter's name, Barnes leaned close to hear. "She retired. She was feeling rather better."

The night was balmy; the bay swells and dipping sweeps that carried them back to the frigate left Bliven with an almost content feeling, allaying for the moment the contest between home and the sea that this tour was intended to clarify. After trading good nights the commodore retired to his cabin, and noiselessly Bliven opened the door of

Sam's berth and left the basket on the table. He closed the door to his cabin slowly and backed against it. Well, he thought, perhaps it said something for his character that he did not feel good about what had happened. He did not feel like a conqueror. He did not feel love or loved; the worst part was that there was from Rebecca something pleading about it, something lonely that he could not fulfill.

His own cabin seemed like a refuge from the whirlwind of the evening's events. He undressed in the dim light of the battle lantern. He had been to the theater with royalty, he had heard music that he never imagined existed, he had possessed a woman for the first time. "Oh, God," he whispered as he remembered that the *Wasp* would sail with them, and would carry letters home from the squadron. He could not be certain of having time the next day; he must write his parents tonight and let them know he was all right. If he didn't they would read about Americans killed at Derna before his next chance to write, and they would not know if he was alive or dead.

And he must answer Clarity, but he must give no sign how she had wounded him with her praise of that handsome, young, passionate, religious—horrid, ridiculous—Beecher. He must write pleasantly, and be reasonably informative, but presume nothing of her emotional favor.

NAPLES, KINGDOM OF NAPLES
AUGUST 10, 1805

My Dear Clarity,

I take advantage of the departure of the Wasp on the day after tomorrow to answer your kind favor of 8th May last.

416

Bliven set the pen in its inkwell and leaned back. This was not right. He was becoming one of them, one of those serial deceivers, one of those detestable other lieutenants who had spent this very evening in the taverns and stews. *Am I not,* he thought, *writing a letter to a young lady I care for tenderly, even while the sweat of mating with another dries on my body?* He rose, emptied a porcelain pitcher that sat on his table into its basin, and washed as well as he could before resuming. If he did not feel more clean, at least he felt more awake.

Dispatches of our latest engagements also go in the same vessel, so it is possible that you will read here, before it is published generally, that the war is over, and brought to a successful conclusion. Successful, at least, in terms of our government having imposed its terms on the pirate Bashaws of north Africa—terms which, at the last hour, were altered so as to be not too unpleasant to our enemies, and so to assure their agreement.

General Eaton, whom I have come to respect so very highly, is nothing short of appalled by the terms—he who enlisted the help of the former and rightful Bashaw of Tripoli, to raise an army, on the pledge of the United States to restore him to his throne—and General Eaton who then had to tell this ally that the United States had concluded a peace behind his back with the usurper, and he should get on his camel and go back to Egypt, with his wives and his children still held captive by his fiend of a brother.

Well, he thought, it wasn't a camel, it was that fine black Arabian stallion, and Hamet Pasha still had his retainers to worship him, so he was not as bereft as though he had risked all for Eaton and lost. He still had his billet in the Mameluke army; he would be all right. But Eaton's point still stood immovable, that the honor of the United States had been compromised beyond respecting. A camel, however—he elected not to change it, for a camel might better suit her novel.

And Mr. Barnes, the new consul whom we have delivered safely to Naples, was scarcely less in umbrage that all he had suffered in the dungeons of Algiers would not be avenged. Arabs treat Christian— that is, infidel to them—prisoners with great brutality. He has not imparted any detail of what he has suffered, but I have no doubt that he has suffered such humiliation—

He could not say "buggery," although he learned from his time in the Libyan Desert that the Arabs felt no scruple against inflicting the practice on others, so long as they suffered it not themselves.

such degradation as must stain his view of the world should he live to be a hundred. Thus, I gather that the thought of his eventual vindication and triumph over them was all that sustained him. I fear he must reconcile these matters, else live out his time a broken man.
   His daughter—

Bliven laid the pen down and pondered what to say of her.

seems to have come through the ordeal in better condition than her father, and she a captive for nine months in a harem! She, however, professes not to have been molested, the Arabs believing that it would diminish the sum of ransom to be paid for her.
   You will recall that I have at sundry times pled the case of the

naval service's lack of sufficient number of men to put such a force on the ocean as to command the respect of other nations. Having now been two long cruises at sea, I can say that I no longer wonder at this. Who would wish to serve in such a fleet? From the bottom up, all is confusion, self-interest, small-mindedness. Of the common seamen, most of them joined the Navy because it was an alternative to be preferred over the Debtor's Prison. To say they are a coarse lot is the only defense I can find for the abhorrent food they must eat; most have probably never known a fine table, and had they done so they must mutiny.

And above them the midshipmen. What one of them would happily serve under the tyranny of lieutenants who are no better than brutes, who make it their study to find useless and demeaning tasks to assign them, then conspire among themselves to make certain that the tasks cannot be done and then punish them when they fail?

Understand me rightly, this is how they treat the most junior officers. Can you even imagine how they treat the common sailors? I will tell you, they treat the seamen with a contempt that can only arise from a hatred not of the men but of themselves. I wonder that they are not murdered in their beds. In good faith, I hope I live long enough to forget some of the things I have seen. And above them the captains— some good, some bad, some mad.

And at the top of the pile, the government, which acts in half-measures so that it may claim to be both at war and not at war, depending on the political need of the moment. For the many late missteps of this war, I do not know where, ultimately, the fault lies. Do we say that Mr. Jefferson sent us to sea with an impossible task, to rescue our ships and sailors, and punish pirates, but for too long gave *us no clear mandate of war to do so? Or do we say that Mr. Jefferson was compelled to this course because his enemies in Congress, had he gone to them for a declaration of war, were so keen to make mischief for him that we would have been put even more in hazard than we were?*

Do we fault the commodores like Morris who, given those handicaps, were reluctant to prosecute a vigorous campaign, or blame the ones who do fight with alacrity? What reward for them? Commodore Preble, as we have only recently learned but you may know by the time you receive this, is being relieved of his command. He is blamed for the loss of the Philadelphia, which was not his fault, but someone must be blamed for it, and apparently a decision has been made—somewhere, by someone, or perhaps it is mere conformity to the popular will—that we need Mr. Bainbridge in the role of a hero, despite his rash actions that led to the loss of a brilliant ship and the suffering of three hundred of his crew for more than a year.

Thus, for Commodore Preble and General Eaton, the two men who did most to force this war to a victorious conclusion, they are to be turn'd out, while the laurels will be placed on men like Mr. Lear, who crafted the questionable bargain, and Captain Bainbridge, because Americans prefer our heroes to be young and handsome, dashing and reckless. This is not the education that I expected to receive.

You see how much confidence I place in your discretion, to keep this letter between ourselves, for if it were made public, I should likely have to fight duels with all concerned.

However to all that, I have saved the good news for last, that the Constitution makes ready to sail in a few days, so I will see you in

perhaps six or eight weeks. I am most keen to do so, and inquire into
the status of the bargain we made when last we parted.
And now I must haste to sleep or be worthless tomorrow.

With affectionate wishes for yr
health and happiness, I am yr
Bliven Putnam, Lt., USN

THE NEXT MORNING, work began in laying in stores for the month's, or more, voyage home. Preble awoke to see out his great windows that a British three-decker had slipped in during the night. He felt his ire rise as a look through his glass confirmed that it was the *Hector*, which he had encountered in Gibraltar.

There was no time to distress over it now, for there would be a full day of laying in stores, and then he must get himself to the consulate for their farewell. All their boats would be shuttling all day—the bosun's lockers, the carpenter's lockers, the bread lockers all had to be filled, tons of salt meats, Cutbush would need to replenish his pharmacy. The jolly boat only had he reserved for his own use, and sent his chef with silver to round up the last and freshest of victuals for the commodore's stores; he would return by late afternoon. Come evening the men would have put in a hard day of toil, and he instructed the bosun to select those who had worked the best and send them ashore in the cutter for a night's liberty. It would be their last chance to carouse, for Preble determined that they would put in only briefly at Gibraltar on their way home. In fact, if relations there had continued to deteriorate, he would not tarry at all. If there were not dispatches to send and receive, he would sail on by.

The officers must have a frenetic day; Putnam only, in his office as aide, would he take with him to the consul's party. It was nearly eight in the evening when the jolly boat landed them at the wharf. No carriage met them, but then he expected none, for this was likely to be a large affair and the carriage would be otherwise employed. It was a pleasant walk up to the consular district.

Bliven was surprised to see Sam on the front porch as they arrived, and they shook hands briefly. "Sam, I missed you today. Where have you been?"

"Transferring to the *Wasp*. We will sail ahead of you. The commodore called me in this morning. He was very kind, he knew this is my fastest route home. You are for Boston and we are for Virginia."

"Did you get your basket?"

"Yes, I came up to thank Mrs. Barton before we sailed."

"How are you, Sam?"

He lowered his head. "Sad, to be truthful. It is harder than I imagined it would be."

Bliven noted for the first time that Sam's epaulette had changed from left shoulder to right, and pointed silently from one to the other and back again.

Sam had to grin. "It is only in an acting capacity."

"Well, then, an acting portion of congratulations to you."

"And you also," said Sam. "Look at you!"

"Equally in an acting capacity, but it seems that we advance together."

"Good evening, Lieutenant Putnam." Rebecca had come out on the porch. She was in a gown of russet-colored silk that suited her well and wore a pendant of topaz at her throat.

"Miss Barnes, you are looking very well." They exchanged bow for curtsy.

"I rested exceptionally well last night. Will you introduce me to your companion?"

"Oh, excuse me. Miss Rebecca Barnes, may I present Lieutenant Samuel Bandy of South Carolina?"

"How do you do?" Sam bowed.

"From South Carolina?" she said with enthusiasm as she curtsied. "I am from Virginia, so we must have many things to talk about."

"Most certainly. I wonder if you are aware, we nearly met some months ago, in Algiers, when we were first there to try to win your and your father's release."

"Is that a fact?"

"Yes. After your being so long sequestered, the commodore felt, in case of our success, that you would be comforted by hearing a voice that sounded, let us say, somewhat close to home. So I"—Sam paused, laid a hand on his chest and made a comical attempt at a court bow— "was brought up to the palace especially to escort you."

"Well, sir! I would have been honored—had I known of it. I was locked in my rooms, in the attic."

Playfully, he took her hand and kissed it. "Ah, you were so near, yet so far."

"Well, I declare! Come, sir, you must have a glass of punch, and pour me one as well." They turned into the hall, and without further prompting Rebecca threaded her hand beneath Sam's elbow and secured it on his arm.

Bliven stared after them in astonishment. "Well!" He'd had no idea that Sam could handle his craft so ably, in the very instant of opportunity. He was so amused, it took a second for him to realize that Sam had also relieved him of any awkward moments alone with her.

He followed, at a distance, to the mahogany sideboard in the dining room and poured himself a glass of punch. He was near enough to hear Sam say, "In the interim, I have been placed in command of the *Wasp*. We will be carrying numerous dispatches concerning the end of the war, so we will be bound for Hampton Roads, being so near the government."

"What extraordinary luck," exclaimed Rebecca. "My father has agreed to let me go home to recover from the past months' imprisonment. If you are bound for Virginia I could come on your ship. If you have no objection?"

"No," Sam said, smiling broadly. "No, you will be most welcome indeed."

"And I will delight in having a Southern gentleman to talk to."

Bliven turned and wandered back into the drawing room. *Good for Sam,* he thought. *This could turn out very well indeed.* For only a second did the icy doubt sweep through him that she might impart to Sam what had passed between them, but he dismissed it quickly. A flirt or a tart might do so, but Rebecca had far too good management of herself to indulge in something so pointless. In fact he had all but satisfied himself that their encounter had weighed more heavily on him than on her.

He made his way back to the drawing room, where Barton had introduced Preble to what it seemed must be the city's entire diplomatic corps, and their ladies. As Bliven took his place at Preble's side, Barton approached opposite them with an angular tall man in British uniform, topped with an old-fashioned powdered wig.

"Gentlemen," said Barton, "I would like you to meet Captain Lord Arthur Kington. He commands that handsome British third-rate you saw newly arrived in the bay."

"His Majesty's Ship *Hector*," added Kington, "seventy-four guns."

Preble found himself sucking at his lips, reckoning the needs both social and political to maintain civility. "Yes, sir, we met in Gibraltar, last year."

"Ah, yes," Kington affected to remember slowly. "The American commodore had some sailors jump ship." He smiled ever so faintly, as though he were enjoying the fading memory of a successful subterfuge, in that English way that Preble could not abide.

"That question is still open to investigation, sir, but tell me, how have they made out as British sailors?"

"Had to hang one of 'em," Kington said lightly. "The blighter turned round and tried to desert again, cheeky bastard. Didn't die well, either—kicked off his shoes when they ran him up the yardarm, almost like he shied them at me. Not much trouble with the others after that, though."

Preble turned over in his mind the possibility that an American citizen had been forcibly impressed into the British Navy and hanged when he tried to escape. It made him sorry they were at peace. "Our previous acquaintance was not social, as at this moment," said Preble. "May one inquire into the nature of your title, sir?"

Kington's clear blue eyes looked down an aquiline nose as his wide, narrow mouth moved. "My father is the marquess of Wexford."

"Ah," said Preble. "One of the new Irish peerages, is it not?"

Kington's gaze became if anything even colder. "It is. It was formed of estates confiscated from traitorous rebels."

Bliven calculated quickly. "Lord Kington, do I recall reading somewhere that you have an elder brother?"

"Who are you?" he asked highly.

Bliven saluted lazily. "Lieutenant Putnam, sir."

"My aide," said Preble.

"M-hm. I do have an elder brother, Michael, the earl of Rosslare. In what connection could you have read of him?"

Bliven's face became blank. "In all honesty, Captain, I do not recall, but I am sure that your family name seems familiar in some way. It is probably of little consequence."

Kington's face seemed to turn to marble. "Your memory or my family?"

"Oh! My memory, of course, I beg your pardon."

Susan Barton joined them, rustling in a gown of brilliant pink silk, curtsying to the rank of bows. "Mrs. Barton," said Preble, "I shall be most heartily sorry to leave you."

"We have enjoyed your acquaintance so very much, and we are delighted at the success of your mission." If she knew that Barron was replacing him, she did not betray it.

"Before I take my leave, I would enjoy one more turn in your garden, in case I do not make it by this way again."

"By all means," said Susan, "gratify yourself. The flowers are at the height of their season. There are some torches along the paths; you should see them well enough."

"Thank you, ma'am." He bowed himself away. "Mr. Putnam? If you please." Bliven replenished his punch on the way out.

The back wall of the garden was lined with those peculiar tall

Roman cedars. Preble held his peace until they were out of earshot of the house. "Putnam, as God is my witness, that man took our sailors and hanged one of them, and I can't prove it."

"Does he not personify every trait about the British that you detest?"

"He does." They took in the perfumed air of the Neapolitan garden for a moment.

"And is it not just like them," said Bliven, "to set up peerages in the countries they conquer? Marquess of Wexford, my left foot. You do know, if we had lost the Revolution, the man might be the marquess of New Jersey, and his elder son the earl of Newark."

"True. But that is bothering me, Putnam. How the devil did you know he had an elder brother?"

"Well, he introduced his father as a marquess, and that estate must include lesser titles, such as an earl, that would be borne by an older son. This peacock was introduced only as Lord Kington, so there had to be a missing link in the chain."

"Well, by God."

"So you see, for all his airs and snobbery, he is a second son, or even further down the line for all we know. He is most likely in the navy to make a way for himself, because he doesn't have an acre of land to call his own. It is the hypocrisy of it, you see! The façade! 'My father the marquess, my brother the earl'—pooh! Of course he means to act as superior as he can because he's got nothing!"

Preble nodded. "I do believe you have the man's measure. I will likely not be around when the time comes you have to fight them, him and his kind. That will be a hard job. Their navy makes twenty of ours. Look you, his ship has seventy-four guns and is only a third-rate."

Bliven shook his head. "As I think of it, perhaps I should go back down to the quay and keep an eye on our men. If this lizard poached our sailors in Gibraltar, there is nothing to stop him doing it here."

"Good thinking, by God, go to it."

"Oh, and also, Mr. Bandy seems quite smitten by Miss Barnes, so it may slip his mind to mention it. She is going back to the States to recover from all this. She is from Virginia and he and the *Wasp* are bound for Hampton Roads. She asked passage, will that be all right?"

"Yes, yes, I am sure we can count on his gentlemanly conduct."

"Good, good." Bliven made his way back into the house and sought out Susan to extend his thanks and farewell.

She took his hand warmly. "Mr. Putnam, we have so enjoyed having you here. I hope you will remember your time in Naples fondly."

"Yes, ma'am, I certainly shall, and for more reasons, perhaps, than you can guess."

She burst out in a high laugh, and much to his surprise poked him in the ribs. "Oh, I do think I can guess." She winked.

He smiled bashfully and bowed himself away. So, she was behind it all. Well done. "Lieutenant Putnam," Kington's cold voice erupted behind him, "I do not believe I am mistaken in having felt your disdain this evening, though God alone knows what superior ground you think you stand on. If I have done something to offend you, say so plainly or be gone and the devil take you."

Bliven could feel the fine spiked punch swirling in his head. He saluted smartly, but with a faint smile. "Sir, you need not have not *done*, you merely *are*."

"Why, you!"

"I am on my way down to the quay, to make sure that no more of our sailors . . . desert, as it were." Abruptly his voice dropped and his words came rapidly. "Take heed, sir, we will not let such a 'desertion' pass a second time. If you have arranged for a press gang to circulate among the taverns this night, you had best find a way to call them back."

"Why, you stiff-necked little colonial brat. You people think your backwoods crudity somehow makes you superior creatures. Well, sir, daily I thank my God that you will never be our equal in culture and civilization."

"That is true, Captain," said Bliven as he began to bow himself away. "We are not like you, for which *we* thank *our* God, every Sunday in church. Good night to you."

Kington had just grasped the hilt of his sword when he felt a soft hand on his. He looked aside and saw Susan Barton threading a stout but still elegant arm through his. "Do not deny it, Captain Lord Kington, for you are restraining yourself so violently you must injure yourself in the effort. What on earth are you thinking?"

Kington glared over his shoulder at Bliven's receding figure. "That one day I am going to have to fight that boy."

THE NIGHT AIR, scented and balmy, cleared Bliven's head by the time he regained the waterfront. Ahead of him down the curve of the quay he made out the Pizzofalcone that jutted out into the bay, and up on its heights he could descry torchères on the terraces of the Palazzo Sessa. Without forgetting his errand to see to the safety of the *Constitution*'s boatmen he allowed himself a smile, and a few moments of a more deliberate walk with his hands clasped behind him. Up there, Susan had told him, above the heat of the streets in that sixteenth-century mansion with its palm-punctuated gardens, was where Lord Nelson and Emma, Lady Hamilton, had so shamelessly cuckolded her aging and no longer virile art collector of a husband. He recalled almost with a start that Susan had imparted this to him in the theater as they waited for the opera to commence, and he realized now her meaning—that romantic assignations need not always be seen as censurable; they can be therapeutic, can even save a lonely person from despair. Bliven as he walked allowed himself a wave of appreciation for her.

And he allowed himself a second smile at what else Susan told him—and it was not commonly known, that Sir William Hamilton did not actually own the Palazzo Sessa, he merely rented rooms there from the Marquis di Sessa, albeit he rented the best rooms that fronted on the terrace, where he and his art became the envy of the diplomatic corps. Such grand pretenders the English are. And Lady Hamilton, despite her beginnings dancing naked on tables for gatherings of gentlemen, she had parlayed her marriage into becoming the confidante of Queen Maria Carolina, procuring vital help for the British fleet, and in return, Nelson's protection of the Sicilian throne.

That was only a very few years ago—but a lifetime as the dice roll in European politics. Sir William Hamilton was recalled, and Nelson bought a large country house that had seen better days for the three of them to live in together—excluding Lady Nelson—raising such a scandal that he was sent to sea again, but not before Emma bore him a daughter. Hamilton had died two years before, in 1803, a broken man after a ship carrying his Greek vases came to grief on rocks off the Scilly Isles. Lady Hamilton was now regarded as a scarlet woman; she was tolerated because of Nelson's protection but not received in society, certainly not so long as Lady Nelson was so expertly promoting her martyrdom. For Lady Hamilton, if anything happened to Nelson, debtor's prison was only a matter of time, for her husband had left her almost nothing. How quickly fortunes change, Susan had pressed upon him; one must seize opportunities and enjoy life as it comes. Nelson had been in Sicily as recently as four months ago, when he received intelligence that the French and Spanish fleets were combining near Spain, and he sortied west to bring them to a decisive action.

Bliven gave a moment's wonder whether the *Constitution* might reach Gibraltar with the British fleet still in port, and whether he might perchance meet the great Nelson and be dazzled by his diamond badges. The story was that he wore his decorations defiantly in battle, daring sharpshooters in the enemy's fighting tops to find him.

Sight at last of the *Constitution*'s cutter, tied up next to their jolly boat, brought him back to the present.

"Good evening, Lieutenant." The single sailor guarding them made his salute.

"Good evening. How is the night passing for you?"

"Quietly, sir, thank you."

"It does not distress you to be standing guard alone while the rest are making merry?"

"Oh, no, sir, I just came on duty a few moments ago to relieve the last man. I have already made merry and he is having a drink."

"I see," said Bliven. "And where are your mates?"

The sailor indicated a well-lit and noisy tavern fifty yards down the quay.

"Mm. Are they all in there?"

"Well, mostly, sir." The sailor gave an embarrassed laugh. "From time to time one of them will escort a lady around the corner to that street you see."

"Well, the captain is not far behind me, let us go round them up."

Bliven stood just inside the door, as close as he cared to experience a prime example of what all sailors knew as a dockside stew. For such it was, a brew of odors of sweaty men and spilled ale, of piss outside the door, of loose-bloused women displaying their wares by barely concealing them, of pipe smoke and hearth smoke and pungent food.

There were no musicians here, so it was easy to gain their attention. "Gentlemen, all sailors of U.S.S. *Constitution* to report outside at once. The captain is returning shortly and we are going back to the ship. Check around among your mates, make certain no one is missing."

As they formed up before the tavern a commotion rose from the dark lane where the prostitutes had been taking the men to their house by turns. There was a clatter of hard-soled footsteps, curses and exhortations shouted in British accents. When they became visible there was one British lieutenant in full uniform, and six vaguely dressed ruffians who followed him. They were hustling along an unwilling man whose shirt had been pulled up over his head, his arms pinned inside.

It was exactly as Bliven had feared. The Americans knew from his shouts and protests that it was one of their able seamen. "Look, boys, that is Shifflett. They are taking him off!"

"Stop! You men, there!" bellowed Bliven. "Unhand that man! Release him, instantly!" With a metallic slink he withdrew his saber from its scabbard.

Without command the British sailors formed a defensive line, screening their captive. Their lieutenant pulled out his sword and took position in the front, as the press gang produced a motley assemblage of dirks and small bludgeons. "His Majesty's business," called back the lieutenant highly. "You dare not interfere."

In a flash Bliven took their measure. They were one officer and six thugs who doubtless could acquit themselves in a fight. He had four rowers from the jolly boat, plus eight rowers from the cutter and the men they brought over for some liberty. Without taking time for arithmetic he figured he had about twenty. "I have no quarrel with you, sir, yet you have taken my man. I am willing to call it a mistake, but you will hand him over or we will take him."

"There is no mistake. We have captured a would-be British deserter and we shall take him on board our vessel." The lieutenant looked back at his detail. "By the right, quick march, march!" They loped off in a body, at a trot, toward their boat.

Bliven faced his sailors and raised his sword. "*Constitution?*"

He was met by a throaty roar as the men withdrew dirks and truncheons and lead knuckles, all standbys that sailors secrete upon their persons when ashore for recreation.

"You three men"—he pointed to them with his saber—"cut straight through and get our man back. You others with me, all right, come on!" They surged forward as fast as they could run, and although they quickly overtook the press gang it was quickly apparent that the British toughs could each account for two of them. Bliven and the British lieutenant met each other blade to blade, and he realized in a heartbeat that his Baltimore saber was at least four inches shorter than the English one. His only help was to attack so furiously and continuously that the Brit must continually be on defense, and give him no opportunity to counter.

At the edge of his vision he saw the three men he detailed seize the American prisoner. They pulled him out of harm's way, finished pulling his shirt off over his head, and in a heartbeat had thrust a bludgeon in his hand and all four joined the fight, assaulting the English from behind their line.

The two men fighting at Bliven's immediate right engaged a massively thick brute of a man, thin hair, heavy brow ridge, bulbous nose, peglike teeth. Where others were hurling curses, he but grunted. Bliven had never imagined how one could grunt with a British accent, but somehow he did, when he walloped the man on Bliven's right a terrific blow over his left eye.

That one shrieked as though his head must fly off, and without meaning to Bliven turned to see if he was going down. The flashing instant that he turned his head, he felt a match-burning agony rip across his stomach from right to left, like a seam opening. At this the British officer stood back, haughty as anything, as though he were waiting for a fencing master to award him the point.

Never regard a wound, Lieutenant Curtis had hammered into him and Sam. *If it is a slight wound, it will be no hindrance. If it is a fatal wound, you will be dead soon enough.* The only response to being struck was to attack with redoubled fury. Your enemy may be so surprised that he will flee, or make a mistake, but you must attack before a loss of blood saps your strength. Without so much as looking down, Bliven slashed his way forward, shouting at each stroke.

Seeing his prey forfeited and his men suffering under an attrition of punishment, the lieutenant jumped back several steps. "Withdraw!" he cried. He pointed with his sword to their boat. "Withdraw."

"Hurrah the *Constitution*!" There was a roar of acclamation. "After them, boys!" the general cry went up. "Teach them a lesson!"

"No!" Bliven stepped to their front. "Let them go, we have accomplished our task." He felt the warm wetness oozing down from his lower belly.

"Why, Mr. Putnam, you are hurt."

He felt himself sink to his knees, and he knew that several

hands took hold of him, strong but gentle, before he floated from consciousness.

He opened his eyes, sitting in the cutter, supported on both sides.
Bliven was conscious of the loop being passed beneath his armpits, but
as the line curled through its tackle and he felt himself being lifted, he
fainted.

When he came to again he was lying on a table. "More light! More
light, damn it!" It was Dr. Cutbush's voice. "Oh, what have you done?
What have you done?"

Three more battle lanterns were hung about the table, and Bliven
recognized the cockpit; at the edge of his vision he made out the rib-
like scantling that imparted brute strength to their ship. He felt Cutbush scissoring away his shirt and the top front of his breeches. "My
good clothes," he whispered.

"Not anymore." Cutbush laid the bloodstained shreds aside.

The added light and activity brought Bliven back to his senses, but
his vision was straight up, not down at his belly. "Am I killed?"

"I don't know yet."

"If you find that I am killed, will you tell me plainly?"

Cutbush ceased his ministrations for a second only, laying a bloody
hand on Bliven's chest as his face appeared in his view. "Yes. Lie still,
now."

He could feel Cutbush probing the edge of the gash across his abdo-
men; he turned his head aside enough to see him take up forceps and
knew he must be spreading the wound to see how deep it extended.
Who would tell Clarity that he had survived battles with pirates only
to be gutted by a supposed ally on an allied waterfront? Would that be
the end of her novel, a cruel and violent irony?

Suddenly a pain worse than the initial cut seared across his belly, and he felt something cold and wet dripping down his sides. He cried out before he could stop himself, and felt Cutbush's hand on his shoulder. "I'm sorry, lad."

"That is not honey! You said the Romans used honey."

Cutbush smiled gently. "Alcohol, Mr. Putnam. Surer than honey."

"The captain!" The voice came from the after ladder. "Captain on deck!"

The cockpit fell silent as everyone snapped to attention, and Bliven saw Preble's face far above him, fixed as granite. "Well?" he asked Cutbush quietly. "How is he?"

"He is a lucky young man, sir. The wound extends almost the width of the belly, it cut through the skin and grazed the flesh. But the belly wall was not penetrated—no guts were exposed. I will cleanse the wound, and sew him up."

Cutbush looked down at Bliven. "That will hurt, I fear." Bliven nodded.

"But with luck and no infection, sir, he will mend."

At those words Bliven resolved to withstand any pain without complaint, as long as Cutbush would vouchsafe him his life. "Sir?" he asked weakly.

Preble leaned down, stiffly, but closer. "Yes?"

"Did we save our man?"

"Yes, he is safely aboard. Well done."

"Was anyone else hurt?"

Cutbush interposed himself. "A few cuts and bruises, and bumps on the head. You were the most seriously injured. And now, Captain, if you will excuse us, I must finish."

"Of course, of course." Preble looked down again at Bliven, who knew he would show no emotion in front of the men, and then the captain looked about the flickering light of the cockpit. "Who was the senior man present at this altercation?"

Bliven heard general agreement that it must have been the master's mate, a man named Richardson. "Well," Preble said wearily, "come give me a report of what happened while it is fresh on your mind."

Bliven heard their footfalls recede even as his belly tightened and twisted against another burning wash of alcohol.

"Do you know what this is?" Cutbush's soft voice was right by his ear.

Bliven opened his eyes and saw a new coin, a long-haired figure of Liberty with a fat, barely draped pair of breasts. "A dollar," he answered.

"Well, you are going to bite down on this soft silver dollar while I sew your belly together. If you can lie still, and not flinch and make me miss a stitch, the dollar is yours."

"I shall have a scar, I suppose."

Cutbush nodded. "Like Caesar's wife. Now, bite down." Cutbush continued to soothe him as he worked surely and swiftly. "Now, unless I miss my guess, you are already wondering whether it will make a better impression on your sweetheart, whether to have me write her a letter telling her you are wounded, so as to let her sympathy grow during the weeks it will take us to get home, or whether your case would be better advanced by letting her discover it in a shock, once you arrive. If you want me to write her, I can make out that your wound is more dangerous than it is to magnify the result."

Bliven made a small vocalization, but Cutbush stopped him. "Don't speak, just bite down. And you should think about what stories the newspapers might dream up, inflating their subscriptions by exaggerating your exploits. Perhaps you took on a whole British ship of the line, or the whole fleet, single-handed. And the celebrity in your hometown? Everyone will want to buy you a drink."

Forbidden to speak, Bliven listened to Cutbush's soft wit-filled monologue, concentrating on that instead of the wicked needle sticks, and the fine silk thread that felt rough as twine pulling through the holes in his skin. Perhaps Cutbush was, in his own way, telling him about life, that it is a duality, that mirth must come with pain, joy with sadness, wisdom with loss.

"Oh, and the politicians. Your winning this war will surely make a senator or two, perhaps even a president. Maybe it will even be you. There. Now, give me the coin back." He pulled it from Bliven's mouth. "Well, you won't want to spend this—you'll want to keep it and show your grandchildren." He inspected the deep tooth marks in the amply bosomed Liberty. "But heavens, I hope you never bite this hard on anyone else's titties."

Bliven exploded with laughter but grabbed his belly. "Ow! Oh, Jesus, ow!" Cutbush blotted the sweat from his brow, affecting not to notice that he also wiped away the tears that traced down from the corners of Bliven's eyes.

"May I have some water, Doctor?"

"Of course." Cutbush held Bliven's head up until he had gulped his fill. He bound the wound tightly with fresh bandages wrapped completely around his middle, then had several men transfer him to a freshly sheeted bed with a pillow.

"Are you comfortable?"

"Yes, I thank you."

Cutbush nodded. "I will sit up with you. You sleep now, you will live to fight another day."

ACKNOWLEDGMENTS

Of all my books, *The Shores of Tripoli* may, at the end of the day, have to be logged in as my favorite, first for the warm associations made or renewed during its creation. I tender my deep thanks to its acquiring editor, Nita Taublib, to whom I credit the initial idea of recognizing that American letters had no early naval hero to compare with Britain's Horatio Hornblower or Lucky Jack Aubrey, and for bringing me on board after reading my other historical novels and believing I might be a suitable author for the Putnam naval series. How lucky could I get that my agent, Jim Hornfischer, is himself also a well-known, front-rank naval historian, and was set afire with the possibilities of the series? I thank Ivan Held, president of G. P. Putnam's Sons, for maintaining the project during changes within the company, and for handing it off to Christine Pepe, Putnam's executive editor, of whom I came to stand in awe at her gift for making the best suggestions with the lightest touch, and for giving the book a full edit not just once but a second time, after requesting that I expand certain parts of the narrative. The entire crew at Putnam, from the copyeditor to the designer to the artist, has been the surest and most professional I have worked with.

Authors of historical novels must make a strategic decision with each book—how close or far from historical fact to steer in order to best serve the story. As the author of numerous history books, I have always maintained that real historical people offer the best stories, and *The Shores of Tripoli* threw down the gauntlet to prove that theory. Therefore I steered the story as close to fact as my Lieutenant Bandy steered the *Constitution* to the whirlpool in the Strait of Messina. The main characters, the Putnams, Bandy, and the Marshes, are fictitious. With very few exceptions whom I needed, as they say, for dramatic purposes, everyone else actually lived: all of the captains and commodores with whom Putnam served, General Eaton and Tobias Lear, Dr. Cutbush, King Ferdinand and Queen Maria Carolina of Naples, Mustapha VI and Hamet Pasha, and many others—all were a thrill to research and are presented as close to their true selves as the needs of the story would allow.

Similarly, the story's background is as authentic as I could make it. Sarah Pierce's School for Girls and Tapping Reeve's law school were indeed thriving institutions in the Litchfield of 1800. John C. Calhoun was a student there, and Lyman Beecher did cross Long Island Sound to preach there. The Putnam family did indeed introduce Vermont Russet apples to Connecticut. The ruins of Cyrene are indeed a day's ride from Derna; their ancient economy was indeed based on an aphrodisiac/abortifacient herb. And so on. Rather than tell a story and hang history on it like Christmas ornaments, my approach was to line up the history and weave a story through it. As a writer, I have never had so much fun in my life. And so I thank those long-dead people, who are as alive and vivid to me as my own friends.

I also thank my own cadre of readers for wading into the manuscript with an eye for continuity, errors, and loose threads: Craig Eiland, Evan Yeakel, Robin Sommers, Brent Bliven, and Jim Kunetka. Any errors that got by them must be so obscure that I am the only one who must bear the responsibility.

GLOSSARY

Ballast—Deadweight carried in a ship's hold to keep her stable in the water.

Barbary states—Semi-independent states of the Mediterranean coast of Africa, from west to east Morocco, Algiers, Tunis, and Tripoli; nominally loyal to the Ottoman Empire and the sultan in Constantinople, but in reality exercising considerable autonomy of policy.

Bashaw—Pasha, or bey, title of the rulers of Tunis and Tripoli, nominally inferior in rank to the dey in Algiers but functionally independent.

Berth deck—On a vessel the size of a frigate, the third deck, beneath the spar and gun decks, containing living space for the crew.

Biscuit—Dietary staple of a ship's enlisted crew, made of flour, water, and salt, baked twice to rock hardness, eaten by breaking it up and soaking in tea or water. Not called "hardtack" until the Civil War era.

Bosun—Contraction of "boatswain," the warrant officer charged with supervising operations of the deck crew.

Bow—Pertaining to the front end of a ship.

Bowsprit—Spar projecting forward from the bow, used to attach the staysail and jibs.

Brig—Smaller class of sailing warship, mounting approximately sixteen to twenty-two guns; among merchant ships, a square-rigged merchantman of up to three hundred tons.

Camboose—The stove in the galley on which the crew's food is prepared.

Cockpit—Station of a ship's surgeon when treating those wounded in battle, typically located lower down in the ship than the regular sick bay, to be more insulated from the fighting.

Cutter—The larger of a ship's boats, used for transporting larger numbers of men.

Dey—Title of the ruler of Algiers.

Epaulette—Shoulder insignia of an officer's rank.

Fighting top—Platform attached to a mast above the lowest course of sail, large enough to hold several marksmen to snipe at an enemy's crew, especially officers, during battle.

Frigate—Second-largest class of sailing warship, after ships of the line, typically mounting twenty-eight to thirty-eight guns. American heavy frigates were rated to mount forty-four guns but usually carried many more, and were far more robust than their European counterparts.

Galley—That portion of the berth deck set aside to prepare food for the crew.

Gun deck—On larger sailing warships, a deck separate from the spar or berth decks devoted to operating the main battery of guns. Ships of the line had two or three gun decks; frigates had one main gun deck but with a varying assortment of guns mounted topside.

Guns—Naval cannons, typically six-, nine-, twelve-, eighteen-, twenty-four-, and thirty-two-pounders, the number being the weight in pounds of the ball fired.

Haul down—The act of pulling a ship when in port over onto her side so that part of the hull normally underwater can be cleaned.

Head—That part of a ship used as a toilet, typically located farthest forward, on either side of the bowsprit.

Hogging—The tendency of a poorly designed ship to be too buoyant amidships, with the bow and stern pulling lower in the water, bending and eventually breaking the keel.

Hold—The lowest portion of a sailing ship, where was stored the heaviest cargo, such as water, and ballast to keep the ship from becoming top-heavy.

Jambia—A type of curved, broad-bladed dagger favored in south Arabia and the Horn of Africa, the style traditionally being heraldic to a particular tribe.

Jibs—Staysails that run from the foremast out to the bowsprit. On a large ship they are, in succession, the staysail, jib, and flying jib.

Jolly boat—The smallest of boats carried by a ship, for ferrying crewmen in a port.

Keel—The central backbone of a ship's hull, to which the ribs are attached; the first part to be laid down and about which the construction centers.

Kentledge—Scrap iron used as ballast.

Lateen rigging—Triangular sails carried on yards mounted at an angle on the mast, making it easier to sail in a direction other than straight before the wind; probably of Roman origin, adopted by Arab mariners.

Linstock—Type of slow-burning fuse put to a gun's touch hole to fire its cartridge; informally called "matches."

Magazine—A storage compartment for gunpowder.

Mainsails—Or "courses," the lowest set and largest of the sails on a sailing vessel.

Mole—Lengthy breakwater meant to shelter a harbor.

Navigation—The art of pinpointing one's location at sea and charting a course that will arrive at the desired destination.

Orlop deck—The lowest deck on a sailing ship large enough to have three or more decks, typically used for storing cables.

Plum duff—A type of pudding made of grease, flour, and raisins, served as a very occasional treat to sailors.

Polacca—Or polacre, a sailing ship common in the Mediterranean and favored by Barbary pirates, typically lateen-rigged on the foremast, which was often leaned forward so as not to interfere with the square-rigged mainmast; the mizzenmast might bear a square topsail over a lateen mainsail.

Port—Pertaining to the left side of the ship, as in "a turn to port," or "located port side"; also, a town or city that engages in maritime commerce.

Quarterdeck—The aft portion of the main deck from where a ship is commanded and steered.

Rigging—The configuration of a ship's sails, differing with each type of vessel.

Royals—The fourth-highest set of sails on frigates and ships of the line.

Schooner—The smallest class of sailing warship, mounting ten or twelve guns, typically with two masts, mainsails rigged fore-and-aft, with perhaps square rigging in the topsails.

Scimitar—A type of sword, of Moorish manufacture, with a broad, curving blade.

Sextant—A navigational instrument for sighting the angle of the sun above the horizon at a given time, used for determining latitude.

Ship of the line—The largest design of sailing warship; divided into classes, a third-rate of seventy-four guns typically mounted them on two gun decks, whereas a second-rate of more than eighty guns, and a first-rate of one hundred to one hundred twenty, had three gun decks.

Skysails—The fifth and highest set of sails on a ship of the line.

Sloop—More technically in this era, sloop-of-war, the smallest class of gun-bearing sailing warships, undifferentiated by rigging, though often described by their specific type or function (schooner, gunboat, bomb scow), they were typically listed as sloops.

Spars—Horizontal timbers on which the sails are hoisted up the masts.

Speaking trumpet—A brass cone used to amplify the voice in hailing ship to ship.

Starboard—Pertaining to the right side of the ship, as in "a turn to starboard" or "located starboard side."

Staysails—Triangular fore-and-aft rigged sails between the masts, which aid in more effective tacking; named for the mast and section from which they descend, as in "main topgallant staysail."

Steep tank—A large barrel in which salt meat is soaked in freshwater to remove the salt and render it edible, typically requiring about four changes of water.

Stern—Pertaining to the rear of a ship.

Studding sails—Typically pronounced "stuns'ls," sails hoisted on temporary extensions of the spars to gain extra speed, especially in a light wind.

Tacking—A sailing maneuver in which a ship turns her bow alternately to the port and starboard of a headwind, allowing her to sail more or less into the wind.

Tompion—A plug inserted into a cannon's mouth to keep the inside of the barrel clean and dry when not in use.

Topgallants—The third-highest set of sails on a sailing vessel.

Topsails—The second-highest set of sails on a sailing vessel.

Xebec—A Mediterranean sailing ship typically used for piracy; similar to the polacca but smaller, with the addition of oars to allow propulsion in a calm.

Weather gage—The advantageous position of a ship in being upwind of the enemy.

FURTHER READING ON
THE BARBARY WAR
AND THE EARLY U.S. NAVY

Interest in the Barbary War has exploded in the past decade, as scholars assess its relevance to the United States' current combat in the same region. The following general titles will be found of interest. I include a biography of Commodore Edward Preble because he died soon after these events. Biographies of other historical participants, such as Bainbridge and Decatur, will accompany the second volume in this series. I particularly commend Fenimore Cooper's 1839 history of the navy. It may be a surprise to learn that this famous early American author of *The Last of the Mohicans* was also a lucid and compelling historian.

Cooper, James Fenimore. *The History of the Navy of the United States of America*. Lea & Blanchard, 1839.

Kilmeade, Brian, and Don Yaeger. *Thomas Jefferson and the Tripoli Pirates: The Forgotten War That Changed American History*. Sentinel, 2015.

McKee, Christopher. *Edward Preble: A Naval Biography, 1761–1807*. Naval Institute Press, 1996.

Office of Naval Records and Library, Navy Department. *Naval Documents Related to the United States Wars with the Barbary Powers . . . Naval Operations Including Diplomatic Background.* U.S. Government Printing Office, 1939–44.

Toll, Ian W. *Six Frigates: The Epic History of the Founding of the U.S. Navy.* W. W. Norton, 2006.

Tucker, Glenn. *Dawn Like Thunder: The Barbary Wars and the Birth of the U.S. Navy.* Bobbs-Merrill, 1963.

Wheelan, Joseph. *Jefferson's War: America's First War on Terror, 1801–1805.* Carroll & Graf, 2003.

TURN THE PAGE FOR AN EXCERPT

At the opening of the War of 1812, the British control the most powerful navy on earth, and Americans are again victims of piracy. Bliven Putnam, late of the Battle of Tripoli, is dispatched to Charleston to outfit and take command of a new 20-gun brig, the *USS Tempest*. On his way, he boards the *Constitution* and sails into the furious early fighting of the war. With exquisite detail and guns-blazing action, *A Darker Sea* illuminates an unforgettable period in American history.

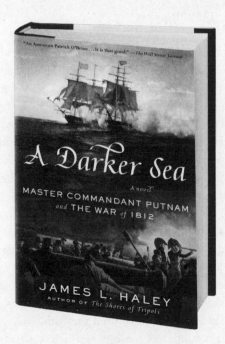

 Penguin Random House

PROLOGUE:
THE HOUND IN BLUE

In his cabin at the stern of the brig *Althea*, Sam Bandy dressed as he sipped the morning's first cup of coffee, rich and full-bodied, from Martinique. Sped into Charleston on a fast French ship with a dry hold, it tasted of neither mold nor bilge water. He was lucky to have gotten it in, avoiding the picket of British cruisers who, in the never-ending mayhem of the Napoleonic wars, sought to sweep all French trade from the seas. It might well have ended in the private larder of an English frigate captain. Now he had brought a quarter-ton of it to Boston, tucked into his hold along with the cotton and rice that one expected to be exported from South Carolina.

Yes, the life of a merchant mariner suited him, and it endlessly amused him. If one wanted a bottle of rum in Charleston, the cane was grown in the West Indies, where it was rendered into sugar and its essential byproduct, molasses. Thence they were taken by ship and, passing almost within sight of Charleston, delivered all the way to Boston, or Newport. There the scores of Yankee distilleries manufactured the rum, which then had to be loaded and taken back south to Charleston, which was halfway back to the Caribbean. And money was made at each exchange.

Sam ascended the ladder topside, coffee in hand, snugging his hat upon his head—a blue felt Bremen flat cap that a German sailor had offered him in trade for his American Navy bicorn. Sam had surprised the German with how readily he accepted the exchange, for in truth he felt no sentimental attachment to it at all. There were several considerations that impelled him to separate from the Navy. The death of his father during the Barbary War and the disinterest of his brothers placed the responsibility for their Abbeville plantation on his shoulders. And the Navy's penchant for fur-loughing junior officers for months at a time, and then recalling them with-out regard for the seasonal imperatives of planting or harvesting, he could not accommodate. Most important, on his voyage home from the Mediter-ranean on the *Wasp*, he had brought the daughter of the American former consul to Naples, and she had become his wife. Naturally he wished to pro-vide her and their growing family the gracious life he had known, and ship-ping provided them a measure of comfort even beyond that of their neighbors.

And this would be a profitable trip. Their South Carolina cotton for the Yankee mills had brought him eighteen cents per pound and paid for the trip, leaving the rice, some indigo, and the Martinique coffee as pure profit. Top-side, he observed his first officer, Simon Simpson, directing stevedores down into his hold. Simpson was astonishingly tall and brawny, dishfaced, with wild black hair; he knew his trade but was not overly bright, but then, apart from captains, what men who became merchant sailors were?

Their lack of schedule suited Sam; they had tied up halfway out the Long Wharf, selling until his hold was empty, and his taking on new cargo could not have passed more conveniently. As he reflected, Boston's famous Paul Revere was in his mid-seventies, but still innovating, still trying his hand at new business. His late venture into foundry was a rousing success, and Simpson lined the bottom of *Althea*'s hold with cast-iron window weights, fireplace accoutrements—andirons, pokers—and stove backs. Nothing could have provided better ballast, and atop these he loaded barrels of salt fish, all securely tied down. This left room for fine desks and book-cases from the celebrated Mr. Gould. Upon Sam's own speculation, apart from that of his co-owners of the ship, he visited Mr. Fisk's shop and bought a quantity of his delicate fancy card tables and side chairs, for which he ex-pected the ladies of Charleston to profit him most handsome. Fisk's lyre-backed chairs were in the style of Hepplewhite of London, and when Sam visited Fisk and Son to make the purchase, it caught his ear that more than one patron expressed his pleasure that Fisk's fine workmanship has soured the market for Hepplewhite itself, so disgruntled had people become with the British interference with their trade.

The Long Wharf, with its glimpse of Faneuil Hall at its head, the taverns he had frequented in their nights here, the dockside commotion, the frequent squeals of seagulls, the salt air beyond his West Indies coffee, all left him deeply happy, but he was ready to go home. "Mr. Simpson!" he called out.

Simpson left his station at the hatch and joined him by the wheel. "Good morning, Captain."

"Good morning, Mr. Simpson. The tide begins to run in three hours. Can we be ready by then?"

"No question of it, we are almost finished."

"Excellent. Now, if you please, divert two of those Fisk chairs to my cabin. There you will find on my desk a package, addressed to the Putnam family in Litchfield, Connecticut. Take it to the post office and dispatch it. The Port Authority is right close by there. Arrange a pilot for us, come back, check the stores, and prepare to get under way."

Ah, the Putnams. Sam did not miss the Navy, but he missed Bliven Putnam. Their midshipman's schooling together on the *Enterprise*, their learning the handling of sabres together, their fighting Barbary corsairs together, even their fumbling attempts to bridge the cultural gap between Connecticut and South Carolina, and their punishment together at the masthead of the *President* mandated by Commodore James Barron for their having fought each other all had bonded them in a way that would have been imperishable even had Barron not compelled them to swear their friendship to each other. Sam could not absent himself from the ship for a week, which would gain him only a day's visit to Litchfield, but he could send Bliven a sack of this rich coffee.

By ten Simpson had returned, and Sam hoisted the flags, signaling his imminent departure. With crew counted and hatch secured, Sam cast off, moving ever so slowly under a single jib and topsail into the harbor. The wind was from the northwest, which could not have served them better.

At the end of the wharf the pilot boat appeared, a small, sleek, low-waisted schooner, which hoisted *Althea*'s name in signal flags. Sam answered and fell in behind her gratefully. In Boston's shallow bay the tides ran swiftly;

once, he visited the other side of the city when the tide fell just to see the sight of Back Bay emptying out as fast as a man could walk; such flats were no place to get trapped. But this pilot very clearly knew what he was doing; the schooner was under a full set, and Sam had to loose his courses to keep up. They passed through the channel between Long and Deer Islands, and could see Lovell Island off their starboard bow. At this point the pilot came about, wishing *Althea* fair sailing; Sam signaled his thanks and steered east-southeast for the northern curl of Cape Cod. If the wind held, they should round the cape and be halfway down that seemingly interminable spit of sand when dark fell. He would be safe on a southerly course and well clear of Nantucket by morning, when he could set a new course, if the wind permitted, west-southwest for Long Island.

If it were not for the knowledge of going home, Sam would not relish the southward voyage. South by west was the most direct course to Cape Hatteras, but that would place him in the very teeth of the irresistible, opposing push of the Gulf Current. More distant in miles but infinitely faster it was to steer closer inshore along the mid-Atlantic and follow the eddying cold-water currents that would aid him.

Their seventh day out, Sam awoke to the accustomed clatter of the cook setting the tray of his breakfast on his desk. He did not mind, for every morning it reminded him of the glorious luxury of not being in the Navy, that every morning there were eggs and bacon and toasted bread for breakfast. On this voyage he did rather feel obligated to share his Martinique coffee with the crew, but it was a small cost to see the men feeling favored, and thus working with a more congenial will.

He dressed and glanced at a chart on the table, estimating in rough how far they must have come during the night. Topside at the wheel he saw his tall, wire-haired first mate, keeping a firm grip on the wheel in a stout wind from their starboard quarter. "Good morning, Mr. Simpson."

"Good morning, Captain."

Sam regarded the wind and the set of sails. "Steer east-sou'east until noon, then make due south."

"Very good, sir, east-sou'east she comes." Simple Simpson eased the helm a few points to port.

There was no need to explain why. Their southerly course had brought them almost to the outer banks of North Carolina. Now it was necessary to stand out far enough to avoid those coastal shoals whose locations changed with every storm, shallows that had brought numberless crews to grief, yet not stand so far out as to meet the strongest opposition of the Gulf Current, which here compressed as it rounded the Hatteras Cape and was here at its swiftest. If they made that mistake they could labor all day with their sails bellied full out and end the day not five miles farther on than when they started. It was a delicate calculation, but they would know if they went too far, for old sailors had many times told Sam, and he had himself once discovered the truth of it, that the inner edge of the warm Gulf Current was so sharp and sudden that in crossing it, water brought up from the bow and the stern might be twenty degrees different in temperature.

AT THE SAME MOMENT in the sea cabin of His Majesty's sloop-of-war Hound, twenty-two guns, Captain Lord Arthur Kington in his dressing gown poured himself a glass of Madeira. Two weeks out of Halifax, bound for Bermuda, but empty-handed. They had not raised a single French sail to engage, nor even an American merchant to board and harvest some pressed men. For days now they had been plowing through the drifting mess of the Sargasso Sea, no doubt snagging strands of the olive-brown weeds that would hang on their barnacles and slow them down.

How in bloody hell could he have fallen from command of a seventy-four- to a twenty-two-gun sloop? For six years he had sailed in purgatory like the *Flying Dutchman*, each morning asking and answering the same question of himself, unable to break the cycle of it. It was difficult to comprehend how that incident in Naples had precipitated such a consequence. In attempting the apprehension of a deserter from a dockside tavern he and everyone else knew he was carrying out Crown policy. His fault, apparently, lay in attending a diplomatic reception while his press gang was assaulted and bested by a clot of drunken American sailors. No captain of a seventy-four would be seen in the company of his press gang; the notion was absurd, and he the son of a duke. What did they expect of him? Apparently, that his press gang prey only upon victims foreign or domestic, beyond the protective circle of their shipmates. It was his lieutenant on the *Hector* who had acted imprudently, but in the long-established calculus of the Royal Navy, he as captain should have foreseen such a circumstance and ordered his lieutenant to greater caution. That junior officer had not suffered for the act, he had later been raised from the *Hector's* third officer to second, but it was Kington himself who, in response to the diplomatic stink that the Americans had fomented, had to be punished. And yet he wondered if there were not more to it, whether some key bureaucrat in the Admiralty had simply conceived a dislike for him.

At least the Admiralty had broken him in command only and not in rank, an admission that they needed his service as one who would willingly overhaul vessels on the high seas and take off what men were needed to crew His Majesty's ships. The need was bottomless, for desertions were constant, and Napoleon simply would not be crushed. Kington's conclusion was that his value to the Navy lay in impressing men in ways that could not be readily discovered, and in six years at this he had come to excel. The Navy needed him but would not acknowledge him; it was a circumstance that left him feeling ill used. Yet, if he did but do his duty, without complaint, and without overmuch using family influence on the Admiralty, he would work his way back up to his former station. This was certain, for even now a new frigate was waiting for him in Bermuda to take command once he brought in the *Hound* with a merchant prize or two, and some well-broken American sailors.

Thus he served, secure in the knowledge that the Royal Navy needed pressed men more than ever—and more particularly they needed him, for after that affair with the American frigate *Chesapeake*, their need for impressment was forced into still greater subterfuge. Infinitely more so than Naples, the *Leopard–Chesapeake* encounter had altered the dynamics of impressment. Doubtless, it had been less than prudent, or at least less than sporting, for Post Captain Humphreys of H.M.S. *Leopard* to pour broadsides into the unprepared American frigate in peacetime, but it was open and obvious that the Americans had been enlisting British deserters into their crews. The American captain, some fellow named Barron, had been court-martialed and suspended for not fighting his ship to the last, irrespective of the hopelessness of the contest.

Kington screwed up his mouth into a smile. That said much for the American frame of mind, but not their practicality. Barron had had no chance. His guns were unloaded, rolled in, their tompions in place. His decks were piled with stores in preparation for a long cruise; when approached by the *Leopard*, Barron, knowing they were not at war with Britain, had not beat to quarters. Had he resisted, his crew would have been slaughtered as they limbered up the guns. As it was, the American was lucky to lose only four killed and eighteen, including Barron himself, wounded. Humphreys had seized four men from the *Chesapeake*, and then, the worst insult of all, refused Barron's surrender—they were not at war, after all—and left him there on his floating wreck. God help them if they ever encountered Barron again, he would sell his life very dearly indeed.

Of the four men Humphreys had seized, one was a Canadian, whom he hanged. They did have some color of justification for taking Canadians, to whom the Americans presumed to grant naturalized citizenship. How dare they? His Majesty's government of course refused to recognize American naturalization. They were naval pretenders even as they were still pretenders as a nation, and no great attention need be paid them except for taking likely-looking seamen.

Now Kington knew that his exile was at an end; a new command awaited him in Bermuda, but he had concluded that he could not enter empty-handed, and he had turned to the northwest, crossing and riding the Gulf Current into the waters of the American coastal trade. Even as he was thinking they must sight a vessel on this day, he cocked his head at the faint cry above the deck overhead, of deck, sail ho. He straightened his dressing gown and seated himself at his desk, waiting for the rap at his door, which came only a moment later. "Enter," he said quietly.

"Beg pardon, m'lord." A lieutenant stood at attention and made his respects. "The lookout has sighted a ship bearing to the southwest."

Kington affected not to look up from the papers on his desk. "What do you make of her?"

"An American merchantman, m'lord, a large brig, low in the water, heading south."

"Very well. Make all sail to overtake her. I will come up."

"Very good, m'lord." The lieutenant made his respects again and departed.

Kington pulled a pair of brilliant white silk stockings up his calves, and then donned equally white knee breeches, which he fastened at the waist and knees. The talk was that the Royal Navy was going to change at any time to trousers for officers, as well as the enlisted men, who already wore them. He hated the notion. Trousers—inelegant, egalitarian, shapeless—suitable for the common sailors but certainly not for officers. After regarding his shiny white calves in the mirror, he buckled his sword about his waist and selected a coat from his wardrobe, the blue frock, undress but bearing the dual epaulettes that signified a captain of more than three years' experience. It was hard to bear how many years, since Naples, but his circumstances would improve soon enough. He took up his glass and ascended the ladder to the quarterdeck.

The courses blocked his view down the deck, and he slung an arm through the mizzen's starboard ratlines, leaned out and focused the American in his glass. Yes, it was a large brig, low and slow; they were gaining on him rapidly and he could not but have seen him. This should be a good day.

"What is your pleasure, m'lord? Shall you hail him?"

"Beat to quarters, Mr. Evans, ready your starboard bow chaser. At six hundred yards put a shot through his rigging. That will hail him well enough."

"Beat to quarters!" Evans barked to the bosun, and an instant later the ship leapt to life in response to the drum's tattoo. Both officers knew this was probably unnecessary when their quarry was an apparently unarmed merchant vessel, but both knew equally that an overawing display of firepower was the surest guarantor of a passive reception.

ABOARD THE *ALTHEA*, SAM BANDY had been alerted to the approach of the British sloop and followed her through his glass, noting the deployment of starboard studding sails to increase her speed. He was studying her even as he saw the flash and smoke of her bow chaser; its booming report reached him almost simultaneously with the singing of a ball through his rigging. He started and shot his gaze upward at a loud pop, and beheld a rip in the main topsail, one edge flapping in the wind. He turned his head to the right, waiting for and then seeing the small splash a hundred yards out or more. Unarmed and laden too heavily to run, he had no choice but to furl his sails and wait for what fate should bring.

"She is bringing in her sails, m'lord," said Evans. "It looks as if she means no resistance."

"Good," said Kington. "Have the bosun swing out the cutter. You and I will go over with ten Marines for escort."

At the cutter's approach, Sam had a rope boarding ladder lowered. Eight Marines came smartly up in coats of brilliant scarlet, flanking the ladder, then two officers in blue frocks, and two more Marines.

Bandy faced them, arms akimbo, several paces in front of his curious and apprehensive crew.

"I am Captain Lord Arthur Kington, of His Majesty's sloop-of-war *Hound*. Are you the master of this vessel?"

"I am Samuel Bandy, captain of the brig *Althea*." Sam squared his shoulders against him. "By what right do you stop an American ship in international waters?" he demanded.

"By the authority of Orders in Council of His Majesty's government," he said highly. "We are at war with France, and we are charged to stop ships, search for deserters, and seize ships which are carrying contraband bound for French ports. What is your cargo?"

"Your orders are of no effect upon American ships."

"Mr. . . . Bandy, my broadside gives me all the authority I need. I ask you again, what is your cargo?"

"Salt fish, and kitchenware, and furniture."

"Where bound?"

"We are seven days out of Boston, bound for Charleston."

"I see. I require to see your manifest, and after that to inspect your hold. Take us down to your cabin."

Sam clattered down the ladder to his small cabin, followed by the two officers and behind them two of the Marines. From a shelf he pulled the log book and extracted the three pages of manifest, detailing his cargo to the last item.

He handed the papers over to Kington, who rattled the sheets as he barely glanced at them before folding them back along their existing creases and tucking them into his coat pocket. "Well, I say, you are a lively-looking fellow," said Kington.

Sam squinted and shook his head. "What?"

"We are searching for a Canadian deserter who bears the singularly appropriate name of Lively. Do you claim that the name means nothing to you?"

Sam was truculent. "Of course it means nothing to me. Why should it?"

"Because"—Kington looked Sam down and up and down again—"he

stands about five feet nine inches, weight thirteen stone, very fair com-plected, reddish to blond hair." He looked more closely. "Blue eyes. Did you really believe we would never discover you?"

"Damn your eyes, I am Samuel Bandy of South Carolina, captain and part owner of this vessel!"

Kington crossed his arms doubtfully. "Well, your accent is plausible. Still, that can be affected. Let me see your protection."

"God damn it, I am the captain! I don't carry proof of my citizenship!"

Kington tossed his head lightly. "Well, then."

"Wait, I have my master's license. Wait." This was a document that he never expected that he would have to produce. He knew it was in a pouch of papers in his sea chest, and he dropped to his knees and flung open its lid.

"Hold!" barked Kington. The Marines who flanked him lowered their muskets at him. "Move very slowly."

"Bastard," muttered Sam. He rose again, unfolding his master's license and handing it to Kington, who glanced about the cabin.

"The light in here is very poor." He ambled over to the stern windows and opened one, sitting on its sill and leaning partly outside. "Now, let us see." He mumbled the lines as he read them. "Oh, dear!" He opened his fingers and the paper fluttered down to the rolling sea.

Sam swelled up but checked himself as the Marines took a half-step for-ward *en garde*.

Kington tapped his index finger against his chin. "Perhaps you are who you say you are, but perhaps not. You answer the wanted man's description too closely to dismiss the matter. Prudence dictates I shall bring you to Ber-muda for more certain identification."

"Wait a minute, I know you!" Sam shook his head. "From where do I know you?"

Kington looked at him with his haughty expectation.

Sam's finger shot out at him. "Naples! After the war, the Barbary War, the American consulate, you had an altercation with Commodore Preble."

"Indeed? I cannot say that I remember you at all. I do remember one particularly impudent lieutenant, but it was not you. Mr. Evans?"

"M'lord?"

"We will select a prize crew to take this vessel to Bermuda. Poll the American crewmen. Those who carry protections and wish to go home we will put ashore when we reach Bermuda and they can catch a ship home as best they can. Naturally, any who wish to volunteer into His Majesty's service will be welcome to enlist." The two officers chuckled. Once carried to Bermuda, it could take months for some neutral ship to carry them home again.

"You're just a damned pirate," spat Sam. He knew that Kington would have no trouble finding enlistments among his crew. In the American merchant service, as in the Navy, a fair portion of his sailors went to sea to escape their problems on land. Among the men were surely some whose fortunes had sunk so low—wanted by the law, or in the shadow of debtors' prison—that a foreign ship seemed as viable an escape as walking into the Western wilderness, with the advantage that there were no bears or Indians. Given that they had no way home from Bermuda, it was tantamount to impressment just the same.

Kington smirked. "Damn fine chairs. Hepplewhite, by the make?"

"Fisk of Boston, damn you, and so stamped on the back of each." He swept an arm out grandly. "But please, have them. They will show very fine in a pirate's cabin."

"That remark," said Kington quietly, "will cost you six lashes, as the lightest of warnings. Provoke me further and you will regret it in proportion. Now, will you come quietly, or must we bind you? Before you answer, let me warn you that if you give me your parole to submit and then resist, I will surely hang you. I have no scruple about it."

"No, I have no doubt of that." He inclined his head toward a pine wardrobe. "Am I allowed to keep my clothes?"

"Certainly not. You will be fitted out in His Majesty's uniform for an able seaman." He glanced down. "You may keep your shoes, however. Shoes are in short supply."

"What of my clothes?"

"We will keep them safe. If your story proves out, they will be returned to you."

"Well, they are too large for you, at any rate. But perhaps your tailor can take them in for you."

"Six more lashes, and I urge you, do not build up a large account."

The swell on this morning was easy, as two Marines descended the boarding ladder to their cutter. Kington scanned about *Althea*'s deck and remembered that he had not inspected the hold. *Ah, well.* He had the manifest, and in this circumstance judged that sufficient. He had the ship; the nature of the cargo they could ascertain at leisure.

"Mr. Evans."

"Yes, m'lord?"

"Inspect the crew for their protections. I will send the cutter back with a prize crew. Those who wish to enlist with us send back across with the boat. With luck, it will be an even exchange and we will both have a full complement. Then you will follow me to Bermuda."

"Very good, m'lord." He made his respects as Kington and the remaining Marines descended to the cutter.

As they approached the sloop, Sam saw that she had turned a bit in the current, and he could make out the name HOUND freshly painted under her stern windows. Given his captivity, Sam debated whether he should open a conversation with this captain, try to reach at least a minimal respect between them, and weighed that against his visceral disgust with him, his almost visual desire to see him swinging on a noose.

"She is a handsome enough vessel," he ventured. "Twenty-two, by the look of her?"

Kington regarded him with some surprise. "You have a practiced eye, Mr. Lively. You have estimated her exactly."

"At fourteen I was a midshipman in the *Enterprise*, twelve, and then a lieutenant in the *Constitution*, forty-four," he stated quietly. "Some of that time we were in company with the *John Adams*, twenty-four, and your ship seems only the slightest degree smaller. And if you please, Captain, my name is Samuel Bandy, as you will discover upon a full investigation of the matter."

Kington perceived exactly what Sam was doing. "We shall see. On my ship, I am addressed as 'my lord,' and you will oblige me by adopting the custom."

Sam felt as though his jaw would break if he did so, but he swallowed his gorge and said, "Whatever you say, my lord." Those two words, from the mouth of any American, sounded ridiculous.

As soon as they tied up, Kington scaled the boarding ladder first, and Sam followed, finding the captain already engaged with his second officer, a smallish, auburn-haired man with freckles, named Crawford. Once the Marines were up, a well-armed prize crew descended and pulled away. It took half an hour to make the exchange on the *Althea*, and the cutter returned with Evans and five of Sam's crew who had determined to throw in with the English.

As soon as they came alongside, lines went tumbling down from the davits that curled out overhead. Crewmen made them fast to the eyebolts on the cutter's bow and stern, and as soon as the last of the men stood on deck the cutter came up after them by jerks. Sam marked which of his men had turned coat and determined not to speak to them, even as he admitted to himself that they were not entirely beyond his sympathy. As the cutter was made secure in the davits Sam heard the orders barked and saw the yards braced up as they tacked and settled on a course east-nor'east, under full sail, close hauled but not straining, running full-and-by. Kington may be a miserable wretch, he thought, but he knew how to use the wind. Sam peered astern and saw his *Althea* following suit. At least, he thought, they were on their way to somewhere.

"Well, Lively." It was Kington's voice, and Sam turned to face him. "I will say that your attempt at conversation was noted down in your favor, as perhaps indicating a quiescent bearing. We are bound for Bermuda, from where inquiries will be made. If you prove to be who you say you are, you will be set at liberty."

"And my ship?"

"That I cannot promise. But I tell you, if we find that you are who I think you are, you must hang. Not from my personal animus, understand, but because it is the law."

Sam's words were ready that when he was discovered to be a fellow officer, Kington would oblige him with satisfaction, but he barred the words from passing his lips, calculating that it would be his own death sentence.

"As it is," said Kington, "you have an account and we must square it. Mr. Crawford."

"Yes, m'lord."

"All hands on deck to witness punishment. Except"—he paused, considering—"except those five new enlistments; keep them below with the purser to get their uniforms." He looked at Sam. "I will spare you that. Bosun, do your duty."

"Aye, m'lord," replied a very deep voice. Sam regarded the bosun, middle-aged, gray and very curly hair, missing teeth, skin so salt-cured that he might well have been pulled from a cask in the meat stores. "Come along with ye," he said.

This shockingly grizzled man seized Sam tightly by an upper arm and led him across the thirty-foot beam of the ship. "Ordinarily," said the bosun so quietly that only Sam could hear, "ripping down your shirt is part of the show, but 'tis such a fine shirt, I will give you the opportunity to remove it yourself and lay it aside."

Glowering, Sam began pulling the shirttails out of his trousers. "I have heard of an officer and gentleman, but never a bosun and gentleman. Thank you."

Four of the crew leaned a heavy hatch grate against the mainmast's starboard ratlines, at enough of an angle that he could not keep balance on his own feet, yet vertical enough that the crew could see the spectacle.

"Now lie you up against it," said the bosun. "Stretch up your arms." As soon as Sam extended his arms, crewmen seized his hands and bound them, threading the rope through the openings in the wooden mesh. From the corner of his eye Sam spied the bosun's mate shaking out a cat, running his fingers down its separate strands of twisted hemp to each end, picking off the bits of flesh from the tassels left from when it was last used, finally nodding to the bosun.

The bosun made his respects to the officers on the quarterdeck, calling out, "Ready to commence punishment."

The officers had been at their ease but followed Kington's lead in snugging his bicorne down on his head. "One dozen," he pronounced.

Sam steadied himself, concentrating at that instant on the lapping hiss of the water as it slid by, the creaking of the rigging, the warmth of the morning sun on his back. He knew that his life, or rather the way he regarded life, would never be the same after this morning. He was parsing how he would change, as he heard the cat's tails sing for an instant through the air before slapping across his back, searing like a great brand of fire laid across the flesh. He snapped taut against the ropes that spread his arms, but he made no sound. His teeth clenched, even as he determined that he would die before giving Kington the satisfaction of hearing him cry out.

"One," announced the bosun, as the bosun's mate shook out the tails behind him for a second strike.

He would withstand all dozen lashes, he would stand them by conjuring in his mind's eye himself, standing over Kington's broken body. Whatever it took and however long, he swore to himself that he would have his vengeance. There was a second quick whish of air and a second burning slap on his back, lower down. He clenched his teeth again but uttered nothing.

"Two," intoned the bosun.

Nor was it lost on him that he had been taken into slavery and whipped. He, who had grown up on a plantation and been wet-nursed and clothed and tended by slaves, and he who was now a master of dozens, had never in his life whipped a slave, nor seen one whipped. He knew that it happened, and he had seen the evidence of it in the scarred-over welts on the backs of others' slaves, mostly on those belonging to white trash who vented their own social envy upon the two or three hapless blacks in their power. Such drivers were not respected. Nevertheless, now he understood what it felt like. Whish, splat!

"Three," declared the bosun.

The Indians, he thought. He had heard of Indians beyond the woods who invent ceremonies and tortures and subject their young men to them, giving them the privilege of demonstrating their bravery, their disregard for pain. Those who passed this test became warriors; those who did not—such shame was not to be countenanced. If Indian boys could stand such, a Southern gentleman must surely be able to bear that, or more. Whish, splat!

"Four," called out the bosun.

After twelve lashes the strain had caused the sweat to pour down Sam's brow. As he was untied from the hatch grate he found himself unable to release the tension knotted in his back. Upon standing straight, he felt liquid trickle down his back, but he had no way of knowing if it was also sweat or blood, and he was glad he could not see it. He had no desire to surmise how his broad white back was now scarred for life. He felt faint, and he summoned every ounce of rage and resolve not to fall; he would not give such pleasure to this horror of a human being who now held him in his power.

An officer in a blue coat, different, not a frock but a cutaway with gold buttons, stepped forward and touched Sam's back in several places with a white handkerchief, which came away streaked with crimson. "I am Dr. Kite," he said quietly, "ship's surgeon. You had best come with me, I will tend to your wounds."

Further civility was the last thing Sam had expected. "Yes. Yes, of course, thank you."

"Can you manage the ladder?"

"I think so."

The bosun handed Sam his shirt and whispered hoarsely, "Well done, Yankee lad. Keep up your courage, and for God's sake do nothing stupid. We will speak at a later time."

Sam held the shirt to his sweating chest and stomach as they went down. The sloop *Hound* was small enough that she mounted all her guns on the spar deck; the ladder descended to the single berth deck.

Kite led him forward of the galley to the sick bay and indicated a narrow berth along the curve of the hull. He pointed and said, "Lie on your belly."

Sam slipped off his shoes and did as he was bidden, watching the surgeon extract a bottle and a white cloth from a wooden chest.

"This will sting," said Kite. "It is an astringent." The pain was sharp and more localized than the lashes themselves had been, but not nearly as overwhelming. As the surgeon dabbed at the slices into his skin he said, "They tell me you served in the *Constitution*. Is that true?"

"Yes."

"Then you were acquainted with the surgeon on that vessel?"

"Dr. Cutbush, yes, very well."

"Did you know he is quite famous? What can you tell me about him?"

"Vastly skilled, but also very amiable." Sam started to turn onto his side to face Kite as he spoke, but a firm hand pressed him down to keep him on his stomach.

"Tell me about him, but lie still, I am not done."

Sam related his and Bliven's first day on the *Constitution*, Cutbush having met them on deck and seen to their comfort, of his fascination with ancient doctors and medicine, an element which he did not know personally but which Bliven had told him about.

"You have gratified my curiosity very well," Kite said at last. "Listen to me now. I want you to lie quietly on your belly until we know the bleeding has stopped. Do you feel like you could eat something?"

"Yes."

"There are things I must tend to, but I will have a meal brought to you.

They tell me we are only two days from Bermuda. I am going to excuse you from duty until then; that will give you a chance to heal properly."

"When I get home," said Sam, not admitting to himself that he was unsure whether or when he would see home again, "and make a report to the Navy, I will mention your kindness prominently."

Kite departed, and Sam heard Evans the first officer accost him. "How is he, Bones?"

"As one might expect after a dozen lashes. Is the captain in his cabin?"

"I believe he is."

Kite strode the length of the berth deck, pausing to instruct the bosun to take Sam a meal when it was time to eat, before rapping on the door of the captain's cabin.

"Enter," the voice issued from within.

"M'lord, I have reason to believe that the captain of that American prize is indeed who he says he is."

Kington was seated at his desk. "Oh, and why is that?"

"Sir, I questioned him as I treated him. He claims to have served in the American frigate *Constitution*. The surgeon on that vessel, Dr. Cutbush, I know well from a call I made in Philadelphia many years ago. He knew the name, and he describes him so exactly, I have no doubt he is telling the truth. He would have been a very young lieutenant during the Barbary conflict, and cannot be the man you suspect."

"Thank you for telling me, Dr. Kite." When he didn't move, Kington asked, "Is there something more, Doctor?"

"M'lord, it occurs to me that when we reach port and an inquiry is opened, you will of course wish me to offer these facts into the record."

The next moment of tense silence freighted infinitely more conversation that what had orally passed to that point, that wonderful silence of polite exchange which indicates that the true message conveyed is other and greater than what was uttered. Both men recognized the impasse, that Kite had interposed himself in a matter not his concern, but to which Kington was vulnerable because he might have been treading at the very edge even of the freewheeling practice of impressment.

"You will be informed," said Kington at last. "You may return to your duties."

"M'lord." Kite made his respects but delayed withdrawing just long enough for Kington to look at him again, into his eyes, and realize that his intention was serious. Kite clattered up the ladder and sucked in the fresh salt air, recovering from his brazenness at challenging the captain in such a way, but also calm and satisfied that he had acted out of conscience, something that he was not sure he could still do.

Sam slept fitfully and had just opened his eyes when he counted the eight bells that signaled the onset of the first dog watch. Heavy steps approached, and he looked up to see the grizzled bosun standing over him, bearing a square wooden plate, a tin cup, a swatch of cloth, and a hammer. "Are ye hungry, Yankee lad?"

"I could eat, yes." He sat up, trying not to crack the new scabs on his back. "May I know your name?"

"You will know me as Mr. White." He set the square plate onto the thin mattress, and Sam beheld a shapeless mass of boiled beef, a small slather of peas, and a large rocklike biscuit.

Years had passed since Sam's last exposure to ship's biscuit. He looked up again, and White gave him a large mug of steaming tea and laid beside him a swatch of white cloth and a hammer. "I expect ye know of naval fare."

"When I was in the American Navy, it was not much different among our men. I was a lieutenant; the officers made out somewhat better."

"A word of advice, Yankee lad," he said quietly. "Do not follow that course. Protesting your identity will gain you nothing. On this vessel your name is Lively, a suspected Canadian deserter who will be used for duty pending your execution. Now, the Navy does inquire into such things, and if you can make your case, you will be set at liberty. But until then, do not provoke the captain's displeasure."

"I understand," said Sam.

"The surgeon has told me you are excused duty until we make port, so be guided by me, make yourself as little noticed as possible."

"Thank you for your consideration," Sam said, as White nodded curtly and disappeared. Left to regard his rations, Sam took a spoonful of peas, chewing them as he folded the biscuit into the white cloth. He pulled the thin mattress aside until the wood of the berth was exposed and hammered at the wrapping until the biscuit was broken up into small sherds, which he dumped into his tea to soften. He plunged a fork as deep as he could into the mass of beef, and he bit off a small chunk of it. It was hot and tasted of brine, and he knew it had not soaked long enough in the steep tub. He should eat it first, he thought, because it would make him devilish thirsty, and save the tea for last, for he did not know when he would be offered water.

Late in the next morning, Sam was roused from his bed by the bosun, who was accompanied by a brawny but dull-looking sailor. Motioned up the waist ladder, he found himself in a line, directly behind others whom he thought must be captives.

"We have raised Nelson Island off the starboard bow," White told him quietly. "It is the practice when coming into port to shackle the pressed men." Sam looked to the head of the line and saw the ship's armorer quickly and efficiently riveting irons to the ankles of each man. "You need not go back down," White continued. "You may stay on deck and take some air, if you feel up to it."

"Yes, I would like that," said Sam. "Thank you. Where are the other men from my ship?"

"Them? They enlisted, so they are not considered pressed men."

Sam nodded calculating what a convenient policy that was to mask the true numbers of impressment, and turned his gaze aft to the unraised quarterdeck, where he saw Kington and a lieutenant quietly observing the armorer hammering the rivets of their shackles against a small anvil.

From this distance Sam and Kington made eye contact, with no sign of acknowledgment. Kington could readily admit that fitting chains to the pressed men was some inconvenience to them, but the sight of land, even such a hopelessly isolated island as Bermuda, might prove too great a temptation to impressed seamen to leap overboard and swim for it—despite the fact that there was no hiding in this tiny colony, separated from North America and safety by six hundred miles of open sea. Shackling them while in port decreased the incidence of desertions, and the subsequent odium of tracking the culprits down and hanging them.

As he waited his turn and then as the manacles were hammered about his ankles, Sam Bandy felt the ship enter a starboard turn, coming due east, and continuing until the sails were put over with the brief, confused snaps of the luffing canvas as she wore completely around, heading southwest. He could see land a half-mile off to port, and a half-mile to starboard the mole of the Royal Dockyard. He had never been here but had seen it a hundred times on the map as he shuttled up and down the coast in his trade and recognized Bermuda.

Kington leaned over to Evans. "You've been here before, you know the channel?"

"Yes, sir."

"Well, come around easy to starboard, you may take us into the anchorage." Kington strode a few paces forward and surveyed the length of the deck. He was fortunate, only a third of his crew had been pressed into service. Through the vastness of the Royal Navy the percentage was closer to half, and sometimes more.

"Mr. Evans," he said at length.

"Sir."

"Anchor us convenient to that frigate. I am going below; keep an eye on the armorer, make sure all the risky ones are chained."

The first officer made his respects. "Very good, sir."

At the top of the ladder Kington peered across the harbor to the much taller H.M.S. *Java*, gazing long enough to count fourteen large gunports down her gun deck, and saw the irregular black stubble of large carronades about her fo'c'sle and quarterdeck. That, he thought, is more like it; he could not wait to transfer over.

It is all Bonaparte's doing, he thought as he descended the ladder. For the English, the decade and more of war with the French had required a breathtaking inflation of the Navy, now more than nine hundred ships—nine hundred and one, he smirked briefly, with this fat American brig. What country on earth could deploy nine hundred vessels with all-volunteer crews? Impressment in the British Navy had been accepted for three centuries; now it was needed more than ever, and it was no time to question it. Of the one hundred forty thousand sailors presently in service, at least eight thousand made good an escape every year, but Kington was satisfied never to have lost one.

As he heard the *Hound*'s cable thunder from its tier and the anchor crash into the water, he opened a large red leather pouch and began assembling his papers—his commission, his orders, his personal correspondence.

Let no one doubt they were about the King's business. Well—the King's business after a fashion. The King himself was now famously imbecile, a raving, wigless waif wandering the corridors of Windsor Castle, or playing

his organ, or holding imaginary conversations and, it was said, pissing purple water. The regency was now firmly in the hands of the Prince of Wales,
who was a great friend of the Navy's, or at least, when he was paying more
attention to frills and laces and the cut of embroidered waistcoats, was
under the influence of high and respectable men in the Admiralty.

The right half of Kington's mouth again screwed up into something like
a smile. Sardonic irony was not his only emotion, but it was his favorite, and
the closest to unaffected amusement as he was capable. One day these
American upstarts must realize what kind of game the English were running there in Bermuda, that they were not just taking the odd American
sailor while capturing "deserters" to round out deficient crews. Rather, they
were harvesting them from America's growing merchant fleet, harvesting
whole strings of them, like hops in August. Bermuda was their principal
clearinghouse, from where they were distributed as needed to their undermanned men-o'-war.

When these Americans did realize how they were being used, great must
be their rage, but greater still would be their impotence, for there is nothing
they can do about it.

Lord Nelson himself, God rest his pickled soul, had endorsed the practice with all his heart. No admiral in the Navy had been so vocal in his disgust, his disdain for America and Americans. He respected those wonderfully
designed heavy frigates of theirs well enough, and no doubt he would have
approved the memorandum circulating within the Admiralty at this moment, a proposed instruction that British frigates not engage them with less
than a two-to-one advantage. That was unduly alarmist, in Kington's opinion. Their ships might be well built, but their seamanship had nothing to
offer against centuries of British tradition. And these United States, these
Americans and their concept of a country and their vision of themselves as
a people—no officer more than Nelson would have more stoutly advocated
reducing them back to their proper station as colonial tributaries of the
Empire.

Kington wondered, if it were not for the satisfaction he had derived from
this business, whether he should have remained in the Navy. The duke his
father was not without friends in the Admiralty; perhaps he had something
to do with rescuing his fortunes, all very well if he did. At least now he was
resuscitated to the point of commanding a frigate. That was a good step.

There came two sharp raps at the cabin door. "Enter."

It was first officer Evans. "All the pressed men are secure, sir."

"Very well. Send a boat over to the frigate, alert them to pipe me aboard shortly."

"Very good, m'lord."

"Oh, and have that Canadian deserter, Lively, taken over as well. I think he is not who he says he is, but he is an experienced seaman and I can use him. Besides, he could raise a good deal of dust if we leave him here. I think we'll just keep him where he can cause no difficulties."

"Aye, m'lord, I will send him over with the boat and let them know the situation."

"Very well, I shall be ready to transfer by the time they get back."

The arrangements took only half an hour before Kington was in a boat, sitting with his back straight and his pouch upon his knees. As he approached the *Java* he could tell that she was but lightly constructed; she was French, a 5th rate, captured at Madagascar with considerable damage only the previous May. He knew she had been refitted at Portsmouth before coming out to meet a seasoned captain. Kington noted darkly that on her stern above his cabin windows he could make out the shadow of her previous name, the *Renommée*, lurking beneath the golden letters JAVA.

Still, he was happy to have read in his briefing paper that she was only four years old, and he knew that her builders, Mathurin & Crucy of Nantes, turned out creditable vessels. Once they had tied up to the ladder, Kington looked up in surprise to see a bosun's chair being lowered to him.

"If you please, sir."

He had barely time to say "Oh" before he was being hoisted up and swung in.

"Welcome aboard, m'lord." Kington beheld a plump lieutenant with dark hair and eyes making his respects. "Lieutenant Freemantle, sir, first officer."

"Mr. Freemantle." He returned the salute and extended his hand, which the first officer took, but not in an overly familiar way. "Did you think I could not manage the ladder?"

"We saw that you were carrying a large pouch of papers, sir. The chair seemed indicated."

Kington inspected him. "Observation and initiative, eh? Very good. We'll get on."

"Will you inspect the ship, m'lord, or see your cabin first?"

"See the ship, yes, at once. I am pleased at what I see already." He gestured up to the fo'c'sle and down the spar deck. "How many carronades?"

"Eighteen, sir. Thirty-two-pounders."

"Excellent." Ordinarily, commanding officers were given a choice of what guns to mount, but *Java* had come out to Bermuda as a completed package. Still, this was exactly the secondary battery he would have chosen, for he preferred close action behind the raking power of carronades over mounting lighter long guns topside. Kington ran his hand lightly down one of the stumpy barrels. "They look new. Are they just from the factory?"

"Yes, m'lord. Each one came on board with its full kit just before leaving Portsmouth."

All knew what that meant. The Carron foundry in Scotland persuaded the Navy to contract for its carronades by delivering them as a complete firing system. Each gun came with twenty-five balls, fifteen double-headed shot, fifteen bar shot, ten charges of grape, and ten charges of canister. They delivered powder, too, in premixed woolen bags that eliminated the need for wadding. Carronades' low muzzle velocity did not overheat the barrels, thus there was no need to worm the barrels before reloading, which made them the most rapidly firing large guns in the world.

"Excellent," admired Kington, as he led the small clot of officers down the ladder to the gun deck. "How many crew?"

"Four hundred and two, m'lord."

"How many were pressed?"

"A hundred and eighty, sir."

"Mm." Kington considered this for a moment. "Round up your worst dozen and send them ashore for other duty. I just took some deserters and new recruits from that American brig. Bring them over from the *Hound*. I think it is better to keep them at sea. But separate them into different watches."

"I understand, m'lord," said Freemantle. He knew that that order embraced not merely understanding what he was to do but understanding that leaving American crewmen ashore could complicate any repercussions of having taken them in the first place. Better to have them safely incommunicado.

1.

DANGEROUS TRADE

My Dear Putnam,

We dropped anchor in this place known so well to yourself on the day before yesterday. Being my first visit here since our salad days as midshipmen, and being a fresh autumn day, it did set me in mind of my time spent in Litchfield with you and your excellent parents, who I pray are still with you and in good health.

Rebecca bade me send you her fond regards straightaway as I made port. I tell you, Putnam, making her my wife was the best and wisest thing I shall ever do. At managing our plantation she has proved herself so capable I have considered dismissing our foreman as a redundancy. I have not done so, for with two lively boys tearing about, and I do not believe we are yet quitted of that enterprise of going forth and multiplying, she must one day be more occupied in being a mother than in running the place. I do confess, however, that to this date she shows no sign of being overwhelmed. Indeed, sometimes to amuse the boys, she repairs to her old trunk in the attic and dons some of the exotic-looking clothes that she purloined from that pirate vessel in which you rescued her.

What a queer feeling it is, to see her playing at pirates with the boys, with no sign of what terrible memories that must arouse in her. She does tell them freely that she was once captured by pirates, and spent many months held prisoner in a castle by the sea, also that she was an honored captive, awaiting ransom and eating dates off a silver platter. And Bliven! Nothing do, but the boys asked, what are dates, and they would not rest until we procured some for them! When she is out of sight, they ask me if her stories can be true, and I am bound to tell them that they are, and that you and I saw her there, veiled and peering out from a window. Ha! It only deepens the adventure for them, and they are not old enough to have inquired into its darker nature.

I am bound to say also, that I marvel at her strength in this, for I did learn just how terrible is her memory of it. I have never written you of this—when we married I discovered that she was, let us say, not unknown to man. When put to the question, she admitted with evident unease that when she was a prisoner she was outraged by one of the bastard pirates. She sank to her knees and prayed that this shame should not come between us.

O, Putnam! I have never before felt so ashamed, that my pride could cause this courageous woman to relive such an anguish. I took her in my arms and vowed that I should never broach the subject again, that her will to survive only deepened my affection and respect for her.

THE VERY BEGINNING OF CROW'S-FEET wrinkled the corners of Bliven's eyes as he broke into a smile. Good Rebecca, he had judged her rightly. Well done, once again. Their private duet during the opera in Naples would remain their secret.

"What is it, son? What has amused you? Who is the letter from?"

"From Mr. Bandy, Father. You remember him, he came to visit us when we were lieutenants on the *Enterprise*."

"Ah, yes. A well-seeming boy, for a Carolinian."

"Do you need help?"

"No, I thank you." Benjamin Putnam had entered from the hall with evident pain. "I give you I walk on sticks," then his eyes suddenly flew open. "But walk I still can, and as long as the good Lord vouchsafe me any use of my legs, I shall do so."

"Did you rest well?" It was close on two o'clock, a nap rather longer than usual.

"Yes."

When his father had become partly infirm, the result of a serious and warning apoplexy, Bliven had pulled a great heavy parson's bench into the keeping room and positioned it near the fireplace, lining it well with cushions. It was large enough that the elder Putnam could recline against one arm and stretch out his legs to the other arm, well tucked under a blanket. Thus he could pass time amid family activity and not feel himself an invalid. It was necessary to elevate his feet during the day, for with too much walking his feet and ankles swelled like bladders by evening. "Where is your mother?"

"Gone hunting."

"What? Ha!"

"Well, she bade me tell you she has gone hunting."

Benjamin Putnam beheld the family's two rifled muskets and fowling piece resting in their brackets above the mantel. "For what has she gone a-hunting?"

"Cloves and cinnamon, and ginger. I told her I had a mind to take a wagon out to the back field and cut pumpkins today. The first thing she thought of was spices, and that she is almost run out."

"Hmph! I hope she is able to find some. One hears that such nice commodities have become very dear for trying to race them past the British cruisers."

"How timely that you mention it. Mr. Bandy was just writing of this. Shall I read you what he sends?"

The elder Putnam touched a brand to his Dutch pipe and nodded, "Aye," between puffs.

"Bandy is no longer in the Navy but commands a merchant ship, and he has just dropped anchor in Boston—here it is."

My good ship Althea is a tight handsome brig, as smart as any you have seen, and passing large for her species, near three hundred tons and of great burthen, which makes her operation the more profitable for her owners, among whom I am happy to number myself, although claiming but a minor share.

OLD PUTNAM SETTLED HIMSELF on the parson's bench and stretched out. "Mercy! He writes a majestic great sentence, does he not?"

"He does, yes." Bliven continued.

We loaded off a full cargo and received very good prices, for being part owner of the vessel I partly pay myself. Is it not so, that in the hearts and spades of commerce, one must take care not to miss a trick?

You may find it of interest that in taking on a return cargo of Fisk furniture, I heard it emphatically expressed that any progress in local manufacturing that spoils the business for British goods occasions great satisfaction here.

"HMPH!" PUFFED BENJAMIN PUTNAM AGAIN. "I shouldn't wonder."

"Indeed," said Bliven, "he goes on in the same vein."

Among these men of business, all the talk is of the endless war betwixt the British and the French, and of their never-ending wars with each other, and of the utter, utter disregard of our own American rights by both sides. Our own veering and yawing policy over the years has cost us hundreds— and I say, hundreds!—of our trading vessels being seized by both England and France, and converted by them into warships, and of millions of dollars of cargo confiscated and never paid for. And worst of all has been—

BLIVEN NOTICED THAT BANDY'S HAND CHANGED as he had written this, more angular and almost slashing.

—the impressment of American sailors, seized even upon American ships on the high seas, put in irons and forced to crew foreign men-o'-war. So prevalent has this become, that I marvel we have not felled every tree

from Boston to Savanna, and built such a Navy, and taught them such a lesson, that they must leave off such damnable molestations. Mr. Madison, now he is President, seems to know not what policy to pursue—yet all here can see a terrible storm gathering.

For my own part I have little at hazard, for my partners and I limit our trade to our own coastal waters. You may likely judge the adventure I have had in procuring you the little gift that accompanies this letter, a sack of the most excellent Martinique coffee.

THE ELDER PUTNAM PUFFED ON his pipe. "That would be what I smelled when I awakened."

"Yes, mother roasted some while you slept, and I just ground and brewed it. Shall I pour you a cup?" He asked this even as he got to his feet, for his father's look of expectation gave a full answer. "Milk?"

"Just a little. Where is that strong-minded wife of yours?"

Bliven smiled as he stirred the coffee. "She is gone into town to have tea with her mother. She will be back before supper."

"Did you take her?"

"No, she hitched Cassius to the carriage and drove herself."

"Where was Frederick?"

"Hauling furniture for a customer."

"So she drove herself alone?" Bliven's father sucked some air audibly between his teeth in disapproval. "Well, that will give our village busybodies something new to talk about."

Bliven handed him the cup of coffee. "I needn't tell you how she declines to be fussed over and waited upon." He lowered his gaze and his voice. "Traits not unknown to yourself."

"Ha! Says he who stirs my coffee for me. Thank you." The elder Putnam relished a first sip. "Tell me truly, does it not . . . discomfit you at all that she spends so much time about her old life instead of here with you?"

"My word, no. I have to cut pumpkins the rest of the afternoon."

"No, son, I mean it generally. Her former life sported so much luxury, she cannot but find our circumstances too humble altogether."

Bliven shrugged. "Can you complain that she has neglected any of her duties here?"

"I cannot."

"Her mother is alone now, and not well. I do not begrudge them what time they have together."

"You will inherit better from her mother than you will from us, that is certain. You married well from that aspect."

"We married in no wise from that aspect, Father." It was telling that Benjamin phrased his observation in the manner that he did, for by their marriage, all of Clarity's property, including what she would inherit from her mother, would belong to him. Not without reason, however, had the Marsh family befriended Tapping Reeve, the proprietor of their famous law school, and obtained his advice on what he called Clarity's pending disability of coverture. As long as she remained single, she was heir to the Marsh fortune, but the instant she married, that was lost. They had been to see old Mr. Reeve in his comfortable manse that abutted his school, and to emphasize the point, Reeve had pulled the appropriate volume of Blackstone off the shelf and traced his finger along the lines for them: *By marriage, a husband and wife are one person in the law; that is, the very being or legal existence of the woman is suspended during the marriage, or at least is incorporated or consolidated into that of the husband, under whose wing, protection, and cover, she performs every thing.*

"I love you dearly," Clarity had said, and even as she smiled added, "but I think I shall not be looking to you as my master when it comes to my family's property." Nor did he wish her to. He might be lost at sea and his fate unknown for months, or years, and her life must continue and be paid for. Theirs was a case in which the law failed in its social purpose, and readily he signed deeds of trust to preserve her interest. The act made old Marsh and his wife trust him all the more, and intensified Clarity's devotion to him. There were still things she could not do—she could not incur debt nor make a contract, but with her unfettered access to money, she should not need to.

Together Bliven and Clarity agreed that there was no need to make his parents aware of their arrangement. Like all parents, they must regard a son's marriage into wealth as additional security for themselves should he die. Even in the Navy he was more likely to survive them than not, so the trust deeds, and Clarity's agreement to provide for his parents should he die, reposed with Mr. Reeve against that unlikely event.

"Besides, Father," Bliven added, "I must go back to sea one day, and we decided together that she should maintain lively interests of her own, and not just sit here and pine for me to come home."

"And that would include interests, such as Reverend Beecher and that too-loud church of his?"

Bliven rolled his eyes. "Well, you have me there, I cannot disagree with that." Until the previous year, Lyman Beecher's visits to Litchfield had been confined to six a year as he crossed the Sound from his home church on Long Island. But now he had relocated to Litchfield itself, with its celebrated intellectual life and prosperous means. Especially, Bliven thought, for its prosperous means. At least Beecher had married and begun fathering children left, right, and center, so his former concern that Beecher's energy might be directed toward Clarity was allayed. He returned to happier thoughts and the last page of Sam's letter.

> *We will stay here and make our presence known, until our hold is full of goods for which we will realize a good return back in Charleston. Providence alone knows when you might be recalled to active service, or when we shall meet again, but until we do, this missal travels with the esteem and affection of—as you remember we were once compelled to swear to each other—*
>
> *Yr. friend,*
> *Samuel Bandy*
> *Cmdg. Brig Althea Bliven Putnam,*
> *Lieut. Comdt., USN*
> *So. Road, Litchfield, Connecticut*

A CHILL GUST CURLED THROUGH the keeping room as the door opened and Dorothea Putnam swept in, well shawled against the cold, clutching a small basket, a scattering of orange and brown leaves blowing in at her feet.

"Welcome and hail!" exclaimed Benjamin. "Diana home from the hunt."

Quickly she removed small packets from her basket and set them on the great pine table. Bliven held each to his nose and inhaled deeply, enjoying the treat of ginger and cinnamon not yet shaved, and cloves not yet ground. "Oh, I sense a pumpkin pie coming tonight."

"Bliven," she said, "may I ask you something?"

His face slackened with surprise. "Yes, certainly."

She seated herself but not comfortably. "Forgive my bluntness, but it is on my mind. I chanced across Mrs. Overton at the mercantile."

Bliven's heart fell as he guessed her meaning.

"You are acquainted with her son, I believe, who was lately second lieutenant in the *John Adams*. She said he has received a letter ordering him back to active service. Were you aware of this?"

"I was, yes."

Dorothea folded her hands in her lap, failing to disguise her anxiety. "And have you also received such a letter?"

"I have, yes."

Her voice rose despite herself. "And was there some point in time at which you were going to inform us of this?"

"Yes, but not yet. Soon, not yet."

"But how can you—"

"Mother." Bliven raised his hands in defense. "I am not ordered to report to the fleet. I am only to go to Washington City."

"Why ever?"

"I have no idea."

"When?"

"End of next week. Come, warm yourself by the fire." He handed her a cup of the fresh coffee.

She seated herself, both cold hands wrapped around the crockery cup for its warmth, her eyes sad and distant.